Deirdre leaned closer to the pool, hardly daring to breathe. All around her the night hummed and whispered its magical song, but as she watched the blank water a waiting stillness descended upon the clearing. Something was about to happen—she could feel it—the entire world seemed to stop in hushed expectancy.

"Show me!" she cried aloud. "Show me my true love."

Across the forest, Alistair noticed a faint glimmer of light. He gulped in air fragrant with damp earth, the scent of life itself. He saw a woman sitting on the edge of a dark pool. She was sobbing, her hands covering her face, and her midnight hair streaming.

"Why do ye weep, lady?" Alistair asked.

Laird of the Mist

Elizabeth English

JOVE BOOKS, NEW YORK

LAIRD OF THE MIST

A Jove Book / published by arrangement with
the author

PRINTING HISTORY
Jove edition / January 2002

All rights reserved.
Copyright © 2002 by Elizabeth Minogue.
Cover design by Marc Cohen.
Cover art by David Stimson.
This book, or parts thereof, may not be reproduced in any form
without permission.
For information address: The Berkley Publishing Group,
a division of Penguin Putnam Inc.,
375 Hudson Street, New York, New York 10014.

Visit our website at
www.penguinputnam.com

ISBN: 0-515-13190-3

A JOVE BOOK®
Jove Books are published by The Berkley Publishing Group,
a division of Penguin Putnam Inc.,
375 Hudson Street, New York, New York 10014.
JOVE and the "J" design
are trademarks belonging to Penguin Putnam Inc.

PRINTED IN THE UNITED STATES OF AMERICA

10 9 8 7 6 5 4 3 2 1

To Janie, who asked what happened next
Sis, this one's for you

Prologue

Ravenspur Manor, the Borderlands, 1375

"*So ye think this is a bad idea?*"

Ian Kirallen asked the question lightly as he swung himself into the saddle. His cheeks were ruddy, his dark eyes snapping as he took up the reins. At twenty-nine, Ian was at the very height and pride of manhood, as restive as the blooded stallion between his knees. The beast pranced and reared, its hooves striking sparks from the frozen cobbles, but Ian brought him easily under control. Having completed this dazzling display of horsemanship, he grinned down at the fair-haired man planted solidly before him.

"Aye, I do," Alistair said, his jaw set in a stubborn line.

The eight knights who were already mounted sat back in their saddles. *They're at it again,* they signaled to each other with rolling eyes and shrugs. Sir Alistair was preaching caution, but he might as well be speaking to the wind. Lord Ian's mind was set upon this venture.

Not that any of them doubted Alistair's courage for a moment. Their captain was without dispute the finest swordsman on the Borderlands, a matter of great pride to his knights. Whether or not it was a source of pride to him, they could not say. Sir Alistair never wasted words on matters he considered trivial. Often silent and always watchful, his cool gray eyes summed up each situation with a composure that never wavered, not even in the hottest battle.

When it came to planning an engagement, they could rely upon his judgment absolutely, for they knew every possible contingency had been accounted for. If the captain said do this or that and thus-and-so will happen, a man could rest assured it would fall out that way exactly.

The same could not be said of their lord. Ian's ideas were bold and striking, always daring and often brilliant, designed for the greatest glory. But once the action started, anything might happen. He was wild and he was fearless, and he threw himself into each new adventure with an abandon that set fire to his men.

Every young squire dreamed of joining Lord Ian's personal guard, whose exploits were recounted in awestruck voices all along the border. Those chosen few would have followed him to hell and back—and counted themselves lucky to have made the journey. And though Ian's impetuous ways might drive his foster brother to distraction, they all knew that in his heart, their captain felt the same.

Once committed, even to a course of action with which he disagreed, Sir Alistair would back his foster brother to the hilt. And if the plan developed some unexpected turnings—as Lord Ian's plans had a tendency to do—it was often Sir Alistair's genius for the split-second decision that turned a potential rout to the stuff of songs and stories.

Two sides of a coin, that's what they were, and for all their disagreements, nothing could divide them.

As Ian grinned down at Alistair, inviting him to share the fun, Alistair steeled himself against his foster brother's contagious high spirits. There was something wrong with this plan. Alistair was sure of it, even if he could not say precisely what the trouble was. But since the night before he had felt a pricking of his thumbs, a stirring of the Sight that sometimes visited him.

"If ye willna be stopped, then at least let's take more men," he argued.

Ian frowned and glanced back at the eight knights ranged behind him. " 'Tis too late for that. We'll go carefully."

For a moment Alistair considered digging in his heels. Let Ian call him coward if he liked, just as he had done the night before when Alistair tried to dissuade him from this venture. It wasn't as though there was any need to ride out this morning. Two dozen stolen cattle meant nothing to the clan, and Ian knew it well enough. But of course the cattle were not the point. Ian would not let the Kirallens be bested over what was, to him, a point of honor.

It was so like Ian. There was nothing Kirallen's heir would not dare to score a victory over the English, particularly if the Englishman happened to be Darnley.

Ian's expression tightened into annoyed impatience, and Alistair knew that nothing he could say would change his mind. With a sigh of resignation, he mounted and took his place at his foster brother's back.

A chill January mist clung to the hollows and hung heavy over the moat. Just as they clattered to the other side, Alistair felt his horse's pace falter. Dismounting, he used his dagger to pry the stone loose from the animal's hoof, muttering a curse when the horse stumbled on its next step.

"I'll have to fetch another," he said to Ian.

Ian sighed, his breath misting the air. "Catch up to us."

"I'll only be a moment."

Ian laughed. "We canna waste the morning waiting about for you! Ye can catch us—and hurry, man, 'tis late enough already."

Alistair felt his temper rise. What was wrong with Ian this morning? His eyes were feverishly bright, his color high—he was drawn as tightly as a bowstring . . . almost fey.

The sharp answer Alistair was about to make died on his lips when he felt the hair stir on the nape of his neck. His mouth went dry, and though he tried to shout a warning, his words came out as hardly more than a whisper.

"Wait—don't go—"

Ian heeled his horse into a canter and looked back with a grin. "Try not to miss all the fun!"

"Ian, don't—*wait*!"

But Ian was gone. Alistair turned and ran back to the stables, shouting for a groom. Ten minutes later he was galloping over the drawbridge, the icy wind stinging his cheeks.

The day was dark and overcast, shrouded in mist, cutting visibility to almost nothing. But Alistair had no trouble following their path. The tracks were clear in the new-fallen snow. Above the dull pounding of his horse's hooves he heard noises in the distance—a cry, cut quickly short, the ring of blades. Then silence.

"Come on, come *on*," he muttered, urging his horse ahead with hands and knees. "Run, ye bastard! Now!"

Over the rise of the hills they flew, toward the outcropping of stone standing at the edge of the moor. Alistair veered around it to his right, following the tracks. More tracks now, leading from behind the outcropping, joining with the others.

He pulled up and listened hard. "Ian!" he shouted, his voice muffled by the fog. "Answer me, damn ye! Where are ye, man?"

It was then he saw the first drops of blood, like rubies scattered in the snow. He looked up sharply at the sound of hooves, and from out of the mist appeared a riderless horse heading back to Ravenspur at a panicked gallop, reins trailing loose behind it. Alistair kicked his mount and raced ahead, drawn sword in his hand. As he reached the open moor, he could just make out the shadowy forms of men on horses vanishing toward the border.

But which men? The ones Alistair had watched riding out of Ravenspur? Or the ones who had lain in wait beyond the rock?

But he knew already. Even before he saw the bodies crumpled on the blood-soaked moor, he knew the ambush had succeeded. Eight, he counted swiftly. Or no, not eight. Nine. Every one of them. And there, a little apart from the rest, was Ian, his blue cloak unmistakable.

As Alistair dropped to his knees beside his foster brother, Ian stirred. He was alive then, Alistair thought with an uprush of relief so strong it left him dizzy. Of course he was. Ian couldn't die, not here, not like this. Not for a herd of cows.

When Alistair touched his arm, Ian opened his eyes and grinned. A weak grin, to be sure, but still Ian's. He could not be wounded so badly, then. Nothing that could not be mended.

"'Twas Darnley—I never expected him to come himself—the bastard! I should have—waited—for ye—"

Alistair pulled back Ian's cloak, searching vainly for a wound. At first glance he did not seem to be marked at all. Yet there was blood. So much blood, rivers of it, soaking Ian's quilted gambeson, staining the snow beneath him.

Backstabbed, Alistair realized numbly. And even he, who had hated Lord John Darnley all his life, was shocked that the Englishman was capable of such a deed.

"Christ, Ian," he said, "we have to get ye home."

But when he tried to lift him, Ian gave a terrible cry of pain and gripped his arm. "Too late—ah, God, Alistair, I'm sorry."

Of course he was. Ian was always sorry afterward. Well, this time he wouldn't find it so easy to get around Alistair with a shrug and a sheepish grin. From now on things would be different. The next time Ian came up with one of his mad schemes, Alistair would make damn sure he listened to reason.

For there *would* be a next time. There had to be. Ian couldn't possibly be wounded so badly as all that. There was no reason, none at all, to think Ian would not be fine. But, oh, God, there was so much blood.

"Alistair—"

Ian's hand slipped from Alistair's arm and fell to the ground. The high color had faded from his cheeks and his skin was ashen, tinged with a greenish-white that Alistair had seen before. But he refused to acknowledge what it meant.

"Quiet," he told Ian. "Save your strength."

He swung the cloak from his own shoulders and draped it over Ian, over the blood-soaked gambeson and scarlet snow. Think, he ordered himself sternly. What is the best way, the quickest way to get him home? But for some unaccountable reason, his mind, usually so obedient, refused to work at all.

"No—no time," Ian said, stuttering a little with cold and shock. "S-say that 'tis all right, say that ye—"

"I forgive ye, all right?" Alistair snapped. "Is that what ye want to hear? Now shut up and let me think a minute."

"Malcolm." Ian's voice was strangely choked as he said his son's name. He tried to clear his throat, then managed a hoarse whisper. "Watch over him."

"Like my own son," Alistair promised, blinking hard against a sudden stinging in his eyes. The wind, he thought. That must be it. The wind was strong and very chill. "But you'll be there, too," he added heartily. "We'll get ye home and—"

Ian coughed sharply and Alistair stared in disbelief at the bright blood gushing from his mouth. He lifted Ian in his arms, holding him as his foster brother's body arched in agony, his mind refusing to accept what was happening even as Ian fought and lost the last terrible struggle against death.

L aird Gawyn Kirallen woke to the sound of the bell tolling in the chapel. When it paused, he heard soft sobs coming from his bedside. Malcolm, he thought. 'Tis

Malcolm. Why is he here? What is wrong? Then he began to remember bits and pieces of the day.

Alistair stumbling into the hall, Ian held before him, both of them covered in blood. Malcolm's cry as he leaped from his seat and ran forward. His own shout of anguish as Alistair laid Ian's lifeless form on the trestle . . . An ambush. That was it. And all Ian's men, those poor lads, were lying dead upon the moor. . . . My heart, Gawyn thought, remembering the shaft of white-hot pain that had lanced through his chest before everything went black. He felt no pain now, only a great weariness. But he had to wake. For Malcolm. There was no one else. Poor boy, his father was dead, and now he was an orphan. . . .

"Whisht," a deep voice said. "Here, now, 'tis all right, just lay your head down, lad . . ."

Thank God, Gawyn thought, relaxing back into his pillow. Alistair is here. It will be all right now, everything will be well. So long as Alistair is here. . . .

When *Gawyn woke again there was silence in the* chamber, though far off, behind the door, he could hear women's voices raised in a keening wail. The entire manor must be filled with mourning tonight. Filled with death. And Darnley was responsible.

This time Darnley—sly and sleekit coward that he was—would be forced to take a stand. It would mean open war between the families, such as had not been seen for many years. With terrible clarity Gawyn remembered the devastating cost of war. Through the years, as far back as memory reached, Kirallen had fought Darnley, years of unrest that periodically flared into open conflict. The last time they had gone to battle, Gawyn had lost his father and his brother. Now that ancient hatred had reached out to take his son.

When would it ever end? How many deaths would it take until someone had the courage to cry, "Enough!"

Ian is dead, Gawyn thought, forcing himself to face the

truth without flinching. Nothing they could do would bring him back. The only thing Gawyn could do for his son now was to give his death some meaning. Ian's name would not be just one more on the long list of the slain. Ian's name would be the last.

When Gawyn opened his eyes, he found that though Malcolm was gone, his foster son was still beside him. Alistair was slumped in his seat, bright head resting on his hand, dressed in the same bloodstained clothing in which he had brought Ian back again.

"Alistair," he said, his voice cracked and harsh.

"Aye, Laird." Alistair was instantly alert.

"Tell me—all of it."

Alistair obeyed, his voice as flat as though he were reporting a routine mission, not the death of his own foster brother, Gawyn's son and heir. Only at the end did he falter.

"He should have waited for me," Alistair said. "He said it himself—asked my pardon—"

"And ye gave it," Gawyn said.

"I did. But I'll never forgive him! Stupid, reckless—I'm sorry. The fault was mine as much as his. Or more," he added bitterly.

"There was nothing ye could have done," Gawyn said firmly, giving Alistair the comfort he could not find within himself.

"It was quick," Alistair said. "He didna suffer."

Gawyn nodded. Whether Alistair spoke the truth or not, Gawyn must believe him. He had no choice. To do otherwise would surely drive him mad, and madness was a luxury he could not afford.

"I want ye to do something for me," he said.

"Have no fear, Laird. Darnley is a dead man."

"Nay. Not that. Not now. I want ye to send for Jemmy."

"Jemmy?"

Alistair repeated the name as if he'd never heard it before. But of course he had. Jemmy was the laird's son, after all, as much Alistair's foster brother as Ian had been.

"Jemmy?" he said again, and now his voice held the beginnings of anger. "Whatever for? Malcolm is Ian's heir. There's no need to be bringing Jemmy back here—if we can even find him!"

"A letter." The laird gestured toward his writing table.

Alistair retrieved the parchment and studied it. "Cadiz," he said. "So he's still in Spain. . . . But why?" he demanded. "Why now, after all these years?"

"He is my son . . . his place is here. I want him with me."

Alistair looked at him sharply, surprise and disbelief etched across his face. He kens me well, Gawyn thought, a bit too well to swallow that lie whole.

"Ye dinna want Jemmy," Alistair said. "Ye said yourself ye have no use for him since he ran off. Now lie back and drink that draught Master Kerian left ye."

"Nay—I want Jemmy, I tell ye—"

He broke off with a choked gasp that brought his foster son instantly to his side, face taut with concern. Gawyn regarded him through half-closed eyes, satisfied with what he saw.

"All right, Laird," Alistair said comfortingly. "If ye want Jemmy, ye shall have him. Though God knows what good he will do ye," he added in a mutter.

Alistair will obey me, Gawyn thought. Though he doesn't understand yet what I mean to do, his loyalty is absolute. Even when he does know, he will obey, because there is more than the fealty of knight and laird between us. But will he ever forgive me for it?

When Alistair understood that Jemmy was to be the instrument of peace with Darnley, he would be furious, hurt, betrayed—but he would stand fast. He *would*, Gawyn thought. He must.

God would never be so cruel as to take both Alistair and Ian and leave him only Jemmy.

chapter 1

The Chevron Hills, One Year Later

Alistair's first thought when he woke was: *God be thanked, I am back in Scotland.* His second was: *Darnley is still alive.*

The ground was cold beneath him, the wind chill, yet he was sweating. When he opened his eyes, faint morning light stabbed into his throbbing head and every muscle ached as he sat up. The sky was gray and the damp air smelled like snow.

Painfully, he got to his feet. As far as the eye could see, there was naught but empty moor. But Scottish moor, he reminded himself. Last night he'd crossed the border and if he had been feeling a bit better, he would have fallen to the earth and kissed the ground.

He looked about, trying to fathom exactly where he was. He'd left Leicester behind two days ago and headed straight north, which should put him . . . square in the middle of nowhere. With fever upon him, a snowstorm on the way, and almost nothing left of his provisions.

Good planning, Alistair, he told himself as he moved stiffly to saddle his horse. Brilliant. As fine an effort as you've managed this past year. Only this one will likely kill you.

And would that be such a bad thing? a voice asked in his mind. Why not just give it up? Everything ye tried has failed . . . why not end it here and now? Just lie down, go back to sleep. God will do the rest.

He slumped against his horse, fighting the temptation to give in and take the coward's way. Who would ever know? the voice asked reasonably. No one but yourself.

"Sod it," he said thickly, pulling himself into the saddle. Once mounted, he tried to get his bearings, but nothing looked familiar and the sun was invisible behind the clouds. Finally he let the stallion have his head.

He rode half in a dream, alternately chilled and burning, and it was hours later that he raised his head and saw the hills rising to the east. Two hills, jagged, with a narrow pass between them. There was something familiar about this landscape. . . . When he realized where he was, he laughed harshly. Turn west, ride hard, and nightfall would find him back at Ravenspur. The one place he could not go.

He stared up at the hills again, his eyes lingering on the narrow passage between. There, just at the top of that rise, stood a cave. Fergus's cave. If Fergus was still alive.

There had been a time when Alistair visited the old man often, but years had passed since he'd ventured up this path. He wondered if Fergus had heard what had happened to him, then knew it didn't matter. Fergus might dwell on the edge of Kirallen's domain, but he was a *taibhsear,* a holy man, owing allegiance to no one but his gods. Surely he would not deny Alistair shelter for the night.

He jerked the reins and started up the rocky slope. Before they had gone half a mile, the first cold snowflake touched Alistair's hot cheek.

• • •

A fterward, Alistair could never remember how he'd come to Fergus's cave. Once the snow began to fall in earnest, there was nothing to his memories but the swirling whiteness and deadly cold, but at last he pushed aside the stiffened hide covering the cave's entrance and stumbled inside.

Fergus was sitting by the fire, white head bent as he studied the parchment spread open across his lap. He looked up at Alistair's entrance, surprised but not alarmed. "Peace be upon ye, traveler," he said courteously. "Ye are welcome here."

Alistair dragged back his hood and the *taibhsear* got nimbly to his feet. "Why, it's Alistair," he said, a smile creasing his weathered face.

"Fergus," Alistair croaked. "Can ye give me shelter?"

"Well, let me see," Fergus said. "I'm expecting the king of France with half his court, but I suppose I could squeeze ye in somehow."

Alistair managed a faint smile as he sank down by the fire. "Good."

Fergus touched his knuckles to Alistair's brow. "Now that's a fine fever you're carrying," he said. "Let's get ye out of those wet things."

Alistair laid his head on his bent knees. "Just let me rest a bit."

With surprising strength Fergus gripped Alistair's shoulders and pulled him upright. "Up, now, there's a lad. Just lift your arms . . ."

A short time later Alistair was warmly covered and propped against a rolled sheepskin with a steaming mug in his hands. He drank the brew down, grimacing at the bitterness. By the time Fergus returned from stabling the horse, Alistair was warm at last and the pounding in his head had subsided to a dull ache.

"So where did ye blow in from?" Fergus asked casually, shaking the snow from his cloak and spreading it to dry.

"London."

"Been doing a bit of traveling, have ye? Seein' all the sights?"

"I went to London to kill John Darnley," Alistair answered shortly.

"Did ye now?" Fergus did not seem the least surprised by this statement. "And is he dead then?"

"Nay."

Fergus nodded. "Good."

"Why, are ye a friend of his?"

"I've had dealings with the man, but that's neither here nor there. 'Tis for your sake I am glad."

He refilled Alistair's cup and then poured a cup for himself. "Drink up, lad, and stop glaring at me. The last thing ye need is murder on your conscience."

"This wasna murder. 'Twas justice."

"So you're God himself now, are ye?"

"I am—I *was*—Lord Ian's foster brother. I *was* responsible for my men. Now they're all dead, every one of them."

"I ken a great wrong has been done," Fergus said gently, "and not only to Lord Ian and his men."

"And do ye ken you're harboring a banished man?"

"I've heard as much. But what I couldna learn is *why* ye were banished. They say ye turned traitor to the clan, tried to seize control and drive Lord Jemmy out. Some say ye tried to kill him—or the laird—or both."

"Are ye no afraid such a desperate character might murder ye, as well?"

"In your condition? I think I'll take my chances."

Fergus smiled and tossed a log into the fire. Then he sat down and waited for Alistair to speak.

"I didna turn traitor," Alistair said at last. "Though 'tis true I did my damnedest to drive Jemmy out. He's weak, Fergus, he isna fit to rule—" He broke off, coughing.

"Whisht, lad, sit back. Take it slowly."

Alistair lay back against the sheepskin. "The laird took the notion to make peace with Darnley," he went on at last, "and Jemmy was all in favor of it. Och, I canna blame the laird. He's aged since Ian died. He isna well, not in body or in mind. But Jemmy is a different matter."

"I remember Lord Jemmy," Fergus said mildly. "He used to come here years ago, bring me animals to mend. He seemed a nice lad."

Alistair snorted. "Nice? He is a fool. Twelve years he was gone, Fergus, twelve years he spent in Spain. But did that make a difference to our Jemmy? Nay, not him; he walked in and started giving orders as if he'd never been away! He stripped us of our honor, made terms with that murdering bastard Darnley and expected the clan to swallow it without complaint. Aye, I fought him. *Someone* had to do it. But when it came to the point, the laird sided with his own blood. And so I had to go."

"Off after Darnley with murder in your heart?"

"I would have had him. God's teeth, I was so *close*. Then he fled to France, the coward."

"So now what, Alistair?"

Alistair leaned his head back and closed his eyes. "I dinna ken," he admitted wearily. "I couldna think beyond getting back to Scotland . . ."

"Dinna fash yerself over that. 'Twas what was meant to be. All is well, ye are here now, just as I saw."

"Ye saw that I was coming?" Alistair asked drowsily.

"Not exactly . . . but someone. I'm no' a young man, Alistair. 'Tis time another took up the burden. And here ye are."

"But—"

"Whisht, we'll talk it through tomorrow. But know this: long ago, when ye were but a bairn, I went to the laird about ye, asked that ye come here to be fostered. He refused me. But ye came anyway, did ye no'? It must be the hand of fate."

Alistair wanted to argue, but he was too weary. Tomorrow, he thought. Tomorrow I will tell him that I canna stay for long. I have to earn some gold, take ship for France, find Darnley . . .

Even if ye could get to France, what then? the voice said

in his mind. Ye would never find him there. Ye canna even speak the tongue. Give it up. Ye tried, ye failed, and there's nothing left to do but join the others now.

"Go on, lad, sleep now," Fergus said. "All will be well, now that ye are here."

The Chevron Hills, Four Months Later

Fergus *lowered himself carefully to the flat stone outside his* cave. The day was scented with new grass and heather, sunlight on earth, blossoms, and fresh breezes. Spring at last, he thought, turning his face up to the sunlight. Just when I had begun to doubt it would ever come again. . . . He chanted softly:

> "Greetings to ye, Sun of the Season,
> As ye travel the skies on high,
> With your strong step on the wings of the heights
> Ye are a happy mother to the stars."

At the sound of footsteps Fergus looked up to see Alistair Kirallen walk over the crest of the hill, a shaggy bull trotting docilely beside him. The familiar weight of helpless pity settled over Fergus as he watched the younger man approach. Alistair's eyes were shadowed, his expression grim, and he kept his gaze fixed on the ground, oblivious to the fragrant sunlit landscape through which he walked.

Taibhsear, they called Fergus in the true tongue, vision seeker, bridge between this world and the next. In his day Fergus had been called upon by lords and lairds and even, once, a king. If they had not been pleased by his advice, at least they had admitted its worth. But what good was all his vaunted wisdom now?

When Alistair arrived, Fergus had been certain he would recover swiftly from his illness and accept the new life that had been offered him. But Alistair did not recover swiftly. He lingered on the edge of life and death for weeks, the fever stripping the flesh from his bones until there was almost nothing left.

Worst of all was the damage to Alistair's spirit. He did not speak of finding Lord Darnley anymore, and though he listened politely enough, it was clear he had not the slightest interest in all that Fergus longed to teach him.

No matter how Fergus might try to deceive himself that Alistair was getting better, he knew it wasn't so. Alistair's spirit was dying, right before the *taibhsear*'s eyes. If things continued as they were, Alistair would be dead before the summer ended.

But Fergus had not yet given up. There was one more thing to try, and today, Beltane, was the day to try it. Whether it would work or not, Fergus simply did not know. But he was well aware that this was his last gamble, and he wagered for Alistair's life.

"Good morning," Fergus called, and Alistair looked up, startled.

"And to ye," Alistair answered courteously. "Here is the bullock ye asked for."

"A fine one he is, too," Fergus said approvingly, standing and looking the animal over.

Alistair leaned his elbows on the beast's back. The sunlight fell full upon the gaunt lines of his face. His eyes held a bitter humor, the closest Fergus had seen him come to laughter since he arrived.

"Well, this is a fine thing," Alistair said with a hard edge to his voice. "Here I come to ye for the wisdom of the ages and ye have me reiving cattle!"

Fergus met his eyes with a bland smile. "Ye object to reivin' cattle, do ye? Well, if ye ask me, 'tis a step up for a banished man."

chapter 2

She was a witch.

Brodie Maxwell sat on the edge of his bed and watched blearily as his wife approached, a cup held carefully before her. A witch. It explained everything.

"Drink it," he ordered.

Deirdre Maxwell glanced from the cup in her hand to her husband's face. "Sure and I didn't get it for myself. 'Tis but the mulled ale you asked for."

"Ye've put something in it," Brodie said with drunken certainty as he rose unsteadily to his feet, one hand moving to the dagger at his belt.

"Of course I haven't!"

Her eyes met his, dark brows slightly raised, the very picture of innocent surprise. Clever witch. That's what she was. What she'd been from the first, when she enspelled him on the windswept cliffs of Donegal four years ago.

She had made him promises. Oh, not in words, for she had barely spoken to him during their brief courtship. But her eyes—so blue, so clear, and yet so distant—her eyes had held depth upon depth of mystery and promise. Her mouth had curved in a secret smile that hinted of ecstasy to come.

Lies, it had been, all lies. She had given him nothing but her body, unwillingly at that. From their joyless mating he'd gotten but one puling girl-child and nothing since.

Who knew what black arts she had used to win him. Had been using since to shrivel his manhood. What potions she'd been slipping into his ale.

The dagger flashed and the point just touched the white skin of her throat.

"Brodie, whatever are you doing? What's come over you tonight?"

"Drink it," he snarled.

One shoulder moved in the slightest of shrugs. And there it was again, the elusive quality that had once entranced him and now drove him to rage. In a single gesture she dismissed him, as though she was so far above him that nothing he said or did could ever truly touch her. He didn't take his eyes from her as she finished every drop and lowered the cup. Then he stepped back and sheathed the dagger.

"Fine, then."

"Are you well, husband?" Her voice held just the right touch of concern. Oh, she played her part ably enough when it suited her to do so, but he wasn't taken in. Not now. 'Twas well known that a true witch could not feel love. But even a witch could bear a son, and by God, he'd have that much from her.

He grabbed her arm and pulled her hard against him. Ah, he'd finally reached her. The fear springing to her eyes sent a thrill of excitement racing through his veins.

"Oh, I'm well, *wife*," he said.

Her slender body stiffened, as though she braced herself against a blow. She'd had blows from him before—well earned, every one of them—but tonight he had other plans.

He released her and walked to the flagon—one he'd fetched himself—and poured, draining the mazer in thirsty gulps. When it was finished, he poured himself another. God knew a man needed something to warm his blood if he was to take this bony, whey-faced witch to bed.

But take her to his bed he would. Tonight was Beltane Eve, and even if Brodie was in name a Christian, he was still half pagan in his heart. Tonight he would beget a son. And then he would rid himself of the witch he'd married, lest she taint the boy who would one day be his heir.

Deirdre Maxwell watched her husband drain the second mazer, then bent her head to hide the relief in her eyes. Brodie thought himself so clever, but he was truly a great fool. What she had brought him was just ale, nothing more or less.

It was the flagon she had drugged.

chapter 3

Alistair stood back, arms crossed, a cynical smile curling his lips as Fergus put one gnarled hand on the bull's head and chanted softly. First he has me reiving cattle, now he's singing to the livestock. And isn't that just my luck? I've left it too late and he's lost what wits he had.

Fergus glanced over at him, frowning. "This is no game," he said. "Listen well and remember what ye hear."

Alistair bent his head. Let the man sing, then. But as he began to concentrate on the words, his skepticism faded into a dreamlike wonder. The chant, a blessing and a prayer, wound through the still spring air, swelling as the light grew. By the time the sun stood straight above the dew-soaked grass, Alistair had become a part of the song. Moving as if in a dream, he drew his dagger and laid it against the animal's throat. Its life's blood pulsed through the steel and up his arm, mingling with his own heartbeat.

The chant rose and held, then stopped abruptly. Alistair drew the blade in a quick, sharp motion. The beast started, tried to run, and Alistair felt its panic in his breast. Then the melody began again, gently now, a song of sunlight and green meadows. The animal snorted and went down, twitching feebly as its blood sank into the thirsty earth.

When it lay still Alistair drew one sleeve across his face, smeared with blood and tears.

"Now what?" he asked hoarsely.

"Skin it," Fergus answered. "Skin it whole. Then bring its hide to me."

Alistair obeyed without question. It was a long job and by the time it was finished, he was spattered head to foot in blood. He dragged the hide to the cave's entrance. Fergus was waiting there, seated on the flat stone, a goblet set beside him.

Fergus looked at the hide and then at Alistair. "Good," he said briefly, picking up the goblet. "Now drink this."

Alistair drained the goblet without thinking. It tasted of herbs and honey and something bitter underneath. By the time he swallowed the last of it, his fingers had gone numb and a peaceful languor was moving through his limbs.

He set the goblet back on the flat stone. The sunlight struck its surface in a shower of golden sparks. He stared at it, transfixed, and an image formed before his eyes, a slender, dark-haired lass—or no, he thought dizzily, no ordinary lass, but a queen—gliding quickly through a forest.

"What do ye see?" Fergus asked softly.

The scene before Alistair's eyes blurred and changed. "Death," he whispered. "Eight men lying on the moor, lying in their blood. And Ian . . ."

With a cry of horror he struck the cup aside.

"It was meant to be me that day, not him!" he burst out angrily. "God—or the devil—made a mistake. 'Twas all wrong, I kent it then . . . and I ken it now. 'Tis as though—as though I *did* die that day—and all that's happened since is but a dream."

He had said it at last, the thing he had sworn never to tell another living soul. But now that it was said, he felt no fear, just relief at having it out. And Fergus didn't seem at all perturbed. The old man didn't look at him as though he had no business walking free. He simply nodded as if what Alistair had said was the most natural thing in the world.

"I see. Is there more or is that the end of it?"

Alistair laughed, the first time he could remember doing so for many months. "More? I'm a walking dead man, Fergus, in every way that matters. Isn't that enough?"

D eirdre Maxwell walked swiftly to the pool, looking neither right nor left. Her hair hung loose down her back, falling well below her waist, and the setting sun struck blue lights in its raven depths. Hurry, hurry, her mind said in rhythm to her steps. But she should have a little time yet. Her daughter, Maeve, was sleeping, and Brodie snored soundly in his bed, helped along by the draught she'd tipped into his ale.

Stupid man, she thought with rising anger as she glided noiselessly through the wood. He blamed her for his impotence when it was none of her doing. She'd never wanted him and had never once pretended that she did. But if a woman's will could strike a man's rod lifeless, there would be few children born into this sorry world.

When she thought of what he would do if he discovered she was gone, she hesitated, a brief spasm of terror shaking her from head to foot. Then she squared her shoulders and hurried on. It was only for an hour. Was that so much to ask? She quickened her steps and ran headlong through the dusk, arriving breathless at the pool.

There she stopped, growing calmer, growing stronger, as she always did when she came to this place. The last rays of the sun fell through the new green leaves to light the tiny clearing. In the center stood a round pool, its surface calm and still. Deirdre sat down on a rock and gazed into its depths, a world of flickering light and shadow. It reminded her suddenly and sharply of the tide pools beneath the cliffs of Donegal.

She raised her eyes to the setting sun. "You sink down into the perilous ocean, without harm and without hurt," she sang in her pure, clear voice. "You rise on the quiet wave like a young queen in flower."

Even now they would be singing that in Donegal, with the bonfire piled high at their backs and the endless sea before them. Deirdre's father would be there, her sister, Siobhan . . . and Ronan. She thought of her childhood friend with a stab of longing, then pushed the image aside.

"Dear St. Brigid, give me courage," she prayed. "Give me strength and wisdom—"

Deirdre did not dare light a fire here tonight, even a small one. Since the first year of their marriage, Brodie had banned the ancient springtime ritual from his lands. He said it was a pagan thing, not pleasing to his god, but Deirdre did not believe him for a moment. Brodie's beliefs were easily twisted to suit his own design. And taking this from Deirdre had pleased him.

She sighed, the familiar weight descending on her shoulders. It was such weary work to live with Brodie, always watching, always waiting, using all her wits to anticipate the moment when his mood would sour, keeping their daughter, Maeve, from sight when he descended into sudden rage. After four years, she was exhausted, that was the truth of it. If not for Maeve, there would be no point in going on at all. . . .

How did I ever end up in this place? she wondered. Once, the future had stretched before her, bright and filled with promise. Fool that she had been, she had actually believed there was a man, one man and no other, whose heart beat in rhythm with her own, whose soul had come to earth in search of hers.

But as Deirdre grew to womanhood and he did not appear, she put away her hopes of a lover spun of dreams and moonlight. She would be mature, she thought. Dutiful. Responsible. If she would not marry for love, she must do so for her family. And so she had accepted Sir Brodie Maxwell, who had come to Donegal to trade for horses.

A good match, everyone had said; extraordinary, really, for a dowerless lass like Deirdre. She had thought so herself, had been grateful to Brodie, and though she told him from the first she did not love him, he only laughed and said that didn't matter. Love often came after marriage, she had told herself, a belief that lasted right up to the moment Brodie backhanded her across the face, knocked her stunned and bleeding to the floor, saying she had been careless in the polishing of his boots.

By the time she knew what Brodie was, it was too late. She was trapped in Scotland, shackled to the brute who was her husband for all time. Her fault. Her own damnably stupid fault!

A mirthless smile twisted her lips as she thought of the man she had wished for, the one she'd waited for in vain. Even if she met him now, she probably would not know him. Certain it was he would not recognize her!

She looked into the pool again but saw only her own re-flection on the surface. Huge eyes stared back at her from a pale strained face surrounded by dark hair hanging straight down to the water.

The clearing grew hushed, as though the forest had drawn in its breath. Then a breeze rushed past, rippling the surface of the water. A smile of startled delight curved Deirdre's lips as she tasted the unmistakable flavor of the sea.

Tonight was Beltane and the veil between this world and the next was very thin. "I am the flow, I am the ebb," she chanted softly. "I am the weaver and I am the web."

There was magic in the air tonight, Deirdre could feel it all around her. A flutter of hope stirred deep within her breast. Maybe he existed after all, the one she'd dreamed of as a child. Maybe he was out there somewhere, looking for her, not knowing he had left it far too late.

"Just a glimpse of him," she whispered. "Is that so much to ask? Just to know if he was ever real?"

She bent her head to the pool and waited.

Alistair climbed the steep rocks to the top of the gush-ing waterfall. By the time he gained the crest, he was soaked to the skin and his shoulders ached from the weight of the hide slung across his back. He splashed through the cataract to the small cave behind, then slipped the ropes from his shoulders and rolled his arms with a sigh of relief.

The evening sunlight struck the water, and the breath caught in his throat. He was inside a crystal, gazing through a prism of endless living color. Then the sun moved, the illusion vanished, and he was back in the small cave, cold and shivering, looking at an impenetrable curtain of water.

Well, I've gone mad, he thought. This is it, I've hit the bottom. Or not quite, he reflected, looking at the hide rolled at his feet. In a moment I will have reached the depths.

Shivering, he stripped and untied the hide, wrapping it around him. It was stiff with blood, and globules of fat glistened on its surface. For a moment he was close to vomiting with revulsion, then relaxed as its warmth began to spread across his skin.

The water was leaden against the fading light. The cave was chill, but inside the bullock's hide, sweat began to trickle down Alistair's chest and back. What did he think he was doing here? Did he honestly expect that he would be granted a vision? Such things were for saints and wise men, not for him.

But he'd said he'd stay a night, and damned if he would fail. The water rushed by, soothing the thoughts from his mind, beckoning him into its depths. . . .

He began to dream without any sense of falling into sleep. One moment he lay inside the cave, the next he was watching himself, a boy of eleven, run through the forest with Ian. They burst through the treeline and into a small clearing where several boys were laughing as they threw rocks at a dark-haired lad who was straining against the ropes about his wrists.

Yes, Alistair thought with one part of his mind, I remember this. The tinker lads we found that day. Ian's younger brother, Jemmy, had disturbed them in some game, and they'd tied him to a tree.

Now he watched Ian glance at him—the younger Alistair—with a hard grin. Five tinker boys, that grin said, every one of them older than the two of us. No contest at all. Alistair joined the fight readily—no one trifled with a Kirallen as these boys were doing. He'd been too angry, too excited, to feel much fear, even when he found their opponents were armed and eager for a fight. It could have gone badly, but it didn't. Because he and Ian found the way to win.

For the first time they took the position that was to become so natural, back to back with daggers drawn. And with the click of a key turning in a lock they were freed and joined, soul-bound into a fighting force that would one day surpass any on the Borderlands. Soon enough the tinker boys were running off with Ian at their heels.

"Take care of Jemmy!" he called, then disappeared down the path.

Alistair remembered well enough what had happened after that. He'd sliced through Jemmy's bonds and taken the boy to the stream. Jemmy had been cut quite badly, once across the brow and once across the hand. Alistair had washed the blood away and clumsily bound up the injuries with strips torn from his tunic. Then he'd sent Ian's brother home again.

But that wasn't what happened in the dream. All at once, as Ian ran off, Alistair wasn't watching anymore. He was inside the dream, a man now, and a terrible foreboding gripped him.

"Ian, wait!" he shouted. "Don't go, 'tis a trap! Darnley's waiting for ye!"

He ran down the path after Ian, calling for him to stop, to wait for him, just as he had done on that terrible morning when Ian rode off to his death. His lungs were bursting, and the muscles of his legs felt as though they were on fire. Small branches slapped his face as he went on, from time to time glimpsing Ian just ahead.

The forest grew darker, the undergrowth more twisted, but he forced his way through with a strength born of desperation. Then the forest was behind him and he was looking over a dark plain toward a tower rising black against a bloodred sky.

A thrill of terror raced through Alistair's body. The tower was a dark and brooding place not made for mortal man. Yet he knew he had to go inside.

Then he *was* inside, the corridor stretching endlessly before him, blank smooth walls on either side. He walked down its length, footsteps echoing in murky gloom, tapping out a doleful rhythm. Lost, it said. Lost for good and ever. You'll never get out again.

Shadows dove and gibbered, and when Alistair turned a corner, twisted gargoyles on the walls bared their fangs and hissed. He walked through the passageway, on and on, a place with no end and no beginning.

"Ian?" he called, his voice muffled in the darkness.

A shrieking howl was his only answer, and he ducked, instinctively raising one arm to shield himself as invisible wings brushed his face. Ian wasn't here. He couldn't be. Please God, let Ian not be here in this desolate place.

But if Ian was not here, Alistair feared that he himself would never find his way out again.

D*eirdre leaned closer to the pool, hardly daring to breathe. It was about to happen, she could feel it . . .* the entire world seemed to stop in hushed expectancy.

And there was nothing. The surface of the pond was blank. Tears started to her eyes, and she clenched her fists, summoning every bit of energy she had.

"Show me," she cried aloud, half plea and half command. "Show me my true love."

T*here—a faint glimmer of light at the end of the passageway.* Alistair made for it, stumbling with weariness, driven on by the certainty that it would vanish any moment. As he drew closer he perceived the dim outline of a doorway. The door was closing, closing—he flung himself outside. Cool wind fanned his face and he gulped in air fragrant with damp earth, the scent of life itself. He did not see the two shadows that slipped from the passageway as the door slammed shut behind him.

As his breathing steadied he looked about. Moonlight streamed through twisted branches to light a path ahead. With a little shrug he followed it, expecting to come out at the waterfall. Instead he stepped into a small bright clearing.

A woman sat on the edge of a dark pool. She was sobbing, hands covering her face, midnight hair streaming like a shining cloak across her shoulders.

"Why do ye weep, lady?" Alistair asked.

She lifted her head and he drew a sharp breath, staring dumbly into the sapphire depths of her eyes, bright with tears and framed by thick dark lashes. Ah, but she was radiant, too beautiful for any mortal. Surely she was a faerie sent to guide him.

"What—" she began, and then stopped, her eyes wide. "How did you come here?"

"I hardly know. There was a waterfall—and a passageway—I couldna find my way. I thought ye must have called me forth," he finished in confusion. "Are you no' one of the Sidhe?"

She laughed softly, and the sound was tinged with bitterness. "No, I am but a mortal woman."

Her voice was low and musical, carrying the lilt of its rhythm falling softly on his ear. He would have been content to listen to her talk forever.

He sat down beside her and looked into the pool, where her reflection shone dimly in the moonlit depths. But though Alistair leaned close to the water, he could not see his own image. Of course, he thought with a ripple of amusement, my body is back behind the waterfall. And this is nothing but a dream.

Deirdre glanced at the man beside her, wondering that she felt no fear. The moment he walked out of the darkness of the forest, her heart had leaped in joyful welcome, though she was certain they had never met before. This was a man she could never have forgotten.

He was powerfully built, with the arms and shoulders of a warrior, and yet for all his size, he moved with a dancer's silent grace. Though the clearing was dim, she could see him quite clearly, down to the twisted pattern of the brooch at one broad shoulder and the small green gems winking in the dagger at his belt. A lock of fine fair hair fell over his brow as he stared into the pool. When he turned to her, his smile was bright as quicksilver and hot as living flame. She looked away, dazzled and a little frightened by the strength of her response.

"Why were ye crying?" he asked again.

She weighed her instinct for concealment against the impulse to confide in him. Why should she trust him with her secrets? But then, why had she trusted him at all? Why had she not run screaming at the first sight of him?

Then she understood. Of course, it all made sense! The way he walked out of the forest without a rustle of leaf or crack of twig to herald his approach, the unearthly glow of him, even her own calm acceptance of his presence was nothing to be wondered at. Worn out with longing and worry, she must have fallen into sleep. And for all her failure to summon an image, Deirdre knew enough of magic to understand that a dream so vivid was bound to have some deeper meaning.

"I came looking for my own true love tonight," she said, gesturing toward the pool. "But he isn't here."

"Is he a silkie then, that ye seek him in the water?" The question was asked without a trace of laughter, confirming her belief. Why not a silkie? Anything was possible in a dream.

"Nay, I sought his image, not himself."

"Why? Is he in Ireland?" he asked, giving her a bright, shrewd glance.

She shrugged. "Perhaps. But it does not matter, for I am here in Scotland, wed these four years past."

"Four years wed and still ye pine for a man ye left behind in Ireland? Why, then, is your own husband such a fool that he canna make ye love him?"

"Ours was not a love match," she answered sadly. "Or, at least—sure and I don't know what it was on his part, desire maybe. But even that"—she made a pretty, helpless gesture with her hands—"whatever it was he wanted, I did not give it to him. Nor have I given him a son. I think he hates me now."

"A fool indeed," he said, his voice deep and soft.

A long slow shiver wound down Deirdre's spine as she looked into the stranger's cool gray eyes. But of course he was no stranger. It was he, the one she had waited for, the one she had despaired of ever finding. Hadn't she always been certain she would know him?

Too late, she thought bitterly. Where were you four years ago when I accepted Brodie? But of course he was not real at all. Such a thing could only happen in a dream. Still, she thought with a sigh, it was a lovely dream, the finest she had ever known. If only it could go on forever. . . .

But then, without quite knowing how she knew, Deirdre was certain it was about to end—or in the manner of dreams, to change into something very different.

"What is it you came to say to me?" she asked, standing and looking warily about the clearing. "Why have you disturbed my dream?"

"Nay, lady." He smiled with a flash of even teeth. "This is my dream, not yours. And a verra pleasant one it's turning out to be."

He rose in a single graceful movement to stand before her. He is perfect, she thought, tall and strong but not so ungainly large as Brodie. She imagined how snugly she would fit against his shoulder, then smiled wryly. Of course he would be perfect! He was her invention, after all!

She was a bit surprised that her imagination had fashioned such a man, when she had always thought dark slenderness the very model of male beauty. But now she saw how wrong she had been. The man before her seemed spun from moonlight, with his silver-gilt hair and fine gray eyes, yet he was strong and solid as the earth. Exactly as she had dreamed of him so long ago, when she was still a child.

But, she realized suddenly, she was a child no longer. She was a woman grown. What would it be like to walk into his embrace, feel those strong arms close around her? For all his strength, his touch would be gentle, Deirdre thought, and a tingle started somewhere in the region of her heart, moving slowly downward. It was a strange feeling, not unpleasant, but unfamiliar and a little frightening.

Four years of marriage had taught Deirdre many lessons, but none of them prepared her for the dizziness she felt when she looked into his eyes. And he knew—he understood without a word between them—for the same dazed wonder was etched upon his face.

This is a dream, she thought, staring wide-eyed as he extended his hand to her. I can do anything tonight and it won't matter.

Yet even as she moved forward, she stopped, knowing she had been wrong. This *did* matter. It mattered very much. Dream or no dream, he was more real to her than anyone she had ever known. And whatever was to happen between them now would change her for all time. She hesitated for the space of a single breath, so short a time that he could not have marked it. But still, it was too long. She watched in horror as his outline shimmered and began to fade.

"Wait," she said desperately. "Oh, don't go—please—"

She reached to grasp his outstretched hand, then cried aloud in wordless disappointment as her fingers met only air.

But Alistair felt the warmth of her touch. It streaked through him like a burning brand. Quickly, before she could vanish altogether, he leaned close and kissed her full soft lips. At that moment a flame leaped between them, searing to his soul, so sharp and sudden that he could not tell if what he felt was pain or pleasure.

She drew a quick breath and stared up at him, one hand pressed against her mouth. She had felt it, too, then, had been burned by the same fire that had marked him for all time. Oh, he did not want to wake. Not now. Whatever she was, wherever she had come from, he would stay with her and gladly, even if he could never have more of her than this.

Her sapphire eyes were large and wondering, shimmering with sudden tears. He moved to draw her into his arms, knowing from the start that it was hopeless, yet powerless to stop his instinctive gesture of comfort. She swayed toward him, then froze with a small gasp of fear, her gaze moving over his shoulder. Turning, he saw naught but the forest and heard nothing but a bird's harsh cry.

"Two ravens," she whispered. "There, just behind you. What does it mean?"

"Ravens?" he repeated. She began to waver before him, as though he viewed her through a veil of water. "Ah, corbies. Twa corbies," he said and was seized with an unreasoning terror, as though he had pronounced his own doom.

"Ah, no—farewell!" Her voice was small and distant, and as his sight faded, he tried once more to reach her.

"Wait!" he cried. "Who are ye? What is your name?"

Whatever answer she might have made was lost in the rushing of the waterfall. Alistair pulled the stiffened hide around him and stared into its depths as dawn slowly lit the sky beyond.

chapter 4

Fergus stepped out of his cave and leaned upon his staff. It was a golden day, bright with summer, but with a fresh breeze blowing from the mountains. Time for harvest, time for hunting . . . time for the restless yearning to grip a young man's heart. Alistair stood at the edge of the clearing, one arm leaning on an overhanging branch as he stared into the valley below. He had put on flesh in these past months, Fergus noted, satisfied. Through constant exercise he had regained his strength, and his eyes were clear and focused.

"You'll be leavin' soon," Fergus said.

Alistair turned with a start. "How d'ye do that?" he demanded crossly. "I never hear ye come or go."

"I canna tell ye *all* my secrets. Ye must leave me some mystery and magic." He brought out the last word with a twist of his lips.

"Oh, you've plenty of that to spare," Alistair said. "How did ye know I was thinking of leaving?"

Fergus shrugged. "I could say I divined it by my arts,

but the truth is it's writ upon your face. And you're right. 'Tis time ye were away. And if you're worried for me, don't be. I've weathered many a winter here before."

He lowered himself carefully to the flat rock, sighing as the sunlight warmed his bones. "This is not the place for ye," he said with some regret. "I'd hoped—but there's no arguing with what's meant to be."

"But where can I go?" Alistair asked. "Have ye forgotten I'm a banished man?"

"Kirallen doesna own the world, just one small piece within his borders. Ride north or west or east . . ."

"East of the sun and west of the moon?" Alistair asked with a scornful curl to his lip. "Is that where I shall find her?"

There was no need to ask whom he meant. Since Beltane Eve, Alistair had spoken only once of the woman of his vision, giving Fergus only the barest outline of their meeting by the forest pool. When Fergus wondered if she might be real, Alistair had laughed and changed the subject. And when Fergus suggested that Alistair go forth and look for her, the younger man had grown quickly angry and refused to hear another word on the subject. But his very silence was more eloquent than words. Whatever had happened that night, Fergus had no doubt it had shaken Alistair to the depths of his soul.

"There's no knowing which way your path will take ye," he said at last, choosing his words carefully. "But whatever ye need, ye will not find it here."

Alistair sat down beside Fergus and brushed the white-gold hair back from his face. "I don't know what to say," he began hesitantly. "What thanks can I give for all you've done for me—"

"Well, since ye ask, I'll tell ye." Fergus put his hand on Alistair's and looked into the crystal-gray eyes. "Ye can live," he said quietly. "That's what ye can do."

Alistair had come a long way from the sick and broken man who had come to him six months ago. He no longer spoke of suicide, though Fergus suspected he still thought of it at times. But the times were becoming far less frequent. For that, Fergus gave silent thanks to Alistair's woman of the forest. Whoever—or whatever—she might be, she had shaken him out of his preoccupation with Ian Kirallen's death.

Yet Alistair's vision at the waterfall had left Fergus deeply puzzled. He had run through the business with the bullock more for Alistair's peace of mind than from any expectation of a vision. It wasn't magic, it was just plain common sense, as any hedgepriest would agree. Get the man to tell him what the trouble was, give him every reason to forgive himself. Then send him through a ritual designed to bring on clarity of thought.

But they had both gotten more than Fergus had bargained for. Alistair had been granted an *immrama,* a true vision, one that Fergus did not fully understand. There was no denying Alistair had brought something back with him from the waterfall, the shadows that followed him on dusky wings. There was more than guilt and grief at work here.

Something had happened to Alistair on that January morning when he had lost not only his closest friend but eight men under his command. If part of Alistair's soul had indeed gone with them to the grave, it was a situation fraught with danger. Alistair alone could find the missing part of himself, and he would not find it here. Perhaps the woman was the key—if she truly lived. But there was no telling if she existed on this plane at all or was as insubstantial as the dark tower Alistair had seen.

Sighing, Fergus recalled himself to the present. "If there is one thing I have learned, lad, 'tis that wherever ye go, your fate is sure to find ye."

"That's what I'm afraid of," Alistair said, and though the words were spoken lightly, Fergus saw the sudden tension in the younger man's form.

A cloud passed across the sun, and the wind turned chill. From the distance came the harsh cawing of a bird.

"The corbies," Fergus said. "Aye, I hear them, too. But ye canna hide from them forever."

Alistair picked up a bit of dried heather at his feet and tossed it high into the air. Fergus watched the breeze catch it and bear it toward the valley.

"West it is," Alistair said, then laughed. "If Ian could only see me now! He used to say I couldna put on my boots without first setting out the options and drawing up a plan. How he would enjoy this!"

His laughter died and he turned away quickly, blinking hard. It was a good sign, Fergus thought, that Alistair could speak of Ian like this, let out his grief for his friend.

"Perhaps ye had to plan so carefully because he never did," Fergus suggested gently. "And now ye have your own path to follow."

"Aye, but . . . Fergus, I am sorry. I ken ye hoped . . ."

"The fault was mine, not yours, for trying to twist ye into something ye were never meant to be. And I havena quite given up hoping yet."

Fergus tried to speak cheerfully, but this morning he felt very old and weary. If the one he waited for did not come soon, it would be too late. He would die without passing on the knowledge that had come down to him in a line unbroken for a thousand years.

"The world changes, lad, whether we will it or no," he said softly. "Perhaps 'tis meant that it should end with me."

"Can I do aught for ye before I go?" Alistair asked.

"Nay." He smiled and laid a hand on Alistair's brow in blessing. *"Go n-éirí do thuras leat,"* he said. "May the one who watches over all speed your journey. And wherever ye might go, Alistair, remember ye are always in my prayers."

chapter 5

The hall at Cranston Keep was a small place, usually dark and cheerless. Tonight it blazed with torch and candle while many voices echoed from the bare stone walls. Knights and squires, men-at-arms, and hired soldiers sat at trestles or walked about the hall. It was a crowd such as Deirdre Maxwell had never seen in all her time in Scotland.

Brodie strode among his men, stopping here and there to talk to the small groups that had gathered. He was in a good humor tonight, for which all the gods be thanked. Tomorrow the men would march forth to meet Johnson and settle for good and all the disputed lands between their borders. The talk of battle was thirsty work.

Deirdre cast a practiced eye over the hall. Varlets scurried about, bearing trays of mugs and pitchers of ale, all of which were disappearing as fast as they could bring them. She turned back to the kitchens to order another cask be opened. As she left the hall, she heard the voices roar out a startled greeting. Another one, she thought with a sigh, and where were they to put him? Well, he'd just have to crowd in somehow with the others in the hall.

A listair smiled as Kinnon Maxwell came forward and took his hand.

"Alistair, where have ye been, man? There have been the strangest tales told about ye lately—"

"Aye, I imagine that there have," Alistair answered with a grin. "And with luck, maybe half of them are true."

Kinnon laughed a little nervously, toying with the fringes of his beard. "Later on, when we've the time, perhaps you'll tell me the truth of it."

"I'll do my best," Alistair promised. "But I've heard tales as well. Is it true Brodie needs men against Johnson?"

"Oh, aye, as ye can see," Kinnon said, gesturing about the crowded hall. "Why, is your sword for hire?"

"That it is."

"Well, that's a bit of luck for us! Sit down and eat—ye look as if ye could use a good hot meal." His small dark eyes moved over Alistair in a quick, assessing glance, taking in the patched cloak and plain leather tunic, devoid of identifying colors. His face was filled with questions, which Alistair supposed was only natural, but good manners kept him from voicing them.

"Alistair! Alistair Kirallen, is that really ye?"

Kinnon's sister, Jennie, ran lightly through the hall. Alistair smiled and caught her hands. "Why, Jennie, look at ye! Just as fair as ever!"

She dimpled, her brown eyes dancing. "Och, go on with ye, and me a mother three times over!"

"Impossible!" Alistair exclaimed. "Ye look just the same as the day we danced at Ian's wedding."

"Such blether!" Jennie said with an unconvincing frown. "But, oh, 'tis good to see ye, Alistair."

It was good to see Jennie and Kinnon as well. Though the Kirallens and Maxwells had never been more than lukewarm allies, Alistair had visited this place many times before. The last occasion had been four or five years ago, with Ian. They had stayed a night, and then, their business done, had ridden back to Ravenspur.

Now everything was different. Alistair wouldn't be given the second-finest guest chamber on this visit. He wouldn't be offered a place at the high table. And when he left, he wouldn't be going back to Ravenspur. Not this time. Not ever.

He was a banished man, an outlaw, cut off from home and kin forever. His mind had known that all along, but the agonizing burden of guilt he carried had blocked out every other pain. If he thought of it at all, it was with a bitter sense of justice. What right had he to warmth or happiness when his foster brother and the men whose safety was his responsibility all lay moldering in cold clay? But tonight his sight had cleared, and he saw that in the madness of his grief, he had thrown away everything that still had meaning for him.

He braced himself against the shattering wave of homesickness that threatened to overwhelm him. He had no home now, no kin, no bonds to tie him. His choices had been made and there was no turning back. All he could do was go on, living one day to the next, taking each moment as it came.

"Tell me about these bairns of yours," he said to Jennie, trying hard to return her smile, then broke off as a crash resounded through the hall.

A tray of wooden mazers lay scattered on the stone floor in a puddle of spilled ale. Above stood a woman, her face bone white beneath her coif. The smile faded from Alistair's lips as their eyes met.

It was her. Oh, it couldn't be, not here and now, and yet it was. "I am but a mortal woman," she had said, but he hadn't quite believed her. It seemed completely incongruous to see such a woman in Maxwell's dingy hall, dressed in the common clothing that ordinary women wore. But it was her. He knew her with a flash of certainty too deep to doubt.

Yet a moment later he *did* doubt it, for this woman was very different than the young lass he had met on Beltane Eve. She looked at least ten years older—close to his own age, thirty, he guessed. Her gown was a hideous high-necked thing that hung loosely on her gaunt frame. A plain linen coif covered every bit of her hair and framed a face too pale and thin for beauty. Her cheeks were sharp, her mouth a taut thin line, so different from the full and lovely lips he had touched so briefly with his own.

But her eyes—ah, once he looked into her eyes he knew her once again. Even at this distance he could see them shining like sapphires. And beneath that ugly coif was hair as black as midnight. But who was she? A servant? Impossible! This was some sort of trick, or a disguise . . . the whole thing made no sense. His heart began to pound and shake within his breast as they faced each other across the crowded hall.

"Clumsy bitch!"

Brodie Maxwell seized her by the arm and drew his hand back. Alistair was across the floor before the motion was complete.

Brodie rounded on him, scowling, and tried to shake Alistair's hand from his wrist. "She's my wife, Kirallen, and I'll thank ye to stay out of it."

Wife? Oh, no, she couldn't be his wife! Not Brodie Maxwell! The eldest of the brood was a blunt and surly man, with a slow wit and fearsome temper. Oh, Brodie could not be wed to this faerie woman. The very thought was sickening! Alistair looked at her and she bowed her head, a muscle twitching at the corner of her mouth.

"Well, wife or no, she's but a wee bit of a thing," Alistair said, keeping his tone light and friendly. "Hitting her won't mend matters. Instead why don't ye come and tell me what you're paying."

Brodie's hand fell from his wife's arm, and he gave a short bark of laughter. "Dinna tell me you've come to fight for us! It must be true then, all I've heard. Banished, were ye? Banished wi' a price upon your head?"

"That is my own affair," Alistair said, resisting the temptation to smash his fist squarely into Brodie's face.

"Not if ye fight for me, it's not."

" 'Tis my sword for hire, not my past. Are ye interested or no?"

Lady Maxwell slipped away back toward the kitchen. She stopped at the doorway and looked over her shoulder with a fleeting smile that stopped Alistair's breath.

"God's blood, ye always were a touchy bastard, Kirallen," Brodie said. "Too proud by half—at least while Ian was alive. Come down a bit, haven't ye, now that he's gone?"

Alistair would have given anything to spin on his heel and walk away. Or almost anything. What he would not give was his hope of seeing the woman once again. He would suffer even Brodie for that chance.

"I've sunk low, indeed, to be seeking work from the likes of you," he answered but he forced himself to smile as he said it. "Now get your long nose out of my business and give me a drink while we settle things between us."

He waited, every muscle tensed. Brodie could go either way. But Maxwell's heir was in a good humor tonight. He roared with laughter and slung an arm across Alistair's shoulder.

"All right, all right! Kirallen's loss will be my gain, and we'll say no more about it! Come and get yourself a mug."

Alistair allowed himself to be led off to a corner. There they bickered back and forth, but he was careful to let Brodie get the better of the bargain. God forbid he'd be the one to put the man into one of his tempers. Not now that he knew who would suffer for it.

O*nce the singing began, Deirdre crept into the hallway* leading to the kitchens, keeping close against the wall. She spied Brodie seated at the corner of the long table, deep in conversation with the golden-haired stranger.

Back in the kitchens Jennie and the other women were all in a flutter, chattering like magpies about the man. Deirdre had felt a cold shock run through her when they named him. She had heard of him, of course. No one could live on this particular stretch of border and not know of Sir Alistair Kirallen, a name shrouded in treachery and scandal.

While no one was quite sure what had happened at Ravenspur Manor last year, on one point the rumors all agreed. Alistair Kirallen had turned traitor to his clan. His own foster father, who it was said had loved him well, had been driven to cast him out.

He was a banished man. An outlaw. A man with no home, no kin, no claim to honor. Deirdre smiled bitterly. Well, at least she was consistent. When it came to men, she had no judgment, as she had proven yet again.

He looked different than he had seemed to her on Beltane Eve; older, harder, with an almost tangible aura of command shimmering about him. Even his plain leather jerkin and old cloak could not disguise the fact that this was a man accustomed to be giving orders, not taking them.

As Brodie talked on, Sir Alistair's eyes moved over the hall, taking the measure of the men he was to fight with. Deirdre noted the keen intelligence in his glance and imagined he had already summed up their strengths and weaknesses, labeled and divided them into fighting units.

They said that when he was just twenty, Sir Alistair had been chief among Kirallen's legendary band of knights. His extraordinary rise to power had made his sudden disgrace all the more fascinating to his neighbors.

Even sitting still, he was filled with a restless energy that showed in the drumming of his fingers on the trestle, the tapping of one booted foot on the rush-strewn floor. His fine light hair had come loose from its braid and caught the torchlight, making a halo around his face. Yet there was little of the angel about this man, unless it was a fallen one.

His eyes were just as Deirdre remembered, large and brilliant, set wide above broad flat cheekbones. For the first time she noticed that his high-bridged nose was slightly crooked, as though it had been broken.

It was a strong face, undeniably attractive. Certain it was that every other man vanished once he walked into the hall. And from the talk she'd heard in the kitchens, she wasn't the only woman he affected in that way.

Whatever had he been doing last Beltane Eve? Deirdre could not begin to guess what strange ritual had set his soul to wandering through the night. But it had been him. Of that she had no doubt. And he had recognized her as well, though all the gods be thanked he'd held his tongue about it. At least so far.

She remembered now the things they'd said and done that night and felt the blood drain from her face. What had she been thinking? Who would have ever thought the man was real—and known to her husband! But how well known? What was he saying to Brodie now? One careless word, one chance remark, and Brodie would fly into a killing rage.

Brodie held out his hand and Alistair took it. From the smile on her husband's face, Deirdre could tell he'd made a bargain to his liking. She breathed again, her knees shaking with relief. It was all right, at least for now. But whatever must Alistair Kirallen think of her? How deep did his friendship for Brodie run?

As Brodie strode off, Alistair frowned and wiped his palm on his jerkin, then turned and looked straight into Deirdre's eyes, as though he understood her fears and was trying without words to reassure her.

Before she could decide whether to acknowledge his gesture, his head whipped around toward the bard seated in the center of the hall. Puzzled, Deirdre followed his gaze, then the words of the bard's song reached her.

> "As I was walking all alone,
> I heard twa corbies making a moan;
> The ane unto the t'other say-o,
> 'Where shall we gang and dine to-day-o?'"

Twa corbies. That's what he had said that night when she spoke of the two ravens behind him.

The talk and laughter of the crowded hall faded into silence. There was nothing but the bard's song, and by the pricking of the tender skin of her neck, Deirdre recognized the presence of strong magic in the room. How could they not feel it? she thought, looking at the laughing faces around her. But they did not.

> *"In behint yon auld fail dyke,*
> *I wot there lies a new slain knight;*
> *Naebody kens that he lies there-o,*
> *But his hawk, his hound, and lady fair-o."*

What did it mean? Alistair had gone dead pale and his eyes were wide as he listened to the tale unfold. He looks like a man hearing his own fate told, Deirdre thought. Then she shivered, knowing she had hit upon the truth.

> *"His hound is to the hunting gane,*
> *His hawk to fetch the wild-fowl hame,*
> *His lady's ta'en another mate-o,*
> *So we may mak our dinner sweet-o."*

Deirdre listened with growing horror as the birds went on discussing the dead knight, planning how they might make use of him.

> *"Ye'll sit on his white hause-bane,*
> *And I'll pike out his bonny gray een;*
> *Wi'ae lock o' his golden hair-o*
> *We'll theek our nest when it grows bare-o."*

She glanced at Alistair, at the wide gray eyes and golden hair, and before she knew it she was across the room, laying a comforting hand on his shoulder. His fingers gripped hers hard, but he didn't take his eyes from the bard as the tale reached its mournful end.

"Mony a one for him makes moan,
But nane shall ken where he is gone;
O'er his white bones, when they we bare-o,
The wind shall blow for evermair-o."

The song ended and the bard stopped his fingers on the harp.

"The twa corbies?" she asked, her voice sounding shrill to her own ears. "Are they with you still?"

He glanced at her with surprise, and with a rueful smile unloosed his grip upon her hand. "Aye, they are. And now we both ken why."

"Nay," she whispered. "It means naught, 'tis just a song—"

"Just a song?" he repeated with a lift of one brow. "Music has its own magic, lady."

She bit her lip and made no answer, knowing he was right. But now, even knowing all she knew of him, she could not accept it as the truth. How many nights had she stared with aching eyes into the darkness, reliving every detail of her Beltane dream? How many days had she clutched its memory against her as she went about her work, the marks of Brodie's hand upon her skin?

And all that time her dream had been a living man, warm and strong and real, not a dream and never hers at all.

"Well, I have neither hawk nor hound—nor lady fair-o, for that matter," he said with a wry twist of his lips. "Perhaps 'tis not time yet."

"How can you jest about it?" she asked in a horrified whisper.

"How can I not?" he answered with a shrug of his broad shoulders. "I've known since spring that they boded me no good."

"The lady—in the song—she must have known the knight was dead if she took another mate so quickly."

"Murdered by his lady's will," Alistair said thoughtfully. "And the man who made the song—'twas he who did the deed, no doubt. Weel, then, I'll just have to steer clear of taking a wife who'd like to see me dead."

Deirdre wrapped her arms about herself and shivered. "Don't say that," she whispered. "You mustn't joke of it."

"I'm sorry," he said at once. "I didna mean to worry you."

"You did *that* just by walking in here tonight."

"Dinna fear, lady," he answered with a grin. "I'm not the kind of fool who goes about babbling his every dream."

" 'Twas *my* dream."

He laughed, his eyes lighting with amusement. Such beautiful eyes he had, the very color of the morning mist in Donegal. And his voice was beautiful, as well. The Scottish accent she had thought so harsh and ugly fell softly from his tongue. She dragged her gaze from his and glanced about nervously. "I cannot stay—"

"Aye, I know," he said gently, and now his eyes were dark with confusion and regret. "God go with ye, lady."

When Deirdre reached the passageway, she looked back to see Brodie holding forth in one part of the room, surrounded by a crowd of men. His fleshy face was red with ale and the excitement of the coming battle. He is Maeve's father, she reminded herself sternly. My husband. With a little shudder she slipped through the door.

chapter 6

D eirdre heard the sounds of Maeve's screams before
she reached the chamber. She had been a delicate
child from birth, prone to sudden fevers, and this last one
had left her with a terrible pain in her ear.

When Deirdre hurried into the room, she found Anice,
the nurse, spinning by the fire as Maeve screamed in her
bed.

"How long has she been crying?" Deirdre demanded,
scooping the child into her arms.

"Not long," Anice answered stolidly. "If ye but leave
her, lady, she'll settle back to sleep."

"Hush, wee one," Deirdre crooned, smoothing the damp
tendrils of black hair from the baby's flushed cheeks.
"Hush, now. Have you given her the onion I left?" she
added to Anice.

The servant snorted. "Onions! Yer haverin', lady."

Deirdre didn't bother answering. She quickly sliced the
onion and wrapped it in a bit of cheesecloth, then bound it
tightly against Maeve's ear.

"There, sweeting," she said. "Soon it won't pain you at all. Have courage."

She paced back and forth before the hearth, then walked to the window and flung the shutter wide. "See?" she said. "All the stars are shining tonight."

Maeve drew a hitching breath and lifted her head to follow her mother's pointing finger.

"Look, sweeting, see how bright the stars are?"

Maeve let out another yell, then broke off to yawn in the middle.

"There's the dog star," Deirdre went on quietly. "A fine faithful hound he is. But instead of chasing rabbits, he chases the comets through the sky. And when he's lucky, he'll catch one by the tail and swallow it down whole. He has the whole sky to run through . . . and when the chase is done, he lies down to sleep at his master's feet."

Maeve's head drooped against her shoulder and the child yawned again.

"Star," Maeve mumbled sleepily. "Sir Star."

"That's right," Deirdre said, smiling a little, remembering her own mother telling her this story. "Sir Star is his master, and he is a wise knight, kind and very brave. Sometimes, when the moon is full and bright and there is none to mark his going, Sir Star slips down to earth to fight for those who have no champion. His sword is made from starlight and his cloak is woven from the mist . . . he can summon the mist at will, my love, bid it come or go at his command. He travels often under its disguise. . . ."

Lost in her own story, Deirdre started as the door flew open. Maeve sat up and began to cry.

"Can ye no' shut the brat up?"

"Hush, Brodie," Deirdre said. "She's near asleep."

Brodie stood swaying by the door, his feet set wide apart and a scowl upon his face.

"Hush, ye say?" he demanded truculently.

"Here, Anice."

Deirdre pushed the child into the nurse's arms, tears

stinging her eyes as she pulled the screaming child's hands from around her neck.

"I'll quiet her," Brodie said, taking a step forward.

"Now, there's no need to upset yourself," Deirdre said, forcing herself to smile as she took her husband's hand in hers. "You must get to sleep and rest for the battle."

Brodie glared at her, then at the child crying in her nurse's arms. Deirdre held her breath, waiting to see what he would do next. From the moment of Maeve's birth he had shown no fondness for the girl but only rage that she had not been born a boy. But thus far he had been content to take his disappointment out on Deirdre.

Deirdre could bear what she must—she had chosen to wed him, after all, and would keep her part of the bargain. But on the day he lifted a hand to Maeve, Deirdre would kill him, even if she hanged.

"Well, keep her quiet," Brodie muttered.

"Anice will," Deirdre said, steering him through the door to their own chamber. "And now you must rest, Brodie. 'Tis very late. Are you not pleased with the muster?" she went on quickly. "They seem good men all. . . ."

He allowed himself to be led to the great bed and fell backward upon it.

"My boots," he ordered.

"Aye, Brodie, I have them," Deirdre said, pulling the first one from his foot and turning her face away from the stench of his woolen hose. She'd made him countless pairs over the years, but he could seldom be convinced to change one for the next.

By the time she tossed the second boot aside, he was snoring heavily. Deirdre breathed a quick prayer of relief.

She went to a small table set before the window and poured water from the pitcher. She washed her hands and unbraided her hair, combed it smooth and plaited it into a shining rope, then bound it tightly beneath the coif.

Brodie did not like for even a wisp of hair to show. He seemed to think the very sight of it might drive a man to lustful thoughts, which would perforce be Deirdre's fault. It made no sense to her, for surely a man was responsible for his own thoughts and actions, but she had learned not to argue with what in Brodie passed for reason.

The chamber was small but snug, warmed by the fire burning in the hearth. For a moment Deirdre remembered her own chamber in Donegal. She had always been cold there, for it had no hearth at all, and the fresh sea wind whistled through the chinks in the old stone walls. When it rained they went about placing buckets to catch the drips from the gaping roof. In the last two years before she left, the drips had turned to steady streams, and even when the rain stopped, the smell of mold had clung to every chamber.

Well, it must be mended now, she thought. Even if Father is a wee bit reckless with a coin, he is not completely without sense. At least part of Brodie's gold must have been put to good use.

She turned back to the table and washed her hands again, then held them up, still dripping. How ugly they were! Twenty years old and look at her, worn to nothing, with hands as rough and brittle as a crone's. Her lip curled in a bitter smile as she remembered Ronan Fitzgerald singing praises to her milk-white hands. But that had been four years ago, in another life entirely.

"Ah, Ronan," she whispered sadly. "I do miss you!"

She could not remember a time when she had not loved Ronan, as well as any sister ever loved a brother. If only he could have been content with that! But he could not, and she could not give him what he wanted. Now she was alone in a strange land, cut off from everyone who cared for her, entirely dependent on a man who was touched with madness.

A hard bargain, she thought, staring at her sleeping husband, but she had made it for herself.

She ached for the old castle by the sea, to hear her father's laugh and see her sister, Siobhan, again. If only she

had not been so hasty in her choice! Better she had jumped
from the cliffs before doing what she'd done.

She wiped impatiently at her wet cheeks and patted her
coif, making sure it sat straight upon her head, then walked
back into the nursery.

At least one good thing has come out of the wreckage of
my life, Deirdre thought, gazing down upon her sleeping
child. Maeve's dark curls were spread out on the pillow,
one hand tucked beneath her sleep-flushed cheek. Deirdre
had never imagined herself capable of the fierce, protective
love she felt for her daughter, a love that grew deeper with
each passing day.

"Angels guard your rest," she whispered, kissing the
child.

She considered lying down beside the babe to catch a
few hours' sleep, but a strange restlessness gripped her. It
had been a mistake to look back. It always was. She
thought she had learned that lesson long ago. But perhaps
it was easier than thinking about the man who had walked
out of her Beltane dream into her husband's hall tonight.
He could not be tucked safely into the past. No, Alistair
Kirallen was very much in the present and all too real.

Taking her cloak from its peg on the door, she slipped
down the stairs and past the hall. It was dark now and the
only sound to be heard was the snoring of the men upon
the floor. So many to be fed before they set forth! It was
hardly worth the trouble of sleeping now, what with all the
work to be started in just a few hours.

The thought of it made her head ache. What she needed
was fresh air and quiet. Then perhaps she could order her
thoughts and feelings into something approaching her
usual resignation.

chapter 7

Alistair lay full length on his side, cheek resting on one hand as with the other he tossed a pebble into the pool. He had found this place easily, his steps leading him down the path as if he'd walked it all his life. But even so he was still a little shocked to find it here, so exactly as he remembered. Just as before, the corbies had been waiting.

He glanced up into the darkness of the branches. "I hear ye," he said. "No need to make such a racket."

He was answered by a rustle of wings and a harsh croak.

"Aye, you're fine ones, aren't ye?" he said, rolling over on his back and crossing his arms beneath his head. "Plottin' and plannin' up there."

On impulse he pitched a pebble into the darkness overhead. He knew it was useless, but it still made him feel a little better.

"Ouch!"

He sat up quickly and peered back along the path. Then he smiled and lay back again.

"Did it hit ye?"

"It did," Deirdre Maxwell answered. "I thought the sky was falling."

"Mayhap it will," Alistair said. "It seems these days anything might happen."

She hesitated on the edge of the treeline, her face hidden by the shadow of her hood. He was annoyed by her hesitation, though he knew she had good reason for it. Given all she must have heard of him, it was a wonder she had not already taken to her heels.

"Well, step out, lady," he called. "I willna bite."

"Are you sure of that?" she answered tartly. "I've heard far worse of you tonight."

She remained just on the edge of the clearing, every line of her slender body tensed, ready to turn and run at the slightest provocation.

"Aye, well, I'm sure ye did. But for all my wicked crimes, I'm no danger to the lasses."

"That's not what Jennie says," Deirdre answered. "She said you were a terrible—what was it? A doup skelper?"

"Who, me?" he said, startled into laughter. "Blether, pure blether."

"Hmm. Well, I heard you are a rare danger to anything in skirts—and harder to catch than any unicorn."

"Jennie said that?"

"You needn't sound so pleased about it!"

"Weel, lady, it's nice to know that someone remembers me as more than a banished man."

There, they had been said, the words that had been hovering between them. Deirdre took a step closer.

"Can you never go back again?" she asked.

"No."

"What did you do?"

" 'Tisn't what I did, lady, but what I wouldna do. Jemmy Kirallen bargained for peace with the Englishman who murdered his brother. I would not stand for it. And so"—he shrugged—"I had to go."

"But they say," Deirdre said quietly, "that the Kirallens are doing well, that this peace has made them prosper."

"Prosperity bought by the coin of their own dishonor! If that is doing well, lady, then I'm best off where I am."

"I see," she said thoughtfully. "But . . . was that not the laird's decision? I would think his son had little choice but to do as his father ordered. And were you not bound to obey your liege lord, as well, whether you agreed with him or not?"

She met his gaze calmly, with only curiosity in her expression, not the condemnation he had thought to see there. For she was right, of course. He *had* been bound, had given his sworn word to obey his laird and foster father. And he had broken it.

"There are times when a man canna stand by silent and let wrong be done," he said defensively. "I made my choice and the laird made his."

"And now? Do you still believe you chose rightly?"

"I do. Of course I do," he said, though for the first time he wondered.

She nodded thoughtfully and sat down at some distance from him, plucking a blossom and tossing it into the pond. Alistair watched it float upon the surface, a faerie boat bound for ports beyond mere mortal ken.

"I understand," she said. "I know all about those kinds of choices. Once made, there is no turning back. Right or wrong . . . well, they cease to matter, don't they? The only thing to do is live with what you've chosen."

Her voice was calm, detached, but he sensed the pain beneath her words. And that was little wonder, given the choice that she had made! But Brodie Maxwell was her problem, not his.

He regarded her with puzzled anger, wondering what point there had been to their uncanny Beltane meeting. But then, what point was there to anything? Life, which seemed to offer so much, in the end gave nothing but disillusionment and disappointment. And love was the greatest deception of them all. He frowned, gazing at her pure profile, outlined against the shadow of the forest.

Was it love he felt for her? He did not know, but no

woman had ever made him feel the things he was feeling now. He wanted to carry her off on a fine white charger, to a place where no one had ever heard of Maxwell or Kirallen and all the wrong choices they had both made could be forgotten. He wanted to build her a tall strong castle, pile bright jewels in her lap, slay a dragon for her sake . . . Was that love? Or was it only madness? What *was* love, after all?

Whatever it is, 'tis not for me, Alistair thought, flinging a stone into the pond and sinking the fragile blossom. Only a fool would give his heart into any woman's keeping. That kind of love was nothing but a trap, one that could break even the strongest man in the worst way, from within. No, thank you, he thought. Married ladies—especially ones wed to madmen such as Brodie Maxwell—were no concern of his. He had quite enough trouble as it was.

Deirdre watched the ripples spread and lap against the edges of her pond. But no, the pond was not hers now, not anymore. It had been spoiled for all time by the man beside her. This place would never feel the same again, she thought sadly. Nor would she. A few words, a smile, one kiss . . . and she had been changed forever. Never again could she resign herself to life with Brodie Maxwell, not now that she understood all that she had missed. She would not have even her dreams to sustain her, only memories of a man she wished with all her heart she had never met.

"What brings ye here, lady?" he asked, an impatient edge to his voice.

"Oh, am I disturbing you?" she answered sharply. "I often come here when I am in need of solitude."

"And as these are Maxwell lands, I should offer to remove myself?"

"Stay if you like. I am going. But I would ask one thing before I leave you."

He glanced at her, his expression wary. "What?"

"That you say nothing to Brodie about our meeting here, either tonight or—or that other time."

She felt the heat rise to her face as she went on. "If I had known—that night—I would never have—I *am* a faithful wife, Sir Alistair," she finished earnestly.

"Aye, I know ye are."

"How can you know that?"

"You're still alive," he answered bluntly. "That tells me you're either faithful or a very clever liar, and ye haven't the face to hide your thoughts and feelings. What happened that night was—well, it was no fault of yours, lady. 'Twas well beyond your ken. And mine, as well," he added with a rueful laugh. "Who would have thought—"

"—that you were real," she finished softly, looking down at the flowers in her hand.

"Oh, I'm real enough. But no threat to your *happy* marriage. Believe me, lady, I am just as eager to forget last Beltane Eve as you."

She rose swiftly to her feet, blinking hard against the tears that stung her eyes. He was right. She should forget it. Beltane Eve had not been the shining magical encounter she had believed it. It had all been a mistake, a terrible, shameful mistake. Coming here tonight had only made things worse.

"Wait."

He was on his feet as well, looking down at her. "Forgive me," he said, and when he smiled, Deirdre's heart began to pound. "I am as surprised as ye must be yourself, lady. But that is no excuse for my rudeness. Of course I will say nothing to anyone of this."

The silence seemed to draw around them, cutting them off from the familiar world. Slowly Alistair held up his hand, and after a moment Deirdre, moving as if in a dream, placed her own against it, palm to palm. A shock ran through her at the touch, and when she heard his sharply indrawn breath, she knew that he had felt it, too.

"Ye can trust me," he said, his voice little more than a whisper.

She nodded, her eyes fixed on his. "I know."

"Deirdre, I—"

"Good night," she interrupted hastily, taking a step back. "I hope one day you find your way home again."

With that she turned and fled. Alistair watched her go, every muscle tensed as he fought the temptation to run after her. When she was gone, he lay back on the hard ground and stared into the dark water of the pond.

From the trees came the cawing of the corbies.

When Deirdre lay down beside her daughter, she was sure she would not sleep. Yet no sooner had she closed her eyes than she plunged into deep slumber that lasted for an hour.

Then the dream began.

It started with a sound; harsh, insistent, echoing strangely through a swirling mist. The corbies, Deirdre thought, an icy dread striking her heart.

The croaking seemed to come from first one direction, then another. Deirdre wanted to run, but she was paralyzed by fear.

The mist lifted and the dark water of the forest pond rippled before her eyes. The sound grew louder, closer, and all at once she realized it was not a bird at all, but a heavy form crashing through the undergrowth. 'Tis Brodie, she thought. He's awake; the potion didn't work. I cannot let him find me here.

"Deirdre!"

Snap. The sound of leather on leather was one Deirdre had heard many times before: Brodie drawing off his belt, doubling it over and bringing the two pieces together. *Snap.* Deirdre's paralysis broke and she ran blindly through the forest, the sound of her own breathing harsh in her ears. In the distance she heard soft music and made for the sound, racing headlong down the path.

She came breathless to a clearing and there was Ronan Fitzgerald, as dear and familiar as her own twin, sitting cross-legged on a boulder. His raven head was bent over the harp in his hands.

He gazed up at her with sorrowful green eyes. "Ah, Dee, how came you here? Why do you seek me now? I would have given you all the world, but 'twas not enough."

"Deirdre!" Brodie roared from the forest behind her. "Dinna think to hide from me."

"Ronan, help me!" she cried, her voice hardly more than a whisper.

"Who is that?" Ronan said sharply, standing and gazing over her shoulder. "Not your . . . ? God's blood, Dee, what kind of trouble are you in?"

She shook her head wordlessly and turned to flee.

"Wait!" Ronan called. "Tell me—"

But Deirdre could not stay to answer. She was running for her life now, and with every step she could hear Brodie gaining. She chanced a quick glance over her shoulder and saw him just behind her, his face flushed with rage. He reached out his hand and she screamed, then ran full into something solid.

"Here, now," Alistair Kirallen said, catching her in his arms. She buried her face against his chest with an incoherent cry. "Dinna fear, lady," he said soothingly. "No harm will come to ye."

She lifted her head and he smiled down at her, one lock of golden hair falling across his brow. With a careless motion he waved one hand and the mist descended like a curtain, hiding Brodie from her sight.

"I can summon the mist as I will," Alistair said. "Bid it come or go at my command. Ye can trust me, lady, 'twas written long ago. Do ye not know that?"

"Aye, I do," she whispered. "I do know that."

He bent to her and she wound her arms around his neck—

"Mam!"

Deirdre shook her head, clinging to her dream, even as it dissolved like sea foam on sand. With a sigh she rolled over and opened her eyes to find herself staring into her daughter's face.

"Mam, hungry! Hungry!"

Deirdre sat up and rubbed her eyes with shaking hands. She summoned a smile and kissed Maeve's dark curls.

"Feeling better, sweeting? I'll find you something to eat, then."

She remembered the men below and jumped guiltily to her feet, realizing dawn was almost upon them. Brodie would be up soon, and judging by all he'd had to drink last night, his temper would be foul.

"Stay here, love," she ordered Maeve. "Quietly now, just as quiet as a mouse, until I come back."

"Aye, Mam," Maeve said, her eyes moving toward the doorway of the chamber where Brodie slept. She put a finger to her lips and nodded solemnly.

She'll be safe enough, Deirdre told herself, so long as she keeps out of Brodie's way. Aye, today she will be safe, and perhaps tomorrow, but what will become of Maeve when she grows to womanhood? She'll be married off at her father's will, and I'll have no say at all.

What if Maeve is given to a man like Brodie?

I have to save her, Deirdre thought wildly. I'll send her to my father—only for a visit—I can say 'tis for her health. If Father writes and says she died, perhaps Brodie won't question overmuch . . . Despair washed over her as she realized Brodie would never allow such a visit, not even if Maeve's very life depended on it.

Unless, perhaps, Deirdre could provide him with the son he craved. Then he might grant her this small thing.

"Deirdre! Damn your eyes, ye lazy bitch, where the devil are ye?"

She jumped at the sound of Brodie's voice, her dream terror vivid in her mind. She remembered the rest of her dream and a hard smile touched her lips. She was twenty years old, no child now, and the time had come to accept things as they were.

There is no help for me, she thought, straightening her

shoulders. But 'tis not too late for Maeve. No matter what I have to do, I will see she gets to Donegal. And once she is gone, I will see she never comes back here again.

"I'm coming, Brodie," she called.

"Mousie," Maeve said, diving under the coverlet.

"That's right," Deirdre said. "That's my good little mousie. Stay here and if you're very quiet, I'll bring you a bit of cheese."

chapter 8

"**D**amn the man!" Ross Maxwell swore beneath his breath. "He's a fool—"

"Quiet," Alistair snapped, crouching against the outcropping of rock that shielded the two men from the fighting. "We have our orders. Now wait for his signal."

The field below was filled with shouting men, and the clash of weapons echoed up the hillside.

"Pitching stones down on the Johnsons!" Ross turned his head and spat into the river raging far below. "Like as not we'll crush our own men and horses along with theirs."

"Aye, we might," Alistair agreed. "But 'tis his battle, his command. Look sharp, lad—"

Ross whirled, sword in hand, to face the two Johnson men who came around the bend, slipping on loose stone. Alistair sighed and held his own weapon ready. Apparently Johnson had come up with the same plan as Brodie Maxwell. Which just went to show that the two men were well matched—in idiocy if nothing else.

Ross engaged the first of the Johnsons, leaving Alistair

the second. Good God, he was nothing but a child! Which was probably why he had been sent up here instead of taking part in the battle below.

And that showed that Johnson at least had a bit more sense than Brodie, who was wasting two good fighting men on a fool's errand.

Ross and the first man were slipping down the slope, their blows falling wildly in all directions. Alistair sighed again and looked at the frightened boy before him. Fifteen? Sixteen? His cheeks were downy with his first growth of beard, but the eyes above were those of a terrified child.

"Raise your sword, lad," Alistair said on an exasperated breath. "Dinna just stand there like a sheep to the slaughter."

The boy lifted the heavy weapon and stood ready. "That's right," Alistair said, feinting slowly to test the lad's mettle. He had no intention of killing the child, but on the other hand, he did not mean to be so careless that the lad killed him.

He felt as if he were back at home, lessoning one of the young men in the yard. Back and forth they went for a time until the boy began to gasp and pant with weariness. Then Alistair disarmed him with one turn of his sword.

The boy sank to his knees and closed his eyes.

And now what? Alistair wondered. Let the lad go and he'd be bitterly shamed. No doubt he'd be armed again in no time, ready to redeem his honor by engaging the next man he saw in battle. Like as not he'd be dead by nightfall.

"Oh, get up," Alistair said. "Here—step over to this tree, if ye please. Have ye kinfolk to pay your ransom?"

"Nay, sir," the boy said in a miserable whisper.

"Christ's blood, lad, ye mustn't say that!" Alistair cried impatiently. "Do ye know nothing about this business at all?" He regarded the boy through narrowed eyes, then said, "I think I may have struck ye in the head and addled your wits. Now, as I was saying, I'll hold ye for ransom. Like as not Johnson will pay to have ye safe again."

He glared at the boy, daring him to contradict, but he stayed wisely silent as Alistair bound him to the tree, pulling the knots tight. There. That should hold him for an hour or two. And by the looks of what was happening below, an hour would see the battle finished.

Ross Maxwell came breathless up the slope, wiping his sweating brow. "That's done," he said cheerfully. "Now what?"

Alistair glanced down to the field below. "Now we wait for Brodie's signal."

"But we'll miss it all!"

"And if we leave now and Brodie signals, then what? Orders are orders, my fine laddie, and I'll thank ye to remember it."

Alistair spoke sharply, for in truth he agreed with every word Ross spoke. Brodie had no idea how to lead his men. Imagine putting him—Alistair Kirallen, a seasoned commander and an able swordsman—up here among the rocks and stones! It was a calculated insult, to be sure, but it was the kind of insult only a fool like Brodie would invent.

"Fine!" Ross flung himself down upon the stone slope. "We wait."

Alistair stood, one hand shading his eyes as he watched the battle below. "Here, now," he said. "It's coming this way."

Ross sat up, his face brightening as he watched Johnson's men scramble up the slope. And Brodie, who should have known better, was leading his own men after them.

"If we push the stone down it will take Maxwell, too," Ross said, worried. "What's Brodie thinking to follow?"

"God only knows, lad," Alistair replied grimly. "Here, now, stand ready—"

At Alistair's signal they leaped forward with a cry, taking Johnson's lead men by surprise. Johnson's men stepped back, loose shards of shale slipping beneath their feet and carrying them right into Brodie's force.

Up and down the slope they fought as the sun rose to its zenith and sparkled on the river far below. Without quite

knowing how it happened, Alistair found himself in command of a dozen men. Save for young Ross they were all
mercenaries like himself, many of them men he'd fought
with—and in some cases, against—before. They had aban-
doned Maxwell in disgust when he ordered them to stand
and fight on the slope of the hill, below Johnson's men. It
was an indefensible position, as was proved by the beating
that the bulk of Maxwell's men were taking.

Crouched in the lee of the highest rocks, Alistair wiped
his streaming forehead and surveyed the battle below.

One of the older men grunted. "Christ, just look at that,"
he said, pointing toward the Maxwells on the hillside.
"Where the devil is Maxwell himself?" he asked, dis-
gusted. "Worst day's work I ever did, takin' siller from the
man."

"Aye, well, let's see we all live to regret it," Alistair said.
"Go there"—he pointed toward an outcropping just above
Johnson's forces—"and wait for my signal. With any luck
we'll drive them right back down the hillside and home
again."

Alistair waited as they made their way toward the outcropping. From the corner of his eye he saw a flash of plaid
among the trees behind him. Damnation, he'd forgotten the
boy he'd tied to the tree. If one of Maxwell's men found
him there, he might kill the lad.

He sprinted into the stand of trees. And there he found
Brodie Maxwell himself, sword upraised as the terrified
lad ducked futilely behind a slender branch.

"Hold, Brodie!" Alistair cried. "That's my prisoner."

"Prisoner?" Brodie roared. "Who gave ye leave to be
takin' any prisoners?"

"Christ's blood, he's but a bairn," Alistair said, dis-
gusted. "Let him be—or here, I'll turn him loose. Go!" he
ordered the boy, jerking his head toward the path as he
sliced through the ropes.

But even as the boy began to run, Brodie put out a foot
and sent him flying. He landed inches from the cliff's edge
and lay gasping, the wind knocked from him.

"Brodie, that's enough!" Alistair cried, really angry now, but had no time for more as Brodie Maxwell raised his sword again and rushed forward. Even as the sword began its swift descent the boy twisted desperately, knocking Brodie's feet from under him. And as Alistair watched, astonished, the force of Brodie's charge carried him straight over the cliff's edge.

Running forward, Alistair saw Brodie fly through the air with a wailing cry. Alistair cried out himself as Brodie struck against the side of the cliff, bounced off, and vanished with a splash into the river far below.

chapter 9

Deirdre rose stiffly from her knees and drew her cloak around her as the priest began his final blessing. Poor old man, she thought with distant sympathy. His stained and mended surplice gave but little protection from the cold. The end of his long nose was red and his words were visible things, coming from his mouth in little puffs. Deirdre shivered, glancing about the dank and miserable chapel of Cranston Keep. Neither Brodie nor his father had ever seen fit to waste a single coin on a place that held so little interest for them.

But even Maxwell's laird could not avoid his chapel altogether now. He was not here today, which was odd, for he himself had ordered daily masses for Brodie's safe return. Day after day the household crowded into the tiny chapel, and though Maxwell had ordered braziers to be lit at every corner, their warmth was quickly dissipated by the ever-present drafts.

Deirdre had spent the fortnight past surrounded by people, all of them with heads bent in prayer. She wondered how many were praying that Brodie might return in good health, and how many, like herself, were besieging God with heartfelt petitions that he would not come back at all.

As the priest hurried through the mass, Deirdre tried to order her jumbled thoughts into coherent prayer. It was wrong, she knew, to be praying that Brodie might be dead. Yet it would be a lie to ask for anything else.

"Dear St. Brigid," she pleaded silently, "you know what is in my heart. All I ask is the strength to bear God's will."

And that was the best that she could do. Brodie's God was a stern and fearsome stranger, but St. Brigid would understand. She would know that Deirdre was suspended on the edge of hope and fear, so tightly strung that she would shatter at a touch.

The three men who had witnessed Brodie's fall all agreed that there was little hope he had survived it. As the days passed, the household began to change "little hope" to "no hope at all." But Deirdre did not yet dare believe it. In her dreams Brodie came back again, skin livid, eyes blank and empty, water weed tangled in his dripping hair. And his anger had been terrible.

Brodie could still return. Any moment now, he could walk into the hall and obliterate Deirdre's every hope of freedom. She could not—she would not—start believing herself a widow, for if it came to naught, she would run mad.

As she left the chapel, a man was waiting by the nave, hood drawn far across his face. But even before Deirdre saw his face, she knew him. Thank you, St. Brigid, she thought with a dizzying wave of relief. All will be well, everything will be all right now that Alistair is here.

She stopped short, hardly noticing the others passing by her, glad she had a moment to compose herself before she spoke to him. He might have news, she told herself sternly. It was for that she felt the gladsome leaping of her pulse.

As the others passed, she drew a bit aside. Alistair waited until they were alone before he spoke.

"I've come from Maxwell," he said. "He has called off the search."

"Called off?" Deirdre repeated, not daring to believe that the words meant what they seemed to mean.

"Aye. He's given up on finding Brodie's body. He will be naming Kinnon as his heir."

What would Kinnon think of that? she wondered numbly. Would he be glad or sorry? Kinnon was always so secretive that it was impossible to guess. He would have to marry now, she thought, and wondered who he would choose. . . .

Then her thoughts stopped with a jerk. What difference did it make to her what happened here now? She was free. I can go home, she thought, the blood draining from her face as the reality hit her. Home to Ireland, to Donegal, her family, where she and Maeve would be safe.

"Lady—" Alistair said, concerned, putting strong hands on her shoulders as she swayed. "Are ye all right? Come, sit down, I know this must be a shock—"

A *shock*? Deirdre felt the wild laughter rising to her throat, and there was nothing she could do to stop it.

Alistair drew her close, and she leaned her head against his shoulder, part of her mind noting that they fit together perfectly, just as she had known they would. He held her as her body shook with helpless laughter that quickly changed to tears.

"Lady—Deirdre—God's blood, I'm so sorry. I shouldna have told ye like this—"

"Oh, aye," she gasped. "Better you—better here—than before them all—"

His cloak was rough against her cheek, and he smelled of woodsmoke and clean fresh air. When he bent to her, murmuring comforting words in his deep soft voice, his hair brushed her cheek. She closed her eyes and leaned against him, and after a time she grew calmer.

"There," she said at last, drawing a shaking breath and giving him the best smile she could mange. "It's all right. I'll be fine now."

"Will ye?"

She looked into his eyes and saw he was still worried, still blaming himself for her outburst. "Thank you for telling me," she said. "I'm glad you did."

She realized that his arms were still clasped around her waist and knew she should step back. Instead she lifted her face to his and closed her eyes.

"Deirdre," he said roughly. "I must go—and—and ye—"

His breath was warm against her lips. They stood so close she could feel his heart racing as wildly as her own. She lifted herself, felt her lips touch his, and then with a muffled groan he pulled her more tightly into his arms and kissed her.

It was very different from the brush of mouth on mouth that he had given her on Beltane Eve. This was no dream, but very real, a shattering burst of sensation that flooded her with heat. His beard was rough against her cheek, his lips firm and supple as they parted hers. She wound her arms around his neck and returned his kiss with desperate need.

When he drew back at last, Deirdre sighed, nestled close in the safety of his arms, his lips moving against her brow, her neck. How perfect, she thought drowsily. How right. Can this really be happening to *me*?

Stop, a voice said in her mind. It was a cold voice, very clear, entirely without emotion. Here you are on the brink of freedom, and what are you doing? Behaving like some witless wanton, throwing yourself at this man—a banished man, an outcast—who can bring you nothing but unhappiness and disgrace! What kind of mother could so soon forget her daughter's future?

She pulled away abruptly. "I am sorry," she heard the cold voice say. "I was—upset."

"Think nothing of it, lady."

Alistair's voice was as impersonal as if she had committed some trifling offense; trodden on his toe, perhaps, or neglected to pass him the salt. But his eyes were bright with the same pain she was feeling now, the same aching loss and emptiness.

She pulled on her gloves, smoothing each finger carefully, trying to match his outward composure.

"Will you be staying?" she asked politely.

"Nay."

"But—" She stopped, controlled herself, and went on calmly. "Where do you go from here?"

He shrugged. "Wherever the wind blows me, I suppose."

Only a man could afford to be so careless! So long as he had that bright sword to protect him, Alistair could come or go exactly as he pleased. But Deirdre had no such freedom. She was a woman, alone and unprotected, a dangerous thing to be in this time and place.

The Normans had succeeded in imposing their laws and customs in parts of Ireland, but they had never gained a firm foothold in Donegal. There Deirdre would have at least some standing under law. But she was not in Ireland now. She was in Scotland, a country that was not only indifferent to women, but positively hostile.

Here she had no rights but those her husband—or now, his father—might grant her. And if she did not succeed in getting Maeve to Ireland, her daughter would grow to womanhood in this hateful place, forever the property of one man or another.

Love might be fine for songs and stories, Deirdre thought, but this was real life. Her life. And she alone would steer her course. Never again would any man have the slightest influence on her decisions. She would be cool and rational, and her choices would be based on reason, not the ebb and flow of her desire.

"God keep you, lady," Alistair said formally. He bowed, turned, and walked from the chapel.

She watched him go, blinking furiously against the weak and foolish tears that stung her eyes. Well, at least she was safe now from her own ridiculous fancies. Having found and lost Alistair Kirallen, no man would ever tempt her into folly again.

chapter 10

𝒟

Maxwell made his announcement that night in the hall. Jennie, seated beside Deirdre, burst into noisy tears and flung her arms around her sister-in-law.

"Poor Dee," she wailed. "Poor lass. Go on, ye can cry, 'tis better if ye do—"

Deirdre closed her eyes and prayed for strength. Jennie was a nice lass, but she was a fool if she thought that Deirdre would ever grieve for Brodie.

I'm sorry for you, Brodie, she thought. I am sorry I feel naught but joy that you are gone. My God have mercy on your soul, for I have none in me for you. And now I'm free!

"There, now, bear up," Jennie whispered, patting her hand.

Deirdre wanted to scream at her sister-in-law's innocent solicitude, to pull her hand away and shout out the truth to them all. Instead she bowed her head and managed a brave smile. Let them believe what they wanted to believe. She was going home.

"I have given some thought to your future, daughter."

Deirdre turned toward her father-in-law with surprise. The man had disapproved of her from the start, and his disapproval had taken the form of ignoring her entirely. When forced to speak to her, he never addressed her by name. "You," he would say when he wanted her attention. "You, pass me the porridge."

Never once had he called her daughter. Until now.

"Have you, Laird?" she said politely. "So have I."

He waved one plump hand, dismissing her thoughts upon the matter.

"Kinnon is in need of a wife," he said. "I've given ye to him."

Deirdre looked past Maxwell to his second son, seated on his other side. Kinnon was a small man with sandy thinning hair and a perpetually anxious expression. Now he caught her eye and smiled nervously.

"Thank you," Deirdre said crisply. "But I plan to return to my father's house as soon as possible."

Maxwell's small eyes narrowed above the pouches of flesh. "Ye'll do no such thing."

"Indeed I shall," Deirdre said with icy dignity. "My father insisted on the arrangement. In the event that I was widowed, I was to return home if such was my desire." With a good bit of gold, she thought, but did not quite dare add the words.

"I know of no such arrangement," Maxwell said. "And I've already decided the matter. Ye should be grateful Kinnon will have ye," he added nastily. "'Tisna every man who'd agree to take a dried-up bag o' bones to wife."

Deirdre let the insult pass, instead seizing on the lie he'd told so casually. He *did* know about the arrangement between Brodie and her father. It was one reason he had been against the marriage from the start, saying Brodie had been swindled. It wasn't for any love of her that he wanted to keep her close, but for the widow's rights she had been promised.

"I am going home," she said firmly. "And my daughter with me."

"The lassie is a Maxwell," the old man said shrewdly. "I am the one to say whether she comes or goes. I suppose I canna stop ye from running back to Ireland, if such be your desire. But I will never give ye leave to take—ah—to take my granddaughter out o' Scotland."

He doesn't even know her name, Deirdre thought furiously. Maeve is nothing but a pawn to him. He knows I would never leave my child behind.

"So that's settled, daughter," he declared. "Ye'll wed Kinnon and we'll say no more about it."

Deirdre bent her head. It wasn't difficult to summon a few tears, not when she could have cast herself on the floor and wailed in rage at the ruin of her plan. Maxwell's lips curved in a satisfied smile as the tears trailed down her cheeks.

Settled, is it? she thought, allowing a tiny sob to escape her lips. We'll see about that, you horrid old toad. Beneath downcast lashes, her eyes gleamed with new determination as she plotted her escape.

chapter 11

Alistair added a few sticks to the fire, then leaned his back against an oak and stretched his feet toward the blaze. The rabbit he had snared was browning nicely, and its scent was carried on a crisp autumn breeze, mingling pleasantly with the scents of woodsmoke and damp leaves. He closed his eyes and listened to the sounds of the evening: the splash of water over stone, the trilling of the birds among the trees, the crackle of the flame and the small hissing sound the rabbit's fat made as it dripped into the fire.

They came seldom, these moments of contentment, rare and precious gifts. Fergus said this state was what all men strove for, which was something of a jest. The essence of contentment was in the very lack of striving. It could not be bought with gold nor won by force of arms. The only way to find it was to stop looking altogether.

It was very strange, Alistair mused. When he left Deirdre Maxwell in the chapel, he had ridden forth in the blackest despair. But for the past two days he had felt curiously empty. He had meant to travel much farther before stopping, for he was a bit too close to Kirallen's border for his comfort. But something about this small sunlit clearing had called to him and he had given in to the temptation to idle away an afternoon. Why not, after all? The day was warm and he had nowhere particular to go. But the afternoon had turned to night and still he lingered, and now another day had passed.

He turned the rabbit on its spit. At least the corbies had vanished from his life. For that, he was grateful. That Deirdre Maxwell had vanished just as surely, he did not want to think about. He resented every moment she occupied his thoughts. Waking, he could keep her at bay, but at night she persisted in invading his dreams.

She came to him as he slept, crowned by a shining nimbus of glowing stars, moving with the regal bearing of a queen. Her hair was loose and flowing as it had been beside the pool, her mouth soft and welcoming beneath his as it had been that evening in the chapel . . . and in the dream things went much further than a kiss. . . .

He muttered a curse and turned the rabbit again, forcing his thoughts back to the present. Tonight he would eat and he would sleep—God grant without dreams—and tomorrow he would see what happened next.

It amused him that he, who had always planned his life—and Ian's, too, as well as Ian's men's—down to the smallest detail, was now content to let tomorrow unfold before him. It would be good or bad, but worrying wouldn't change that. Fergus would say that good and bad were an illusion. The day would simply be what it was. It was he who put his judgment on it.

He walked to the edge of the clearing, then through a small belt of trees and looked down into the sweep of the valley below. The afternoon was drawing on, and a chill mist crept up from the river, shrouding the bottom of the valley. Sunlight caught the edges of the vapor, turning it to a glittering web.

He perched on a rock and drew one knee up, clasping

his arms around it. He was waiting, he realized, but for what? For some sense of purpose to magically appear? For the death the corbies had seemed to promise? Or was he simply waiting for the mist to rise? He had a clear image of himself upon the rock as the mist enfolded him, muffling all sight and sound. When it cleared, the rock would be empty.

He smiled and rested his chin upon his knee. There was no hurry. Sooner or later something would happen. He would wait.

D eirdre paused on the edge of the forest, every muscle tensed as she peered back through the trees. Damn this fog! She could not see above ten yards. But then, she thought, the Maxwells could not see her, either.

"Mam—"

"Hush," Deirdre ordered sternly.

Maeve's chin quivered and her eyes filled with tears. Deirdre was stricken with remorse.

"I'm sorry, love," she said, catching her child in her arms. "You've been a good lass, very good. Just be brave a little longer, all right? Can you do that? Soon we can stop and rest."

"Aye, Mam," Maeve said, her head drooping.

Deirdre listened hard. No hoofbeats. No hounds baying. No horn winding through the forest. They were safe—for now. But tomorrow the hunt would start again.

A wave of weariness hit her, but she straightened her back and lifted Maeve to the saddle, leading the mare carefully through the wood. When she caught the scent of roasting meat she stopped. Maxwell's men? She did not know, but she could take no chances. Moving slowly, wincing at every crackle of twig beneath the horse's hooves, she turned to her left, preparing to go around them.

Half an hour later Deirdre knew she was lost. The sun was hidden, and without it to guide her, she feared she had turned around and was going back the way she had come.

Stop, she thought, leaning wearily against an oak. Think
a bit. Don't go off in a mad rush, for that will gain you
nothing. She looked around carefully, seeing that over to
the right, the trees thinned.

"This way," she said to Maeve, heading for the edge of
the treeline and passing through it. A moment later she
stopped in her tracks, hands white-knuckled on the reins.

The entire world had vanished. She and Maeve stood on
the edge of nowhere, surrounded on all sides by an impenetrable wall of mist. A panicked cry rose to her lips, but she
bit it back, mindful that the Maxwells could be anywhere
and sound traveled in the fog. Heart pounding, palms
sweating, Deirdre forced her mind to work. This could not
last forever. She must be patient, that was all, and it would
clear.

A light breeze ruffled her damp brow. The mist parted
and a shaft of sunlight shot through its depths. Deirdre
stared, too surprised to move, her mouth dropping open in
astonishment. Not thirty paces away, a man was seated on
a rock, the sunlight falling squarely upon him. He lifted his
head and turned to her. She just had time to see the spun
gold of his hair, to note the surprise in his cool gray eyes,
before the mist swirled over him again, hiding Alistair
Kirallen from her sight.

chapter 12

❦

Alistair lifted the two sticks on which the rabbit was suspended and planted them beside the fire. The flesh was crisp but not burnt, he noticed. So he could not have been gone more than a few minutes.

Just long enough to lose his mind.

He shook his head and sank down beside the fire. Was Deirdre Maxwell going to haunt him forever, then, popping in and out of sight like some demon in a pageant? And was he to spend the rest of his life chasing a will-o'-the-wisp as he had just done, scrambling over rough stones and bracken to search vainly for any trace of her?

Well, why not? he thought bleakly. It isn't as though I have anything better to do!

He dropped his head into his hands with a groan, then straightened, his gaze going to the thicket to his right. A horse was approaching down the road beyond. The Maxwells again, he told himself. It must be. All day the wood had been crawling with them, riding to the hunt. So far he had managed to avoid them. Now he sighed, hoping the rider would simply pass him by, though he knew it wouldn't happen.

As the hoofbeats slowed and finally stopped, he glanced at his sword, propped behind him against the tree. Then he shook his head, instead loosening the dagger in its sheathe. It should be enough. He sat back, legs crossed, hands lightly resting on the earth beside him. It was a deceptively relaxed pose, for the slightest pressure on the outsides of his feet would bring him upright in an instant.

The thicket rustled but he pretended not to notice. Let the stranger have a look at him. With luck, whoever it was would go away again and leave him to his meal. As the seconds passed it was almost irresistibly tempting to turn his head and glimpse whoever stood concealed. Go or stay, he thought impatiently. But don't stand there all night gawking.

"Alistair Kirallen?"

The words were hardly more than a whisper, but he was on his feet before the first syllable was complete, the dagger in his hand.

"Who is there?" he called sharply. "Show yourself."

A small cloaked figure stepped from the trees.

"Deirdre?" Alistair whispered, then blinked hard. When he opened his eyes again, she was still there, looking at him uncertainly. "You're really here! But how—"

"Oh, Alistair!" she cried, her voice shaking. "It *is* you! I thought—before—"

"Aye, it's me," he said. He was not mad, after all. She was truly here, standing in the flesh before him. He wanted to laugh out loud, catch her in his arms and kiss her until both of them were breathless. . . .

"Mam!"

For the first time Alistair noticed that Deirdre was not alone. An enchanting sprite of two or three stood just beside her, hands fisted in Deirdre's skirt. She took one look at Alistair and began to cry, turning to clutch her mother's knees.

"This is Maeve, my daughter. She is afraid of men,"

Deirdre said apologetically, caressing the child's curls. "Hush, now, Maeve, he isn't going to hurt you," she added to the child, then looked at Alistair with the question in her eyes.

"Of course I'm not," he said gruffly, annoyed that she thought it necessary to ask. "What happened to ye? Are ye lost?"

"No. Well, yes, perhaps a little—"

"A little? Lady, ye are a full day's ride from Cranston Keep."

"A day?" she repeated, putting one hand against a tree trunk and leaning upon it as though suddenly exhausted. "Is that all? I've been riding since dawn yesterday."

"Sit down," Alistair ordered. "Here, by the fire. Have ye eaten?"

Deirdre sank down on the grass, one arm wrapped protectively around her daughter. The little girl gave Alistair a wary glance and moved to stand behind her mother.

"Not since dawn. I took what I could, but we have to be careful if it's to last us to Annan."

Alistair seized on the one word she had spoken that seemed to make the slightest sense. "Annan? Lady, ye are nowhere near Annan. What are ye doing out here all alone in the first place? Has Maxwell lost his wits, letting you travel—"

He broke off as the baby's chin began to quiver, and she buried her face in her mother's shoulder with a little sob.

"Later," Deirdre said. "Please."

"Of course," Alistair said at once. "Forgive my lack of manners. I have not welcomed you to my castle!" He waved a hand about the clearing.

"Well, Maeve, it seems we are in luck," Deirdre said, her lips quirking in a smile. "I did not expect to find a castle here! And how cleverly you have disguised it, sir! It looks exactly like a forest clearing."

Maeve lifted her head and looked around, her eyes wide and wondering.

" 'Tis all part of the magic, ladies," Alistair said gravely.

"King of the Glen, are you?" Deirdre asked lightly, pleased to see Maeve begin to smile. "Laird of the Mist?"

"Precisely," Alistair agreed. "Did ye no' see how I bade them come and go before? I needed time to prepare a feast worthy of my guests." With the air of a conjurer, he began to lay food before them on the ground. "We have rabbit, bread, and cheese," he announced, and Deirdre's mouth began to water as the scent of the food reached her. "Hazelnuts and, for later, a bit o' honeycomb."

"But we can't eat your entire supper!" Deirdre protested.

"Of course ye can. I'll go catch a fish or two, just over there. Call if ye have need of me."

He walked to the burn and crouched on the edge of the rushing water, pulling a line and hook from the purse at his belt. He was an indifferent fisherman at best, but to his surprise he caught two fine trout, one after the other, almost as soon as his hook went into the water. He cleaned them and wrapped them in leaves, then plastered the whole thing in clay before walking back to the fire.

Maeve scooted closer to her mother when she saw him, but she didn't hide this time. He smiled at her and set the fish to cook among the coals, and after a moment she smiled shyly in return.

"Did ye eat your supper, lass?" he asked. "Oh, I see ye did. Then this is for you."

He held out a bit of honeycomb. She looked from it to his face, every muscle of her small body tensed, reminding Alistair of a wild cat he'd once befriended as a child. He waited with the same patience he'd learned then for her to make up her mind.

She glanced up at her mother and Deirdre nodded. With a frown almost comical on one so young, Maeve set her shoulders and held out her hand as though expecting a blow instead of the offered sweet. Alistair dropped the comb into her palm and stepped back quickly.

Deirdre looked up at him with a smile that warmed him to his toes.

"She's had but few treats," she said as Maeve retreated behind her once again.

Few treats and a fear of men, Alistair thought, shaking his head. Brodie Maxwell's gifts to his daughter.

As he waited for the fish to cook, Alistair slipped back into the timeless contentment he had felt before. All the questions he meant to ask melted into the shaft of deep golden sunlight slanting through the trees. Time enough for questions later. For now it was enough to sit by the fire, from time to time taking in the picture of the woman and her child against the backdrop of the forest.

Deirdre had shed her cloak and leaned against the oak, her eyes half closed as she stared into the flames. The coif had slipped back on her head and a few wisps of hair escaped, startling against the whiteness of her skin.

She was still too thin, he thought, and worn out by her journey, but her face looked soft and far younger than she had seemed that night at Cranston Keep. And that was no surprise. Being wed to Brodie Maxwell would surely age a woman quickly.

The child beside her yawned, her cheeks flushed a brilliant red, her lips sticky with honey. She put her head in her mother's lap and brought the honeycomb to her mouth. And thus, between one heartbeat and the next, she fell asleep.

Deirdre looked down at her with a tenderness that transformed her thin, pale face. Alistair's breath caught in his throat. Had his own mother ever looked at him like that? It did not seem likely.

And yet . . . he remembered a warm presence, a sweet voice, a gentle touch. Surely that had been her. How could he have forgotten that for all these years? And yet, he realized with some surprise, that memory had always been with him, nestled close and secret in his heart.

The afternoon faded into twilight and the fire brightened. When he judged the fish had cooked long enough, he pulled it from the coals and broke the hard clay, sniffing appreciatively as he peeled back the leaves.

"Will ye have some?" he offered.

Deirdre looked up, her eyes wide and startled, as though she had forgotten he was there.

"No," she said. "I've eaten enough of your food already."

" 'Tisn't mine, lady. It comes from the forest and there's enough for all."

She smiled back, somewhat wryly. "Not when you don't know how to find or catch it. I fear I did not bring near enough to last us."

"Two days or three, if ye kept on as ye were going, ye'd have reached Ravenspur. The laird would have welcomed ye."

She shook her head. "I wouldn't have stopped there, not unless we were starving in truth."

"Why not, Deirdre?" he asked directly.

"Because he must know by now that Maxwell is looking for us," she answered. "And I don't mean to be found. I'm going home and Maeve with me."

She put one hand on the child's dark head. "They won't keep her," she said with quiet vehemence. "I will not let them. And I won't stay there myself. He can say what he likes, but I'll not marry at his bidding. I am going back to Donegal and no one, not the Maxwell himself, will stop me."

"Ah, I see," Alistair said. He frowned, picking at the fish. " 'Tis a long way to Donegal."

"The journey has been made before," she answered briskly.

"Not by a lone woman and a child with the Maxwells hunting them."

"Have you seen them?"

"All day I've heard men passing through the wood."

She paled and the strained look returned to her face. "We should go on, then."

"What, at night? Don't be ridiculous," he said, more sharply than he'd intended. "Stay here where you're safe. Ye look like ye could use the rest. And your horse—"

"The horse!" She sat up straight.

Alistair sighed. "I'll get her."

He found the mare tethered loosely just off the path. He swore softly as he considered that any one of Maxwell's men could have seen her there. For that matter, his fire could draw them still.

He led the stumbling horse to a patch of grass beside the burn and hobbled her beside his own. Then he stamped the fire out.

"Deirdre," he said, sitting down beside her. "I ken that ye want to return home, but ye canna just run off into the wood with no idea where you're going."

"I can do what I must."

Her voice was calm and very, very certain. She straightened her shoulders and looked at him coolly, as if he was a rather dim-witted servitor with no conception of royal duties.

"Perhaps ye can," Alistair said grudgingly. "But what of the child? Is it fair to drag her from her home and—"

"Fair? Aye, 'tis fair, Alistair Kirallen. Else she'll live all her life a prisoner at Cranston Keep. I will not have it," she said, as though issuing orders from a throne. "Not for her nor for myself. But that is not your worry."

"D'ye think I'll leave ye to wander until ye starve or Maxwell's men take ye?"

"Neither of those things will happen." She waved a hand, dismissing his words with an arrogance that astounded him, given her complete lack of resources. "Tomorrow or the next day we shall be out of Maxwell's demesne. Without his men to trouble us, we can keep to the path and make good time. I thank you for the meal and fire," she added graciously. "But from here on in we shall be fine."

She meant it. Every foolish word that came from her lips was spoken with complete conviction. She was lost in the forest, without food, without a plan, without the slightest idea of what she was facing. Yet for all that, he had been dismissed. She did not want his help.

"Fine?" he snapped. "That I doubt. Maxwell will never

give up until he finds ye. Best go back and seek his mercy now."

"I beg no man's pardon when I am in the right," she answered proudly. "My father had Brodie's word that I would be free to return home if I was widowed—and I should have the gold to do it. It was the one thing Father insisted upon, and Brodie gave in at the last. But now old Maxwell denies it. Damn his lying tongue! I will not go back there—they cannot make me—"

"Whisht," Alistair said quickly, hearing the tremor in her voice. "If ye willna go, ye willna."

"That's right." She sniffed. "I shan't. Nor will Maeve. We are going home, the two of us together. I have enough for our passage once we reach Annan."

"Then ye best get some sleep," he said, thoroughly exasperated. " 'Tis a long way ye have to travel."

Stubborn, foolish female, he thought as he wrapped himself in his cloak and settled down to sleep. But about one thing she was right: it was none of his concern.

He twisted on the hard ground, trying to get comfortable. There was really no need for him to worry. Even if she insisted on traveling on, it would all come to naught. Maxwell would likely have her back again before she came to any harm. It seemed a pity that the old man was so quick to break the bargain his son had made, but that was typical of Maxwell. He was a tight-fisted bastard, always had been. Age had only made him worse.

Deirdre didn't stand a chance against him, Alistair thought, giving up the attempt to sleep and sitting up. Not one woman all alone, burdened with a helpless child. The whole plan—if such a wild, ill-judged venture could be dignified by such a name—was absurd. But brave, he admitted reluctantly. He'd have to give her full marks for courage. She must want to get home very badly.

It was the man, he decided. The one she'd spoken of the first night they met, the one she'd left behind in Ireland. He wondered who the man was and if he was worth all this trouble. Well, he must be worth it to Deirdre. If it was a

song or story, he supposed he would admire the loyalty
that drove her to this desperate act.

What kind of story was her tale, he mused, drawing his
sword and taking the whetstone from his pouch. One that
ended happily with the lovers reunited? Or a sad one in
which she was caught—or set upon by thieves or tinkers—
or she and the child starved together in the forest—and the
man she sought never even knew that she had tried?

How the devil did I get dragged into her story? he wondered irritably. She had made it clear—not once, but twice
now—that she wanted nothing more to do with him. And
that was fine with him. The very last thing he needed was
to entangle himself with any woman, no matter how
sweetly she fit into his arms. Let her save her kisses for the
Irishman or, if her luck failed, for whatever man Maxwell
decided should have her slim white hand in marriage. It
was naught to him.

The branches up above his head fluttered without any
breeze to stir them. They are back, he thought with weary
dread. The damned corbies had found him once again.

God's blood, but he was tired of them. And he was sick
to death of tales that ended badly. His own ending he knew,
and it wasn't a nice one. But what was nice about any
death?

It all goes by so quickly, he thought, listening to the
woman and the child breathing softly in their sleep.
Nothing—not rank or gold or skill at arms—could save
anyone in the end. Death would always win.

"Oh, what the hell," he muttered, loosening the dagger
in his sheathe. He might as well use the time that he had
left to see that Deirdre's story turned out a bit more happily than his own.

chapter 13

❦

The forest was coming alive around them as Alistair knelt by the mare, one hand running down her foreleg.

"When did she begin to limp?" he asked, not looking up.

"Last night she was a little lame," Deirdre said, kneeling beside him and looking anxiously at the mare. "I checked, but there was no stone that I could see—"

"The muscle is strained. She canna carry ye."

Deirdre's hands clenched into fists, but her voice was even when she said, "Then she'll have to find her own way home. She'll be all right until she does, there's plenty of grass and water."

Alistair looked up at her and she glanced away, not wanting to see the expression in his eyes. He'd made his opinion of her plans clear enough last night, and she had no intention of arguing the matter further.

"If we must walk, we shall walk," she said firmly. "Come, Maeve, it's time we left."

Maeve obediently gave her mother her hand, looking up at her so trustingly that Deirdre's throat ached with sudden tears. Oh, God, what was she doing? What kind of mother was she to even think of risking Maeve's life this way? But what kind of life would Maeve have ahead of her at Cranston Keep? She straightened her shoulders and smiled encouragingly at her daughter.

"There will be no need for that," Alistair said as he pulled a currycomb from his saddlebag and began to groom his own horse. "Germain can carry the both of ye."

"You'd give us your horse?" Deirdre asked, stunned by the generosity of the offer.

"Weel, nay, not exactly. I need him, ye ken. I'm afraid you'll have to take the both of us."

"Take you?" Deirdre repeated weakly. "Take you where?"

"I've always wanted to see Annan."

His hands moved over the horse's back in quick, competent strokes. But then, everything about Alistair Kirallen screamed competence. From the moment she had stumbled upon him last night, he had taken charge of everything, making sure they had enough to eat, giving Deirdre the first decent rest she'd had since old Maxwell made his announcement.

Twice during the night she'd woken with a start of fear to see Alistair sitting at the clearing's edge, a faint outline against the darkness of the forest, the drawn sword across his knees glittering coldly in the moonlight.

"Mam!" Maeve tugged on her hand, pulling Deirdre down to her. "It's him. Sir Star. Laird of the Mist, Mam. Ye said so."

"Oh, nay, sweeting," Deirdre said, caught between tears and laughter. "'Tis only Sir Alistair Kirallen, as I told you—"

Maeve shook her head and her dark curls flew in wisps about her flushed cheeks. "Nay, Mam. Look at his sword!"

Of course his sword was bright, Deirdre thought. He'd had the entire night to sharpen it! And all because he'd stayed awake and watchful.

He would protect them. She was sure of that. But what

did he expect in return? She felt badly even asking the question after all his kindness, and yet it must be asked. She was not about to enter into any bargain she did not fully understand. Not again.

"It is very kind of you," she said firmly, "but I don't see why you would take such a risk. We'll have to go through Kirallen's lands, and you know that isn't safe for you—"

" 'Tis no so great a risk as all that," he answered, swinging the saddle from the branch onto the horse's back. "I know the paths they ride and others, too." He rested his arms on the saddle and looked at her, his gray eyes very steady. "I'm doing it because I want to. There's no more to it than that. Ye needn't fear I'll ask for something in return."

"I didn't mean—"

"Och, of course ye did. And quite rightly, too. 'Tis natural enough for ye to wonder. The truth is," he added lightly, bending to tighten the girth, "I've taken quite a fancy to Mistress Maeve. Every knight needs a lady to serve—'tis the rule, ye ken, and I'm all for following the rules—so I've decided she'll be mine."

He knelt before the child. "My lady," he said gravely, holding out his laced fingers. "Your steed awaits."

Maeve smiled, two dimples appearing in her cheeks. "S-Star!" she said.

"Weel, his name is Germain—or at least it was—but I suppose—"

Maeve shook her head and touched Alistair's cheek. "Star," she said firmly.

Alistair's mouth twitched and Deirdre held her breath, certain he would burst out laughing. She had only meant to set the child at ease with her nonsense last evening, and now Maeve had somehow tangled Alistair with the enchanted knight of Deirdre's stories. But if he laughed at her now, Maeve would be devastated.

It was seldom that Maeve spoke to anyone save Deirdre. She was a very quiet child, existing in a world of her own imagination. Deirdre was well aware that the Maxwells thought her simple. They made no attempt to understand her, and their unkind laughter had moved Maeve first to tears and then to stubborn silence.

But Alistair did not laugh. "That's Sir Star," he said to Maeve, and the girl smiled brilliantly. "At your service."

Deirdre blinked back sudden tears as Maeve put her tiny foot into Alistair's waiting hands. It was a small thing he had done, but Maeve was staring at him as though he was in truth the shining knight straight out of legend. She asked so little, Deirdre thought. Just a bit of kindness. Brodie had never cared enough to show her even that.

"Will ye ride, as well?" Alistair asked, turning to Deirdre.

"I can walk."

He took the reins and began to lead the horse down the path. "Come along, then. Let's walk."

The day was warm with a brisk little breeze that kept them comfortable as they passed quietly along the sun-splashed path. They kept a good pace, and the miles melted away beneath Deirdre's eager feet. Home, home, it grew closer with each step she took. She could almost hear the mewling gulls, feel the ocean breeze upon her face. Oh, she couldn't wait to show it all to Maeve. They would explore every one of the secret places she'd discovered as a child, and Maeve would grow strong and well and happy in the salty sea air.

Deirdre thought of Ronan Fitzgerald then, so much a part of her own childhood, and her heart faltered. She had dreamed of him last night, a strange dream, very clear. He had stood beside her as she lay sleeping.

"I'll be there soon," he had said. "Don't worry, Dee. I'll find you."

Well, everyone had dreams, and far stranger ones than that! Yet a part of her feared that Ronan was indeed on his way to find her. And if he was, the fault was hers for letting her thoughts dwell on him so much the night Alistair had arrived at Cranston Keep. Ronan had always known when Deirdre was in trouble or had need of him.

Years ago, when she was still a child, Deirdre had fallen down the cellar stairs and sprained her ankle. Ronan had appeared moments later, saying he had a feeling something was amiss. And once, when she had walked out to a small island and been stranded by the tide, Ronan had led her father straight to her. Even Father had been impressed by that! And so had Deirdre. But then, she had never denied there was a special bond between them.

There was no one's company she preferred to Ronan's, no one she trusted more completely. If she could have loved him as he wanted, she would have done so. But she could not. And if Ronan had a bit more sense, he would have realized she was doing him a favor by refusing him. But though Ronan had many gifts, sense was the one thing he had always lacked.

In his last letter Deirdre's father had said Ronan was back from his travels, still unmarried, still pining over Deirdre. And when they met again, their friendship, so precious to her, would be shattered beyond mending. If he asked—and he would, she was sure of it—she would refuse, as kindly as she could, but very firmly. She had no intention of marrying again. Once had been quite enough.

No doubt Ronan would compose a new song lamenting Deirdre's cruelty, and when he sang it the most hardened warrior would weep into his ale. Oh, Ronan's pain was genuine, she thought with quick remorse, and she was sorry to have caused it. But she would have been a good deal sorrier had he not been so quick to turn his pain to verse and find a fitting melody!

Now she stole a glance at Alistair, walking along with an easy, loose-limbed stride. Somehow she could not imagine *him* wasting a moment in pining for a lady. No, it was far more likely that he would use that slow smile and deep soft voice to win her for his own.

Jennie and the others had giggled like girls in the kitchen the night that Alistair had arrived at Cranston

Keep, saying he knew a thousand tricks to woo a woman to his bed, jesting about his prowess between the sheets.

"Now, there's a man who kens how to pleasure a lass," one of them had said, a grin tugging at the corners of her mouth. Pleasure? Deirdre had wondered with a shudder, even as the others burst into eager laughing questions. What possible pleasure could there ever be for a woman in *that*?

She glanced at Alistair again, and a shiver, half fear and half excitement, started at the pit of her stomach and rippled slowly downward. What exactly did he *do* with a woman in his bed? It must—surely it *must* be something very different than Brodie had done with her. She studied his eyes, so cool and distant, and wondered how they would look at a woman lying in his arms. Her glance lingered on the sensual curve of his lips, the breadth of his shoulders, moved down to his hands, so strong, yet capable of gentleness, as well. . . .

But whatever it was he did, she wouldn't be finding out. For Alistair Kirallen, who had bedded every lass from Aberdeen to Berwick—at least to hear Jennie tell it—now seemed content to have her as a friend and nothing more.

For which I should be on my knees, thanking all the gods, she reminded herself sharply. A friend was exactly what she needed now, and this man's friendship most of all. And it was best that way, because of one thing she was certain. After Alistair had wooed the woman, taken her to bed and did whatever it was he did there, he would go on again. Alone. In the end Alistair would always walk alone.

She laid a hand on Maeve's small leg and smiled at her daughter. They were going home together. And once they were safe, she'd never trouble about any man again.

chapter 14

H*e was awake.*
 Grianne Nixon knelt down beside the pallet, careful
of her aching joints. The man lying on the straw tried to lift
himself but fell back, one hand clutching his bandaged head.

"Lie still," she said in the toneless voice of the deaf.

His lips moved, and though she could not hear his
words, the meaning was plain enough.

"My grandson pulled ye from the river," she said, offering
him a spoonful of hot broth. "I've been tending to ye since."

His lips formed the words, "How long?"

"About a fortnight," she answered, putting the spoon to
his lips. He accepted the broth hungrily, but before the
bowl was empty, he lay back and fell asleep.

She rose stiffly to her feet and shuffled back to the fire,
picking up the torn plaid the man had worn and squinting
as she threaded her needle.

Not a word of thanks did he think to give me, she
thought, shaking her head. But then, what could ye expect
from a Maxwell?

chapter 15

Deirdre woke with a start, heart pounding in her breast, Maeve's panicked screams ringing in her ears.

"What?" she said, straining to see into the darkness. "Maeve—"

Maeve twisted beside her on the forest floor, tangled in her cloak, her small fists flailing wildly. Deirdre caught her hands and held them close. "What is it, Maeve? Are you hurt?"

"Ugly!" the child cried. "No—get away—"

"It's just a nightmare."

Alistair's voice was deep and calm as he bent over Maeve, thrusting his dagger back into its sheathe.

"Wake up, love," Deirdre pleaded. "'Tis a dream, no more, it can't hurt you—"

"Nay!" Maeve sobbed. "Ugly! Mam!"

"I'm right here, love, just beside you. Wake up now."

The child stopped struggling and lay very still. "Mam?"

"That's right," Deirdre breathed. "I'm here."

Maeve was crying in soft, heartbroken sobs that tore at Deirdre's chest. "What is it, sweeting?" she asked.

"The man," Maeve sobbed. "Ugly."

"Hush, now," Deirdre said. "'Twas just a dream, 'twasn't real."

Maeve twisted from beneath her hand, her breath coming in great noisy gulps. "No!" she cried. "Real—"

"Was it a monster, then?" Alistair asked.

The child trembled in Deirdre's arms. "Monster."

"Ah, well, then you've naught to fear," he said. "I've fought more monsters than ye can count. Why, there was one I met just the other day, a great hairy fellow with long arms and huge white fangs. But after we'd fought a bit, he ran off, crying for his mam."

"He did?" Maeve gulped.

"Oh, aye. And then there was the other one, a huge great dragon with red-gold scales and teeth as long as my arm, sitting on the biggest pile of gold you've ever seen. He riddled me three times and three times I answered. Dragons are no so clever as they think they are," he added confidentially. "The trick is to keep your sword to hand and your wits about ye. We parted well enough in the end, for I let him keep his gold, all but a pretty bauble I took, just in case one day I should meet a lady who needed one."

Maeve's body was soft and heavy against Deirdre's now. "Dragon," she whispered drowsily. "Giants?"

"Oh, so ye know about giants, do ye?" Alistair said.

"Finn Mac Coul," Maeve said with a sleepy smile.

"Well, I'm sorry to say I've never met him in particular," Alistair said, "though one time, way up in the hills on a fine spring morning, with the sun shining bright and the birds all singing and the sky the same blue as your bonny eyes . . ."

As his voice grew lower and finally died to silence, Deirdre laid the sleeping Maeve back on the ground and covered her again. Alistair added wood to the fire and drew his sword and whetstone.

"You're very good with her," Deirdre said, sitting down beside him and holding her hands out to the blaze.

"I like bairns." He shrugged, running the stone against

the blade and testing it with his thumb. "And ye ken I've had my share of nightmares."

Deirdre nodded. Not a night had passed that Alistair didn't start at least once from his sleep, waking her from the fitful doze that was all she usually could manage.

"Do you dream of monsters, as well?" she asked lightly.

"Nay." For a moment it seemed he would say no more, then he sighed and added, "I dream of Ian. I thought I was finished with all that, but these past days the dream has started up again. It always begins the same way. . . ."

He told her of the day when he and Ian had found young Jemmy tied to a tree, the way he and Ian had fought the tinker lads, and how Ian ran off after them.

"Up until then, it's all just how it happened," he said, "Once Ian was gone, I saw to Jemmy as he bade me, but in the dream, every time, when Ian runs off, I know that he's heading straight for Darnley's ambush. I chase him, but I never reach him in time.

"Sometimes I end up back at Ravenspur. And the laird—he looks at Ian and then at me and I know what he's thinking, why are you alive when he is dead? It all comes back then, knowing how I failed him, failed Ian, failed my men . . . and then the laird gives a great cry and falls down senseless, just as he really did that day.

"But usually I come out of the forest and I'm on the moor and there they all are—my men—lying in the bloody snow with Darnley riding off. And then I stay with Ian while he dies again—and again—" He stared into the dark forest, his face strained and pale. "If only I could catch him," he whispered. "If only I could reach him in time . . ."

"Then what?" Deirdre asked gently. "What could you do if you reached him? He's dead and gone."

"He may be dead, but I think—at times I wonder if he is truly gone."

Deirdre shot an uneasy glance about the clearing, then gave herself a shake. "Of course he is gone," she said briskly. "'Tis yourself you should be worrying for now."

He ran a hand across his face and shot her a wry smile. "Thank you, lady," he said. "You are quite right, of course."

He bent to his sword again, his expression chill and shut.

Deirdre watched the competent movements of his hands, sensing he regretted confiding in her. She could hardly blame him. She had handled it badly, she knew that, but while tales of spirits might be fine around a winter's fire in a crowded hall, out here in the dark forest it was a bit unnerving.

"Do you not miss Ravenspur?" she asked, breaking the awkward silence. "Are you not wanting to be home again?"

"Nay," he said flatly. "Oh, I miss Malcolm, even the laird, at times, but Ravenspur is—" He broke off, frowning. "There's too much hatred there, too many old wounds that canna heal. 'Tis a bad place these days, at least for me. I don't belong there anymore." He stopped, looking faintly surprised. "It's taken me a long time to see that."

"Then what will you do next?"

"Who knows?" He glanced up into the trees. "I'm just marking time, Deirdre. One road's much the same as any other these days."

She glanced up, as well; it seemed an icy finger was laid upon her neck as she heard the faintest flutter of dark wings above.

"So you mean to wander rootless through the world until you die?" she burst out, fear sharpening her words. "Is that it? Just go from here to there as the wind blows you?"

"The wind blew me into your path, lady," he reminded her. "But for that, you would be back at Cranston Keep."

"But what about when I am gone? What then, Alistair?"

He shrugged. "I'll see what happens next."

She had the sudden desire to slap him hard, just to see if she could rouse him from the dark dream he wandered in.

"You'll see what happens next?" she repeated derisively. "Sure and that is the most pathetic, cowardly thing I have ever heard!"

He looked at her, his eyes kindling with anger. "I dinna recall asking your opinion on the matter."

"I *dinna* recall it, either," she snapped. "Consider it a gift. There are a thousand things you could do, but no, you want to skulk about the forest like some poor doomed outcast, wasting all your talents!"

He laughed shortly. "My talents, is it? My men are dead, my pledge is broken, and my kin have turned me out. Oh, I'm a fine prospect! Of course, there are still some things I can manage. I can kill a man in twenty different ways—now, there's a talent for ye! Makes me verra popular among men who need killing done. The trouble is, I've had my fill of fighting battles that have naught to do with me and killing men who've done me no wrong. And that is all I'm good for now."

"Don't be ridiculous. You could leave this place and start again, try something new. But no, of course you wouldn't do that—'tis too much effort!"

"Well, lady, since ye are so free with your advice tonight, where do ye suggest I go?"

"To Ireland," she said, then stopped, surprised. "Yes, to Ireland," she said after a moment. "Why not? You could take service there. . . . My father would welcome you to Tullyleah, and he knows every family in Donegal."

Alistair glanced at her, brows raised. "Ye mean I should try my hand at killing a few Irishmen? It seems hardly worth the journey. From all I've heard, they bleed and die just the same as we do over here."

"You don't have to be a hired sword," Deirdre said with exaggerated patience. "You are a seasoned commander, Sir Alistair, and your reputation—"

"—is black as pitch," he said flatly. "Oh, it may not have carried as far as Ireland, but there is enough coming and going that it willna stay secret long. Who would want me then?"

"My father," she said at once. "He would. When he learns what you have done for us, he'll find a place for you. He won't care what anyone says about it, either. He never does. Father is . . . well, he goes his own way, always has. And he would be very grateful."

Why had she not thought of this before? Alistair deserved some return for all the trouble he had taken, and she was pleased to offer him such a perfect solution to his problems. Perfect in more ways than one, she thought, looking at him sideways.

Just the thought of Alistair living at Tullyleah, where she would see him every day, made her heart beat a little faster. He could redeem himself in Ireland. He could be more than a homeless outcast. If he wanted to, he could be a very eligible suitor. If he wanted to. But did he?

"I thank you, lady," Alistair said stiffly, "but I have no been reduced to taking charity just yet."

"Charity?" She laughed. "Oh, it wouldn't be that. We cannot afford charity. We cannot afford *anything*! Between the O'Neills and the O'Donnells, there's precious little left for the MacLochlanns. But we still have Tullyleah."

Oh, if only she could tell him how wonderful it was! She could almost see it, the ruined walls and one standing tower, just at the top of the cliff, with the sea below and the endless sky above.

"It is so beautiful, Alistair—oh, 'tis old and a bit crumbly, I suppose, not grand at all. But it is always full of music and dancing. . . . *Everyone* comes to Tullyleah! Even if the rain does drip on their heads, it doesn't matter. They come anyway, and we have such good times. . . ."

He was staring at her in surprise, and she let her words trail into silence, suddenly embarrassed at her enthusiasm.

"MacLochlann?" he said. "That is your family?"

"Well, yes," Deirdre answered, puzzled. "Why?"

"*Thus fell the MacLochlanns,*" Alistair chanted softly.

> *"Kings of Aileach and monarchs of Eire,*
> *Deprived of a kingdom*
> *Through the fortunes of battle*
> *And the schemes of their rivals;*
> *Trapped between swords,*
> *Red ran their blood,*
> *On the hills of Caim Eirge."*

In his own voice he said, "That is your family? Kings of Aileach and monarchs of Eire?"

"Several hundred years ago," Deirdre said, surprised and a bit embarrassed. "Wherever did you hear that bit of song?"

"We had a tutor when I was younger, came from Ulster way." He was looking at her very strangely, as though he had never really seen her before. "Aye," he added quietly, seeming to speak to himself. "That explains it."

"Explains what?"

He grinned suddenly. "The way ye order me about, for one thing."

"It doesn't seem to do me much good," she answered grumpily. "You never listen."

"Och, I wouldna say that. Are we not bound for Annan, exactly as Your Highness desires?" He made her a mock bow, very graceful, and she couldn't help but laugh.

"You should think about the rest of it, as well," she said. "Coming to Tullyleah."

"Leave Scotland?" Alistair looked troubled. "Forever? I've never thought of it."

"I don't see why not," Deirdre said shortly, pulling her cloak around her and standing. "'Tis a horrid place."

chapter 16

They woke to rain that went on and on, sometimes in a downpour, sometimes in a drizzle, slowing their progress to a crawl. The sodden earth squelched beneath their feet, and their clothing would not dry, even when Alistair succeeded in igniting a sullen little fire. By dusk they were all exhausted, and Alistair, who knew this stretch of forest well, insisted they seek shelter at a woodsman's cottage. The old man who inhabited it was hardly welcoming, but when Alistair showed him a coin, he let them inside.

Alistair went to stable the horse and Deirdre cast a nervous look around the filthy room, very much aware that the woodsman was watching her with sly, sideways glances. His enormous dog, surely the biggest she had ever seen, sprawled between them and the fire, stealing a large measure of its heat.

Deirdre eyed the hound apprehensively. It stared back, then yawned, exposing enormous fangs that glinted in the firelight. Deirdre stepped back a little and stumbled into the woodsman, who was standing just behind her.

"I've naught to give ye," he said.

"That's fine," she answered quickly. "We have dried meat and bread—will you share it?"

"Aye. I will."

She had just turned to their small bag of provisions when a movement caught her eye.

"No, Maeve!" she cried. "Stand back!"

The child had walked over to the dog. It lifted its head from its enormous paws and looked straight into her eyes. Before Deirdre could move, the hound sniffed Maeve's outstretched hands, then put his tongue out and licked the girl's face.

"That's enough, sweeting," Deirdre said, picking up her giggling child and setting her on a bench.

"Nice doggy," Maeve said.

"*Big* doggy," Deirdre answered. "Too big to be playing with tonight. Here, now," she added quickly, putting a bit of bread into Maeve's hand. "Eat."

The woodsman walked over to the dog and kicked it in the ribs. "Out!" he commanded.

The hound cringed away, and as Alistair opened the door, it slipped past him into the night. The woodsman gave Alistair his sideways stare. "Mayhap I've seen ye before."

"Mayhap ye have, grandfather," Alistair answered, shaking the rain from his cloak and spreading it on the earthen floor before the fire. "But whether or no, I think ye'd best forget ye saw me here tonight."

The old man nodded quickly. "Aye, well, 'tis none of my affair."

"That's true," Alistair agreed. "'Tis not."

There was no more talk as they consumed their meager meal. With another of Alistair's coins clutched in his hand, the woodsman took himself off to an outbuilding to sleep. Deirdre squeezed into a tiny alcove beside Maeve, but though the straw was fresh and fragrant, she could not sleep. She didn't like the way the woodsman looked at them and then their baggage, as though weighing up his chances.

The night was halfway through when she rose to replenish the dying fire. When the logs began to blaze, she sat back on her heels and held her hands out to the flame, then jumped with a startled cry as a hand touched her shoulder.

"Go back to sleep," Alistair said. "Ye need your rest."

"I'm nervous as a cat tonight," she whispered back. "That man—he looks at us as if he means us no good."

"Perhaps he doesna," Alistair said, amused. "But you mustna lose any sleep over him. He won't dare try anything tonight. He kens well enough who I am."

"And he could earn a piece of gold, perhaps, if he went to Ravenspur with his information," she said, voicing one of the fears that kept her wakeful.

"I'm sure he means to," Alistair agreed. "But 'tis half a day's walk to Ravenspur from where we sit. By the time he gets there and finds someone to listen to his tale, we'll be long gone."

The sound of his voice, so calm, so unconcerned, loosened the tight knot of worry in Deirdre's stomach. Alistair had realized the danger already. For all he might claim to live from one moment to the next, apparently he was quite capable of thinking ahead.

There was no denying that she and Maeve would never have made it this far without him. And in return he had received exactly what he asked: nothing. Except, of course, her unwanted advice, delivered with the rough side of her tongue. And her offer to come to Tullyleah, which he had apparently rejected out of hand.

"Alistair," she said contritely. "I haven't even thanked you for everything you have done for us."

He smiled, head bent as he tested the edge of his dagger. "No need for thanks, Deirdre."

They sat in silence for a time, as the rain lashed against the roof and the wind gusted down the chimney. Alistair put his dagger down carefully and dropped the whetstone beside it. Then he turned and looked straight into her eyes.

"A man gets weary of traveling alone."

Oh, Jennie had been wrong, Deirdre thought, her heart pounding. Alistair Kirallen was not the sort of man who would trick a woman to his bed. No, he was very honest about it. He wanted her, right now, tonight, and made no attempt to hide behind pretty words or empty promises. It was all there in his eyes: his loneliness, his need, all there for her to see, offered with a shattering directness that stole her breath away. And yet he made it easy to refuse; she only had to glance the other way and make some remark about the lateness of the hour, the need to rest. . . .

She felt the blush rise up her neck and flood her face, but still she could not look away. Did not want to look away. A log cracked in the fire and fell apart in a shower of bright sparks; the wind gusted against the shutters, rattling them in their frames. Slowly she reached out one shaking hand to brush the tangled hair from his brow.

This would not be forever, she thought. He was not the sort of man to commit himself beyond a single night. But for this night he wanted her. He *needed* her. And, she realized with a shock of violent longing, she needed him, as well.

A shiver ran through her body as he caught her hand and brought it to his lips. When his mouth moved lazily across her palm, a surge of unbearable anticipation rushed through her, sent her spinning into a place of shimmering light and warmth.

Right or wrong ceased to matter. They were distant concepts that held no meaning for her now. He was the one. She had known it from the first. Her choice had been made already, long ago in some other place, and she no longer had the will to fight it.

Alistair closed his eyes as Deirdre's fingers brushed his face. It had been so long, too long since he had lost himself in a woman's arms. And this chance might never come again. Tonight she was alone and frightened, completely at his mercy. It would be so easy to take advantage of her momentary weakness. But it wouldn't be like that, not really. He would see that she did not regret it.

She slid easily into his arms, her body flowing against his, and her mouth was soft and sweet. He kissed her slowly, sensing her uncertainty, knowing instinctively that she had never experienced anything like this before. And come to that, he thought, surprised, neither had he. Though what the difference was, he could not say.

When he parted her lips, she dug her fingers into his shoulders and arched against him, so wantonly inviting that he was tempted to lie her down on the floor and take her then and there. But as his hand moved up her waist to cup her breast, she pulled back, eyes wide open and every muscle tensed.

"What is it?" he asked softly.

"Nothing. Nothing at all," she answered, giving him a false, bright smile. "I'm sorry."

She pressed herself against him again, but it was not the same. Her body was stiff, and though she tipped her head back, inviting his kiss, her eyes were dark and frightened.

Brodie, he thought, and a surge of violent anger tore through him. He had used her badly—blind, stupid bastard that he was. If the man wasn't dead already, Alistair would gladly have murdered him at that moment. But Brodie was dead. The question now was how to banish his memory forever and undo the damage he had done.

"It's all right," he whispered, cradling her against him. "There's nothing to be sorry for, nothing at all. . . ."

He held her then, as the fire dwindled and the shadows grew, until he felt the tension leave her. Then he pushed the coif back from her hair and deftly unwound the long black braid. Her hair was cool, sliding between his fingers, around his wrists, and it smelled faintly of some wildflower. He buried his face in its darkness and felt her heart pounding against his chest. Like a little bird, he thought, his throat aching with wild tenderness. So beautiful. So right.

Moving slowly, careful not to frighten her, he eased her down beneath him and looked into her eyes. She gazed up at him, still a little hesitant, but curious, as well, trusting him to make it all come right between them. And he knew that he could do just that. There was nothing he wanted more than to give her all the joy that she had missed, and in giving, find something more than pleasure.

She drew him down and he went, his mouth closing over hers. This time her lips parted eagerly beneath his. One night, he thought, deepening the kiss. That was all that he could hope for. Tomorrow she would see, as he already did, that there could be no more than that. Deirdre MacLochlann Maxwell, daughter of the kings of Aileach and monarchs of Eire, was not meant for the likes of him. If he had any sense, he would stop this right now.

When he broke the kiss she sighed, her lips warm against his neck, her fingers tangled in his hair. Her leg bent, slid up his thigh, and his resolve wavered, then crumbled into dust. He ran his hand slowly up the slim line of her waist, tracing the curve of her breast, feeling her nipple harden beneath his palm. A searing flame of desire shot through him as she moaned softly, her leg tightening on his. Tomorrow be damned. Tonight she would be his.

But when she drew back a little, her lips parted and her eyes glowing, he knew one night would never be enough. No, not one night or two—even a dozen would not begin to teach him all he longed to know. It would take many nights, and many days as well to know her fully. Days spent loving her, talking with her, listening to her laugh, watching each expression as it passed across her face.

He wanted to know everything about her—what touch would make her shiver with delight, the games she had played as a child, what she believed would happen after death. . . . One night could never answer all his questions. With Deirdre it would take a lifetime.

But he didn't have a lifetime. And even if he did have years before him, what difference would it make? There was nothing he could offer her save disgrace, dishonor, and the bare existence of a gypsy tinker.

He could still have the one night, he thought, smoothing the hair back from her face, kissing her brow, her eyes, the sweet curve of her cheek. One night of joy. One night that would surely break his heart. For in the morning they would both know he had taken advantage of her loneliness to win a single night of pleasure. In her eyes—and in his— he would be no better than Brodie, taking what he wanted with no thought of what was best for her. He would lose her trust, her friendship, the chance simply to be near her and sometimes make her smile.

He could not bear to lose her. Not now, not yet. She was so brave and beautiful, so very much alive, the only brightness on the dark path he was traveling. With an effort that seemed to tear him in two he sat up and took his arms from around her.

"I'm sorry, Deirdre. I—oh, Christ, I'm sorry," he repeated helplessly. "'Tis verra late and we both are tired. Too tired to be thinking clearly."

"Oh."

Just the one word, but it was enough to pierce him to the heart, and when he saw the tears shining in her eyes, it took all his strength not to reach for her again. Instead he said deliberately, "Ye never told me about the man ye left behind in Ireland."

"Who?" she said, obviously bewildered. "What man?"

"There is a man, is there no? Someone waiting for ye?"

"Oh! Well, I suppose. . . ."

"What is his name?" Alistair insisted, some devil prompting him to hear what could only cause him pain.

"Ronan," she said, her voice choked.

"Ah. And what sort of man is Ronan?"

"He—he is a Fitzgerald—at least, his father was. His mother was an O'Donnell."

A Fitzgerald. Of course. Even if it was a Norman name, not quite so noble as Deirdre's, the Fitzgeralds were a powerful force in Ireland these days. The old nobility and the new, he thought. A good and proper union for them both.

Deirdre began to braid her hair, pulling it with quick, vicious jerks that looked as though they hurt. He wanted to grab her hands and still them against his lips. Instead he bent to the fire.

"Really?" he said, surprised to hear his voice come out so calmly. "And have ye known this Ronan long?"

"All my life. We were betrothed—a cradle match. After King Edward outlawed marriages between his Norman lords and the Irish, the match was broken. But he still visits Tullyleah—my father wrote that he was there just last spring—and we are still—friends."

"I am sure they will all be pleased to have ye back," Alistair said evenly. "Sleep now. We'll start at dawn."

As she went back to her place beside Maeve, he threw a stick into the fire and watched the cinders leap. Friends, indeed! He saw the whole thing now, the two young lovers torn apart, Deirdre's forced marriage to Brodie Maxwell. But they were not helpless children anymore. And if young Ronan Fitzgerald—noble, wealthy, in every way a fitting match for Deirdre—did not still want her, the man must be either a eunuch or a fool.

But Alistair himself was neither. He ached for her—literally, he thought, shifting uncomfortably on the hard-packed earthen floor. And he would just have to keep on aching, for Deirdre MacLochlann Maxwell was far out of his reach. She was meant for a man of wealth and rank, not the bastard offspring of a crofter's daughter and the smooth-tongued, lying knight who had so basely used her.

At least I haven't repeated his mistakes, Alistair thought. There had been no virgins for him, no rings or empty promises. He had made damned sure that any woman who shared his bed understood exactly what he offered. If any of them had ever come to him and claimed him as father to her child, Alistair would have welcomed the bairn with joy and given it his name. But that was when he had a name that meant something. If he and Deirdre had begotten a

child here tonight, she would have no choice but to pass it
off as Brodie's get. It would never have even known who
its father was.

He had done the right thing. The only thing. But when
he picked up a stick and broke it across his knee, he took
grim pleasure in imagining it was Ronan Fitzgerald's neck
he snapped.

chapter 17

❧

The rain stopped mid-morning, though the sun still hid behind heavy clouds and the wind blew cold and damp. They trudged along in silence until they halted for their noontime meal. Maeve seemed tired. Deirdre hoped the child wasn't coming down with a chill. If only the rain would hold off long enough to make a fire tonight . . . and they could find some dry ground to sleep on. . . .

Hold on, Maeve, she thought. We're going to make it. We're going home.

"In Donegal," she began, then stopped, rigid with fear, as an enormous shaggy shape burst through the undergrowth.

Alistair was on his feet in an instant, drawn sword in his hand.

"Nay!" Maeve cried. "Doggy!"

She threw herself before the dog, who began to wriggle with excitement, his enormous tongue lashing the child's face until Maeve fell laughing to the ground.

"Doggy!" she cried, burying her hands in its springy pelt. "My doggy."

"Nay, Maeve, he's not yours," Deirdre said. "He belongs to the man who gave us shelter yestere'en."

Maeve made a face. "Mean man. Kicked the doggy."

She put her arms around the dog's neck and kissed its muzzle. "Mine."

The dog flopped onto the ground and turned over on its back, long legs sprawling awkwardly this way and that.

"You're a fine fierce fellow, aren't ye?" Alistair said, kneeling down to rub its belly. "Some sort of wolfhound, would ye say? Mixed with God alone knows what. Look at his paws, Deirdre. He's still a pup."

The dog's tail whipped from side to side in the sodden leaves. When Alistair smiled at her, Deirdre's heart did a giddy little dance. But it meant nothing, she thought. It was just a smile. He did not want her.

How could he act as though nothing had happened between them last night? Why had he turned away from her so suddenly? What had she done wrong? She could not bring herself to ask the questions, for she was afraid to hear the answers.

"We cannot keep him," she said sharply, rubbing her temples against the dull ache that had started there. "We can barely feed ourselves, let alone—"

"I dinna think 'tis so much a matter of us keeping him as him keeping us," Alistair said, rising and brushing his knees. "He'll probably go home when he gets hungry."

"Unless he decides to make a meal of us," Deirdre muttered.

"Finn," Maeve said suddenly, reaching to touch the dog's head. "Finn Mac Coul."

Deirdre laughed. She couldn't help herself. She, like Maeve, had always loved the stories of Finn Mac Coul, the wily Irish giant.

"A fine name," Alistair declared. "He is a very giant among dogs."

Maeve smiled happily. "Finn," she repeated, and the dog

looked at her, tail wagging, for all the world as if he knew his name already. "My Finn."

B y dusk it began to rain again. Alistair made a shelter of pine boughs that kept the worst of it off their heads, but he could not coax a fire from the sodden wood. They huddled miserably together, chewing on dried meat and hard bread.

Alistair was very much aware of Deirdre just beside him, shivering in the darkness. It was with some effort that he restrained himself from putting his arm around her and drawing her beneath his cloak. That would warm her, he thought. It would warm both of them quite nicely. But then they would be back where they had been last night. Just the thought of it, her limbs twined with his, her lips parting in sweet invitation, made his stomach clench with longing.

"Here," he said brusquely, unfastening his cloak. "Take this. Maeve is cold," he added, cutting off Deirdre's protest.

"Maeve, here—stop that!" Deirdre said sharply. "You cannot give your food to that dog!"

"But he's hungry, Mam."

"Then let him go home. Now say thank you to Sir Alistair and go to sleep."

"Thank you," Maeve said obediently.

Alistair tossed the dog the rest of his meal. "Here, Finn," he said, loud enough for Maeve to hear. "Eat up."

He smiled a little when he heard Deirdre's exasperated sigh.

"Good night, Alistair," she said, sounding annoyed. "I hope you don't freeze."

He piled pine needles on the wet ground and stretched out on top of them. "'Tis a small price to pay for your comfort, Your Highness."

"I wish you wouldn't call me that," she said, but her words held a trace of laughter.

Alistair turned over on his side, pulling a branch over

his shoulders. It was worth it, he thought. Worth the cold and the discomfort, worth the hard ache he carried with him always now. It was all well worth it if he could make her smile.

But all journeys have to end, he thought. This one would not last the week. In four or five days they would reach Annan, and Deirdre would take ship for home.

I could go with her, he thought. It will be a new start, a whole new life . . . a life with Deirdre? Was it possible? He would work as hard as he had to, do anything at all if there was the slightest chance of winning her. When he looked at it calmly, he knew it was not hopeless. She desired him, and while that wasn't near enough, it was something to begin with.

Whether he could earn her respect was another matter altogether. Pathetic, she had called him, cowardly, and her words had stung like snow rubbed against a frozen limb. Once the sting began to fade, feeling had rushed in . . . and the first stir of hope.

He was not too old to start anew. He still had his strength, his skill—and all the knowledge he had gained as captain of Kirallen's knights. Surely that was worth something!

I'll do it, he thought. I'll go to Ireland, to Donegal. With Deirdre. On that thought he fell asleep, a smile on his lips.

T*he next morning, when Deirdre woke, Finn was still* there, his back pressed close against Maeve, her small fingers wound in his thick gray coat.

"Wretched hound," she said with something approaching affection as she woke her daughter. At least he had kept Maeve warm. Which was more than she or Alistair had been.

They gathered their things and went on again. By midmorning Deirdre was plastered with mud and stumbling with exhaustion. Alistair looked no better. His eyes were rimmed with red and his cheeks downed with golden stubble. Yet he was smiling as he strode along and once or twice whistled a cheerful tune. Maeve dozed in his arms; she had taken to insisting that he carry her and refused to ride the horse. Germain trailed along after them, head hanging, Finn padding along happily beside him.

"Where are we?" Deirdre said when they stopped to rest beside a clear swift burn.

"At this rate, four or five days out of Annan. We'll have to stop this afternoon, though, and see what we can catch."

Deirdre nodded. She knew well enough their food was running dangerously low. And perhaps they could all have a wash and dry their damp clothes by a fire. "Then let's get on," she said.

Alistair stood and pulled her to her feet. When his hands closed over hers, she felt the heat rise to her face. He hadn't touched her since that night—her face burned as she thought of it, the way she'd lain in his arms. She must have been mad to forget herself that way. Shameless, she had been, forgetting everything but the dizzying rush of her own desire.

She should be grateful that he had stopped it when he had. She knew that. But she wasn't. It must be as Brodie had so often said, that there was some terrible lack in her, a coldness that killed a man's desire.

"Deirdre," he said slowly, her hands still clasped in his. "I have been thinking about the other night—"

"No," she said, her voice a choked whisper. "It doesn't matter."

"—and I think I will come with ye as far as Donegal."

"What?" she said, confused, then realized he had not been talking about *that* night at all. "Oh. Aye."

"I find skulking in the forest is no so pleasant in the rain," he said with a smile. "I imagine it will be even worse when the snow comes."

She smiled in return, feeling as though the sun had just come out again. "That's fine, Alistair," she said warmly. "Just fine. You won't be sorry, I'm sure of it. 'Tis very beautiful in Donegal, and—"

She clamped her lips shut against the tide of words, feeling an utter fool. He released her hands and bent to pick up the saddlebag.

"Well, after all I've heard about it, I'd like to see the place!"

"Come, my love," Deirdre told Maeve, nervously straightening her coif. "Time to be going on. And I want you to ride Germain for a bit. I think he's lonely."

Maeve got to her feet and stood, her head hanging. "Nay," she said. "Star."

"Sir Alistair is weary," Deirdre said. "Mind me now and get up on the horse."

Maeve shook her head. "Willna."

Deirdre stopped Alistair with a gesture and knelt before her daughter. "That is enough," she said severely. "This is no time for your whims and fancies."

Maeve raised her head and looked at Deirdre with fever-bright eyes. Her cheeks were flushed a brilliant red. "Hurts," she said. "Hurts, Mam."

"Where exactly does it hurt, sweeting?" she asked, touching her knuckles to Maeve's brow.

Maeve put one hand to her throat. "Here. All over."

"I'll make a fire," Alistair said.

"Aye," Deirdre said, running one hand distractedly across Maeve's hair. "Let me think—willow bark will ease her."

"I think I saw some back—"

Finn growled deep in his throat, and Deirdre turned with a start of terror. But the dog was looking back into the forest, the hair standing out stiffly on the ruff of his neck.

And then Deirdre heard it for herself, the sound of horses moving through the trees. Her eyes met Alistair's as they waited to see which way the riders would go. A hound bayed and then another in the unmistakable sound of dogs who had caught their quarry's scent.

"This is what ye do now," Alistair said. He spoke in a voice she'd never heard before; crisp, authoritative. "Take

Maeve and get into the water. They canna track ye there. I wish I could give ye Germain, but I need him now."

As he spoke, he tossed the bag of provisions to Deirdre, then turned and flipped open the saddlebags. "Walk upstream until ye reach a waterfall, then—are ye listening, Deirdre?"

Deirdre, who had turned toward the sounds coming from the forest, jerked her gaze back to his face. "Aye."

He gave her a small pouch, tied securely at the top. She felt the weight of it, heard the dull clink of coins as it changed hands, and looked up at him sharply. "What is this?"

"When ye come to the waterfall, take shelter in the thicket," he went on, ignoring her question. "Wait for dusk, then head north. Tonight, or early tomorrow, ye will see a break in the hills, verra sharp, like this"—he held up two fingers to illustrate—"there is a cave just between. Make for it as fast as ye can. An old man dwells there, Fergus is his name. Ye can trust him. Tell him I sent ye."

Deirdre thrust the pouch at him. "This is yours—"

He waved it aside impatiently. "Now what did I tell ye to do?"

It was all happening too fast. Deirdre could hardly understand that he was leaving her, when just a moment ago he had promised to come to Donegal. She stared down at the pouch holding his entire fortune and knew he did not believe they would meet again.

"Wait," she said.

"Nay, Deirdre we canna wait. Tell me." When she did not answer, he put his hands on her shoulders and shook her. "Say it! What are ye going to do?"

"Walk upstream. Go north. Look for a break in the hills."

"Aye, that's right."

"But—"

He leaned down and kissed her hard, his beard scraping against her cheeks. Then he scooped Maeve from the ground and hugged her briefly. "Be a good lass. Mind your mam."

"Aye, Star," Maeve whispered, her eyes round.

"But—" Deirdre said again, and he put a finger to her lips.

"Take Maeve home to Donegal. Ye can do it, lass. Nay, Finn!" he added sharply as the dog began to run from the clearing.

The hounds bayed again, and a man cried out, "To me! This way, they have something!" His voice was so close that Deirdre's heart leaped to her throat.

"Now *go*," Alistair said, giving her a push.

"Finn, come," she called over her shoulder as she sprinted toward the water. The dog bounded over to her side, tail wagging. Just as she stepped into the icy burn she looked back and saw Alistair leap onto Germain's back. He turned toward her, and when he smiled, Deirdre felt her eyes fill.

"God go with ye," he said. "I'll find ye if I can."

The water was deeper than it looked. It swirled about Deirdre's knees, clutching at her heavy skirts, trying to drag her under. She staggered on, Maeve heavy in her arms, but froze as she heard raised voices. Finn looked back, whining, but stilled when Deirdre laid a hand on his head.

It could mean only one thing. Alistair was trying to hold them off to buy her time to get away. She stood in the foaming water, her legs numb from the cold, and felt Maeve burning with the fever. Enough, she thought. This has gone far enough.

She struggled to the bank and ran toward the voices, hampered by the weight of the child and her wet skirts. Her breath came in sobbing gasps as she stumbled through the clutching undergrowth.

She reached the road in time to see a group of Maxwells on horses, watching something she could not see.

"Ye have no right to take me. I've done ye no harm."

She sagged against the tree, dizzy with relief, as she recognized Alistair's voice.

"We heard ye were travelin' with a woman and a child," a deep voice answered. "Where are they?"

"Ye heard wrong," Alistair said flatly. "Now stand aside and let me pass."

"This is Kirallen land, ye fool," the other man answered contemptuously. "And 'tis well known ye've been banished by the laird's own word. But if ye give us the woman and the bairn, we'll let Kirallen settle it—if he can find ye."

"Weel, thank ye, Dougal," Alistair answered. "But I'm afraid I canna oblige ye. I told ye already that I travel alone."

Deirdre's heart sank a little further. Dougal Maxwell had been Brodie's closest friend and was renowned for both his skill at arms and his utter contempt for anything female. Deirdre could not remember him speaking a single word to her in all the weary years at Cranston Keep.

"Then we'll bring ye to Kirallen," Dougal answered. "And I think he'd far rather have your carcass than to trouble about ye any more."

"Ye can try," Alistair said, and though Deirdre could not see his face, he sounded more amused than frightened.

The men shifted and Deirdre could see him then, standing with his back against a sturdy oak. He looked completely unconcerned, almost bored as he regarded Dougal and another man who stood before him, both with drawn swords pointed at his heart.

You fool, Deirdre thought, watching through a shimmer of tears as the rest of the Maxwells dismounted. Do you think you can stand against them all?

She stepped into the road and opened her mouth to cry out, then stopped, speechless, as Alistair's blade appeared in his hand. How did he do that? she wondered, confused. I never even saw him move. Dougal Maxwell was equally surprised. A moment later he dropped to his knees, one hand clutched to his bleeding thigh.

The second man engaged Alistair, but he was out-matched from the start. In the time it took Deirdre to draw breath, he was disarmed and backing swiftly toward his horse.

That left eight of them against a single man. But if the odds alarmed Alistair, he gave no sign of it. He was even smiling a little as he waited for the next attack to come. The Maxwells nudged each other, but none stepped forward. Alistair grinned, lifting his sword in an invitation none was quite ready to accept.

Deirdre's heart was pounding furiously, and much as she longed to cry out, she was afraid that matters had gone too far for her to stop them now. The next few seconds seemed to stretch on endlessly as they all stood frozen in their places, like painted figures on a frieze.

The taut silence was shattered by the sound of galloping hoofbeats, and a dozen mounted men rounded the bend. Kirallens, Deirdre thought, recognizing their colors as she stepped quickly behind a tree. Ah, God, there was nothing that could save Alistair now.

Their leader sat astride an enormous gray stallion. He pulled up so sharply that the horse pranced beneath him, but he brought it easily under control and surveyed the men before him with a long cool look.

"What is this?" he called. "Did you find the lady?"

"Nay," Dougal Maxwell answered, rising to his feet, hand clutched over his bleeding leg. "Not yet. But we did find something that might interest ye."

Alistair leaned against the tree and crossed one ankle over the other. "Hello, Jemmy," he said casually.

The man on the stallion went very still. His dark eyes were hooded, and his expression revealed nothing of his thoughts. "Hello, Alistair. I did not expect to find you here."

"Aye, well, 'tis a bit of a surprise to me, as well," Alistair admitted. "But here I am."

"He ran off with the woman," Dougal said. "A woodsman said he gave them shelter two nights ago. He stole her away and now he's hiding her."

"Did you steal the Maxwell lady?" Jemmy Kirallen asked, never taking his gaze from Alistair.

"Nay."

"Lying bastard!" Dougal cried. "Take him—alive. We'll have the truth from him—"

"He says the woman isn't with him," Jemmy said calmly.

"He lies!"

"Do you?" Jemmy said, raising one brow as he turned back to Alistair.

Alistair looked around, as though inviting them all to see he was alone, then shrugged.

"And what difference does it make to ye if he lies or no?" Dougal demanded. "He's a banished man! Give him to us, and we'll have the truth from him—and we'll make sure he never troubles ye again."

"That's very neighborly of you, Dougal," Jemmy replied. "But I think I can handle him myself."

Alistair smiled.

"Listen, Kirallen," Dougal said, his face reddening. "'Tis the woman we want—"

"Then I suggest you go and look for her," Jemmy said curtly. "For myself, I begin to think she never came this way at all. We've scoured every acre for three days now and seen no sign of her."

"But what about him?" Dougal cried, pointing to Alistair.

"He is none of your concern. This is a Kirallen matter, and I'll thank you to stay out of it."

"But—"

"Go, Dougal," Jemmy said softly. "Just take your men and go. *Now.*"

Deirdre watched, hardly daring to breathe, as the Maxwells mounted and rode off. Jemmy turned to his men. "Ride back and see they find their way home again," he ordered sharply. "All but Donal and Conal."

The men wheeled their horses and galloped after the Maxwells, not without some regretful looks over their shoulders. Two young red-haired knights pulled their horses to either side of Jemmy's.

"Well, Jemmy?" Alistair asked. "I suppose 'tis too much to hope you'll let me go upon my way?"

"I'm afraid I cannot do that."

"Wait!"

Deirdre ran out from the shelter of the trees, tripping on the sodden hem of her skirt to fall hard upon her knees.

"Please!" she cried. "You can't—please—it wasn't his fault at all, he was but trying to help me—"

"Oh, Christ," Alistair muttered, thrusting his weapon into the soft dirt and coming to help her to her feet. "For God's sake, Deirdre, ye should have been long gone—"

"I couldn't," she said, and all at once the days of fear and hiding caught up to her as tears of exhaustion spilled over to stream down her cheeks. "I wouldn't run off and leave you. Tney meant to kill you—I was about to come out, truly, Alistair, but then—then—"

Some of the anger died from his eyes and he brushed the tears from her face. "Whisht, now, dinna cry."

Maeve struggled to sit up. "Star," she croaked, holding out her arms.

"I'm right here, sweeting," he said, taking the child from Deirdre. He put her over his shoulder and turned to Jemmy.

"The Maxwell lady, I presume," Jemmy said politely.

Alistair sighed. "And her daughter."

"He didn't lie," Deirdre said, the words stumbling over one another in her desperate haste to make Jemmy Kirallen understand. "Not really. He didn't steal us, my lord, we left on our own, that's the truth of it. Brodie did promise—my father made him—but the Maxwell wouldn't listen—and—and he said he would keep my child—" Her voice broke on a sob but she hurried on. "So I had to run off, my lord, I had to take her home. Sir Alistair but met us in the wood—he helped us out of kindness—and now—now Maeve is ill, and then the Maxwells came and—"

She began to cry with frustration, knowing her words made no sense at all but too tired to begin again.

"Donal, Conal," Jemmy ordered. "Please escort Lady Maxwell and her daughter back to Ravenspur. I would rather no one knows of our visitors quite yet," he added, and the two young men nodded their understanding. "Take her directly to my lady's bower and explain what's happened. Lady Maxwell," he added gently to Deirdre. "Go with them. My lady will know what to do for your daughter. As for the rest—we'll sort it all out later, when you have had a chance to rest."

"But," Deirdre protested, "what of—"

"Go," Alistair said firmly. "And you too, Finn," he added to the dog who stood before him, teeth bared and hackles raised.

A light rain began to fall, and Alistair watched Deirdre and the child ride off through a shimmer of moisture. Deirdre turned once and lifted her hand, and from somewhere he summoned the strength to smile as he returned the wave. The sound of the horses faded into silence, broken only by the patter of rain upon the leaves. And finally he and Jemmy were alone.

chapter 18

⚜

Alistair stared at his sword. It stood point down in the damp earth at his feet, raindrops sliding off its shining surface. He could pick it up and fight for his life, but the last time he and Jemmy had matched blades, it ended with Alistair disarmed and the point of Jemmy's sword against his throat. Of course, he thought dispassionately, Jemmy had surprised him. There was a good chance things would go differently today. But though he tried to summon his old anger against Jemmy, he felt nothing but a chill distaste at the thought of killing his foster brother, no matter how little he might like him.

Of course Jemmy would have no such scruples. Why should he? Jemmy, after all, was merely carrying out his father's orders. They had both heard the laird pronounce Alistair's banishment. "If ye are found on Kirallen lands, any man may slay ye out of hand." And here he was, and here was Jemmy, and there seemed little doubt of what would happen next.

Alistair knew he should feel something—fear seemed

the appropriate response of a man who was staring into the face of his own death. But now that the moment had come, he seemed to have used up every emotion save regret.

The rain continued to fall and finally he raised his head to find Jemmy staring at some point in the far distance, apparently lost in his own thoughts. He looked ill, Alistair noticed for the first time. The skin stretched taut over his high sharp cheekbones held a grayish tinge, and his long dark eyes were shadowed. One hand was absently rubbing his shoulder as though it pained him.

"Come on, man, what are ye waiting for?" Alistair said roughly. "Let's get on with it."

Jemmy started and looked down at him. "Get on with what?" he said, sounding as annoyed as Alistair felt himself. "Oh, I see, you think—" He grinned suddenly, looking so like Ian that Alistair felt the breath catch in his throat. "Ah, Alistair, I could almost say I missed you. I should have known you'd be snapping orders right up to the end."

He leaned back in the saddle and laughed, then winced a little, his hand going back to his shoulder. "So, you have it all planned out? Well, go on then, what is it to be? Should I string you up on yonder oak? Or did you have something else in mind?"

Alistair stared up at him in confusion. Jemmy had been a solemn child who had returned from his travels a grim and brooding man. In all the weeks they'd spent together the year before, Alistair had seldom seen him even smile, let alone laugh as free and easy as he'd done just now. He's picked a strange time to develop a sense of humor, Alistair thought sourly. Especially one so like Ian's had been. For a moment it could have been Jemmy's brother sitting there, laughing at Alistair as he'd often done before.

"Or," Jemmy said, his dark eyes narrowing, "did you hope I'd come down so you could cut me into pieces?"

Alistair picked up his sword and flung it into the woods, followed by his dagger. After a moment he pulled the knife from his boot and tossed it after them, then held out his hands.

"I dinna ken what game you're playing," he said stiffly. "But I trust ye are satisfied the now."

Jemmy nodded. "Aye, I am." He toyed with the reins, then added quietly, "Even so, I'm afraid you'd be more than my match today. But it doesn't matter, because I have no intention of fighting you. I haven't really been looking for the Maxwell lady these past days. I've been looking for you."

"Why?"

Jemmy slumped in his saddle, looking suddenly exhausted. "My father is dying," he said.

Of all the things Alistair had thought that Jemmy might say, this was the last. The news hit him like a blow. In that moment he forgot the anger that had been between him and the laird and thought only of the thousand kindnesses his foster father had shown him.

He remembered the laird's face when he had pronounced the sentence of banishment, the tears that had stood in the old man's eyes as he bid Alistair farewell.

"I have to see him," he said.

"He wants to see you, too. Go on, then, and get your things."

chapter 19

Riding the path to Ravenspur felt very odd to Alistair, strange and yet familiar. His eyes moved over each well-remembered landmark with the joy of finding something precious he had believed was lost for good. Every turn of the road, each stream and tree and field held a hundred memories—some good, some bad, but all a part of him. Leaving here, he had left most of himself behind. To see it all again, even once, was a rare and unexpected gift.

And then with a suddenness that took his breath away, there was Ravenspur itself, rising from the moor. There was no pretension of grace about its grim towers and tumbled battlements, no artistry in its design. On the very doorstep of the enemy, it was only strength that mattered. Ravenspur was what it was, a border fortress, the finest of its kind, no more and certainly no less.

The horse stopped, but Alistair made no attempt to urge him forward. He simply sat and stared, seeing himself reflected in the stark lines of his home. Yet he was different now—or was he? Suddenly he wasn't sure. In his own uncertainty the building before him was as foreboding as the black tower of his vision.

Jemmy reined in beside him.

"Ugly pile of stone, isn't it?" he asked lightly.

Alistair looked sharply at his kinsman, remembering that Jemmy had said the same thing on his own return to Ravenspur. He remembered, too, the contempt with which he had greeted his foster brother's words a year ago. Now he saw that Jemmy was the only one who could possibly understand what he was feeling now.

Jemmy had been exiled from Ravenspur as well—by his own choice, aye, but then, the same could be said of Alistair himself. And the pain of exile had been no less for that. What had driven Jemmy to make that choice? he wondered suddenly. What had *he* felt when first seeing his home after so long an absence?

Well, at least Alistair had the answer to that question. Now, too late, he understood exactly what Jemmy had felt that day. And it was beyond words.

"Hideous," he said roughly, to hide the sudden tremor in his voice. "But 'tis still there, isn't it?"

"Aye." Jemmy sighed. "It always is."

Their eyes met and at the same moment they laughed. Alistair hadn't meant that to happen, and from the way Jemmy frowned and spurred his horse forward, he guessed his kinsman hadn't expected it, either.

They continued toward the manor without speaking, and as the silence grew between them, Alistair found himself wanting to break it, though he wasn't sure exactly what he needed to say. Perhaps he *had* been unfair to Jemmy when he first came home from Spain, but had events not proved him right?

Never once had Jemmy listened to Alistair's warnings, never once had he admitted that Alistair was right to suspect Darnley's motives and that he himself had been wrong. Even when Alistair had succeeded in exposing Darnley's treachery—and who had thanked him for it? No one!—Jemmy had gone on, headstrong, willful, insisting that young Haddon, Darnley's heir, be fostered at Ravenspur to ensure the peace. And all of them, including Darnley himself, had bowed beneath Jemmy's will. All but Alistair. The laird, forced to choose, had sided with his son. And Alistair had been sent away.

So why did he still feel he owed Jemmy an apology?

It was because of the woman. Alistair could justify his every action—save for his treatment of Darnley's baseborn daughter, Alyson. She had been sent to marry Jemmy, all the while pretending to be her half sister Lady Maude, a part of Darnley's plan to destroy the Kirallen clan. On the face of it, she had been as guilty as her father, but she had been driven into the plan against her will. Jemmy had come to love her, in the end had married her—and always, deep in Alistair's heart, had lurked a sneaking admiration for that decision. Alyson was a lovely lass, brave and loyal, and though Darnley was her father, her mother had been Clare McLaran, the kindest lady who ever lived.

He wondered if the clan had accepted her and suspected that they hadn't. And he was quite sure the laird had not forgiven Jemmy for defying his will and taking Alyson to wife.

But still, there was no need to be feeling bad for Jemmy. After all, Jemmy had seen Alistair banished and married the lass he loved. Jemmy had won. Or had he? What had been going on at Ravenspur during the past year? Why had the laird sent for Alistair now? In Jemmy's place, Alistair knew that he would have been both angry and deeply worried.

Well, Jemmy has naught to fear, Alistair mused. Not from me. Alistair was grateful to have the chance to see the laird once more and to say his farewells properly, but once that was done, there would be nothing to hold him to this place. He would be finished with Ravenspur forever and ready to start again. Tomorrow or the next day I'm off to Donegal, with Deirdre, he thought, his spirits rising sharply.

Jemmy rode on silently, growing paler by the moment,

his mouth set in a grim line. When they drew up in the stableyard, he made no move to dismount. He sat, his head bowed, hands clutching the edge of his saddle.

"Go in," he said hoarsely. "Father's waiting. And would you send Conal to me?"

Alistair started to obey, but the memory of how kindly Jemmy had spoken to Deirdre halted him. For that, if nothing else, Jemmy deserved something in return.

"Here, I'll help ye down," he told Jemmy. "There's no need to wait for Conal."

Jemmy half slid from the saddle, his face gray as ashes by the time he was on his feet. "Thank you," he said. "I'll be all right now."

"What happened to ye?" Alistair asked.

"A bit of a stramash with McInnes," Jemmy replied, trying to pass it off lightly even as the sweat broke out on his brow. "Hasn't had the chance to heal yet."

Alistair was fairly certain that Jemmy would never make it into the manor under his own power, so he slowed his steps to match his kinsman's, wondering what the devil was going on here.

"Tell me what's been happening since I left," he said.

"Not much," Jemmy answered. "You know how it is. The same from day to day."

"How is Malcolm?"

"Oh, well enough." Jemmy stopped to lean against the doorpost. "Missing you, of course, but otherwise"—he drew a hissing breath as he straightened—"quite all right."

"Let me get someone to help ye," Alistair offered, but Jemmy shook his head.

"No!" he said vehemently. "I'm fine."

They walked into the hall. It was dim inside after the brightness of the afternoon. As Alistair's eyes adjusted, he realized it was filled with people, but a silence fell as he stepped into the room. A moment later the voices all broke out again in excited speculation as Jemmy drew himself up and walked firmly into the crowd, Alistair just beside him.

"My lord," an anxious voice said. A small, gray-haired

man gave Alistair a quick, rather nervous smile, before continuing. "I have the accounts ready if ye'd care to look at them—"

"Thank you," Jemmy said calmly. "But I cannot stop just now. Perhaps this afternoon."

"Aye, my lord," the man said with a quick bow. "But I did just want to talk to ye about—"

Jemmy smiled, though his pallor deepened even further. "Later," he said carefully. "I promise I'll make the time."

The crowd parted to let them by, every face alight with speculation to see the two of them walk in together. Alistair noted it with half his mind, while the other part was busy watching Jemmy. He could tell exactly how bad the pain was now by the lines bracketing Jemmy's mouth. It was just how Ian used to look when he was hurting and didn't want anyone to know. And the way he walked—it was Ian to the life, the same set of the shoulders and tilt of his head. Strange how he'd never noticed how alike they were before. He'd always been too busy noticing the differences between them.

"My lord, a moment!"

Jemmy stopped and turned. "Aye, Sir Calder?"

The knight gave Alistair a sly smile. It said more clearly than words that Calder knew Alistair had a plan and what's more, he was ready to be part of it. Jemmy stood very straight, his gaze moving quickly from Calder's face to Alistair's and back again. He closed his eyes briefly, as though his strength had reached its final limit, but when he opened them his gaze was steady.

"Dougal Maxwell sent a message back wi' us," Calder said.

"I'd be most interested to hear it," Jemmy replied. "But I cannot stop now. I'll send for you later."

"Alistair," Calder said, putting a hand on his arm. "Wait a moment. What—?"

"Not now," Alistair interrupted. "I must see the laird."

"Ah," Calder said with a knowing glance at Jemmy. "I see."

What exactly Calder saw, Alistair couldn't begin to guess. And he found he didn't really care. After the quiet of the past year the crowded hall was almost more than he could bear; there were too many emotions swirling about the room, too many faces, too much noise. Instead he watched Jemmy, wondering if he could possibly make it all the way across the hall and why he didn't simply ask for help. Even Ian would have admitted the need of Alistair's arm by now.

"I'll see ye after," he said to Calder, and the knight dropped him a broad wink before turning away to speak to several other men. They all listened, huddled in a group, their eyes following Alistair and Jemmy as they went on. *A year ago I would have been among them,* Alistair realized. *Now all their plots and plans seemed very small and sordid.*

He and Jemmy reached the stairway without further interruption and started up. But when they reached the first turn, Jemmy motioned him ahead. "I'll be along."

"Christ, Jemmy, what's the matter with ye?" Alistair demanded. "Let me help."

"I do not need help," Jemmy said distinctly. "I am a little tired, that's all, and the wound is troubling me a bit. 'Tis nothing—"

"Right," Alistair said, putting one arm beneath Jemmy's shoulder and half carrying him up the stairway. "'Tis nothing. Ye are fine and ye don't need help. I ken ye well enough, all right?"

By the time they reached the chamber, Jemmy had fallen into white-lipped silence. Alistair flung open the door and helped him to a chair. There was a small sound behind him, and he whirled to see Jemmy's wife rise from her seat by the window.

Lady Alyson was dressed in a blue gown, cut far more simply than those she used to wear when she had first come among them, pretending to be someone that she wasn't. The style suited her much better than the finery had done. Her hair was uncovered and the sun's rays fell upon it, lighting the golden strands within its auburn depths. She looked older, Alistair thought, worn with care and worry. Though it had been not quite a year since they had last met, he saw it hadn't been an easy year for her.

He stood awkwardly, words deserting him. He should have known she would be here, but he wasn't thinking very clearly today. The truth was that during the past year he had done his best not to think of her at all.

The last time he had talked to Jemmy's lady, it was to bring her a sentence of death and an offer so shameful that he could not bear to remember it. "There's no help for ye," he heard his own voice saying. "Ye are a traitor and a spy . . . but for all that you're a pretty doxy and ye seem to know your business well enough . . . name your price."

Later he had realized his mistake. She was not the scheming harlot he had thought her; was not for sale at any price. But by then the damage had been done. Now he wanted to turn and flee, go back to the solitude of the forest and find the peace he had so briefly glimpsed before Deirdre dragged him back into the world with all its shameful memories.

What would Deirdre think if she knew how he had threatened Jemmy's lady? She would despise him. But no more than in that moment he despised himself. Why hadn't Jemmy simply killed him when he had the chance? he wondered wearily. If anyone had said such things to Deirdre, Alistair would have run him through without a second thought.

Alyson looked at him, surprise and fear and wariness passing quickly across her mobile features. But she wasted no words on him before turning to her husband. And all at once Alistair knew the answer to his question. Jemmy hadn't killed him because he didn't know. She hadn't told him. From some protective instinct, Alyson had kept the details of that last terrible interview to herself.

"'Tis all right," Jemmy mumbled. "I'm fine."

"I'm certain you are," she said briskly, though Alistair saw her hands were shaking as she unfastened his cloak and pulled it back. "But if it's all the same to you, I'll just have a look at this."

The gambeson beneath was soaked with blood. Jemmy laid his head back against the seat as she unlaced it and pulled the edges of the fabric from the wound.

"I'll have to cut it. 'Tis ruined anyway," she added with a brave attempt to sound annoyed.

At last Alistair could see the extent of the damage, and he whistled softly between his teeth. Alyson bit her lip, then blinked several times and drew a deep breath.

"Well, you've gone and torn the stitches," she scolded, patting gently at the shoulder with a dampened cloth. "And such a pretty job I made of them! This time you'll have to rest, Jemmy."

"We'll see," he said between clenched teeth.

"Oh, no, we won't," she answered tartly. "Besides, you found them, did ye no? Conal and Donal told me all about it." She cast Alistair a swift glance over her shoulder. "The lady and her bairn are resting."

She went to the hearth and stirred the small pot hanging over the coals. After a moment she pulled out a strip of fabric and let it drip into the bowl as it cooled.

"Can you get to the bed?" she asked.

"Aye."

Jemmy's knuckles whitened on the arms of the chair as he tried to lever himself upright. Alyson twisted the rag between her hands, but she bit her lip and did not speak a word. She knows him well, Alistair thought. He would only snap at her if she offered help.

Alistair gripped Jemmy's good wrist and pulled him up, ignoring his furious protest. "Ye can shout at me later if you like. For now why don't ye stop being such a selfish, stiff-necked bastard. Do ye think your lady likes to watch ye suffer?"

That shut him up, just as Alistair had intended that it should. He got him to the bed and eased him down. "That looks terrible," he said, peering closely at the wound.

"Stop making light of it. Let someone else tend to your affairs and rest."

"There isn't—" Alyson began, but Jemmy cut her off.

"I'll think about it," he said. "Now go and see Father. Tell him I'll be there soon."

"Aye. My lady," Alistair said, bowing in Alyson's direction. "I—" He stopped, confused, with no idea of what he had meant to say. But she was bending over Jemmy and didn't seem to notice.

He slipped from the chamber and leaned against the wall, praying for the strength to face his next ordeal. After a moment he pushed himself upright and started toward the laird's chamber.

chapter 20

D eirdre woke with a start and looked around, her heart beating hard and quick. Something was wrong. Where was she? Where was Maeve? She breathed again when she found the child curled beside her, dark ringlets plastered damply to her cheeks and one thumb tucked between her lips. The fever had broken, Deirdre realized, touching one hand gently to her baby's head.

She sat up, pushing the tangled hair back from her face. Finn looked up questioningly from his place beside the bed, then yawned and laid his head down on his paws. Yes, she remembered now, they were in the tower room, where Lady Alyson had brought them. She and Maeve were safe here—at least for the time. But where was Alistair?

Lady Alyson had not been able to tell her that, for neither Alistair nor Jemmy Kirallen had returned by the time Deirdre lay down beside Maeve. She'd had no intention of sleeping until she'd learned what happened out there on the road when she rode off and left Alistair to face his kins-

man all alone. And yet she could not hold exhaustion at
bay any longer.

The sun was westering, she saw, going to the narrow
window. Late afternoon sunlight washed the cobblestones
with rich gold light and a scullion walked whistling to the
kitchen carrying two pails. It had been hours, then. They
must be back by this time. Or had the corbies caught up to
Alistair at last? Did he lie there on the deserted stretch of
road as they went about their work?

> *"Ye'll sit on his white hause-bane,*
> *And I'll pike out his bonny gray een;*
> *Wi'ae lock o' his golden hair-o*
> *We'll theek our nest when it grows bare-o."*

She paced the small chamber, ten paces and turn, ten
and turn again, but the hateful melody still jangled through
her mind until she thought she would go mad. She wished
that she could cry, if only to ease the terrible pressure
building inside her. But this pain went beyond tears. And
so she walked ten paces, turned and walked, round and
round as the tune went round inside her head. When the
door opened, she whirled to see Lady Alyson step inside.

Deirdre studied her through dry and burning eyes, taking in the rich blue gown, the veil flowing over her lustrous
dark red braids, the rings shining on her slender hands. She
knew she should feel nothing but gratitude toward this
lady who had taken her and Maeve, fugitives that they
were, into her own home. But in that moment Deirdre
hated her with all her heart.

There she stood, this Englishwoman—rich, cherished,
with her shining jewels and her fine manor and her bonny
husband, the man who'd said so carelessly, "Take them to
my lady's bower." With a woman's ear, Deirdre had heard
much in that simple statement. The way he said, "my
lady," with such possessive pride, the implication that *his*
lady could be trusted absolutely. It all told Deirdre that on

top of everything else this lady had, she held her husband's heart, as well.

"You're awake," Lady Alyson said with a friendly, somewhat anxious smile. "Good. How does the bairn?"

"The fever broke, just as you said it would," Deirdre answered stiffly. "I think she'll be well when she wakes."

"Aye, and hungry," Lady Alyson said practically. "I'll have something sent up and a bath for you, as well."

"Thank you."

"Do you have need of anything else?"

"Nothing."

The coolness of Deirdre's tone seemed to reach Lady Alyson. She gave the other woman a questioning look, and the smile faded from her lips.

"Well, then," she said, stepping back toward the door. "If you think of anything, let Maggie know."

"There is one thing."

"Aye?" Lady Alyson turned in the doorway, brows raised in question.

"Can you tell me if Sir Alistair—is he—"

She could not force herself to say the final word, the one that marked the end of him forever.

"Sir Alistair returned some time ago. He is with the laird now."

"Oh."

Deirdre's knees buckled, and she sat down hard on the narrow window seat.

"I thought—when I left him—I thought that—"

"That my lord would kill him?" Lady Alyson finished, and Deirdre nodded helplessly, for now the tears she had wished for earlier had risen to her throat, choking off all speech.

"Well, he did not. For good or ill," she added quietly, as though speaking to herself, "he did not." Then she looked at Deirdre and her expression softened. "I see that pleases you, Lady Maxwell."

"Yes. Sir Alistair has been—very kind to us. And earlier,

if you had but seen him, the way he faced the Maxwells all
alone—"

"Donal told me something of it," Lady Alyson said. "No
one has ever doubted Sir Alistair's *courage.*"

"'Tis his loyalty you question? But that's the very thing
has been his undoing! Misguided loyalty, mayhap, to a
man who's dead and past all caring, but still loyalty for all
that. Mayhap he isn't a fine *English* knight," she continued
in a burst of reckless anger, "and he speaks too blunt for a
lady like yourself. But he does not lie—"

Lady Alyson's face was working—with anger, Deirdre
thought—but then she realized that the other woman was
trying not to laugh.

"I don't see what you find amusing about this!" she
cried indignantly. "'Tis a man's life we speak of!"

"Oh, I know," Lady Alyson said, struggling to compose
herself. "It isn't funny—not really—and you've the right
of it, of course. I've often thought how terrible it must have
been for him last year, knowing what he did and no one listening to him—save for me, that is, and I wasn't about to
admit that I credited him at all—"

Deirdre watched, too surprised to speak, as Lady
Alyson's laughter took on an edge that sounded dangerously close to tears. She sat down beside Deirdre and drew
a shaking breath. "'Tis a long tale, Lady Maxwell, and I
see that Sir Alistair hasn't told you the whole of it."

"Nay, he never did say much, and though we heard some
at Cranston Keep, 'twas all a terrible muddle."

"That about describes it," Lady Alyson said wryly.

"Yet now that I know Sir Alistair, I'm sure he could not
have been so much at fault as rumor has it."

"In some ways he was wronged, but he brought much of
it upon himself. And when it came to the point, he defied
an order from his laird, though he knew full well what the
consequence would be. He was bent on vengeance and no
one could make him see it differently—"

"I think he does see it differently now," Deirdre said.

"'Twas his pride that kept him wandering. Foolish, aye, but men are foolish creatures when it comes to pride."

"They are that," Lady Alyson said with feeling. "Great fools, every one of them. I suppose that's why God sends them women to watch over them." She glanced at Deirdre sideways and smiled.

"No, my lady," Deirdre said gravely. "'Tis not as you might think. Sir Alistair is but a—a friend to me and Maeve. Indeed," she added, looking at her sleeping child, "I think 'tis for Maeve's sake he agreed to help us. The child loves him well."

"Aye, he does have a way with bairns." Lady Alyson sighed.

"Why did they bring him back here?" Deirdre asked. "What will happen to him now?"

"The laird is very ill," Lady Alyson answered. "He wanted to see Alistair once more before the end. After that . . ." She shrugged. "We shall have to see."

"My lady, if you could speak to your lord—"

"On Alistair's behalf?" She stood and smoothed her skirt, then added quietly, "That I cannot do. Ah, dinna glare at me like that, Lady Maxwell. Even if I would speak to Jemmy, 'twould do no good. There are many things you do not know. And if I do not take Alistair's part as you would have me, there is reason for it. For him to come back now, with things as they are—"

She was frightened, Deirdre realized, frightened of what Alistair's return would bring. On impulse she reached out and took the lady's hand.

"'Twill be all right," she said. "I see there *is* much here that I do not understand, but I think—I believe—that whatever drove Alistair away has changed—that *he* has changed."

"God send that you are right, lady."

"Deirdre."

Lady Alyson squeezed her hand and smiled. "And I am Alyson."

"I have not thanked you, Alyson. Forgive me. I am grateful for what you've done for us."

Alyson gave her a mischievous smile that lit her blue-green eyes, and for the first time Deirdre realized how young she was, perhaps younger than Deirdre was herself. "I was glad to do it—and I'm very glad you're here," she added with an impulsive warmth that left Deirdre in no doubt of her sincerity.

"Now, I promised myself that I'd not trouble you with questions . . . but I'll tell you truly, Deirdre, I can hardly wait to hear your tale. You mustn't speak until you're ready, of course, and not to me at all if you'd rather not. And yet . . . if there are some things easier said to me than Jemmy . . ."

"Aye," Deirdre said. "I would like to tell you. I think— I hope that you will understand."

"I'll try. But I won't listen to a word until you've bathed and eaten. Rest for now and I'll be back."

chapter 21

Deirdre hung back in the shadow of the archway, feeling suddenly unsure that coming to the hall had been a good idea after all. Alyson had said she should join them there that night, since apparently the news of her arrival had already spread throughout the manor.

"I dinna ken how it happened," Alyson had said with a sigh when she came to Deirdre's tower room, a gown folded across her arm. "Maggie would never talk, and I trust Conal and Donal—but in this place there are no secrets. But the news can hardly get as far as Cranston Keep tonight, so you might as well enjoy a proper meal. And here, I think this will fit you well enough," she added, holding out a gown across her arm.

Now Alyson gave her an encouraging smile as they stood together, looking into the noisy, crowded hall. It was grand, Deirdre thought, staring about with wide eyes, at least twice the size of the hall at Cranston Keep, with hangings on the wall and two long windows filled with bits of colored glass stretching almost to the ceiling. But even this enormous space seemed barely enough to hold all the people within. People who would look at her with curious eyes, knowing—or thinking they knew—what brought her here.

"Aye, they'll stare," Alyson said, as though reading Deirdre's mind. "But what canna be changed must be borne. Chin up now, Deirdre."

Her brisk kindness was exactly what Deirdre needed. "Well, then," she said. "Let's go in."

She hadn't taken two steps before she saw Alistair. He stood across the room, a crowd of men around him. At her entrance his head turned sharply toward the door.

Deirdre was aware of the curious eyes upon her, but they meant nothing to her now. For Alistair was coming toward her, and a warm blush rose up her throat to stain her cheeks. She touched a fold of her gown, the heavy velvet soft beneath her fingers. It was the finest gown she'd ever worn, midnight blue trimmed with silver, and Alyson had twined bits of silver ribbon in her dark braids.

Alistair looked fresh and rested, his hair shining like burnished gold in the torchlight. He was clad in a fine wool tunic that just matched the color of his eyes. But, she noticed, he still didn't bear the Kirallen colors anywhere about him.

"Deirdre," he said, taking her hand and bowing over it. "Ye look—verra well tonight. How is Maeve?"

She smiled, for she'd caught the hesitation in his words and knew that he had been about to say something else. He had been about to say that she looked beautiful. "Maeve is quite well, thank you. Sleeping, now."

"I'm glad."

There was so much she wanted to ask him, but this was not the time or place for questions. Even now Lady Alyson was waiting for them to take their place at the table.

"My lady," Alistair said stiffly to her.

She nodded coolly. "Sir Alistair."

They began to walk across the hall, but before they reached the dais, the bearded knight Alistair had been talking with swept an elbow across the table, upsetting a pitcher of ale that splashed the hem of Alyson's gown. Instead of apologizing, the man turned away, but not before Deirdre had caught the flash of teeth in his dark beard.

"Why, the clumsy churl!" Deirdre exclaimed.

"'Tis all right," Alyson answered shortly. Two bright spots of color on her cheeks were the only indication that she had even noticed the man's rudeness as she made to walk on.

"Nay, 'tis not!" Deirdre protested. "Alistair, did you not see?"

"Leave it, Deirdre," Alyson said.

But Alistair was already at the man's side, speaking to him in a tone too low to hear, though from their gestures it was clear they were arguing. A moment later they both came forward.

"Forgive me, my lady," the man said sullenly. "I didna see what I had done."

"Very well, Sir Calder," Alyson said, and the knight returned to his seat, giving Alistair a puzzled, resentful glance as he went.

"He did it deliberately," Deirdre said, staring after him. "But why?"

Alistair looked distinctly uncomfortable for a moment but was saved from answering when someone cried his name across the hall.

A boy hurtled through the crowd and threw himself into Alistair's arms. "It *is* you! They said—but I didna believe it—" The words came out in jerky bursts as he buried his face against Alistair's chest.

"Aye, Malcolm, 'tis me," Alistair murmured, holding him close. "Whisht now, I'm here, dinna greet, lad . . ."

After a long moment they drew apart. Malcolm dragged an arm across his eyes and smiled shakily. "Ye look the same," he said.

"The same canna be said for ye! Why, you've grown half a foot! Deirdre," he said, "this is Malcolm, the laird's grandson. Malcolm, this is Lady Deirdre Maxwell."

The boy swept her a graceful bow. "Lady Maxwell, welcome to Ravenspur. Your presence does us honor."

Alistair smiled proudly. As well he might, Deirdre thought as she curtsied to the young Kirallen. Malcolm was a tall young man of twelve or thirteen years, with curling brown hair and bright blue eyes and a dangerously charming smile. In a few years—a very few years, Deirdre judged—he would be turning heads and breaking any number of hearts.

"Where's Uncle Jemmy?" Malcolm asked Alyson.

"With the laird," she answered, a worried frown passing quickly across her face. "He won't be down tonight."

Poor lady, Deirdre thought. She has troubles, sure enough. What with the laird so ill, her own husband distracted, and the puzzling rudeness of the dark-bearded knight, Alyson had much to worry her. She was bearing up bravely—for what could not be changed must be borne—but it was clear that she had care enough without an errant Maxwell lady on her hands.

And yet, Deirdre thought, struck again by Alyson's kindness, she had still found the time to bring her a gown and see to the dressing of her hair.

"Come, Malcolm," Alyson said now, smiling at her nephew with an effort Deirdre was fairly sure none of the others could see. "You must take Jemmy's place tonight."

"Aye—but—" He glanced back over his shoulder.

"Who's that?" Alistair asked, following his gaze. "Is it young Darnley? Bid him join us, if ye would. 'Tis all right," he added as Malcolm hesitated. "Tell him I willna bite."

Malcolm grinned and ran off, returning a moment later with a smaller boy with red curls and a wary look in his blue-green eyes. This must be Alyson's brother—or was it half brother? Deirdre wasn't sure. But either way, the resemblance was strong. Alyson stood back watching, her expression unreadable, as Malcolm presented Haddon Darnley to Deirdre. The boy made her a courteous bow, but all the while he watched Alistair from the corner of his eye.

"Ye remember Sir Alistair, of course," Malcolm added brightly—too brightly, Deirdre thought.

"Aye," Haddon said. "I do."

"And I remember ye, as well," Alistair said with a smile so menacing that Deirdre didn't blame the Darnley boy for paling visibly.

"My quarrel is with your father, not with ye," Alistair went on. "And both of us are guests in this hall. So if ye please we'll eat our meal and say no more about it."

"Aye." Haddon's voice cracked on the word, but he did not back away or take his eyes from Alistair's. "That will suit me."

After a very long moment Alistair nodded briefly. "That is well."

Deirdre let out a breath she hadn't realized she was holding as the tension between them slackened. This place is like deep water on a sunny day, she thought dizzily. You never know when you'll hit an icy current that steals the breath right from your body and turns your limbs to lead.

"Then let's eat!" Malcolm cried with a determined cheer that Deirdre found brave and rather touching. "I'm famished. My lady." He turned to Alyson and held out his arm.

Deirdre slipped her hand into the crook of Alistair's elbow, feeling the iron tension of the muscles beneath her hand.

"Did you have to do that?" she asked.

"I did nothing."

His voice warned her to drop the question there and then. This was a man she'd never seen before, grim and almost frightening, with eyes like chips of ice. No wonder they sent him away, she thought. No wonder they fear him still.

She waited until she was seated, then said with equal coolness, "You frightened that poor boy. It was ill done."

He sat down beside her, his mouth tightening into a hard line. "Did I not tell him he'd be safe?"

"Don't try to frighten *me,* Alistair Kirallen," Deirdre said tartly. "You know well enough what I'm saying, so there's no use pretending that you don't."

He glared at her, then smiled wryly. "And as Her Highness says, so must it be!"

"Don't call me that," Deirdre snapped, and Alistair laughed shortly.

"Then mind that tongue, lady, or someone might get cut! And ye can stop shooting daggers at me with your eyes. I did the boy no harm, nor will I."

"You did him no good, either," she said repressively. "Nor any of the others. Oh, sure and 'tis a fine homecoming you're making for yourself! You can see as well as I that there's trouble enough brewing here without *you* stirring up the pot."

"This is no homecoming. The laird sent for me and I came. There's no more to it than that. And might I remind Your Ladyship," he added sardonically, "that ye have troubles aplenty of your own without putting your nose into mine."

"Forgive me," she said stiffly. "You are right, of course. You tend to your own affairs—no matter how sorry a job you make of it," she added beneath her breath.

She accepted a slice of venison from a kneeling squire, though after the meal she and Maeve had shared earlier, she wasn't really hungry. Alistair *is* right, she thought. Who am I to tell him what to do? Soon—tomorrow, perhaps—Maeve and I will be gone. Now that Alistair had been summoned back by the laird himself, it seemed unlikely he would want to leave again.

Would Alyson convince her husband to let her and Maeve go free? Or would he turn them over to the Maxwells? With everything here at sixes and sevens, she could hardly blame him if he did just that. The last thing he needed was trouble with a neighbor. And even if he did let them go, how long would it be before the Maxwells found them again?

I'll see what happens tomorrow, she thought, then almost smiled, thinking she was beginning to sound like Alistair. Or at least the way he used to sound. Tonight he was a very different man from her carefree companion of the forest. He was home now, back in the place where he belonged. And she did not.

She kept her gaze fixed on her trencher as she cut the meat into tiny pieces and bit by bit became aware of the flow of conversation going on around her.

". . . should have been there, Alistair," Malcolm was saying. "The McLarans had such a feast! Emma kept Robin there, but he should be back again any day now. . . ."

". . . no, Bryce, not like that," Alyson said patiently to the squire. "You must kneel and hold it so—yes, that's it. . . ."

"Well, there's no tellin', is there?" one knight was saying to another at the table just to Deirdre's side. "But ye know that Calder said it's just a matter of time—and now that Alistair is back, I see he spoke true. It will be young Malcolm for sure. . . ."

". . . they say the pair of them ran off together and the Maxwell is sore angry!" a woman's shrill voice exclaimed. A second woman answered, too low for Deirdre to catch the words, though whatever she said caused a burst of laughter. "Aye, he's too canny to be caught by the likes of her! Now he's back again, he'll be looking a good deal higher than *that* whey-faced strumpet!"

"Deirdre."

She looked up, her face burning, to meet Alistair's eyes.

"I'm sorry. For what I said before and"—he nodded toward the women seated down the table—"and for that, as well."

"No need to be sorry for that," she said clearly. "They're naught but silly women clacking their silly tongues."

Alistair grinned and squeezed her hand. "That's right, lass."

And as simply as that, it was there again between them, exactly as it had been that night in the woodsman's hut.

She turned her hand in his, their fingers twined, and suddenly it was true, the women *didn't* matter. Let them say what they wanted, it made no difference, none at all, because Alistair was holding her hand and smiling into her eyes.

"I must to see the laird," he said. "He sent for me and—and I must see him once again. But once that's done, we're off to Donegal."

"Oh, Alistair!" she cried. "Do you mean it? But I thought—"

He cocked a brow. "I gave my word I'd see ye home. Did ye think I'd break it?"

Before she could answer, Malcolm spoke to him, and he released her hand. But Deirdre felt the warm glow of his touch even after he had gone to wait upon the laird and she lay wakeful in her bed, wondering what was to happen on the morrow.

Even as she wondered, she touched her hand to her lips and smiled in the darkness.

chapter 22

"Well then," Jemmy Kirallen said, "they are an hour out of Ravenspur. What do we tell them?"

Alistair, Deirdre, and Alyson sat beside him in the hall. It was empty now and the weak morning sun barely lit the tumbled rushes and stacked trestles, all that remained of last night's gaiety.

"An hour?" Deirdre cried in dismay. "How could they get here so soon?"

"Someone sent word." Alistair swore, then struck his fist upon the table. "Damn him!"

"I won't ask who it was," Jemmy said. "It doesn't matter now. The question is, what do you want me to say, my lady?"

"I—oh, my lord, the last thing I want is to bring trouble between you and the Maxwells. But—but I do want to go home again. And it was agreed that I might do so."

Jemmy shifted in his seat, and Deirdre wondered if he always looked like this, so gaunt and pale, or if it was the strain of waiting upon his dying father.

"Go on," he said.

"My father made an agreement with Brodie. I was to have widow's rights, some gold, some land, but I don't care about that now. I only want to take Maeve home."

"Was the agreement written?"

Deirdre nodded. "It was. My father showed it to me so I might know. If we'd had a son, it would have been different, he would have had to stay. Brodie insisted upon that. He never thought to mention what might happen to a daughter. But," she added, forestalling his next question, "I cannot say what became of the agreement. If the Maxwell found it, no doubt it's ashes, though Father does have a copy."

"There's no time to get word to your father," Jemmy said, drumming his fingers on the tabletop. "Without that agreement, my lady, Maxwell is in the right to ask for your return."

Alyson nodded reluctantly, though her face was wrenched with pity. "Deirdre, I wish there was something we could do to help you."

Jemmy continued to tap his fingers, frowning. "A bit more time, and mayhap we could think of something. But with them so close—still, even if he takes you back today, I can get word to your father. He'll come for you."

"Sure and he will," Deirdre said, trying to smile.

"But it will do no good if Maxwell has you married off again," Alistair pointed out, speaking Deirdre's own fears aloud.

"Well, then, I'll have to see he doesn't," Deirdre said with a courage she was far from feeling. "I thank you for your courtesy, my lord, my lady. I'll go get Maeve ready."

"Wait."

She stopped, halfway out of her seat, and looked at Alistair.

"If ye were wedded, they could not take ye back again."

"Aye, well, if I was, that might be true," Deirdre said. "But—"

"A betrothal will do," Alistair went on, staring down at his clenched hands.

"Aye," Jemmy said slowly, "that might serve."

"But—"

"I'd do it," Alistair said abruptly. "If it would be of any help."

"I—well—" Deirdre stammered, completely confused. Did he really mean it?

"I think 'tis a very sensible suggestion," Alyson declared.

"Then—if you're quite sure, Alistair—" Deirdre said.

"Aye," he answered in a strange, choked voice. "I'm sure."

She wished he would look at her, just once, so she could be sure he meant what he was saying. But what exactly *was* he saying? Was this but a trick or an honest offer for her hand? She couldn't really marry him, of course, it was completely out of the question. Or was it? She couldn't think for the sudden pounding of her heart.

"And of course it could be broken later," Jemmy added thoughtfully.

He can look higher than that whey-faced strumpet. Was that what Jemmy thought? What they all thought? But what did Alistair think?

Oh, if only he would look at her, she was sure she could read the truth of it in his eyes! But he kept his head bent as he waited for her answer.

"All I ask is to take Maeve home again," she said with as much dignity as she could muster. "And if this is the way—then yes, Sir Alistair. I thank you."

Then, at last, he did look at her, but his expression told her nothing. "Of course, my lady," he said formally. "That is what we all want. Isn't it?"

And with the question still hanging in the air, he went to fetch the priest.

"Ah, Christ, Jemmy," Kinnon Maxwell said, *running one hand through his thinning hair. "This is a proper mess. My father will not take it well."*

"Aye, Kinnon, I know," Jemmy said sympathetically. "But what are we to do? It is all signed and witnessed, if you care to look. . . ."

"Nay, there's no need," Kinnon said gloomily. "I'm sure 'tis all in order."

They were once again in the hall, though now it held a dozen Maxwell men and the same number of Kirallens. Deirdre stood to one side of Jemmy's chair, her cold hand held fast in Alistair's grip.

Kinnon glanced their way. "Damn you, Alistair," he said without heat. "So this is how ye return our hospitality?"

"Och, Kinnon, since when is it a sin to fall in love?" Alistair said, just as though he meant it. "The lady is free and so am I, so where's the trouble?"

"My father is the trouble, as well ye ken. But—"

There was a scuffle in the lower hall, and Jemmy rose from his seat, a spasm of pain passing quickly across his face. "Sir Calder, stand back," he called in ringing tones. But the knight either did not hear or chose to ignore him. Calder drew back his arm and struck one of the Maxwells—and the hall erupted into a brawl.

"God *damn* him," Jemmy muttered, starting forward. "Kinnon, call your men off—"

Before Kinnon could move, the men tumbled forward and one drew a dagger from his belt, springing with terrifying speed from the fray toward Jemmy, who stood alone before his chair.

Alistair let go Deirdre's hand and leaped forward. Even as Alyson cried out a warning that would have come too late, Alistair seized the man's wrist but was carried backward by the force of the charge. He stumbled into Jemmy and the three of them went down.

In a moment Alistair was on his feet again, turning to pull Jemmy upright. The Maxwell man lay still in a widening pool of blood.

Now, at last, Kinnon spoke. "Stop!" he cried, his voice shrill with fear. "I order ye to halt!"

"To me!" Jemmy cried. "At once! Sir Calder—the rest of you—that's enough."

He pulled Calder back by the neck of his jerkin and the crack of his hand across the knight's face rang through the hall. "I said stand back," he commanded into the sudden silence. "All of you."

The men obeyed, each side drawing to an opposite corner of the hall. "Jemmy, are ye hurt?" Kinnon asked anxiously, peering into Jemmy's ashen face.

"I'm fine. He didn't touch me. I think 'tis best you take your men and go."

"Aye," Kinnon said, glancing down at the still form lying on the floor. "I am sorry—I canna imagine what Duran was thinkin'—come on, men, take him up."

Jemmy stood until the Maxwells were gone, then fixed his knights with a stern eye. "Every one of you was at fault here today," he said. "I will—" He staggered a little and groped for the back of his chair, missed, and collapsed facedown on the floor.

Alyson ran forward and fell to her knees with an anguished cry.

"Turn him over—'tis all right, he's just fainted—Conal, Donal," she ordered. "Get over here. Lift him—gently now—and get him to his bed."

Deirdre was beside her in an instant, her hand firm on Alyson's elbow. Together they followed Jemmy from the hall. Alyson turned when she reached the doorway, her eyes going over each of the knights in turn. More than a few bent before her searching look, staring at the rushes covering the floor.

When the women had vanished through the doorway, Alistair stood and faced the knights, arms folded across his chest. "Now," he said. "Someone tell me what just happened here."

"I will," Calder said, rubbing his cheek where the mark of Jemmy's hand showed redly. "The rest of you get out."

When they were alone, Calder perched on the arm of Jemmy's chair and scowled.

"What the devil are ye playing at, Alistair?" he demanded. "What were ye thinkin' to get in the way as ye did?"

"Instinct, I suppose," Alistair said casually. "It all happened very fast. I'm afraid I didna think at all."

"Well, ye'd best start thinkin'. Christ, man, there it was, the chance we've all been waitin' for. But mayhap it willna matter. That shoulder is still troubling him—it may yet take him off. Even if it doesna, he'll no be laird after the old man is dead. I've been busy while ye were away."

"What have ye been busy about?" Alistair asked, forcing himself to smile as he spoke.

"Weel, it's like this. The council is all for Malcolm. The lad will be guided by us every step along the way. Is that no what ye wanted?"

This *was* what Alistair had wanted a year ago. In that year he had changed—but everything here was still the same. It was all going forward, everything he had put in motion.

"I *never* said I wanted Jemmy murdered. Never that."

And God be thanked that was the truth, or there would be more on his conscience than he could bear.

"'Tis the quickest way." Calder shrugged, and Alistair felt a slow chill run down his back.

"And then the council will choose Malcolm," he said.

"Why, I've got the council right here." Calder laughed, holding out his hand. "Ye might say I *am* the council, and ye wouldna be far off from the truth. But it would be better for us all if Jemmy . . . well, if he didna survive his wound. Quick and clean and then Malcolm is the heir."

"I see ye *have* been busy!" Alistair said in admiring tones.

"I have. But what of ye, Alistair? What game are ye playing here? I thought I kent, but now . . . well, now I'm not so certain. Ye seem different, somehow."

"I've been away a long time."

Calder gave him a considering look. "Mayhap that's all there is to it. Mayhap not. But know this, Alistair: with ye or without ye, the council will rule until Malcolm is of age.

And by that time," he added, his teeth gleaming in a smile, "he'll ken who his friends are."

"And if he doesna?"

"That's no concern of yours. We'll handle the lad."

Calder stood and looked down at Alistair. "You're either in or out. Ye canna have it both ways."

"Aye. Well, you've given me much to think about."

"Think all ye like. But do it quick. Time is running out—and not only for the laird."

"Calder!" Alistair called, and the knight turned back. "Who gave Jemmy that wound?"

"'Twas a bit hard to tell exactly what was happening that day—ye ken how it is in the heat of battle. Could have been one man, could have been another."

"Or it could have been your blade."

"Aye, it could have," Calder agreed blandly. "But if it was, I wouldna be admitting it, now, would I?"

"L̲ie down, my lady," Maggie ordered firmly, straightening from the bed where Jemmy lay. "I can tend to this well enough."

Deirdre put a hand on Alyson's arm. "She's right. Come and rest—" She could feel Alyson shaking beneath her hand, and added very quietly, "'Tis not only yourself you have to care for now."

Alyson gave in without further protest and allowed Deirdre to lead her to the tower chamber, where Maeve played happily on the floor with the sweet-faced lady who had been sent to tend her. "Mam!" Maeve cried. "Look!"

"Come, bairn, let's go see the garden," the lady said, taking one look at Alyson's face and scooping Maeve into her arms.

"Go on, love," Deirdre said, kissing the child's upturned face. "I'll be down soon."

Alyson lay down upon the bed. "How did you know?" she asked.

"I can't say I did know," Deirdre answered with a shrug.

"From time to time I make a lucky guess. Do you have any pains here—or here—"

Alyson put one hand on her belly and shook her head. "Nay, I think all is well." She closed her eyes and leaned back against the pillow. "We've wanted this," she murmured. "But now—" Her eyes flew open and she struggled to sit upright. "Deirdre, you mustna tell anyone! Promise me!"

"I promise," Deirdre said, puzzled. "But whisht, lie back, you *must* rest now. I'll send for someone—who would you like?"

"No one."

Deirdre's puzzlement deepened. "Surely there is some woman—a friend?"

"Nay," Alyson said in a small voice. "They all—oh, Deirdre, you dinna know, do you?"

"Know what?"

"About how I came here."

"Well," Deirdre said cautiously. "There was some talk. They said your father tried some trick, and it all went wrong."

Alyson's pale lips curved in a smile. "That's what they're still saying here. But I think it all went right—at least for me. And Jemmy. Though lately I've wondered . . . I've brought him nothing but trouble from the first. . . ."

Deirdre took Alyson's cold hand in hers. "Tell me," she said gently. "If you want to."

"Aye. I do want to. Better you hear it from me . . ."

Deirdre listened with astonishment as Alyson's tale came out, of the deception she'd been forced to undertake, her growing love for Jemmy and his for her. When Alyson reached the part where Jemmy had defied his clan and father to wed her, Deirdre wiped her eyes and laughed.

"I knew from the first he was mad with love for you," she said. "Oh, Alyson, if you could have heard the way he spoke of you—he doesn't regret it. Don't ever think it."

"He should regret it. It turned the clan against him—and

he had enough to overcome as it was. We could have won them over, though, I'm sure of it, if not for—"

"For Alistair?"

"Aye. Once he was gone, they all started to talk of him as if he were a holy martyr. The laird could have stopped it, but he didna. It was the guilt," she said quietly. "He looked at Alistair like his own son, the only one he had once Ian was gone. He and Jemmy—they never got on well. That was why Jemmy left in the first place. Once he came back again, things began to get better between them. Until Jemmy married me instead of Maude."

"But I don't understand." Deirdre shook her head. "What difference did it make by then? The laird had the peace he wanted."

"He had it at the price of losing Alistair. The laird always thought that if Jemmy had only married Maude, Alistair would have accepted it—that the clan would have accepted it. But there's a great difference between having Maude, Darnley's true-born daughter as their lady, and the baseborn kitchen slut Darnley foisted off on Jemmy. They hate me, Deirdre—"

"Oh, Alyson," Deirdre cried, "surely that can't be so! They can't all hate you!"

"Mayhap not," Alyson agreed listlessly. "But the ones who don't, don't dare quite offer friendship. They're standing back, waiting, watching to see which way things will go. Now that Alistair's back again, the waverers will be sidling over to his camp if it seems he's winning."

"Winning what?"

"Power," Alyson replied flatly. "Isn't that what all this is about? The council is using Malcolm, but he's just a pawn; they don't intend for him to rule. 'Tis Alistair they really want. And that's what Alistair wants, too. He made no secret of it before he went away. Now, he's back and"—she began to shake.

Deirdre stroked her hand. "Hush, now. Why, he saved your laird's life today! Mayhap he was bitter when he left," Deirdre said slowly. "Who could blame him if he was? But he has changed. He didn't mean to come back here at all, he told me so himself. He was just guiding us through your lands on our way to Annan."

"Are you certain of that, Deirdre? Verra, verra certain?"

Deirdre thought back over everything that had happened since she met Alistair on Beltane Eve.

"Aye," she said at last. "I am certain."

I am, I *must* be, she thought. Because if I am wrong, then Alistair is not only a liar, but the most accomplished liar I've ever met. And that she could not accept.

"He is coming with me to Donegal," she said. "I see now we should leave as quickly as we can."

"Oh, Deirdre—I hate to say this, but I hope you will."

"Now rest," Deirdre said firmly. "Whatever is to happen, you must have a care for yourself—and the babe."

She sat by the bed, stroking the bright hair back from Alyson's pale face until her breathing slowed and Deirdre knew she slept.

When someone knocked softly on the door, she was up and across the floor in an instant.

"Hush," she said, pulling open the door, surprised to find herself face-to-face with Alistair. His cheeks were flushed, but his lips and the skin around his nose were white, as though he had sustained a shock.

"How is she?" he asked, looking past her into the room.

"Resting," Deirdre said briefly.

"Poor Deirdre," he murmured. "Ye look worn out yourself. Come and get some air."

Deirdre glanced back over her shoulder.

"She can spare ye for an hour," Alistair said. "And where is Maeve? I hoped to see her."

"In the gardens," Deirdre replied. "Let me send someone for Maggie, and then I can go."

"I'll see to it," he offered.

A few minutes later Deirdre walked into the Ravenspur garden, a riot of bright colors and sweet scents. Deirdre inhaled deeply, then pulled the coif from her head and let the sun beat down upon her head.

"It is beautiful," Alistair said, his gaze moving over the flowerbeds and neatly clipped lawn. "She's done much in just a year."

Then he smiled, catching sight of Maeve. "Hello, sweeting," he called, and she looked up, her small face lighting with pleasure.

"Star!" she cried, running across the lawn and jumping into his arms. He swung her around until she screamed with laughter, then held her high above his head and looked into her face.

"And what have ye been about, poppet?"

"Horsey!" she said excitedly. "There—"

Deirdre followed her pointing finger to see Malcolm rise laughing from his knees.

"So you're the horsey, are ye?" Alistair said, swinging Maeve onto his shoulders and walking over to the boy.

"A very fine steed, too," he replied with a grin. "Good morning to ye, Lady Maxwell."

"Again!" Maeve cried, tugging at Alistair's hair. "Horsey—again!"

"All right, then," Malcolm said agreeably. "Have another ride if ye like."

Alistair led Deirdre to a stone bench set among the roses and stretched out on the grass at her feet, looking up at her through his lashes with a smile. He could not be plotting murder and treachery, she thought. He simply could not. It was impossible that he could look at her like this, his eyes so bright and clear, if that was so.

"The Maxwells have gone, I trust?" she said lightly.

"Aye, God rot them."

"What do you think happened, earlier, in the hall?"

He looked down at the grass, avoiding her gaze. "Things got a bit out of hand. Apparently the man was a bit the worse for drink—" He shrugged.

"It seemed as though Sir Calder started the whole thing."

"That is not what the knights say," he answered evasively.

So he was defending Sir Calder now, the man who had behaved so rudely toward Alyson, the man who had defied Lord Jemmy earlier today and nearly caused his death. Deirdre's heart faltered, but she forced herself to smile brightly.

"And have you seen the laird?"

"I've seen him, aye, but he has not seen me. He was asleep yesterday. I must go back to him soon."

"What do you think he'll say to you?"

"I canna know until he says it, can I? Forgive me," he added quickly. "I didna mean to snap at ye."

He rubbed his temples as though they ached. "The laird is verra ill," he said. "They think he may not wake again at all."

"Then we should go, right know, today."

"I cannot do that."

"But if the laird isn't going to wake—"

"There are . . . things happening here. Things I canna explain."

"I spoke to Lady Alyson earlier," Deirdre said carefully.

He sat up, every muscle tensed. "What did she say to ye?"

"I think she would be—well, relieved—if we were to go."

Alistair laughed shortly. "I'm sure she would be."

"Then why stay where we're not wanted?"

"Because I swore an oath. With his last breath Ian asked me to watch over Malcolm and I promised him I would. I will *not* be forsworn."

He jumped to his feet and began to pace the grass.

"But Malcolm is fine!" Deirdre protested. "You've seen him for yourself. What is it you feel you must—"

"If the laird had only listened to me from the first!" Alistair burst out angrily. His back was toward her, but she could see the tension in the rigid set of his shoulders. "Malcolm is Ian's son; he should have been named as heir right after Ian died."

When he turned to her, his expression shut and grim,

Deirdre's heart plummeted. Could Alyson have been right after all? Was Alistair still determined to see Malcolm set in Lord Jemmy's place?

"That question was settled long ago," she said firmly. "It was the laird's decision and he did what he thought best."

"The laird was wrong," he said flatly.

Holy St. Brigid, Deirdre prayed, show me how to help him. Alyson is surely mistaken about one thing: Alistair would never use Malcolm as the means to his own ends. Whatever he means to do, he feels himself honor bound to do it, and 'tis with Malcolm's good at heart.

"What of Lord Jemmy?" she asked, almost fearing to hear his answer. "What's to become of him?"

Alistair sighed heavily. "God only knows."

Deirdre stared at him in shock. "He is your own kin—"

"D'ye think I have forgotten that?"

He sank down on the bench and dragged his hands through his hair, until the fine bright strands broke free of their braid and shimmered like molten gold in the sunlight. "Christ's wounds, this is a damnable mess."

"But why? What has Lord Jemmy done, save follow his father's orders? Do you, too, blame him for marrying Alyson?"

Alistair glanced at her, surprised. "That's the one thing he's done that shows any sense! This has naught to do with either of them, really. Malcolm is the one who matters, and Ian—"

"Alistair," she said with swift urgency. "You must stop thinking about Ian. You must. Don't you see that what he wanted doesn't matter now? He's dead but you are still alive! You have a choice—*your* choice, not Ian's. It has nothing to do with him."

"You're wrong. This has everything to do with Ian. I told ye he wanted something of me still. This is it, and it's my one chance—my last chance—to put right what went wrong when he died."

"I don't see—"

"It was my place to protect him and I wasn't even there.

I failed him and he's dead. And now—" He looked up at her, his eyes stricken. "If I fail Malcolm, as well, I will be damned forever."

"No!" She took him by the shoulders and turned him to face her. "Oh, Alistair, you said yourself this was a bad place for you, don't you remember? You said you wanted to make a new start, a new life . . ."

Without a word he pulled her close and laid his head against her shoulder. She put her arms around him, one hand stroking the fine soft hair, and felt him draw a long shuddering breath.

"If only it could be so simple, but it isna simple, not anymore," he said, his voice muffled. "I canna walk away from this."

"From what?" she cried. "Alistair, tell me what you're planning."

"I canna do that. I'm sorry, I wish I could—I ken ye don't understand, Deirdre, but I'm asking ye to trust me." He drew back and looked into her eyes. "Please. Just trust me."

She nodded helplessly. "I will. I do."

"This is something I must do, and—and I fear there isn't much time left to me." He lifted his head sharply. "D'ye see them? They're with me all the time now—"

"Whisht," she said, pulling his head back down on her shoulder. "I don't see anything, there's nothing there, *nothing*."

But she *had* seen them, sitting motionless among the green leaves and bright red fruit of the cherry tree above them. Two dark winged shapes, hideous, terrifying, implacable as death itself. She tightened her arms around Alistair, as though somehow she could protect him, and a sharp stab of fear shot through her as she prayed the prayer of every living being confronted with the reality of death.

Not yet, she pleaded silently. Don't take him now. It isn't fair, it isn't right. Oh, please, just a little longer—

He lifted his head and wiped a tear from her cheek with one callused thumb. "I'm sorry," he murmured. "I shouldna have gone on like that. I must be more tired than I thought. Please dinna cry, Deirdre, 'twill be all right."

But how could it be right? she wondered as she tried to summon a smile. How could anything ever be right again?

"We all must die one day," he said. "'Tis naught to fear. But what I do fear—the only thing I fear now—is that I'll die without a chance to put things right."

"You'll find the way," Deirdre said fiercely. "I know you will."

He smiled, then leaned forward and kissed her lightly. "So long as one of us believes that, I suppose 'twill have to be enough."

He sighed and touched her cheek. "And then there's you. What's to be done about ye, Deirdre?"

Before she could answer, he slung an arm around her shoulder and pulled her close. "No, forget I asked that. Can ye do that? Do ye mind very much if we dinna talk about it yet?"

"I—well, nay," she answered, feeling suddenly a little breathless.

"Let's talk of something else. Something different. Tell me what ye liked to do when ye were a child," he suggested. "What was your favorite game?"

Completely disconcerted by this abrupt change of subject, Deirdre felt herself begin to blush.

"Oh! Well, let me think—I always liked to go down to the cliffs. Sometimes I'd see a seal and would pretend it was a silkie come to carry me away so I could live on the bottom of the sea."

"I wouldna blame any silkie for trying," he said softly.

The sunlight was strong on her face, the scent of flowers heady enough to make her dizzy. And all the time there was the solid strength of his arm around her shoulders, the feeling of his fingers as they twined in hers.

"And then I played the games all children play," she continued, with a nod and smile to acknowledge his compliment. "Counting and jumping—and wishing at the old well."

"What did ye wish for?"

She glanced at him, wondering how he could possibly care about something so trivial when he had so much on his mind. But he was looking at her as though her answer was terribly important.

"Oh, foolish things." She laughed. "A new horse or a ring with a blue stone—"

"And did ye get them?"

"The horse I did get," she said. "My father won at dicing and came home leading a dappled palfrey. He usually did win, but not so much as he did that time. We ate well for a month."

"He gambled, then?" Alistair asked, frowning a little.

"Oh, aye. 'Twas rather a haphazard sort of life, I suppose, though I never thought about it then. I thought it was all great fun. One day it would be new gowns and wax candles and meat at every meal, and then Father's luck would turn and it was back to porridge and rushdips. But no matter what we had upon the table, there was company to share it. And we would be merry, always. . . ."

Alistair was looking down at her hand, still held in his. "Ye should have rings," he said, lightly teasing. "One for this finger"—he set it to his lips—"and this one—and this—"

His lips were soft and warm upon her hand. She closed her eyes and sighed.

"Ye should have had at least one ring today," he said, and she opened her eyes at the sudden seriousness of his tone. "I'm sorry."

"Hush, now," she said, with a nervous laugh. "Where would you have found one in the time?"

He smiled without answering and ran one finger along her palm. She shivered in bright sunlight.

"Well, ring or no ring, it was good enough to convince the Maxwells," he said. "Poor Kinnon—I wonder what he'll tell the old toad?"

Her laughter sounded strained to her own ears, and so

quickly, before he could notice, she said, "They won't be back, will they?"

"They might. And we really should decide what to do next, what ye *want* to do next. But I canna stay now. I must see the laird and hear whatever it is he brought me here to say."

He rose to his feet in one fluid motion and bowed. "Until tonight, then."

She watched him walk away, her eyes moving over his broad strong shoulders and straight line of his back. Then her eyes turned to Maeve, laughing delightedly with Malcolm. For all its troubles, this could be a good place. A good place for Maeve, a good place for her . . . and Alistair? Oh, if only he would give up and accept things as they were, perhaps he could stay here after all. Then they could make their betrothal real . . .

She closed her eyes and imagined herself and Alistair here in the garden, with Alyson and Jemmy and their child . . . Oh, she was a bonny lass, with her father's dark hair and long dark eyes. . . .

"Mam!"

Deirdre sat up quickly, still half dazed with her dream, as Maeve ran toward her, and for a moment it seemed another child ran beside Maeve, a boy so like Alistair it twisted her heart, with yellow hair and bright blue eyes. . . . Then she blinked and realized that this part at least was true. Maeve was hanging on the hand of the golden-haired boy as she dragged him forward, Malcolm following behind.

"Lady Maxwell," Malcolm said, "this is Lady Alyson's brother, Robin."

"How do you do?" Deirdre said, studying him with interest. So this was the boy who had been held hostage by Lord Darnley to force Alyson into her near-fatal deception the year before. He was not much like his sister, Deirdre thought, not as Haddon Darnley was. With his sky-blue eyes and golden hair, Robin had the look of a young angel, an image accentuated by the sweetness of his smile.

"Your sister will be glad to see you!" Deirdre smiled.

"And I her," the boy answered shyly.

"Robin's been off with his mother's people, the McLarans," Malcolm explained. "They live in the Highlands."

"Did you enjoy it?" Deirdre asked.

"Oh, aye. It's very beautiful."

Maeve was gazing up at him, her small face glowing.

"Did ye see the giants?" she asked suddenly.

"Giants?"

"Star said they have giants up there."

"Sir Alistair," Deirdre explained. "He was telling her stories."

"Ah," Robin said. He knelt down and looked at Maeve seriously. "Do ye know, lass, I didna see a one. I looked and looked, but they must have all been sleeping."

Maeve smiled brilliantly. "They sleep a lot," she said confidentially.

"Aye, I've heard the same." Robin stood and added, "I must see Ally now."

"Robin." Deirdre inclined her head. "And Maeve—come here, now, turn Robin loose."

"Another ride?" Malcolm suggested.

Maeve looked from Robin to Malcolm, her eyes large and serious. "All right," she said, turning her smile on Malcolm. "Horsey!"

But even as Malcolm bent to take her on his back, Deirdre noted the way her daughter's eyes lingered on Robin as he walked from the garden. And so it begins, Deirdre thought, and then shivered, wondering what she meant by that.

chapter 23

"I dinna think he'll wake tonight," Master Kerian said, straightening from the bed and giving Alistair a sympathetic glance. "I'll send for ye if he does."

"I'll bide a while."

The physician shrugged and moved to the far end of the chamber, where he busied himself at a long table holding the various tools of his trade.

Alistair regarded Gawyn Kirallen sadly. It seemed unlikely the laird would wake again. Maybe it was best that way. His profile was hawk-sharp now, the flesh stripped from his bones, and his breath rasped in and out in a slow unchanging rhythm.

Alistair settled back in his seat and at length fell into a light doze.

"Alistair?"

He snapped awake and saw that the laird's eyes were open.

"Aye, 'tis me, I'm here." Alistair gripped the laird's frail hand carefully in his own.

"Alistair, I'm sorry—" Gawyn rasped, his eyes bright in his pale lined face.

"Hush, now, dinna worry about that."

"—I was wrong, so wrong, how can ye forgive me?"

"I do. Ye were not wrong—I left ye no choice—"

"Nay!" Gawyn struggled to rise, then fell back with a moaning gasp. "I was! Listen to me, Alistair, I've been waiting for ye, for I had to tell ye—"

He broke off, wheezing, and Master Kerian hurried over, slipping one hand behind his head and holding a cup to his lips. The laird drank, then waved the physician away.

"Hush, now, 'tis all right," Alistair soothed. "Please dinna fash yourself this way."

"But 'tis not all right," Gawyn said heavily. "I was wrong, I tell ye. I should never have brought Jemmy back here."

Alistair stared, too surprised to speak.

"He's no' the man to take my place. Ye were, but I wouldna see it. Jemmy cares nothing for the clan—he showed his colors when he married *her*. Ye were right, Alistair—"

"Nay," Alistair said numbly.

"—Jemmy doesna belong here. All the knights are against him. His fault. His damnable pride. He doesna have the first idea how to hold them all together."

But it is not Jemmy's fault, Alistair thought. 'Tis mine. *I'm* the one who set them all against him.

"Laird—"

"God knows I tried to put things right, but he wouldna listen. He never listens. He cares for nothing but the woman. Och, I canna blame her overmuch—'tis Jemmy who should have known better than to keep her here."

'Tis no wonder he kept her, Alistair thought with sudden understanding. Who else did he have?

"Jemmy isna the one to blame. 'Tis I."

"Whisht, dinna be taking it all on yourself. The thing with Darnley—aye, we disagreed on that, but still, ye acted according to your honor."

"Ye dinna ken what I did," Alistair said desperately. "'Twas I who turned the knights against Jemmy—he never had a chance—"

Gawyn waved a hand. "I ken that you're the man to follow me, then Malcolm after. If it means war wi' Darnley, then so be it. Just return the lad, Alistair, that's all I ask. Send Haddon home again before it starts. Can ye do that for me? Can ye promise not to hurt him?"

"I—of course, I wouldna hurt the lad," Alistair said, revolted at the thought.

Did the laird actually think he was a danger to a *child*? He did, he must, or he would never ask such a thing. But even believing that, he would still hand Alistair leadership of the clan.

If the laird had time to worry for Haddon Darnley, surely he'd had time to consider Jemmy's safety. Yet not a word, not a single promise had he exacted for the sake of his own son.

He's dying, Alistair reminded himself. He does not know what he is saying. Else he would never leave Jemmy at my mercy this way. He kens too well how it's always been between us. Why, for all he knows, I'd slit Jemmy's throat before the funeral was over!

Gawyn lay back with an exhausted sigh, eyes sunken in his ashen face. "I couldna die until I saw ye home again. It broke my heart, sending ye away. Did ye ken that?"

"Aye, I know. I know ye didna want to. I made ye do it. But it was for the best."

"Where did ye go?"

"To Fergus."

Gawyn closed his eyes. "Another sin upon my conscience. He wanted ye years ago, said ye had the makings of a *taibhsear,* and I would not let him have ye. I thought—for Ian—well, we'll say no more about Ian the now. I'll be seeing him soon enough."

His breathing slowed, and Alistair thought that he had fallen asleep, but then his eyes opened once again.

"You," he said very clearly. "*You.* D'ye ken?"

"Aye, Laird. But—"

"Then 'tis well."

Though Alistair sat a while longer, holding the laird's wasted hand in his, Gawyn Kirallen didn't speak again.

chapter 24

Well, there it is, Alistair, he said to himself an hour later as he sat down upon his own bed. The knights are with me, and the laird has given me his blessing. It's mine now, all I ever wanted. All I need do is reach out my hand and take it.

He clung to the detachment he had won so painfully during the past year, away from the close confines of Ravenspur. From that greater distance he could see that it was Jemmy's destiny to rule here, not his, no matter what the laird might say. And Malcolm's to stay with his uncle.

Let Jemmy fight the battle; Alistair was past the squabbling for power that went on within these walls. He did not belong here anymore. Once he had seen Malcolm safe, he would ride for Donegal, never to return.

He was almost resigned to it, save for one thing. It was all well and good to be Deirdre's protector, but what he wanted was to make good the vows they had exchanged today.

He closed his eyes and saw her in the garden, felt her

hand, so rough, so small, within his own. He smiled, re-membering the way her eyes had lit as she described her childhood in Donegal. She'd been happy there and would be again one day. But once she had reached home, she would be finished with him.

Oh, she might not mean to be, but it would happen just the same. Deirdre would be back in her own place, among her own people, the ancient nobility of Ireland. Alistair had forgotten the unbreakable rules of rank and station, but now that he was back at Ravenspur, he could not forget them any longer.

He would have no time with Deirdre in Donegal. If he was lucky, he might see her from a distance now and then, perhaps even exchange a word or two. But even if he ac-cepted the place her father, from charity and duty, must offer, he would be nothing, the lowest of MacLochlann's knights. While Deirdre would be restored to her rightful place as daughter of the house.

And of course the suitors—with that young Fitzgerald at their head—would soon arrive to pay her court.

Ye dinna have to lose her, a voice whispered in his mind. If ye but do as the laird asked, ye could keep her with ye. Every day ye would be with her; every night. . . . He shifted on the narrow pallet. Just the thought of the nights he would spend with Deirdre roused him with swift ur-gency.

He couldn't do it, though . . . or could he? If Jemmy could be persuaded to go back to Spain, then he, himself, would have everything to offer Deirdre. They would have chil-dren . . . black-haired, gray-eyed sons and daughters. . . . And Malcolm would be with him every day, learning the way of ruling. When the time came, Alistair would step back and see Malcolm just where he belonged, in Ian's place.

Would it be so wrong? So very wrong to do as the laird commanded? Jemmy had his lady . . . she was a brave lass, too, and bonny, and loved him well. Why should Jemmy have everything? Jemmy had run off to please himself, but Alistair had spent his life in service to the clan. It wasn't fair that Jemmy should take it all and leave him nothing. . . .

His thoughts dissolved into hazy images of the future as he drifted off to sleep. There he found the dream waiting for him once again.

It began just as it always did with Ian and Alistair walking down the forest path, discovering the tinker's boys tormenting Jemmy. Alistair and Ian faced the lads, outnumbered five to two. But once they moved to stand back to back, there was no fear, only the joy of battle running taut and bright between them. Then the tinker's boys were running off with Ian after them, calling back over his shoulder for Alistair to look after Jemmy.

"Ian, wait!" Alistair cried, just as he always did. He sprinted after Ian, who was disappearing around a turn, though he knew already it was hopeless. "Wait, don't go, 'tis a trap!"

But this time the dream was different. This time Ian was waiting for him around the bend.

Alistair bolted upright on his bed, heart pounding furiously. The room was in darkness now, twilight barely lighting the casement. With a shaking hand he lit a candle and stared into the flame, his eyes glittering coldly in the flickering light.

All his hesitation was gone, all his questions answered. Come morning, he knew what he must do.

chapter 25

"Well, Alistair, what's it to be? Are ye in or out?"
Calder's voice echoed hollowly from the cold
stone walls of the council chamber. The knight's brawny
arms rested on the long table before him as he regarded
Alistair with stony eyes. The six men around him sat so
quietly that Alistair could hear the faint sound of bird-
song through the narrow windows. Outside there was
sunshine, open air, while what remained of the council
was huddled in chill darkness. Like rats, Alistair thought.
Like traitors.

He repressed a shiver and took his accustomed seat just
beside the laird's empty place. Of course that chair was
empty; the laird was dying, and Jemmy had not been invited to this particular meeting of his council. It felt good
to sit here again, Alistair thought. It felt *right*.

He drew a deep breath and met Calder's gaze.

"I'm in."

Calder's eyes flickered, though a moment later he
smiled broadly. I surprised him, Alistair thought. He ex-

pected I'd refuse. And for all his smile, he's not the least bit pleased.

"Well, that's fine," Calder said. "Isn't it, lads?"

"Oh, aye," they agreed quickly. "Just fine."

Alistair glanced around the table. Four of those seated there were new men like Calder himself, barely known to Alistair. The other two had sat on Kirallen's council for years without ever saying more than "yea" or "nay."

"Where is Sinclair?" he asked. "And Gregor and Logan?"

"Sinclair is dead," Calder answered. "Gregor is away just now, and Logan—well, Logan couldna make it here today."

It was more likely that Logan did not even know the council met today. He was the laird's man, always had been, and would never stand for Calder's arrogant assumption of power.

How had this happened? Alistair wondered. How could the laird have given Calder, a knight with no ties of blood to the Kirallens, so much power? Well, it didn't matter how it had happened. The fact remained that Calder was in charge here. But that would change. In time.

"The laird gave me his blessing last night," Alistair said. "Jemmy's out and I am in. Until Malcolm comes of age."

Calder smiled slyly. "Right. So that's the tale, is it? Well, I hear the old man willna wake again, so who's to say? Now, 'tis time the boy learned what's to come when the laird is dead. He's waiting just outside."

Alistair repressed the protest he wanted to make and simply nodded. He had known this moment must come. He just hadn't expected it to come this soon.

Malcolm walked into the council chamber and stood hesitating, his bright eyes moving quickly across the men and settling on Alistair with relief.

"Where is Uncle Jemmy?"

"He's not needed," Calder answered before Alistair could speak. "This is between ye and us, my boy."

Malcolm drew himself up. "I am not *your* boy, Sir Calder. What have ye to say to me?"

Alistair kept his face carefully expressionless. "Malcolm, I saw the laird last night. He told me his will. Ye are to follow him, not Jemmy."

"But, Alistair, he didna really mean that! He's been angry with Uncle Jemmy, and since his last illness he has been—"

"Hold your tongue," Calder ordered. "No one gave ye leave to speak."

Malcolm's eyes flashed. "I shall speak when and how I please, Sir Calder. I take orders from my grandfather and uncle, not from you."

"And from me?" Alistair asked quietly.

"Of course," Malcolm said quickly. "I didna mean—but Uncle Jemmy *is* my guardian. He already named me his heir, even over the children of his own body. Did ye not know, Alistair?"

Alistair hadn't known. It was a clever move on Jemmy's part, one he hadn't expected. But it wouldn't help him now.

Calder laughed. "And ye actually believe that?"

"Of course I believe him. Why should I not? *He* doesna lie," he added pointedly, glaring at Sir Calder.

He is so damn much like Ian, Alistair thought. The same reckless pride and hasty tongue. The same disregard for danger.

"Watch yourself, lad," Calder growled. "I'll stand only so much from ye."

"And then what?" Malcolm challenged.

Before Calder could answer, Alistair spoke sharply. "That's enough, Malcolm. You'll hold your tongue and do as ye are bidden."

"By him?" Malcolm said, pointing to Calder.

"By your council," Alistair said firmly.

Oh, this was hard, much worse than Alistair had expected, seeing the shocked hurt spreading across the boy's open face.

"*My* council?" Malcolm said, his voice cracking. "These men? Do ye no ken what they are? Traitors, every one of them. But ye"—for the first time Malcolm looked like the young and frightened boy he was—"Alistair, ye are no like them—ye *canna* be—"

"Be quiet," Alistair snapped. "Do ye not ken I am acting in your interests. Now run along. We've work to do."

Malcolm stared at him in disbelief, but Alistair kept his own face carefully expressionless as the boy walked out of the chamber, his shoulders stiff. But in the moment before he turned, Alistair had seen the tears shining in his eyes. He clenched his hands tightly together and looked at the men remaining.

"He'll come around."

"He'd better," Calder rumbled angrily. "But whether or no, we have five years before he's of an age to act. By then, he'll be with us, or . . ."

"Or what?"

Calder shrugged.

"Dinna even think of hurting him, Calder," Alistair warned. "I willna stand for it."

"Oh, *ye* willna stand for it? Well, Alistair, 'tis time ye learned there's no room here for a man who canna pull with the rest. If ye should decide to leave with the Maxwell wench, we'll carry on. D'ye understand me?"

The men around the table stayed silent. Calder might speak of pulling with the others, but he meant nothing of the sort. He was in command now, him alone. And left to Calder, Malcolm had no chance at all.

Alistair held Calder's eyes for a long moment, then dropped his gaze to the table before him.

"Aye. I understand. But still—I would not see Malcolm harmed. He's Ian's son."

"Then teach him to hold that tongue of his."

"I will."

Calder nodded. "Good. Now, ye say ye saw the laird last evening. How much longer does he have?"

"Master Kerian said a few days—a week at most."

Calder nodded. "Just as ye said, Hamish."

The man thus addressed smiled eagerly. "'Tis true, Calder. Ye can count on me."

"A week," Calder said, frowning. "Well, we can wait that long. And then Jemmy will be taken care of."

Alistair cleared his throat. "I had thought—if we gave him gold to buy a ship—he'd be happy to go back to Spain."

Janus, an older man who had sat on Kirallen's council for many years, nodded his agreement. "I think he would."

"But what if he doesna want to go?" asked Sir Dunstan.

Calder sliced a hand through the air. "Spain? Nay, I think not. Master Jemmy is bound for . . . more distant points."

"Calder," Alistair said strongly, "Jemmy is the laird's son and my kinsman. I—"

"Dinna fear, Alistair," Calder interrupted. "There will be no blood guilt on your hands."

Alistair glanced around the table. Janus looked troubled, but the rest of them were smiling their approval. The room seemed to draw around them, dark and cold and stifling.

"I dinna like it," Alistair said.

"Ye needn't take any part in it," Calder said with a shrug. "Just stand back and let it happen, man."

"I dinna like it," Alistair repeated, though his voice held little strength now.

"'Tis not the way ye'd have it," Calder said, not unkindly, willing to give a little in return for Alistair's obedience. "We all ken how ye must be feeling. But when 'tis done, ye will see it was the only way."

Alistair considered arguing further, then bowed his head. His silence was the only answer Calder needed.

chapter 26

Alistair blinked in bright sunlight as he walked into the courtyard. He drew a long breath and tried to banish the chill of the council chamber.

"Alistair."

Malcolm touched his arm. "In there—ye didna really mean it, did ye?"

"Aye, Malcolm, I did. The council is control now, and ye had best get used to it. There's no use in angering Calder any more, ye hear?"

Malcolm drew back, his eyes sparking. "I'll not take orders from that traitor. Nor any man on the council."

"I'm trying to protect you, Malcolm, can ye no see that?" Alistair said urgently, putting his hands on Malcolm's shoulders. "They hold the reins, and there's nothing either one of us can do about it."

"But d'ye no ken what they mean to do? They mean to get rid of Uncle Jemmy."

"The laird said—"

"My grandfather is wrong! And he never meant for

Uncle Jemmy to be hurt. D'ye think they'll just let him walk away?" His eyes widened and he took one step back, shrugging Alistair's hands from his shoulders. "But ye ken that already! Ye hate him, too, ye always have. . . . I wanted you to come back!" he cried, wiping one sleeve across his eyes. "I prayed for it every day that ye were gone. But now—now I wish ye'd stayed away!"

Alistair leaned against the wall as Malcolm ran off. He wasn't going to make this easy. But if losing the boy's trust was what it took to save him, then that was what would have to be. He only wished it didn't hurt so damn much.

The courtyard was full now, the servants hurrying about their work. Alistair let his gaze wander over the battlements, each stone so familiar. Up on the highest tower sat two shapes, dark against the sun-bright sky.

When he looked back at the courtyard it was gray and dim, the people no more than walking skeletons, clad in borrowed flesh. None of them was real. *He* wasn't real. He was but a living ghost and the corbies were waiting with endless patience to strip the dead flesh from his bones. He shuddered, gripped with horror. How could any man see what he was seeing and still go on, pretending that anything they said or did actually mattered? It was all vain, all hopeless. . . .

And then Deirdre walked into the yard. She was bathed in light, shining like a brand in the empty darkness. Alistair's gaze fastened on her with desperate hunger. *She* mattered. She was real and true and beautiful beyond all words.

The grayness receded before her and the courtyard was just a courtyard again, filled with people who were hurrying about their business. For the first time he noticed Alyson was with Deirdre, skirts tied about her waist and a linen coif covering her hair. When Deirdre saw him, she waved and smiled. Finn, just beside her, barked once in greeting.

Alistair pushed himself away from the wall and walked over. "Good morning," he said, bowing to the two ladies.

Deirdre smiled brilliantly, but Alyson turned away without speaking. She knows about the council meeting, Alistair thought. Even if she doesn't know exactly what was said, she understands what's happening.

Damn them, he thought with weary anger, why do they not run? Why doesn't Jemmy take her out of here and go back to Spain?

But he knew the answer to that question. Jemmy was a Kirallen and had been given his full share of reckless pride, just as Malcolm had. Alistair sighed. He'd forgotten what weary work it was to keep Kirallens from cutting their own throats. And how dearly it could cost.

Deirdre was looking up at him, one hand shading her eyes against the light. How different she looked now from the woman he'd seen in Maxwell's hall! Like a gem covered in dust, she'd been, but now she blazed in sunlight. In her shining eyes he could see the man of honor she still believed him.

When she smiled at him he smiled in return. He couldn't help it. If he lay upon his deathbed, Deirdre's smile could not fail to call an answering response.

"Would ye care to join me for a ride?" he asked.

"Right now?" she said eagerly, and he nodded, his heart twisting in his breast. How could he bear to part with her? Yet it must be done, and quickly. Calder had already found one weakness in him and hadn't hesitated to exploit it. Malcolm would be safe enough for now; Calder needed him. But Deirdre was a different story. He had to get her out of here before the game he had begun this morning turned deadly.

"Alyson, do you mind if I—" Deirdre began.

"Go along," Alyson said, not turning. "I can manage here."

"Do you think she was angry with me?" Deirdre asked as she and Alistair walked toward the stable. "She sounded very strange."

"A woman's moods." He shrugged. "She'll get over it soon enough."

Casting about for some other topic of conversation, his eye fell on a spray of wild roses hanging over the stone wall.

"For you, my lady," he said, breaking off a blossom and presenting it to Deirdre with a bow.

"Why, thank you," she answered, dropping him a curtsy as she buried her nose in the fragrant spray. "Oh, just smell this!" She sighed. "Do you think Alyson would mind if I cut some?"

"I am sure she would not. Here," he added, drawing his dagger. "Use this."

She turned it in her hand, looking at the finely wrought stag's head set with chips of emeralds. "Such a pretty thing," she said. "I've often noticed it before."

"It was a gift from the laird," Alistair answered, his gaze moving to the mews, where a small, golden-haired boy was peering out at him from the door. He looked familiar, but Alistair could not quite place him. "There was a set— one for Ian, one for Jemmy, and this one for me."

"Sir Alistair!" the boy called. "Can ye spare a moment?" Then he saw Deirdre and smiled. "Good morning, Lady Maxwell."

"Hello, Robin."

Robin Bowden, Alistair thought. Lady Alyson's brother. Clare McLaran's son. My kinsman, even if a distant one. And whatever can he want with me?

"Sir Alistair," the boy said in a rush. "My grandmother, Emma McLaran, that is, sent ye a gift some time ago. It was"—he blushed painfully—"well, before she heard that ye were gone. I've been looking after it, but now that ye are back . . ."

"What did Emma send?" he asked.

Robin stepped out of the door and extended his arm. A hooded falcon sat upon it. "She is a rare beauty, is she no? Will ye come see her?"

"Go on," Deirdre said, dropping a handful of blossoms at her feet and reaching to cut another spray.

Alistair stepped into the soft dimness of the mews as

Robin deftly unhooded the falcon. The boy handed him a feather and he gently stroked the bird's breast, whistling softly as the falcon regarded him with baleful yellow eyes.

"Do ye have the care of her?" Alistair asked.

"I do," Robin said, drawing himself up proudly. "She eats from my hand now. I think she's ready to fly to the creance."

"Well done!" Alistair said, impressed that such a slight young boy could have persuaded this fierce animal to trust him.

"Ye should take her out soon," Robin said seriously. "Now that she's yours, she must learn to know ye."

Alistair looked at the bird, then glanced out the doorway toward Deirdre. She was busily cutting flowers, Finn sitting just beside her.

My hawk, he thought. My hound. And my lady fair.

It was happening, just as it had been foretold. Everything was in place now. And there was nothing he could do to stop it.

He stared unbelieving into the bright fresh day, then started, frowning, as Calder walked toward Deirdre, a false smile on his face.

"Good day to ye, Lady Maxwell," Calder greeted her.

Deirdre looked up, her hands full of flowers. "Sir Calder," she replied coolly.

"Ye are as lovely as the morning," Calder said, seeming not to notice her tone. "Would ye no say so, Alistair?"

"Aye." Alistair bit off the word, watching Calder narrowly as he took Deirdre's arm. "Come along, my lady, we have things to do. Good day, Calder."

"And to the two of ye, as well," Calder said genially. "'Tis a fine day, is it no? Ye had best enjoy it while ye can. I fear a storm is coming."

Deirdre began to gather up the sprays of blossom at her feet. "I want to get these into water."

"Leave them," Alistair snapped. Seeing her start of surprise at his abrupt change of mood, he deliberately light-ened his voice. "If we're going to ride, we best get started."

"But—" Deirdre took one look at his face and obviously decided this was not the time to argue. "Robin!" she called. "Can you see that these are taken to my chamber?"

"Of course, my lady," he answered brightly. "I'd be glad to."

As the boy bent to gather the fragrant blossoms, Deirdre took Alistair's arm and slanted him a smile from beneath her lashes. "He's a fine lad, isn't he? Maeve was quite taken with him."

"Aye," Alistair answered absently. "He's very much like his mother. She was—"

"What was she?" Deirdre asked curiously.

"My first love, I suppose," he said with a smile and a shrug. "I was ten and she was a very grand sixteen, and I used to follow her about like a puppy. She was very kind to me. She'd known my mother a bit—they were distant kin."

"Your mother was a MacLaran?"

"Aye. She died when I was six."

"And your—"

"What say ye we race to yonder oak?" Alistair said quickly, before she could start asking questions about his father. He had no desire even to think about the man, much less tell the whole squalid little tale to Deirdre.

Deirdre looked at him as if she would say more, then let the matter drop and tossed her head. "Fine, sir. But when I win, *I* shall name the forfeit."

chapter 27

Deirdre *crouched low in the saddle, the horse's mane mingling with the hair whipping back from her face.* When they reached a low hedge, she urged the horse forward, laughing as they cleared it in one mighty leap and the animal surged up the hill. When she reached the solitary oak standing on the crest, she pulled up, breathless, as Alistair's mount thundered up the slope.

"Whisht, woman, ye ride like the wind itself," he said, laughing, as he halted beside her. His cheeks were flushed, his hair in disarray, and he looked far younger than his thirty years.

She laughed again, the wildness of the ride still humming through her blood, and patted her horse's steaming neck.

Alistair dismounted and put his hands about her waist, swinging her easily from the saddle. "Well, lass, ye look a proper hoyden," he said, sounding so like Deirdre's old nurse that she slipped back into childhood and stuck her tongue out at him.

"Say what you like, sir, I won and you lost and that's the end of it!"

"Quite full of ourselves, aren't we? Well, truth is truth and ye did win. What will ye have of me?"

A kiss. For a moment she almost thought she'd said the words aloud, and the blush that still plagued her, despite her twenty years, swept from the neck of her gown to the roots of her windblown hair.

He laughed and caught her from behind as she turned away. "How now, miss, cat caught your tongue?" he asked. "Take your time and think of a proper forfeit. . . ."

They stood together, looking back over the purple moor toward the dark lines of Ravenspur against the sky.

"Ah, 'tis beautiful," she whispered. A light breeze ruffled the long grass about her knees, and she leaned against the solid strength of Alistair's broad chest, letting her head fall back against his shoulder.

I'll never forget this moment, not ever, she thought. Not the scent of heather or the sunlight on the moor, the hawk swooping through the sky or the jingle of the horses' harness. I'll be remembering it all when the last breath leaves my body.

For she knew, with a certainty too deep for words, that Alistair was about to speak. And she knew what her answer would be. Her heart filled with joy. It was right, so right. Let them say what they would, she knew Alistair was a good man in his heart. No matter what might happen here, they would see it through together.

Beautiful, indeed, Alistair thought, though it wasn't the view before him that he meant. His eyes were fixed upon the spot where Deirdre's neck met her shoulder, a spot so sweet, so vulnerable, that it seemed made for kissing.

He'd bend and put his lips there—just there, where the skin was so white and soft. And then he'd move slowly upward. He wouldn't hurry—oh, no, he'd take his time about it. She would lean back farther, her eyes falling shut, and he would feel the weight of her against him. He'd move his hands, now clasped loosely about her waist, and cup her breasts.

He knew exactly how they would feel, soft and full, fitting perfectly to his palm. Then he'd trace the outline of her perfect ear with the very tip of his tongue. And when she was shivering in his arms, he would whisper, "Stay with me forever, Deirdre, marry me, for my life is nothing if you're not here to share it."

He saw each movement with crystal clarity, and he knew what her response would be. She would say yes.

She would say yes because she wanted him, he had seen that in her eyes that night in the woodsman's hut. And if wanting and loving were two very different things, surely one could grow from the other. He would happily spend the rest of his life seeing she never regretted her decision. If only things were different.

He straightened and let his arms fall from her waist.

"Aye, 'tis beautiful to me," he said. "'Tis my home, the place where I belong. I see that now. I hope that ye will remember it—and me—kindly when you're gone."

"When—when I'm gone?" she faltered.

"When you're home again, in Ireland."

And if this was the price he had to pay, seeing the hurt spring to her eyes as she turned to face him, then he would pay it. Best she go in anger than in pity—for go she would, and soon, he'd see to that.

"I'm afraid I canna leave here after all," he said. "But I will arrange an escort and ye can go tomorrow. Will ye miss it here?" he added, then cursed his reckless tongue. Deirdre had a way of coaxing words from his mouth that he never meant to say.

"Will I *miss* it?" she repeated. "You mean the moor, the burns, the heather? Is that what you're asking? If I'll pine for *Scotland* when I'm gone?"

"Aye," he said inflexibly.

"I'll miss the heather and I'll miss the moor. But I won't miss *Scotland*!" she cried. Her cheeks were red and her eyes flashing, wisps of dark hair flying behind her in the breeze. She had never looked so beautiful as she did now in her anger, against the backdrop of the endless sky.

"Oh, no, I won't miss Scotland one bit. I'll be glad to leave, glad to see the back of this wretched country, and when I reach home I won't forget it. No, I'll be sure to re-member it every single day so I can give thanks that 'tis behind me!"

She stopped, breathing hard, hands fisted on her hips.

"There's no need to shout," Alistair said mildly. "I hear ye. So, I imagine, does everyone from here to Ravenspur."

She turned with an incoherent sound of rage and put her foot in the horse's stirrup, then turned to him, eyes blazing.

"I should thank you for all you've done for me, and what thanks are due I give you. Now 'tis finished. Leave me be, Alistair Kirallen!" she cried, her voice breaking. "Just let me alone! For I never, ever want to speak to you again."

And without giving him a chance to answer, she jumped on her horse and galloped back to Ravenspur.

T*he stableyard was empty now, for which Deirdre was* thankful as she vainly tried to smooth her hair and compose herself before walking into the manor.

Alistair rode into the yard behind her. She watched from the corner of her eye as he took her horse and his own back to the stable. Let him go, she thought. Let him stay far, far away from me.

She stopped at the well and drew a bucket, taking the ladle from its hook and drinking deeply before splashing her burning face, her eyes lingering on the stable door. She was using a corner of her coif to dry her cheeks when she stopped, every nerve in her body thrilling as though some-one had passed a practiced hand across her heartstrings.

Slowly the coif drifted to the ground as she covered her mouth with her hand to still her cry of shock. Slowly she turned, already knowing what she'd see, and found herself looking straight into Ronan Fitzgerald's eyes.

Her heart stopped, then resumed with a lurch, and she touched the well behind her, thinking that this must be a dream. But no, it was no dream, for though she had imagined meeting him a thousand times, her dreams had never taken into account the four years that had gone by.

Dark hair streamed over his shoulders, framing a face both known and unfamiliar. It was a face that four years had changed, stripping away the last softness of his boyhood, digging deep hollows beneath his high sharp cheekbones, emphasizing the elfin slant of his emerald eyes. Different yes, but still the same, still Ronan, with his patched green cloak—it couldn't, surely it *couldn't* be the same one—and his high dusty boots, looking tired, looking weary to the bone, for of course he'd hurried to her, just as she had known he would.

"D-D-ee?"

His voice, warm and smooth as new cream, the voice that had never faltered in the longest and most complicated lays, stumbled a little over her name. He started to say something more, then stopped, his eyes pleading with her now, and just the thought of Ronan pleading—*Ronan,* whose arrogance was as much a part of him as the harp slung across his shoulder—broke through the shock that held her frozen to her place. She stumbled forward, he took a step to meet her, and then she was laughing and crying against his chest as he caught her close and held her as if he'd never let her go.

"Dee, I thought I'd never find you," he said. "Since Beltane I've been dreaming of you—lost—and so I made for Cranston Keep—they said you were gone but wouldn't tell me where—"

"I know, Ronan. I knew you were coming. Why didn't you get here sooner?" she cried, then laid her head against his shoulder and burst into tears.

A moment later, warned by some instinct, she raised her head and saw Alistair walk out the stable door. He stopped and took in the two of them with one assessing glance. His face went very still.

"Ye must be Fitzgerald."

His voice was flat, expressionless, and Ronan nodded briefly.

"And might I be askin' who you are?"

Their eyes locked, emerald and silver, in a flash of instant and mutual dislike. Then Alistair's glance flicked down to Deirdre, and he was once again the terrifying stranger she'd glimpsed before, his lips curling in a smile that chilled her to the heart.

"Well, Deirdre? Will ye no tell the man who I am?"

"Ronan Fitzgerald, this is Sir Alistair Kirallen," she said, stepping away from Ronan and nervously brushing back her tangled hair. "He is—well, Ronan, he is—"

And while she hesitated, wondering how to possibly explain, Alistair turned and walked away.

chapter 28

"I'm sorry, Alistair, but he canna be seeing anyone just now."

Donal moved to stand directly before the doorway of Jemmy's chamber, a drawn sword in his hand.

"Look here, lad, I need to speak with him—"

"Sorry," Donal said. "Not now. Do ye no' ken the hour?"

"Of course I do," Alistair answered tightly, glancing up and down the deserted torchlit hall.

"Then just take yourself off, and if he wants to see ye, he'll send."

"Will ye no at least tell him—"

"Who is it?" Jemmy called from behind the door.

"'Tis Sir Alistair," Donal called back. "But—"

"Well, let him in!" Jemmy cried impatiently.

"All right," Donal said. "But I'll have that sword first, if ye please."

Alistair handed it over and reached for his dagger, his fingers brushing the empty sheath before he remembered he'd

given it to Deirdre. Donal opened the door and stepped back
for him to pass.

"Did you disarm him?" Jemmy called from the bed,
where he lay propped up on several pillows. "I hope you
got the knife in his boot. And while you're at it, you'd best
take the ties from the bedcurtains—he might decide to
strangle me." As Donal hesitated, Jemmy added smoothly,
"Oh, and don't forget the pillow. 'Twould be easy enough
to smother me as I lie here helpless in my bed."

His face was grave, but his dark eyes were gleaming in
their shadowed hollows. Alistair bent his head to hide his
smile. This was exactly how Ian used to talk when he felt
Alistair was being overly cautious. He knew from experience that Donal was not the least bit amused.

"Go on, Donal." Jemmy sighed. "'Tis but a jest. Go
back to the door."

He shifted a little on the pillows, grimacing. "Here, hand
me that, will you? And pour for yourself."

Alistair passed the cup and filled his own, letting the
spirit slide down his throat in a warming glide. Half a
dozen candles in an iron stand cast a glow over the crim-
son-hung bed, but the rest of the room was in shadow, save
the fire burning faintly in the hearth.

"Where is your lady?" Alistair asked.

Jemmy nodded toward a door leading to an inner chamber. "Best she bide there for the time. She couldn't sleep
for fear of disturbing my shoulder."

Alistair sat back in his seat, relieved. He had been wondering how he could pry Alyson from Jemmy's side. What
he had to say was for Jemmy alone.

"Donal's right, ye know," Alistair began, gesturing toward the outer door. "Ye should be guarded."

"'Tis a bit late for that," Jemmy said wryly. "And I suppose that's what's eating at the two of them. Ah, well,
they're good lads and they do their best. But the danger's
not so simple as they would have it. Unless, of course"—
he cocked one brow—"you did come to murder me? In

which case, I hope you'll have the decency to let me get thoroughly drunk before you do it."

"Shut up, Jemmy," Alistair said roughly. "I didna come here for that."

"I suppose not," Jemmy replied evenly. "So why did you come? To tell me about the council meeting?"

How cool he is, Alistair thought. Surely he knows it was his own death we spoke of there.

"It was . . . interesting," Alistair answered. "Malcolm stood up to them like a man. A *foolish* man," he added, shaking his head. "But no more foolish than other Kirallen men I've known."

"Aye, he told me something of it. He never did care much for Sir Calder. No more did I."

"Then why the devil did ye let him and his cronies on the council in the first place?" Alistair asked bluntly.

"Father did it," Jemmy told him wearily. "I tried to stop him, but—I'm afraid that during this past year Father and I haven't gotten on as well as I had hoped. He never did forgive me for marrying Alyson. And after the last attack he grew . . . unreasonable."

"Ye mean his wits left him."

"You could put it that way. Or you could say we disagreed. But either way, Calder took your seat on the council, and soon he got some others on, as well—oh, why am I bothering to tell you? You know it all already, don't you?"

"I ken what they told me today."

Jemmy smiled. "Aye. Of course. You haven't been in contact with him all along."

"No, Jemmy, I havena. Whether ye believe it or no, 'tis the truth. Even if I thought Malcolm should be laird, I would never have gone about it this way," he said, gesturing toward Jemmy's bandaged shoulder. "Calder is the traitor Malcolm named him—but then, ye must be thinkin' I'm no better."

"Well, the thought had crossed my mind. But it wouldn't be fair to put you in the same boat with Calder. He's out for everything he can get, while you—I suppose you're acting in Malcolm's interests. Just as you were last year."

"Aye, well, there's no denying I did some foolish things last year," Alistair said uncomfortably. "All I can say is that they seemed the right things at the time."

Jemmy sighed, looking suddenly exhausted. "I know that. And who's to say they weren't? Father has come round to agreeing with you."

Alistair shifted in his seat. "I spoke with him last night."

Jemmy held out his cup again for Alistair to fill.

"How was it, then?" he asked casually.

"Good." Alistair turned the flagon in his hands, staring into its depths, then laughed shortly. "Terrible."

"Ah."

"He seemed glad that I was there."

"I think he was holding on until he saw you. I know he regretted what happened between you last year. It was another of the things he held to my account. Not without reason," Jemmy added judiciously, taking a small swallow. "I forced his hand that day, and he never truly forgave me for it. He still thinks if I had married Maude, you would have given up and accepted the way things were."

"He was wrong," Alistair said flatly. "Nothing would have made me give up. Except, of course, what did happen."

"It isn't easy to carry on a war when one side leaves the country," Jemmy said mildly. "I don't suppose even you can manage it."

"Not for lack of trying," Alistair admitted. "I followed Darnley as far as London and made sure he knew of it. He kept a guard around him day and night, but still, he was always looking over his shoulder. I suppose I might have gone to France. . . ."

"Why didn't you?"

Alistair hesitated, then said, "My purse was stolen. Down at the docks, while I tried to find the ship the bastard booked passage on."

Jemmy maintained a tactful silence, his face studiously blank.

"Oh, go ahead, laugh if ye want. God knows Ian would have laughed his fool head off if he could have seen me."

"Nay, I don't think he would. I think he would have told you to give it up and get on with your life."

"Well, I dinna have much choice but to give it up. For now."

"Maybe Darnley's dead already," Jemmy mused. "God knows I hope he is. Rotting somewhere on a French battlefield."

"He's not. I'd ken if he was dead."

Jemmy raised a brow. "The Sight? Ian always said you had it."

"And ye never did believe it."

Jemmy shrugged, then muttered a curse as the movement disturbed his shoulder. "Well, here's your chance to prove me wrong. Go on then, Alistair, tell me the future. Isn't that why you came here tonight?"

Alistair felt a surge of admiration. Here Jemmy lay, wounded, helpless, surrounded by enemies at every turn. Even his own father was against him now. Yet when he lifted the cup to his lips, his hand was steady, and his dark eyes held no trace of fear.

"We'll get to that," Alistair said. "But first I wanted to talk about Ian."

"Ian? Oh, I see. Well, let's have it, then. I was a bad brother to him when I left and a worse one when I came back again. Now he walks the halls of Ravenspur, crying out for vengeance."

Alistair shuddered, for Jemmy was closer to the truth than he wanted to admit.

"Ian never blamed ye for leaving," he said abruptly.

Jemmy stopped, the cup halfway to his lips. "I thought he was furious."

"Well, he wasna. The rest of us were, but never him. He—" Alistair swallowed hard. "He was proud of ye for doin' so well. And he used to read your letters over and over."

"He might have answered one."

"Ah, ye knew him, Jemmy. Never picked up a quill if he could help himself. But he always enjoyed your news. All he cared about was that ye were happy."

There, he'd said it. He felt better now, lighter, as though a burden had fallen from his shoulders.

"Thank you," Jemmy said softly. "I'm glad you told me."

Alistair took a long breath. "And that's why I canna do as your father asked me."

"But I thought—did he not tell you to—" Jemmy stopped, frowning.

"He did. Take it all, he said. Let Malcolm rule after."

"Which, if I recall, is exactly what you said you intended to do last year."

"It was. But not now."

"Why?" Jemmy asked, his voice hard with suspicion.

Alistair gripped the cup tightly between his hands. What should he say next? How could he possibly make Jemmy understand?

"Ye willna believe it if I tell ye."

"Try me."

"All right, then. It started last Beltane Eve—but no, I willna go into that, you'll think me mad for sure. Just know that Fergus sent me on a—well, a journey, and I had a—a dream. A Sending. Of Ian. It's been with me ever since, over and over again, always starting the same way. But I didna ken what it meant."

"Now you do?"

Alistair nodded.

*H*e was running down the forest path, chasing Ian, and then with shocking suddenness Ian was there before him, not a boy now but a man.

"Stop following me!" Ian cried. "Ye canna help me now, 'tis too late! Do ye no' see that?"

"Then what?" Alistair demanded. "What is it ye want?"

"I want ye to do as I asked! Think, man, think!"

"Well?" *Jemmy prompted.* "Are you going to tell me what the dream meant?"

"'Take care of Jemmy,'" Alistair whispered, staring down at his empty cup. "That's what he said. The dream was always a bit different, but that part never changed. I didna mark it until yestere'en."

Jemmy leaned back against the pillows. "I'm hardly in a position to question something that benefits me so profoundly. But I must confess to some concern. What if you have another dream?"

"This was no ordinary dream, but a Sending," Alistair snapped. "Believe or no as ye choose. But I ken what he bade me do and I mean to do it."

Jemmy grinned. "Whether I want you to or not?"

"That's right."

"Well, then, having no choice in the matter, I suppose the only thing to do is thank you."

"Then ye believe me?"

"Does it make a difference?"

Alistair slumped back in his seat. "I suppose not."

"Well, for what 'tis worth, I do believe you mean what you say. As for the dream—" He frowned. "A year ago I would have laughed, but I've seen some strange things myself since I've come back. May I ask how do you intend to go about it?" he added quickly, before Alistair could ask what he meant. "All along I thought ye were the one making the plans, but if that's not so, then Calder is more dangerous than I thought."

"He is. But not nearly so dangerous as I can be if I put my mind to it."

Jemmy smiled. "I do believe that's true."

"I have my seat on the council back, that's the first thing. And now I ken what they mean to do. You're safe enough until the laird goes, but after that—well, we'll have to fight. I see no other way. Who can we count upon?"

After they had decided which of the knights could be trusted, Alistair said, "Have Donal talk to them—"

"No," Jemmy replied firmly. "I will do that."

"But—"

"Leave it to me, Alistair. I am not entirely helpless, no matter how I look just now."

Alistair smiled. "Aye. Right. The fewer who ken I'm involved in this, the better. We'll tell no one, Jemmy. Not until we must. And no one knows what was said here tonight. Not even your lady. Let them all think I'm Calder's man—or he's mine."

"Which is it to be?" Jemmy asked. "Calder's been in charge for some time now. Has it occurred to you that he may not *want* you back?"

"He doesna. But 'tis too late, isn't it? After all, I'm here with the laird's blessing. I suppose I'll have to challenge the bastard, though. He'll be expecting it."

He was committed now. There was no turning back. And no point to thinking how it might have been if he had simply bent his head and kissed the soft skin of Deirdre's neck. He had chosen his path and he must follow it to the end.

"Calder might decide that it's easier just to get rid of you," Jemmy warned.

"Aye," Alistair said wearily. "He's already holding Malcolm hostage to my good behavior, but that might not be enough."

"Have you considered Lady Maxwell's safety?"

"I have. She'll be going back to Ireland with that Fitzgerald lad who came today."

"I thought—the two of you seemed to be—"

"She's leaving," Alistair said shortly. He couldn't talk of Deirdre, not now, or he'd start remembering this afternoon, the way she'd leaned against him so trustingly—

"I think that your wound should keep you abed the next day or two," Alistair said, forcing his mind back to the present. "I dinna need ye in my way just now."

"I can't say I'd mind that," Jemmy admitted. "Damn this shoulder—'tis taking too much out of me. I suppose 'twas Calder who did it."

Alistair nodded. "And that Maxwell lad—he was Calder's man, as well. I dinna ken if he's the only one, but I wouldna be welcoming any of them here if I were ye."

They sat in silence as the fire subsided, leaving only the illumination of the candles against the darkness. Alistair threw a fresh log into the fire and leaned both arms on the mantel, staring into the flames.

"There is one thing more I'd ask of you," Jemmy said from behind him. "If I don't make it, see that Alyson gets back to her kin."

"Whisht, man, you're drunk," Alistair said, forcing himself to speak cheerfully as he took his seat again. "Of course you'll—"

"I mean it. I ken how you keep your promises, and 'tisn't lightly I burden you with this one. But I must."

"Even if something was to happen to you, there would be no danger to her. Unless—" He broke off, staring. "Oh, Jemmy. Dinna tell me she is— What the devil are ye thinking to keep her here? She must go at once!"

"Try telling her that."

Alistair laughed unwillingly. "Aye, I see the problem. She's a braw lass, Jemmy. Much better than ye deserve."

Though he'd spoken lightly, Jemmy didn't smile. "She is. For myself I don't mind, but—I cannot rest thinking of what might happen to her after—"

"Enough of that. Ye will be fine. But just to put your mind at rest, I promise. Now lie back and go to sleep before ye waste all the fine spirit ye just poured down your throat."

Jemmy obeyed, but not before Alistair had seen the shimmer of relief misting his dark eyes. Poor bastard, Alistair thought, rising and looking down at him. He's about reached the end of his strength. But maybe now he'll begin to mend.

He walked to the door, hesitated, then summoned all his energy and flung it open. "Sleep well, Jemmy. Ye stupid, stubborn fool!" he added beneath his breath, but loud enough for Donal to hear.

Staggering a little, he glared at the young knight. "I'll thank ye for my sword," he said thickly, then made a show of missing his scabbard as he tried to sheathe it. "Listen, Donal," he added with drunken confidentiality, leaning close to the young knight. "You're a braw lad, I ken that. Time was ye rode with *me*. So I'll just whisper in your ear that you're backing the wrong horse." He nodded wisely. "Mark me, now. There's still time to save yourself."

Donal stiffened, his eyes flashing.

"To think I used to admire ye," he spat. "Now—"

"Oh, spare me," Alistair said contemptuously. "If ye want to be a fool, dinna blame me for it."

With that he staggered down the hall, satisfied that Donal would spread the word of his treachery. Calder would surely hear of it ere morning.

But later, as Alistair hovered on the edge of sleep, he wasn't thinking of the promises he'd made or the impossible burden he had shouldered. He was finally remembering the images he'd pushed from his mind all day: Deirdre leaning back against him, her head against his shoulder. Deirdre standing on the hillside, dark hair flying about her face, crying out for him to leave her be, that she never wanted to speak to him again. And worst of all was Deirdre, tears of joy running down her cheeks, clasped in the Irishman's arms.

With a hoarse cry Alistair turned his face into the pillow. But even the sound of his own anguish could not drown out the flutter of dark wings above.

chapter 29

"I hear ye were visiting Jemmy last night."

Alistair was kneeling on the hard-packed earth of the paddock, adjusting the spur around his boot. He finished the job, taking his time about it, then rose to his feet. The wind was chill against his bare chest, and he picked up the jerkin folded across the fence. The horse he had been engaged in breaking stood trembling on the end of the long lead rope. Alistair motioned to a groom, who led the exhausted stallion to the stable.

"That's right," he said briefly, tilting his head to meet Calder's eye.

"Well, what did ye say to him?"

The three men behind Calder stood, arms folded, and regarded Alistair with stony eyes.

"I told him to go back to Spain," he answered briefly, pulling the leather jerkin over his head.

Calder let out a hissing breath of annoyance. "I thought we agreed—"

"No, you agreed. I did not. And I decided I didna want to stand back and let things happen around me."

"Ye should have come to me first," Calder began furiously. "Who the devil do ye think ye are?"

"I know exactly who I am," Alistair snapped. "'Tis you who seem to have forgotten."

Calder's hands gripped the front of Alistair's jerkin, pulling him close. "We dinna need ye here, Alistair."

Alistair brought his hands up between Calder's, breaking the man's grasp. Then his fist shot out and buried itself in Calder's stomach. The breath went out of Calder in a startled gasp, and before he could recover, Alistair struck him squarely on the jaw.

Calder's men were slow, Alistair thought as the three of them sprang forward. He easily evaded them and seized Calder by the hair, jerking his head upright, instinctively reaching for the dagger in his belt. He cursed silently when he found it was not there and bent instead to pull the small knife from his boot.

"Back," he ordered the men. When they did not obey at once, he touched the point to the soft skin of Calder's neck.

"Ye heard him!" Calder shouted. "Get back."

When the men had retreated to a safe distance, Alistair released Calder and bent to sheathe his knife as the larger man struggled to his feet.

"I thought ye knew me better," Alistair said, shaking his head.

"I thought I did, too," Calder said, leaning against the fence and rubbing his throat. "But ye havena been yourself since ye came back."

"These are dangerous times, Calder," Alistair said. "A man does well to keep himself to himself. Otherwise, a man can make mistakes. Ye made one yesterday—but I think ye ken that now. Am I right?"

"Aye." Calder bit off the word.

"Malcolm is mine. Dinna forget it. As for Jemmy—well, he's my kinsman and I had to give him a chance to see reason. Just as I am giving ye today. He was fool enough not to take it, but I dinna think you'll make the same mistake."

"I willna," Calder said, and though his tone was conciliatory, Alistair was more interested in his fingers, clenched white-knuckled on the fence.

"That's good," he said, just as though he accepted Calder's words as truth. "Now the laird has sent for me. I am here at his command and he has given me his blessing. 'Twould be foolish to do anything to make the clan doubt his judgment. Do ye hear that? We do *nothing*."

"But Jemmy—"

"Once the laird is gone, I will deal with Jemmy. But for now I am the laird's obedient foster son and care only to fulfill his dying wish. 'Tis clear as glass, Calder."

"For ye, maybe," Calder muttered.

"Aye, that's right. For me. As I said, these are dangerous times," he added, leaning on the fence beside Calder and squinting up at the sky. "A man needs to know who his friends are—and his enemies. Which one d'ye intend to be?"

"A friend, of course," Calder said with a smile that did not reach his eyes.

"Of course," Alistair agreed, noting the cold fury in the depths of Calder's gaze. "Then we'll say no more about it."

As he passed Calder's men he clapped the largest of them on the shoulder. "Next time you'll have to be a little faster," he said with a friendly grin.

The man did not return his smile. "Next time I will be."

Alistair laughed and walked away, but he had no doubt the man had meant it. Next time—and there would be a next time, of that he was quite sure—he would have to be that much quicker himself.

chapter 30

"I've never heard the like!" Alyson exclaimed as they sat in the hall that night, watching Ronan in the center of the floor. His hands moved over the harpstrings as gently as a lover's, drawing forth a melody of piercing sweetness.

"Nor I," Jemmy said. "I don't imagine many people have."

Jemmy looked better tonight, Deirdre thought, with the lines of pain eased from his face and some color in his cheeks. When he smiled at Alyson, she lit up like a flame. Deirdre was happy for her friend. Maybe now things would settle down here, and Alyson could bear her child in peace.

Then Alistair took his seat beside Deirdre. At once the table grew still. Malcolm, on Jemmy's other side, gave Alistair a miserable, bewildered look. Haddon Darnley stiffened. And the glow faded from Alyson, leaving her pale and weary. Only Jemmy seemed unaffected. He did not even acknowledge Alistair's presence as he gestured for a fresh goblet of wine and brought it to Ronan.

It was an honor, but though Ronan smiled and thanked him, he didn't look particularly grateful. But then, Ronan never did. He just accepted the cup as if it was his due and chatted easily with Jemmy without bothering to rise from his seat.

But when Jemmy returned to the table, he was smiling, obviously unoffended. "He has played at more royal courts than even I have seen. What luck to have him here."

"Luck?" Alistair muttered darkly, resting his chin in his palm. "Aye, well, there's all sorts of luck."

Deirdre glanced at him nervously, but his eyes were fixed on the center of the hall. Though she had seen him once or twice since Ronan arrived, he had not spoken a single word to her.

No doubt he was glad that Ronan had come. Now he would not have to even bother to arrange her escort to Donegal. Ronan had relieved him of his burden, and he was free to stay here and wreak havoc among his kin.

Maybe Alyson was right about him after all, though Deirdre still could not quite believe it. He had been so different in the forest, so ready to help her when she needed him, content to take each day as it came. Laird of the Mist, she thought and blinked hard, remembering how he had annoyed her with his careless ways.

Now he was someone else entirely, a stranger with cold eyes and a ruthless edge to him, a man who frightened even those who had once loved him. Or was this who he had always been and she had been too blind to see it?

Once the meal was finished and the trestles taken down, Ronan stopped the pretty tunes he had been playing and sat without moving, waiting for the talk to cease. So commanding was his presence that the hall soon fell silent. He let the anticipation grow and build until every eye was fastened upon him. Then he took his hands from the harp and began to sing without accompaniment. He sang to Deirdre as though no one else was present, the song he used to sing for her so long ago.

"Black, black, black,
is the color of my true love's hair.
Her face is something wondrous fair.
Oh, I love my love and well she knows
I love the ground whereon she goes."

His voice had deepened and grown in power since she'd heard it last. Not a person spoke, not a single foot shifted as he paused between the verses. They were all under his spell.

"Black, black, black,
is the color of my true love's hair.
Alone, my life would be so bare.
I would sigh and I would weep,
Never, never would I sleep
For my love is far beyond compare,
She of the wondrous hair.
Black, black, black
is the color of my true love's hair. ...."

His voice held the last note, then faded slowly into a sigh. The people paid him the tribute of their utter silence.

Before they could recover themselves, he began again, this time a merry tune that he played upon the harp, and his bright green gaze was fixed, not on Deirdre, but on Alistair.

"There was a gypsy came to our door.
He came brave and boldy-o.
And he sang high and he sang low,
And he sang a raggle taggle gypsy-o."

Feet were tapping, hands beating out the time as they caught the familiar rhythm of the song. But Alistair sat very still beside Deirdre.

"It was late that night when the knight came in
inquiring for his lady-o,

and the servant girl she said to the knight,
'She's away wi' the raggle taggle gypsy-o.'"

Ronan grinned as he played between the verses, obviously enjoying his jest. All around the hall people began to dance. Why, Ronan? Deirdre wondered. Why must you shame Alistair in his own hall? People would remember this later when she was gone. They all believed she was betrothed to Alistair. They would think she had run off, just like the lady in the song, and left him behind. Her face was crimson with embarrassment as Ronan began the verses that told of the knight's final meeting with his lady.

"'How could you leave your house and your land?
How could you leave your money-o?
How could you leave your own husband
all for a raggle taggle gypsy-o?'

"'What care I for my house and my land?
What care I for my money-o?
I'd rather have a kiss from the gypsy's lips
I'm away wi' the raggle taggle gypsy-o!'"

When the last verse was done, the music still went on. Deirdre had never heard anything like it, not even from Ronan. His fingers danced over the harpstrings, faster and faster, weaving a melody that wound into fantastic flights of fancy. Yet it always came back again to the original tune, changing it, playing with it, all of it done with an apparent ease that stole Deirdre's breath.

Oh, Ronan had been good before, he had been *brilliant,* but now such words were too pale and ordinary to describe what he was doing. Indeed, it hardly seemed to be mortal music at all. There was magic in him tonight, fey and wild, that held his listeners in thrall. Deirdre wondered a little uneasily if the people could have ceased their dancing even if they wanted to.

And then, at last, it ended. As the last strains faded to silence, there came a great sigh of loss.

"I didna want it to stop," Alyson said, wondering. "I wanted it to go on and on forever."

Alistair lifted his goblet to his lips. "Aye, he plays tunably enough. But I canna say I cared much for the song."

Alyson stared at him as though he must mad, but Jemmy only looked at him gravely. Deirdre wondered how much Jemmy knew and what he must think of her, a silent—if unwilling—partner in Ronan's cruel game.

"I thank you, Master Harper," Jemmy called. "You have gifted us beyond all words."

Ronan inclined his dark head in apparent humility, then glanced up at Deirdre with a wink so broad not a person in the hall could miss it.

She could take no more. As he began to play again, she jumped to her feet, murmured a quick excuse, and fled. The corridor was deserted and she leaned her burning brow against the cold stone wall. Oh, that was ill done, Ronan, she thought with rising anger. She had *told* him all the kindness that Alistair had shown her. But that was Ronan, whose humor often held a malicious edge.

And yet he *had* come for her. She couldn't forget that. He had come all this way to find her. While Alistair couldn't wait to see the back of her.

She bit back the tears that threatened when she remembered that moment on the hillside, that perfect moment she could never forget, no matter how hard she might try. The moment that Alistair had broken her heart. But at least I have Ronan, she thought. He still loves me.

And she loved him, as well, though her love would never approach the feeling she had for Alistair. When Ronan held her, she felt no quickening of her pulse, no desire to run her hands through his hair or feel his lips on hers. And Ronan felt none of those things for her. Had never felt them. But he still believed that what they had between them was true love.

If not for Alistair, she might have grown to believe it herself.

Lost in her own thoughts, she jumped with a startled cry as a heavy hand descended on her shoulder. She turned to see a burly man staring down at her.

"What—?" she began, jumping back against the wall. "Who are you, sir, and what do you want of me?"

"Whist yer clabber and listen," the man said in a harsh whisper. He loomed over her, and she shrank back against the wall. The corridor stretched empty to either side, torch-lit. From the hall came the sounds of laughter and voices raised in song, and she knew that even if she screamed, no one would hear her.

"What is it?" she asked with a brisk confidence she was far from feeling.

"Tell Alistair we're watchin' him."

"I have no idea what you are talking about. Now step back, if you please, or—"

The man grinned. "Ye dinna need to understand. Just remember. And tell him we have ways o' makin' sure he minds us."

"What—"

She had no time for more, for his hands were about her neck. She struggled, beating against his chest, kicking vainly at his shins, and his laughter was mingled with the pounding of the blood in her ears as black spots danced before her eyes.

And then, when the black spots began to merge and the sound of music thinned to a distant hum, he released her and stepped back. She fell painfully to her knees, one hand at her throat, and at last managed to draw a ragged, sobbing breath.

"Will ye tell him?"

When she said nothing, he wound his hand in her hair, jerking her head upright. "Answer me, lady, when I speak to ye."

She nodded frantically, furious at her own helplessness to stop the tears trailing down her cheeks.

"Do it soon. We are not patient men."

And then the corridor was empty again. She struggled to her feet and nausea rolled through her. She clamped a hand over her mouth, willing herself not to vomit, trying desperately to breathe.

"Deirdre, where have you been? You missed—"

It was Alyson with Jemmy beside her, both of them looking at her with concern.

"What happened to you, lady?" Jemmy asked. "Are you ill?"

"Deirdre, what happened?" Alyson asked, her voice sharp with fear. "Did someone—hurt you?"

Deirdre clutched her throat, trying to force the words to come. But it was like a nightmare; she couldn't speak, she couldn't make so much as a sound. And then Alistair was there, pushing between Alyson and Jemmy, and without a word he lifted her as easily as if she was a child and carried her swiftly up the stairs.

He kicked open a door and brought her into a small chamber, then sat down with her on the bed—his own bed, she realized dizzily.

"Deirdre, lass, calm yourself," he said urgently. "Ye must calm yourself now and talk to me. Who hurt ye?"

"I—I don't know who he was."

The words came out in a hoarse croak, and Alistair took her hand, still clutched about her throat, and held it tightly in his own. His eyes narrowed into ice gray slits as he saw the mark that lay beneath.

"He—he said—" Deirdre whispered, her teeth chattering from shock and fear. "Tell you—th—that they're watching you."

"Calder is a dead man," Alistair said with a calm that was somehow more terrifying than any shouted threats. "Did he say more?"

Deirdre shook her head. "N-no."

He pulled her against him in a convulsive movement, crushing her hard against his chest. "If I had known—if ever I imagined he'd move so swiftly, I would never have let ye from my sight."

Deirdre pressed her cheek against his shoulder, and beneath her fear a savage joy swept through her heart. Alistair had said he'd kill the man who hurt her. And in saying it he had claimed her as his to protect. Why would he do such a thing if he didn't care for her?

Then his words reached her and she lifted her head. "You knew that he might do this?"

"Not now," Alistair said. "Not yet."

"But you thought I might be in danger?" she insisted in a strained whisper, and he nodded reluctantly. "And 'tis for that you wanted me to go?"

"I—oh, Christ, Deirdre, yes. Ye must go at once."

"No," she rasped.

"Dinna be a fool!" he said roughly. "Think of Maeve if ye willna think of yourself. We both know what we saw last Beltane Eve. When I'm dead, who will you have?"

She stared into Alistair's eyes, seeing the fear reflected in their depths. Not fear for himself, but for her. And now she could see beyond the fear to something else, something that lit his eyes from within and made them glow like molten silver. She reached up and traced her fingertips across the stubborn line of his mouth.

"You should have told me," she whispered.

She closed her eyes and sighed as his lips brushed hers, teasing them apart, and with a strangled groan he crushed her against his chest, deepening the kiss. She was flying, she was melting, and as his hands tightened on her waist, they burned through the velvet of her gown.

Slowly he lifted his mouth from hers.

"Ye must go, Deirdre," he said, his lips against her hair.

"Then come with me!" she cried hoarsely, abandoning all pride. "Oh, Alistair, please come away from here!" She bit her lip, searching for the words. "They're all afraid of you, even Malcolm—he said such terrible things, Alistair, I couldn't believe them—I *won't* believe them—but . . .

Please, just walk away, right now, before something awful happens. Come with me. We could be so happy."

He looked at her with such longing in his eyes that she was certain he'd agree. Then he shook his head.

"I canna. I must stay and ye must go. Yon harper can see ye home. God knows he's come far enough for the honor." He smiled wryly. "He is a rogue, that one, but 'tis plain he loves ye well. Nay," he said as she would have spoken, standing and setting her on her feet. "Please, no more. Ye leave tomorrow."

chapter 31

When dawn came, it was all but invisible for the rain pouring down in sheets.

"I can't take Maeve out in this," Deirdre said, gesturing toward the stable door.

"She's wrapped warm enough," Alistair replied briefly, swinging the saddle over her palfrey. "She'll be fine."

"But—"

"Mount up."

Ronan leaned against the wall, green eyes shining from the shadow of his hood. "Do it, Dee," he said. "Sure and a little rain won't hurt the child."

Deirdre shifted the weight of her sleeping daughter in her arms. "But she'll want to say farewell."

She knew it was a pitiful excuse, but she was running out of better ones. Since she'd been roused from sleep an hour before, she'd used every argument she could think of to delay her departure. None of them had earned her more than an impatient answer from either Alistair or Ronan. Now that the two of them had joined forces, Deirdre was definitely outnumbered. Alistair didn't even bother to answer as he jerked his head toward the horse.

Deirdre handed Maeve to him and mounted.

"Fernan and McTavish and I will ride with ye a time," he said, and her heart lifted a bit.

Ronan heaved himself aboard his horse with a martyred sigh. Deirdre felt a pang of guilt. He seldom stirred before the morning was far gone, yet for her sake he was doing this without complaint.

Alistair kissed Maeve's forehead, then lifted her to Deirdre. "Ye give her my farewells," he said, a suspicious roughness in his voice.

"Alistair, I still think—"

"Aye, I ken what ye think. But you're going just the same."

Deirdre glared at him with impotent anger. Damn him for his pride, his twisted honor, his warped sense of loyalty. Damn him for being everything she had ever wanted and was about to lose forever.

As he tucked the cloak more firmly about Maeve, she caught his wrist. "When you've done what you must do here, you come and find me. Do you hear me? You come to Donegal and I'll be waiting."

"I fear 'twill be a long wait, Deirdre," Alistair said, so matter-of-factly that tears rose to her eyes.

"How gallant," Ronan drawled.

"Shut up!" she cried, rounding on him in sudden fury. "You know nothing about any of this."

"I know that we had best get moving before those knights drown," Ronan replied, nodding toward the two figures huddled stolidly in the downpour.

And then, before Deirdre could think of anything else to say, they were out the door and the rain was beating down upon her hood. They rode out of the stableyard and over the drawbridge, the horse's hooves hollow on the wood. Then they were in the lane, and the rain began to ease into a drizzle.

The fog was so thick around them that Deirdre could

scarcely see two paces ahead. The world had drawn down to herself and Alistair, riding side by side, through an eerie landscape that didn't seem quite real. It was more like a nightmare where monsters lurked unseen. She tried to shake the impression off but her unease grew with every step. Unconsciously she clutched her sleeping daughter closer as her eyes darted this way and that, finding blank whiteness in all directions.

Ronan began to sing, but Alistair stopped him with a sharp command. "Sound travels in the mist," he said and for once Ronan made no argument. Perhaps he sensed it, too, the menace in the mist, and his song was but a whistle in the dark.

The rain had stopped completely by the time they turned into the lane and a little breeze tore ragged holes in the fog. The ground dipped and the fog enveloped them again.

"There's the road," Alistair said, pointing. "Turn right and follow it straight to Annan. Go on," he added sharply as Deirdre hesitated.

She looked as though she might speak, but in the end only nodded and turned her horse's head. Alistair sent the two knights back to Ravenspur, yet he did not follow. Long after Deirdre had vanished into the fog he still sat, staring after her, clenching his jaw against the impulse to call her back, to beg her not to leave him. . . .

Deirdre would be safe now, he reminded himself fiercely. This was the right—the only—thing to do. But though that belief had sustained him through the past days, all at once it rang hollow in his mind.

Oh, he had removed her from one danger, but the world was filled with countless others which she must now face without him at her side. How could such a thing be right? Anything could happen to her now and he would never even know.

Before he had any idea what he meant to do, he had kicked his horse into a trot and was heading down the road to Annan. Fool! he raged at himself. Ye weighed the facts, went over every option, and came to the only possible decision. Ye *know* that. Deirdre will be fine without ye; 'tis naught but your own pride that makes ye doubt.

They began to canter through the mist, Alistair cursing himself at every step. He *would* turn back, he *must*; it would be wrong and selfish to keep her at his side. Then Germain was galloping headlong down the road and Alistair was urging him ahead, for he knew that whatever might come of it, he could not let her go.

Fitzgerald turned his horse sharply at Alistair's approach, a long knife glinting in his hand. When he realized who it was, his face grew dark with anger.

"Deirdre!" Alistair cried. "Wait—"

Deirdre whirled, her smile blazing across the distance between them.

"I knew you wouldn't—" she began, but Ronan cut her off.

"Listen. Do you hear it?"

And then Deirdre did hear the ring of bridles in the distance. Her mouth fell open as a strong gust parted the fog before them, and she could glimpse the force of men coming down the hillside.

"Maxwells," she breathed. "Good God, how many are there?"

"Too many," Alistair replied succinctly.

The concealing mist was ripped away and they were in the open. Deirdre watched the lead riders halt and point, and then they were cantering down the hillside, the others following.

"Back," Alistair ordered, wheeling his horse around. "Get back to Ravenspur. Come on, harper," he added impatiently as Ronan hesitated, staring at the approaching force. "Or we'll go without ye."

Ronan turned his horse and clapped heels to its side. He was a good rider—in Donegal every child who could find or steal a horse rode like the devil himself—and Deirdre was just behind him. Maeve stirred and began to cry, and Deirdre held her fast as with the other hand she slapped the reins, urging the horse forward.

They swept across the drawbridge just ahead of the pursuit. There was no time to have it raised before the Maxwells were upon it. Alistair leaped from his horse and helped Deirdre to dismount. "Inside," he said. "Find Jemmy. Guard!" she heard him cry as she handed Maeve to Ronan. "Guard, to me! Lower the portcullis!"

Deirdre ran into the shelter of the manor, crying out a warning to the startled guard within the door as she flashed by.

She ran through the empty hall and pelted up the stairway, hardly noticing the sharp stitch in her side. When she reached Jemmy's door, she found Sir Conal on his feet.

"Wake him!" she cried.

But Jemmy, all the gods be thanked, was already awake. He opened the door and stepped out, naked to the waist. The bandage on his shoulder was very white against his skin.

"I see the Maxwells have come to call," he said with a lift of one dark brow. "They picked a damned inconvenient hour. Don't fear, Lady Maxwell," he said to Deirdre. "The main force is still beyond the portcullis. Only a handful made it through. My lady," he added, offering his arm to Alyson as she walked out of their chamber. "Shall we go to greet them?"

Alyson was rosy with sleep, and she yawned and passed a hand over her auburn hair, tumbled in glorious disarray over her chamber robe.

"Of course, my lord," she said with a rueful shake of her head, as though the Maxwells were guilty of nothing more than lack of manners. Oh, they are well matched, Deirdre thought with a sharp stab of envy as they exchanged a very private smile. "But I think we should dress first."

"Perhaps it would be best if you wait here, Lady Maxwell," Jemmy added kindly. "There may be words exchanged that would disturb you."

"Oh, no. Maeve is down there—"

"As you like. But stay close. Conal," he added casually. "Would you be so kind as to attend me?"

"Aye," the red-haired knight said. He put his fingers to his lips and gave a piercing whistle. A boy with sleepy eyes popped his head around the corner. "Get Donal," Conal ordered. "Tell him to bring the others to the hall. *Now.*"

The boy nodded once and vanished. Conal drew his sword and set his shoulders.

"Whenever ye are ready, my lord. I'm at your back."

W hen Deirdre descended the stairs, she found a dozen Maxwell warriors standing in the center of the hall. Alistair stood at the bottom of the stairway, sword in hand. Ronan sat in the shadows with Maeve upon his knee. The child was yawning hugely and staring about wide-eyed.

"Kinnon," Jemmy said as he and Alyson reached the bottom of the steps. "I give you greeting. Would you care to break your fast?"

Maxwell's heir looked nervously behind him, seeming relieved to see a cloaked and hooded warrior looming over his shoulder.

"Nay, Jemmy—though I thank ye," Kinnon added quickly, his small eyes darting nervously over the scant dozen of his men, then passing over the force of Kirallen men-at-arms surrounding them.

Jemmy followed his gaze and smiled genially. "Then perhaps you would tell me what brings you here at such an hour."

Kinnon licked his lips and darted a sideways glance at Deirdre. "Well, Jemmy, 'tis like this. Ye see—'tis a long tale, and perhaps it would be best told—"

"Oh, enough of this!" an impatient voice growled, and the hooded man shoved Kinnon aside. Deirdre's mouth went dry. I should have stayed upstairs, she thought numbly. I should have kept running when I had the chance.

And then the man pushed back his hood.

Deirdre's knees refused to hold her. She sat down hard on the bottom step. Ronan rose to his feet, tense and wary, and drew a long knife from his belt. There was not a sound to be heard until Maeve, who was playing contentedly with a bright clasp Ronan had given her, looked up. And when the child saw the man thus revealed, she gave a scream that ripped through the silent hall.

"No! No! Mam!"

And then Deirdre could move again. "'Tis all right," she said, going swiftly across the room and picking up her child. "I am here."

"No!" Maeve sobbed. "Make him go!"

Brodie Maxwell fixed his wife and daughter with a hard stare. "So that's the greeting I get, is it?"

He walked toward them and Deirdre retreated, step by step, her eyes fixed upon her husband's face.

"Brodie, I thought—we all thought—" she said, her voice hoarse from the bruising of her throat and trembling with fear.

"Well, ye were wrong. It took me a while to get back to Cranston, only to find ye up and gone. Now give me the bairn, and we'll be going home."

"Mam! No!"

"Ronan, don't!" Deirdre said, not taking her eyes from Brodie. But even without looking, she knew that Ronan was tensed to spring. "Don't move, don't say a word."

"That's right, laddie," Brodie said with a smile that showed every one of his teeth. "Ye listen to Deirdre. She kens me well."

Jemmy moved forward with lightning swiftness. "Brodie, why, I'm clean amazed! Come and sit and tell us what—"

"Get back, Kirallen," Brodie spat, shrugging Jemmy's hand from his shoulder. "I've come for what's mine and I'll have it. Dinna think to get between us. For Deirdre and I have some talkin' to do. A *lot* of talkin'."

Deirdre went cold with terror as he spoke the words she had heard so often in the past and tried so desperately to forget.

"Time to have a talk, Deirdre," Brodie had announced cheerfully soon after their marriage. She had followed him willingly enough to their chamber that first time, thinking he meant exactly what he said. She had no idea he was angry until he slammed the door behind her. Then she found herself alone with a blank-eyed stranger who looked through her as if she wasn't there at all. "Come here, lass," he'd said in a strange hoarse voice, "we have a bit of talkin' to do."

Now she fought against the paralyzing sense of inevitability that stole over her, the voice whispering in her mind, "No one will help you, he's your husband, and fighting only makes it worse." She hated that voice with its cowardly weakness, and her greatest fear was that one day she would give up and admit that it was right. Or, she amended, that *had* been her greatest fear. Until today. She suspected that the conversation Brodie had in mind would be something far worse than she had ever known.

Jemmy stood directly opposite her, hands fisted at his sides, and said nothing. But at least he didn't look away. Usually they did that, just as Kinnon was doing now, staring down at his feet as though they were the most fascinating things he'd ever seen. And later, when the *talking* was all done and she came back to the hall, they wouldn't look at her directly. They glanced at her sideways— asklent, they called it here—pretending that nothing at all had happened. Pretending they didn't see the bruises.

She stood rooted to the floor, head held high, as Brodie approached. She had married him, had stood up in the church and said the vows. And by the laws of Scotland and Brodie's God, she had become his property, to do with exactly as he pleased.

I didn't know, she wanted to cry out. *It isn't like this in Donegal! There a woman counts for something.* But she held her tongue. If justice was denied her, she would not beg for pity. It would accomplish nothing but to demean her even further. She knew from long experience that no one in this place, no matter how well intentioned they might be, would interfere between a man and his wife.

"I don't think so, Brodie," Alistair said quietly, stepping

from behind Deirdre. "Whatever ye have to say, ye say to *me*."

"Get out of my way, Alistair," Brodie said, sounding more surprised than angry at this turn of events.

"Nay."

"Jemmy," Brodie said, his eyes never leaving Alistair. "Call him off. The woman is mine and the bairn, as well. I have my rights."

"And I have mine," Alistair shot back swiftly, before Jemmy could reply. "Deirdre and I were married yesterday."

Jemmy's mouth shut with a snap.

"Married?" Brodie's heavy face looked completely blank for a moment, then he threw back his head and laughed. "Ye daft bugger, ye *canna* be married, for she has a husband living."

"Well, we didna know that then, did we?" Alistair said reasonably. "And now the deed is done."

The Kirallen men-at-arms looked dumbfounded as they stared at Jemmy, who shook his head briefly, cautioning them not to move.

Kinnon cleared his throat. "Who witnessed this marriage?"

"I did," Ronan answered quickly.

"And the other?"

Silence descended on the hall and Deirdre bit her lip.

Alistair might mean well, but his story had just made everything worse. And now it was about to be exposed for the lie it was.

"'Twas I."

All heads turned toward Alyson. "Forgive me, my lord," she said to Jemmy. "I have grown so fond of Deirdre that I could not refuse her."

Brodie shook his head like an oxen throwing off a cloud of flies. "It makes no matter who was there! Kirallen, we've been allies until now, but before God, if I dinna leave here with my woman, I'll tear this place down stone by stone."

Deirdre caught her breath. Brodie would do it, she knew he would. Or at least he would try. After all the kindness the Kirallens had shown her, she would not bring war upon their heads.

"Alistair, we cannot—" she began, but he rounded on her with a furious scowl.

"Hold your tongue, woman," he snarled, and she stepped back a pace, too shocked to voice a protest as he turned back to Brodie with a shrug.

"She talks too much, but for all that I would keep her. She warms my bed quite nicely," he added in a low, suggestive voice. "She's sweet, Brodie, verra sweet, and so eager . . . but then, ye ken that for yourself. Or," he added with silken malice, his gaze flicking down and up again, "perhaps ye don't. Why not give her to a man who's . . . capable of enjoying her?"

Brodie went first white, then red, and shot Deirdre a look of such concentrated hatred that she felt the blood drain from her face. Had Alistair gone mad? Or did he *want* to see her dead? For nothing he could possibly have said would have sealed her fate as completely as the words he had just spoken.

Brodie's lips drew back from his teeth and the veins corded on his brow, a sure sign that he was in a killing rage. Without meaning to, Deirdre took another step back, holding Maeve more tightly.

"Ye had her, did ye?" Brodie said, his voice strangled.

"Several times." Alistair flicked a speck of dust from his sleeve and smiled slowly. "Each finer than the last."

"By God, I'll kill ye—"

"You? Do ye really think you're man enough?"

And with an insolence that took Deirdre's breath away, Alistair turned his back.

"I'll kill ye with my own hands!" Brodie screamed. "I'll cut you into ribbons, ye swiving churl. I'll slice off your balls and stuff them up your—"

Alistair whirled to face him. "Tomorrow. Kendrick's Field. At midday."

"Aye!" Brodie tore the gauntlet from his hand and flung it in Alistair's face. "So be it."

Alistair bent and retrieved the glove. When he straightened, his eyes were gleaming above the thread of blood winding down his cheek.

"A challenge given and accepted!" he cried in ringing tones, holding the gauntlet aloft. "With all of ye as witness."

For the first time Brodie seemed to realize things had not gone as he meant them to. He glared about, his low brow furrowed in confusion, as Kinnon came forward and took his arm.

"Come, Brodie, let's get back home again."

"You, bitch," Brodie said, thrusting a finger at Deirdre. "Dinna think ye can hide behind Kirallen for long. Tomorrow I will come for ye. And then—"

"Come *on,*" Kinnon said anxiously, tugging at his brother's elbow as he cast Deirdre a nervous, apologetic glance. "Let's go."

chapter 32

"Well played, Kirallen," Ronan said, leaning casually against the doorpost of Jemmy's chamber. "Very well played."

"Well *played*?" Jemmy repeated tightly. "God's blood, Alistair, what were you thinking? I should kill you myself, right here and now, and save Brodie the trouble!"

"I wouldna have let it come to war," Alistair answered. "I would have drawn the line at that."

"Really?" Jemmy snapped. "I didn't think you were capable of drawing any lines at all."

"Now, Jemmy," Alyson began anxiously, and he rounded on her with a scowl.

"Oh, and now we hear from my lady! Tell me, Alyson, when did you find time to witness this marriage? For I was with you all of yesterday."

"If you're waiting for an apology, you will not get it," Alyson answered sharply. "'Twas the only thing to do."

As the argument continued, Deirdre walked back and forth before the fire, crooning softly to Maeve. The child clung to her with arms and legs, head buried against Deirdre's shoulder. Malcolm and Haddon Darnley sat beside the fire, watching her with wide eyes. They should never have had to witness such a thing, Deirdre thought, and nor should poor Maeve. No child should be subjected to such hatred.

"'Tis all right, sweeting," Deirdre murmured. "All is well now. No one is going to hurt you."

The others were talking, but Deirdre heard them with only a small part of her mind. Let them talk. It didn't matter. Nothing mattered but the child in her arms.

As Maeve's tense form relaxed, Deirdre drew a long breath.

"Ronan," she said quietly. "You must take Maeve to my father. Right now. Don't argue with me," she ordered as he opened his mouth to answer. "Just do as I say. Go on, saddle your horse!" she added impatiently. "Why are you just standing there?"

"Brodie will have thought of that already," Alistair said. "He'll have men watching the road."

"Then go around them," Deirdre retorted.

"He'll be expecting that," Alistair said gently.

"I don't care how you do it," Deirdre said with quiet vehemence. "Whatever it takes, get Maeve out of here right now."

"My lady," Jemmy put in. "You are upset. Sit down and—"

"Upset?" Deirdre said, her voice cracking. Maeve stirred and Deirdre lowered her voice with an effort. "Aye, I am upset, my lord. As would you be in my place. Maeve cannot go back to Cranston Keep."

"But why?" Jemmy asked.

Deirdre did not answer immediately. She waited until Maeve was quiet, then laid her daughter on the window seat and turned to Jemmy.

"My lord, if I return to Cranston Keep, I go alone. I fear I will—I will not be able to protect my daughter from Brodie's anger."

"Maeve is Brodie's daughter, too," Jemmy said. His voice was very quiet, very reasonable, as though he addressed a madwoman.

"She is," Deirdre agreed, trying to match his tone, though what she wanted was to scream at him, to shake him into awareness. "But he means to punish me for what has happened. And he will not scruple to use Maeve to that end."

Jemmy sighed and rubbed the back of his neck, looking uncomfortable and faintly embarrassed.

"You are distraught," he said. "Rest and we can talk of this again—"

"When?" Deirdre demanded. "When it is too late to get Maeve to safety? No, my lord, we will talk of this *now*. You do not know Brodie as I do. If I return with him—"

"Which you will not," Alistair put in, but she did not even glance his way. She could not think of Alistair. Not now. She could not allow herself to imagine what might happen to him on the morrow. If her thoughts once started down that road, there would be no stopping the terror that threatened to consume her. No, she would—she must—keep her mind on Maeve.

"If I return with Brodie," she repeated firmly, "he will be angry. I accept that. And I will be in no position to protect my daughter. Not for some time. Perhaps not ever. *You* must accept *that*, my lord, for it is no more than the truth."

"You believe that he will—"

"He has beaten me," Deirdre said with desperate calm. "Many times. With no cause at all. Now he believes I have been unfaithful to him. I do not think I exaggerate the danger."

"Then you cannot possibly go back with him!" Alyson cried.

"If I do not, it will mean war. No, my lady, I thank you, I will return to Cranston Keep if—if—" She stopped and swallowed hard. If Alistair was defeated tomorrow. If Alistair was lying dead in Kendrick's Field, she would go back with Brodie. She felt herself begin to shake and gripped the back of the settle hard as she continued. "But I must know that Maeve is safe. Then . . . well, I will not stay to let him hurt me."

Alistair turned to look at her.

"But, Dee, you can't!" Ronan protested. "He'll never give you another chance to get away!"

"Do not fear," she said, and though her words were directed at Ronan, it was to Alistair she spoke. "I will find a way."

"Not that way," Alistair said with instant understanding.

"Yes, that way!" she cried. "And if it comes to that, I swear by all that's holy hc's going with me!"

"Lady Maxwell!" Jemmy said, shocked. "What are you saying? You could never do such a thing!"

Jemmy did not understand. How could he? He had no idea what it was to live in constant fear, to guard every word and action and have it never be enough. If anyone laid hands on Jemmy as Brodie had done her, Jemmy would fight back. It was his right—the right of every man. He would never be expected to suffer such insult, not only without retaliation but without complaint. To do so would mark him as a coward.

Why should a woman's dignity leave her no recourse but silence? Why must it be assumed that if her husband chose to hurt her, some measure of the fault was hers? How long was a woman expected to appease her tormenter before she fought back?

"Oh, yes, my lord," Deirdre said simply. "I could do it. And if you were in my place, you would do the same."

Still Jemmy did not understand. But Alyson did. Deirdre could see it in her eyes. Whether from experience or imagination, Alyson knew what it was to be the victim of an evil man. God send that this gentle lady would never feel the rage that had been building inside Deirdre for four long years.

"Sure and there's no use talking of this now," Ronan said uncomfortably. "There's always the chance Sir Alistair might win."

"Thank you," Alistair said dryly. "I intend to."

Jemmy stared from Deirdre to his wife. Whatever he saw on Alyson's face made him change his mind abruptly.

"Very well," he said. "If it will put your mind at rest, Lady Maxwell, we'll find a place for Maeve."

"Thank you—" Deirdre began.

"How?" Ronan interrupted. "You say the roads are watched."

"The road to Annan is watched," Malcolm put in. "But not the others. Let me take her, Uncle Jemmy. We'll go to—to Dunforth!"

Jemmy smiled at his nephew. "Aye. To Dunforth. Take her to Master Johnston—or no, best keep him out of this. Take her to Tavis, the shepherd. Tell him—" He frowned, considering. "Tell him she is under my protection. That should be enough."

"Yes!" Alyson exclaimed. "Oh, Jemmy, that's the perfect plan. Malcolm, how clever of you to think of Dunforth!"

The boy blushed. "I ken Uncle Jemmy has friends there."

"And I doubt Maxwell will be watching that road," Jemmy added, giving his lady a quick smile.

"Then you, Ronan, will take her to my father," Deirdre said. "Brodie will be angry," she added, "but he will not go to war over her."

Not if he has me. She did not speak the words aloud, but from the way Alistair stiffened, she had no doubt he heard them just the same.

"If it makes ye feel better, then send Maeve off to Dunforth," Alistair said. "But ye are upsetting yourself over nothing."

He meant that. He thought that he would win. But Deirdre's life thus far had given her no reason to hope for such a happy outcome. He would die, she thought with sudden certainty. Had he not seen it long ago? Never again would he walk into a room and set Deirdre's heart to leaping. Never again would he make Maeve laugh with his

tales of giants and dragons. And never, never in this life
would Deirdre know the joy of waking in his arms.

Oh, this was not like any pain she had ever felt before.
It was cold and bitter and far too deep for tears.

"For nothing? Perhaps. But 'tis well to be prepared."

Deirdre heard her own voice with disbelief. It was so
distant, so terribly detached, as if the outcome of tomorrow's contest meant nothing to her beyond Maeve's safety.
Alistair turned quickly, but not before she had seen the expression in his eyes.

No, wait, she wanted to cry, I didn't mean it, not like
that! But even as she stood, frozen to her place, he walked
from the room without a backward glance.

chapter 33

R onan leaned against the stone wall overlooking the
moat, chin propped in his hand. The day had cleared,
but he did not lift his head to see sunlight and shadow
chasing each other across the hills. From time to time he
sighed, his shoulders drooping sadly.

Now there is a lovesick young fool if ever I saw one,
Calder thought, watching from the shadow of a tree. He'd
been making inquiries about the Irishman all morning and
was satisfied with what he'd learned. A bard, young
Fitzgerald claimed to be, with a harp bequeathed by his
grandsire, a lordling of the Sidhe. He had dreamed that
Lady Maxwell was in danger and so had come hot-foot
from Ireland to rescue her.

A fine story to impress the serving wenches, Calder
thought with some amusement, though from all accounts
Fitzgerald was immune to their charms, a cause of great
lamentation in the kitchens.

And a lot of good his fidelity would do him. Alistair
meant to have the woman and was prepared to slay the

dragon Brodie Maxwell for her sake. And where did that leave young Ronan? Out in the cold, angry, bitter, with a head full of romantic drivel.

In short, he was the perfect tool.

"So here ye are."

Ronan glanced to one side. "I am. What do you want?"

"To talk a bit."

Calder pulled himself up onto the wall and looked down at Ronan with a grin.

"Just look at yourself, man! Mopin' about while Sir Alistair carries your lady off right from under your nose!"

"What is that to you?" Ronan asked shortly.

"Weel, lad, 'twould seem we have a common cause here. Alistair is no friend to me or to any o' the Kirallens. He's out for all he can get and doesna care too much how he gets it, either. Why, ye saw it for yourself before! There was no wedding yesterday, I ken that well enough. It was a clever trick—but then, Alistair was never above bending the truth to have his way."

"What's your point, Sir . . . ?"

"Calder. Just a word in your ear, laddie. I've seen it happen a hundred times before. There isna a lass who can say him nay, but when he's done with them, he's *done*. Off to the next one, that's Alistair, not caring what he leaves behind. Many a fine lassie has he ruined and never once looked back."

A flush of anger rose to the boy's fair cheeks. "He won't do that to Deirdre. I'll talk to her—warn her—"

"And what good will that do?" Calder said derisively. "When I say there's no lass who can deny him, I mean just that. He's uncanny, lad, fey as hell. Why, he spent the last few months up in the hills with an old sorcerer, learning all his tricks and charms. He'll put a glamour on your lady— if he hasna done so already—and she'll be clay in his hands."

Ronan's flush faded and he shivered. "That can't be true," he said, though his words lacked conviction.

"But it is. 'Tis no secret that Alistair and I aren't the best

of friends just now. 'Twould please me no end to do him a
mischief over this. Then you could take your lady back to
Ireland where she'll be safe."

Calder looked down at him kindly, an older man advis-
ing a younger one with only the lad's good at heart. "She's
a fine lady, Ronan. Far too good for his tricks and games."

"Aye," Ronan agreed fervently. "Far too good for him."

"Then let's do us both a favor. I know a woman in the
hills can break his spell, but I need something of his to
bring to her."

"Like what?"

Calder hid his smile. "Well, there's a dagger he carries
always. 'Tis a pretty thing, shaped like a stag's head and
set with two green stones for the eyes. *Green* stones, lad.
Mark that. 'Tis part of a set the laird had made long ago.
Lord Jemmy carries one set with rubies, young Malcolm's
has his father's with chips of diamonds. Ye want Alistair's."

"With the green stones."

"Aye. And I need it today. Tomorrow will be too late."

Ronan bit his lip. "I don't know. . . ."

"Suit yourself, lad," Calder said with a shrug as he
jumped down from the wall. "If ye want to take Sir Alistair's leavings, ye need only wait until he's done with her.
Shouldn't take too long. It never does. Once he beds them,
he tires of them quickly."

Three paces. Five. He was just losing hope when
Ronan's voice halted him.

"Wait!"

"Aye?"

"Where can I find you? Later."

"I'll be in the hall. But don't leave it too late."

Through the window of the tower room Deirdre could
hear the men-at-arms drilling in the practice yard. She
wondered if Alistair was out there, but didn't have the will
to rise from the bed and walk to the window.

Instead she stared down at her hands folded in her lap. It was very lonely in the small room since Maeve had gone. Should Alistair lose tomorrow, she would never see her child again. But on the other hand, if Brodie was the victor, she would not have much time to grieve.

She looked up as a light knock sounded on the door, then set her shoulders and called, "Come in, Ronan."

He entered and stood before her. "You knew that it was me?"

She sighed. "I did."

"Then you know why I have come."

"Yes. Sit down," she said indifferently.

He perched on the edge of the mattress beside her. "No matter which way it goes tomorrow, you will not go back to Brodie Maxwell. If we leave while they are fighting—"

Deirdre shook her head. "Brodie will expect me to be there. And I want to be there. I must see it for myself."

"And if Sir Alistair wins? Will you leave with me then?"

"I don't know," she answered honestly. "It depends on what Alistair wants."

Ronan jumped to his feet and began to pace the small chamber. "Listen, Dee, this has gone far enough. You were meant for me, you know that just as I do. My grandfather had no right to interfere—"

"He was acting under orders from his king," Deirdre reminded him.

"Edward!" Ronan spat the name. "He is not my king! His edicts and decrees have naught to do with us. I was too young to fight my grandfather then, but now I am a man. I *will* have you!"

"No, Ronan, you will not," Deirdre said as gently as she could. "My answer has not changed."

"So if Brodie wins, you mean to be Deirdre of the Sorrows, is that it? Dragged back by your husband as a prisoner! And will you cast yourself upon the rocks as she did? Well, I won't have it. You are coming with me if I have to kill Brodie Maxwell myself."

Deirdre glanced at him, taking in the bright flush on his

cheeks, the dangerous glitter in his eyes. It was all too easy to dismiss Ronan as a mere musician, but his slender form concealed an iron strength that had not been earned by practice on the harp. No, John Fitzgerald's grandson had spent many an hour in the tiltyard, training with sword and lance. As little as Ronan liked the exercise, Deirdre remembered now that he excelled at both.

But Brodie was twice his weight and had ten years more experience. Ronan would never stand a chance against him.

"You must promise me you will not fight," she ordered sharply. "If you want to help me, then take Maeve home."

"I'll take the both of you," he said. "Whether Brodie Maxwell wins or loses. And then, Dee, we will be married."

His calm insistence snapped the last thread of Deirdre's patience. "How many times must I tell you no?" she flared. "I am sorry, Ronan, I do care for you, but I will not marry you. I have finished with marriage altogether."

"Oh, have you?" he shot back. "And if Sir Alistair was to ask for your hand, would you give him the same answer?"

Deirdre looked away.

"But he has not asked, has he?" Ronan demanded. "No, and he will not. He wants you—I think he's made that plain enough. He wants to use you as his whore! You! Good God, Deirdre, have you forgotten who you are?"

"How dare you!" Deirdre cried, jumping to her feet.

"You're too good for this sort of thing!" he cried, gesturing toward the bed. "Too good for him—"

"This sort of thing? Can you not even bring yourself to say the words? When a man and woman love each other, 'tis right and natural that they should want to lie together."

Ronan jerked back as though she had struck him, with a sound of horrified disgust. "What has happened to you?" he cried. "Listen to yourself! It's him—Sir Alistair—he has bewitched you—"

"Don't be ridiculous," Deirdre said, holding her temper with an effort. "Alistair needs no magic to win my heart."

"You say that—mayhap you even believe it—"

"Because it is the truth!" With a tongue made reckless by anger, she went on, "You say you love me, and I know you believe it, but you don't know the meaning of the word. It's all a dream to you, a fantasy—"

"It isn't!" he shouted. "I love you, Dee, and that's no dream, that's reality! I love you far too much to stand by and watch you debase yourself this way. He is no better than an animal, and he would drag you right down with him. Why can't you see that?"

"Oh, I see!" she shouted back furiously. "I see you understand nothing about me at all. You don't want me, Ronan, not as I really am. You want a plaster statue to put on a shelf and make pretty songs to! That's all I am, all I've ever been to you. But I want—I *need* more!"

"You want *him*," Ronan spat. "The traitor! Do you not know what they say of him? He has murder in his heart, that one, and will stop at nothing to get exactly what he wants."

"I know what they say."

"And you know it is the truth. The man has no honor. He is a murderer, a kin-slayer—"

"Stop!" Deirdre cried, pressing her hands over her ears. "Get out! I won't listen to you—"

"You are a fool!" he cried, starting for the door. "Or else he has beglamoured you in truth."

She turned her back to him and stared out the window, her back stiff. As Ronan passed the table, he hesitated, glancing at a pile of wilted greenery piled on its surface. Among the greenery sat a dagger. He stared at it, noting the beauty of the finely wrought stag's head, the emeralds winking in the sunlight.

"Dee, won't you listen to me?" he cried desperately. "Can't you see how you have changed, what he has done to you?"

"Get out," she said, not turning. "Just leave. I don't want you here."

"Fine. I will."

His hand shot out and grasped the dagger. He thrust it into his belt and hurried from the room.

chapter 34

Water dripped from the eaves of the deserted croft tucked away among the hills. Inside it was cold and drear; the hearth was dark and empty, save for the swallows' nest halfway up the crumbled chimney. The one room held only a table on which a smoking lantern had been set. It lit the faces of the two men standing above it, sharpening their noses and making shadowed hollows of their eyes.

"What news?" Though all was deserted for miles around, still the smaller of the men spoke in a whisper.

"Och, fine news," the larger man said. When he laughed his hood fell back, revealing the bearded face of Calder. "The laird is dying. He'll no last out the night. And tomorrow we'll be rid of Alistair."

"Fine for ye. But what of Brodie?"

"Dinna fear, man. I havena forgotten ye." Calder laughed. "Alistair and Brodie will both be dead by sunset."

"How?" the smaller man asked sourly. "'Tis hardly likely they'll kill each other on the field."

"They'll never even have the chance. Listen, friend, and tell me what ye think. . . ."

Calder bent and lowered his voice even further. As he spoke, the smaller man began to laugh.

"Damn, if I don't think it will work!"

"Of course it will. If ye do your part."

Calder held out his hand and the dagger glittered in his palm, the emeralds catching the lantern light.

"Oh, that's good, Calder. Verra good."

Calder handed off the dagger and followed his companion to the door. With a flash of Maxwell plaid, the man mounted and rode off.

chapter 35

Deirdre rolled over onto her back and sighed, staring up at the shadows dancing on the ceiling. A moment later she turned on her side and shut her eyes, then, with an impatient gesture, threw off the twisted coverlet and rose from the disordered bed.

Finn whined and twitched in his sleep. Deirdre sank down on the settle and laid a hand on his shaggy gray pelt. He quieted, then jumped up with a startled "woof" and ran to the door, his tail whipping furiously from side to side.

"Deirdre?" Alistair's voice was hardly more than a whisper.

She leaped to her feet and hurried toward the door. And if I had a tail, it would be wagging like the hound's, she thought wryly as she drew the latch.

"I'm sorry," he said. "Did I wake ye?"

"No."

When he walked inside, the frozen ache in her heart began to thaw and the tight muscles of her shoulders relaxed. The very air seemed different with him in the room.

The fire gave more light, the candles burned more brightly. All at once the rain was falling sweetly outside the window, making the chamber a warm and homely shelter from the storm.

He stood before the hearth as Finn whined and nosed at his hand. "All right, lad," he said, stroking Finn's head. "That's enough, now. Down."

Finn flopped down at Alistair's feet and gave a snort of sheer contentment.

"That's a good fellow," Alistair said and reached down to give him a pat. Such a perfectly domestic scene, Deirdre thought. If only it could really be like this, if only it could last. . . .

"I shouldn't have come," Alistair said, straightening. "'Tis late. . . ."

"Is it my reputation you're worried for?" Deirdre asked lightly, pouring wine for them both. "Or yours?"

He accepted the wine and sipped, leaning back against the mantel with his own peculiar grace. "I have no reputation left to worry for."

She flushed, remembering his words to Brodie earlier in the hall, when he'd claimed to have taken her to his bed. "No more have I. After today, what was left of it is gone."

"I dinna blame you for being angry," he said, his bright head bent as he gazed into the fire. "I'm sorry. But I could think of no other way to bring Brodie to the point."

"I know that. And I'm not angry, Alistair, not with you. I'm sorry if I sounded that way earlier. I don't want you to fight him! What if—"

He moved quickly across the few steps between them to touch his finger to her lips.

"No *what ifs*," he said. "We've been through that before. I knew what I was doing, Deirdre."

A gust of wind made the fire dance and flicker in the hearth. The chamber seemed to grow a little smaller as she stared into his eyes, and she was suddenly aware that she was clad only in her shift with a thin chamber robe thrown over her shoulders. As though following her thoughts, his gaze moved downward, and she shivered, pulling the robe more closely around her throat.

"You're cold and 'tis late and I'm sorry I woke ye," Alistair said abruptly. "I'll go."

"Oh, don't go! Not yet," she said quickly. "I was wakeful anyway."

Alistair sat down on the settle, and she sat beside him. They were quiet then, sipping at their wine, watching the fire.

"Deirdre," he said at last. "The laird is dead."

"I am sorry. Was it—?" She bit her lip, not knowing if he would want to speak of it.

"He didna wake," Alistair said. "His breathing changed and then . . ." He held out his hands and stared at them. "They said—the physician and priest—it was a blessed release. And I suppose it was. But—"

His voice broke and he leaned his head in his hands, shading his eyes.

"You loved him."

Alistair nodded. "Always. He was more of a father to me than my own ever was."

Alistair had spoken of his mother once or twice, but Deirdre realized now that he had never once mentioned his father.

"Who was your father?" she asked.

"He name was Niall Gordon. He was one of Kirallen's knights."

"Gordon?" Deirdre said, surprised. "But you—" She broke off in confusion.

"He met my mother at a gathering," Alistair said, his eyes fixed on the floor between his feet. "She was fifteen then, a crofter's daughter, young enough to be dazzled by a knight's attentions and innocent enough to believe his lies. He left her with a ring and a promise he never meant to keep." Alistair looked up at her. "And with me."

There was a small silence during which Deirdre was very conscious of Alistair watching her, waiting for her reaction. She hesitated, trying to find the right words. She could hardly say it did not matter who his parents were, when it obviously mattered very much to him.

"At least she had you," Deirdre said at last. "A fine son. I'm sure that was—that *you* were a comfort to her."

"Hardly that," Alistair answered bitterly. "Her parents never forgave either of us for her disgrace."

"But—well, these things do happen," Deirdre said lamely. "She was very young. Did she ever marry?"

"She never had the chance. Her parents kept both of us well out of sight. When she died, they could hardly wait to get me here to Ravenspur. They said I had been a burden to them long enough, and it was my father's turn to care for me."

"Did he?"

"He refused to acknowledge me," Alistair said. "Oh, he was a bonny laddie in his silk and velvet, fancied himself quite the gallant. But it was all paid for by his lady wife. She was much older, ye ken, and verra jealous of her fine young husband. The last thing he wanted was for her to find out what he'd been up to.

"He tried to give me back to my grandparents, but they wouldna have me. It was quite a scene," he said with a wry smile. "There we were in the laird's antechamber, Gordon denying everything at the top of his voice and my grandparents shouting at him, pushing me back and forth between them—"

Quite a scene indeed, Deirdre thought. A terrible thing to happen to any child, let alone one who had just lost his mother.

"How did they settle it?" she asked.

"They didna. God knows what would have happened if the laird hadna heard the noise and come out to see what was going on. He—he took my hand and brought me into his chamber, sat me on his knee, and said they were all a pack of fools and I mustn't mind anything they said. Then he called Ian in and bade him look after me while they decided what to do."

"Is that when the laird took you to foster?" Deirdre asked.

"Nay, that came later. I think the laird kept hoping he'd come to his senses and acknowledge me, especially as he had no children of his own. But he never did. Instead, he apprenticed me to the manor blacksmith. I saw him only once, when he stopped to collect a horse my master shod. He didna even speak to me. Just looked right through me as if I wasna there. But the laird didna forget me. Nor did Ian. Not a week passed that he didna ask to have me up to the manor."

"You must have made quite an impression on Ian," Deirdre said, a bit surprised that a nobleman's heir would be so friendly with a common child.

"None of the manor lads could keep up with him." Alistair laughed, remembering. "Ian would always go a bit further than anyone else, just to prove that he could do it. And I was not about to let any boy—especially a noble—get the best of me. We became . . . friends. Blood brothers, in fact," he added lightly, holding out his hand.

Deirdre traced her finger across the tiny scar on his thumb and smiled, remembering the solemnity with which she and Ronan had sworn just such a pact. How much more important such a pledge must have been to a child like Alistair, who had no family at all.

"Ian sounds like a fine boy," she said approvingly, giving Alistair's hand a squeeze.

"He was verra headstrong and more than a bit spoiled, but so good-natured that it was hard to fault him for it. He taught me how to laugh," Alistair said, his fingers tightening on hers. "I'd never had much practice at it before. I— well, I looked after him. *Someone* had to! And he let me do it. He listened to me—not always, but often enough that his father took notice. The laird canceled my indenture and brought me to live at the manor as Ian's companion. When Gordon died, the laird asked if I would be *his* son now and would I like to take his name? He was so kind to me,

Deirdre. So kind. I canna believe that he is gone—that both of them are dead—"

He turned to her blindly, and she held him hard against her.

They sat quietly for a time, her head against his shoulder and his cheek resting on her hair. His hand moved slowly over her neck and shoulders, and her heartbeat quickened as he stroked her hair. She sat quite still as he untied the knot about her braid and loosened the plait, just as he had done before, though her every muscle in her body tensed as she remembered how she'd failed him in the woodsman's cottage.

What did I do wrong that night? she wondered. What should I do now? I must—I have to get it right this time.

"Ye have such lovely hair," he murmured. "Did ye know that? I thought so the first time I saw ye, by the pool. . . ."

She wondered what she should say, what answer would be right, but then she realized it didn't matter, for he wasn't waiting for her to speak. He pushed her hair aside and kissed the place where her neck met her shoulder, sending shivers down her back.

"And this . . . ah, Deirdre, there are no words for this, or not words that I know. . . ."

She closed her eyes and turned to him, her arms reaching to clasp his neck as his lips moved against the pulse beating madly in her throat.

She yielded her mouth to him, leaning back against his arm. The kiss deepened until she lost all sense of time or place, until nothing existed but the fascinating dance of lips and tongues and hands. When he drew back, she made a wordless sound of protest.

"Shh . . . 'tis all right, 'tis only that my arm has gone to sleep—"

He smiled and she was smiling, too, as she stood and pulled him to his feet. They walked together toward the bed, but once she lay down, she went rigid with fear. Whatever should she do now? She didn't know—she'd never known—and her failure had moved Brodie to rage.

But no, it was shame to think of Alistair as being no different from Brodie. Just lie still, she told herself, squeezing her eyes shut. Let him take what he wants. And pray
God he finds joy in it.

"Here, now, what's this? Don't tell me I've put you to
sleep?"

She opened her eyes and Alistair was leaning over her,
smiling, a lock of bright hair falling over his eyes. "Let me
take this off."

"Oh, no." She put her hands firmly on the skirt of her
shift.

"No? All right, then, I won't. But I thought ye wanted—"

"I did. I do. But—but I—well—"

He looked at her, brows raised. "Then I take it your husband never—"

She was glad he didn't speak Brodie's name, but it made
no difference. He was here between them anyway. Brodie
with his rough hands and hurtful words. "Useless, that's
what ye are." That's what Brodie had said on their wedding night, and he was right, there was some lack in her,
something wrong, and now Alistair would see it, too—

Oh, God, she thought, panicked, sitting up and swinging
her legs over the side of the bed. I cannot do this. Not
again. Not even for Alistair.

His hand touched her hair, very gently, stroking down
her neck. "Deirdre," he said softly. "I'll make you a bargain. When it comes off—*if* it comes off—you'll be the
one to do it. Fair enough?"

She nodded warily, not sure what he meant but anxious
not to drive him away. His arm went around her, and she
leaned against him, wondering what he thought was supposed to happen here. It was obviously something different than she had experienced with Brodie.

"Alistair," she said, staring down at her clasped hands.
"I—I don't know what to do."

"Dinna fash yourself," he said, bending to her. "It
doesna matter."

But it *did* matter, she was quite sure it mattered very

much. As he drew her close, she lay stiff in his arms, afraid
to move yet fearing that something was expected of her.
After a moment he sighed and released her, rolling over on
his back and folding his arms beneath his head.

"Well, then," he said. "What am I doing wrong?"

"You? No, it isn't you, it's me—"

"All right," he said agreeably. "What are ye doing
wrong?"

She gave a choked laugh. "I was hoping you could tell
me."

"If you're asking me—you are asking me, aren't you?"
He propped himself on one elbow. "Nothing. You're
everything a man could want—silly lass!"

He rolled over to face her, then rubbed his nose against
hers and crossed his eyes.

And when she laughed it was all right again, it was the
two of them and not just her alone. He kissed the tip of her
nose, her eyes, and then his lips were on her neck, his
breath warm in her ear. She shivered, her fingers moving
through his soft fine hair, trailing over his shoulders, so
broad, so strong, feeling the separate muscles beneath his
rough wool tunic.

His hair smelled of rain and heather and the faint scent
of sandalwood clung to his clothing. When he lifted his
head and looked down at her, she traced his lips with one
finger, marveling again at the way the hard line of his
mouth could relax into such a charming smile.

He bent to her and began to kiss her mouth, so softly
that she could barely feel his lips on hers, and it was like
the night they had first met in the forest, a kiss that wasn't
a kiss at all but the seal of a pledge made long ago, in another place, another life. . . . Oh, they belonged to each
other and always had—how could she ever have forgotten
him?

When he teased her lips apart, she opened to him with a
little sigh. His fingers trailed over her foot in light, caressing strokes, moving to her ankle, her shin, but stopping always at the hem of her shift. She edged the skirt a little

higher, and when he found the soft spot behind her knee she gasped with pleasure, and then she knew it was all right; that everything would be well between them now.

She leaned up and kissed his lips, then threw off her shift, laughing at her own boldness. Feeling very wicked and delightfully wanton, she whispered, "Why are you still dressed?"

In one fluid motion he was on his feet and pulling the tunic over his head, then untying the laces at his waist, and kicking his trews aside. She caught her breath, staring.

Brodie had only ever removed the necessary portions of his clothing—and that under the coverlet. But she suspected that he would have looked nothing like Alistair did now, with his broad shoulders and slender hips, the breadth of his chest covered with a mat of golden hair that narrowed as it trailed over his hard, flat belly . . . She followed the line of it with her eyes and caught her breath.

He stood without moving, letting her look at him, and when her eyes moved at last to his face, her fear vanished, for this was Alistair, not Brodie, and she could see how dearly his control was costing him as he waited for her to make the next move.

"Can I—?" she said, reaching out a tentative hand.

"Oh, aye, you can. Please—like that . . . ah, Deirdre, wait."

"What?" she asked, pulling her hand back. "Did I do something wrong?"

"Nay. 'Twas right. Verra right. Just—wait—while I think of something—something verra dull—"

"What?" She sat up. "What are you talking about?"

He gave a choked laugh. "I almost—that is, ye nearly— ah, God, I'm no better than a boy with ye!"

"But what—?"

"Later. I'll explain it all later, I promise, anything ye want, but now—" He lay beside her and looked deep into her eyes. "Nay, not now," he whispered, kissing the corner of her mouth. "Not yet. Not until ye ask, I swear it."

"I—I'm not sure what you mean," she said with painful honesty. "What exactly am I supposed to ask? And when?"

He bit his lip, his eyes bright with something that looked like laughter. "Deirdre, don't worry about any of that now."

"But I want to—"

"Shh."

He drew one finger across her lips and the laughter faded from his eyes as he eased her down beneath him.

"You'll know," he whispered.

She nodded, not really understanding, and slid her arms around his neck.

"There's naught to be afraid of," he promised, bending to her.

Deirdre reveled in the heat of his body against hers, the strength of his arms enfolding her. But as his hands and lips moved over her with increasing urgency, the wonderful feeling of abandon began to slip away as she instinctively braced herself against the pain to come.

But she would not let him guess. This meant so much to him, and he was trying so very hard to please her. She deliberately relaxed her muscles and quickened her breathing to keep pace with his. When he kissed her breast, she allowed a tiny moan to escape her lips.

Alistair sensed that he was losing her. She returned his kisses eagerly, sighed at his touch, gave every show of pleasure. But none of it was real. Even as she pressed closer to him, he could feel her body vibrating with tension. He redoubled his efforts, using all his skill, every trick he'd ever tried or even heard of to kindle an answering response, as though somehow the mere force of his desire could *make* her want him. But the harder he tried to draw her with him, the more surely she slipped from his grasp.

"Now," she whispered. "Please, Alistair," and he knew it was not excitement that brought the tremor to her voice, but anxiety to have it over. And she was right to be frightened, for if he took her now, unready as she was, there would be no joy in it for either of them.

Fool, he raged at himself. It was too soon; God *damn* him, he had known that, and he should never have come here tonight. But he had needed to see her, to talk with her, and now he had made a damnable mess of everything.

He wanted to tell her it didn't matter, they didn't have to do this now, that he would be content just to hold her while she slept. But the moment for that had passed. She was offering herself to him, at God knew what cost, and if he refused her now she would be humiliated beyond bearing.

Christ's wounds, how did this happen? I love her so much, but whatever I do now, she will be hurt. Never in his life had he felt so completely helpless. And looking into her eyes, he knew she felt the same.

But, then, he thought, seeing the faintest glimmer of light in the darkness, that was how Deirdre expected to feel when lying with a man. It was all she knew.

With a sudden movement he flipped over on his back and pulled her with him so she sprawled across his chest.

"What—?"

"Wait," he ordered gently. "Here, now . . ."

He raised her until she sat astride him. Then he fell back and rested his hands beside his head, palms upward.

"There we are," he said, speaking as though this was perfectly ordinary, the most common thing in all the world. "'Tis your turn, Dee."

"My—?" She bit her lip uncertainly. "What do you mean?"

"I mean 'tis up to ye," he said easily. "Do what ye like with me . . . or nothing at all."

Just as he had begun to fear he had made things even worse, a smile touched one corner of her mouth.

"So I have you at my mercy?"

"Entirely. Go on, lass, do your worst. I can take it."

She traced a hesitant fingertip across his chest and down his belly, her smile deepening when he drew a hissing breath.

"So I can do that?"

"Aye."

"And this?" she said, her hand dipping lower.

"Oh, aye," he said. "And—and—ah, Dee, that, too . . . especially that."

She pulled her hand away. "And if I said to stop now . . . ?"

"Then we would go to sleep," he said, his voice a little ragged. "Together, if ye like, or I could leave. 'Tis for ye to say."

She drew both hands down his arms, then bent and nipped his bottom lip, her breasts crushed against his chest and her hair falling softly about his face. "But I thought that once a man got started on this sort of thing, he could not stop," she said.

"Some men, perhaps," Alistair said, his breath coming more quickly as the sweet curve of her bottom shifted against him. "Not me."

She kissed his neck, then traced her tongue lightly over the curve of his ear. The feel of her warm breath sent a shiver racing through his body when she spoke again, a hint of laughter in her voice. "You sound very sure of yourself."

She sat up, shaking the hair out of her face, and he stifled a moan as she deliberately rolled her hips.

"I am. Quite. Sure."

She took his hands and brought them to her lips, then laid them on her breasts. He caressed her, fingers trailing lightly over her taut nipples, lingering on the curve of her waist and the flare of her hips. She began to move against him, tentatively at first and then with deepening excitement as she began to understand her power over both of them.

"Ye are so lovely, Dee," he whispered. "Ye canna know."

She shifted and for a moment Alistair thought his heart would burst as he felt them on the verge of joining. He began to reach for her, but her voice halted him.

"If I said this was enough . . . ?" she asked breathlessly.

"'Twould be . . . enough. But please, ah, God, Dee . . ."
He groaned as she lowered herself slightly.

"And this?" she insisted. "Would you still stop if I asked it?"

He nodded, beyond speech now, and turned his face into the crook of one arm, his breath coming in ragged gasps as he fisted his hands in the coverlet. Gently but insistently, she turned his face to hers and looked into his eyes, and oh, God, he couldn't wait, not now, but still she hesitated and sweet Jesus, what did she want from him?

He did not know how he managed it, but he lay unmoving, and just as he was certain he could not bear another moment, she found whatever she sought in his eyes. He held her gaze, gasping with a pleasure so intense it was inseparable from pain when finally, drawing out the torment almost past endurance, she took him inside her.

He waited, barely breathing, as she grew accustomed to him. Heart pounding, hands clenched, sure that he would die at any moment, he let her take her pleasure of him.

But it was worth it. Oh, God, it was worth it all, for he had never seen anything so beautiful as Deirdre at this moment; cheeks flushed, lips parted in a soft moan as her eyes fell shut and she lost herself entirely. She threw back her head, her back arched; he saw the flush spread down her neck, felt the silken brush of her hair against his thighs . . .

"Now, Alistair," she cried. "Now. Come to me."

His own cry mingled with hers as he thrust deep inside her, and at last, at last they came together, bodies taut and straining, and she was able to accept all he had to give her with a joy he felt more keenly than his own.

L ater they lay curled together, Alistair's head resting on her breast, his legs twined with hers. It wasn't possible to be this happy, Deirdre thought. And yet she was.

"There are so many things I understand now," she said, not realizing she spoke aloud until he stirred and kissed the hollow between her breasts, then lifted his head to look into her face.

"Such as?"

"Oh, the songs and stories," she answered vaguely, "things people have said . . ."

His hair was tousled, his eyes sleepy, and he looked very young and vulnerable.

"They said things about you, Jennie Maxwell, and the others. One said that you knew how to pleasure a lass and she laughed—"

That girl had seen him like this, Deirdre realized with a sharp stab of jealousy, had held him in her arms and felt his warmth against her.

"You did this—with her—and others, too," she added, surprised and a little angry, unfair as she knew that to be. She remembered the girl's curling brown hair and bright blue eyes, the way she had blushed and laughed as she talked about the night she had spent with Alistair. But I could never laugh about this, never, Deirdre thought, suddenly desolate and alone.

"Who is this 'her' you're speaking of?"

"Annie Maxwell," Deirdre said reluctantly.

"Oh."

"Oh? That's all you have to say about it?"

"What do ye want me to say? She's a nice lass and we had—well, we had good times together—"

Deirdre rolled over and buried her head in the pillow. "I have no wish to hear about it."

"Then why the devil did you bring her up?"

"I don't remember. Good night, I'm very tired now and I think I'll go to sleep." With that she pulled the pillow over her head.

"Annie Maxwell enjoyed a tumble with me and any other lad she fancied," Alistair said distinctly. "I'm glad to know she remembers me kindly, as I do her—" He pulled the pillow away. "I liked her and she made me laugh, and there was no more to it than that."

"But when I think of you, with her . . ."

"'Twas a different matter altogether," he said gently. "I never loved her, Deirdre, nor any other woman, only you."

Joy swept through her, more powerful than anything she had experienced tonight, a feeling so new, so unexpected, that she was speechless with the wonder of it.

Her silence lasted but a moment, but to Alistair it seemed to stretch into eternity. She cared for him, he knew that, but he had believed—had hoped—there was more than friendship and desire between them.

"You did this before, as well," he pointed out a bit more sharply than he'd meant to. "With your husband."

"But that—that was nothing like . . ." she said uncertainly.

Why? he wanted to cry out. What was the difference? But he stopped himself. It would be wrong to press her for what she was not ready to give.

"No more was it for me," he said, forcing himself to speak in the light, teasing voice he'd used so often in the past, when the woman lying in his arms meant nothing beyond a shared pleasure.

He brought her hand to his lips and kissed her fingertips, ending with a playful nip on the soft pad of her thumb. "Sweet Christ, lady, ye nearly killed me," he said with a lazy smile.

"Did I?" She sat up, instantly contrite. "Oh, Alistair—"

"Whisht, I'm not complaining. I didna mind at all." He laughed and pinched her cheek. "One day we'll change places and I'll show ye what it's like."

"Will you?" she asked wistfully, and his heart lifted.

"My word upon it. Or . . . we could try it now."

With that he pounced and she squirmed away with a shriek of laughter. At last he lay on top of her and pinned her hands beside her head.

"Well, well," he said. "Look what I have here."

"And what is that?" she demanded, breathless with laughter.

"The most beautiful lady in all the world."

"Don't," she said, pulling her hands from his and turning her face away.

"Don't what?"

"Don't say that, Alistair, not now. Not tonight."

"Ye really dinna ken, do ye? Ye don't believe me. Oh, Christ, Dee," he said roughly, pulling her against him and rocking her as if she was a child. "What did he do to ye?"

She hid her face against his shoulder.

"How did you know about Brodie?" she asked. "What you said to him—earlier in the hall—how could you have known those things?"

"It didn't take the Sight for that! 'Tis the fear every man carries, that he's not man enough for his woman. In Brodie's case, I suppose it was well-founded. And he blamed ye for his failure, did he?"

The question was asked so matter-of-factly that Deirdre did not even feel ashamed. She simply nodded.

"And this? Did he do this?"

Alistair kissed the tiny scar beneath her brow and she fisted her hands in his hair, holding him against her as quick tears stung her eyes.

"That was the first," she said, trying to control her shaking voice. "Later he learned not to mark me."

"He will never hurt ye again. I swear it."

"Don't swear," she said quickly. "'Tis bad luck."

"I don't need luck," Alistair answered, raising his head. His eyes were flat and hard as disks of silver.

"You mustn't say such a thing!" she said, a little frightened. "Anything could happen— You cannot know—"

"Oh, but I do. Brodie Maxwell has hurt ye for the last time. I swear it by St. Andrew and the Blessed Virgin. Tomorrow Brodie Maxwell dies."

chapter 36

D eirdre yawned and stretched *deliciously. She was*
    aware of every muscle of her body in a way she never
experienced before. Her eyes still closed, she reached toward the other side of the bed and found only chill emptiness. She sat up, pushing the tangled hair back from her
face.

"Alistair?"

Finn lay curled by the door, but save for the dog the
chamber was empty. Rising quickly, Deirdre ran to the
window and looked out, searching for a glimpse of golden
hair among the crowd gathered in the courtyard below.
Finding none, she dressed quickly and ran down the winding steps into the hall.

The morning meal finished, servants moved among the
long trestles, emptying the last of the porridge and bread
into buckets. Deirdre grabbed a heel of bread and went out
into the courtyard.

"Malcolm!" she cried, spotting the boy across the yard,
talking with Haddon Darnley. "Where is Alistair?"

He shrugged. "Dinna ask me, lady. I havena seen him."

"I did, earlier," Haddon put in. "He rode out this morning."

Jemmy and Alyson joined them. "Where is Alistair?" Jemmy asked. "I thought he was with you, lady."

"No." Deirdre shook her head. "Haddon said he rode out earlier."

"He'd best hurry back," Jemmy said. "We'll be leaving in an hour. It will take nearly that long for him to get armed and ready."

"He was armed," Haddon told them. "I saw his mail as he went by."

Deirdre's stomach knotted. Where had Alistair gone all alone? Why hadn't he waited for the rest of them?

"Maybe he wanted an early start." Jemmy spoke easily, but Deirdre saw the worried glance he exchanged with Alyson.

"You don't suppose he—well, ran away, do you?" Haddon asked, and Malcolm shrugged.

"Of course not," Deirdre snapped. "Malcolm, how could you even think such a thing? You know him better than that!"

"Do I?" Malcolm said, his casual façade crumbling as his eyes filled with tears. "I thought I did, but . . ." He blinked and swallowed hard. "Maybe he did run. I hope he did. I hope he never comes back here again!"

"So do I," Haddon said, putting a comforting hand on Malcolm's shoulder. "Begging your pardon, Lady Maxwell, but you can't expect any of us to feel differently."

"I'm sorry, Deirdre," Alyson said quietly. "What he did for you yesterday was a fine thing, but it changes nothing. Whatever happens with Maxwell today, Alistair will have to go."

"He can come with me, then," Deirdre said, her eyes flashing.

"That would be best," Alyson said with a tight smile.

"What of you?" Deirdre said impulsively, turning to Jemmy. "Do you think he ran away?"

"Nay," Jemmy said gently. "I think Alistair cares for you very much, my lady, far too much to run off and leave you to Maxwell. He'll be waiting for us at Kendrick's Field. And I suggest we get ready to go and find him there."

A listair reached the field with a quarter of an hour to spare. He dismounted and pushed back the mail coif, running one hand through his sweat-soaked hair. He had feared he would be late, yet he was the first to arrive. Smiling a little, he checked his stallion's hooves and saddle, thinking back over the last few hours with satisfaction.

Straightening, he looked over the clearing, pacing the ground to check for holes and hillocks that might catch Germain unawares. When he reached the far side of the meadow he stopped, staring at a splash of color against the darkness of the pines.

Approaching cautiously, he found a man lying huddled at the edge of the clearing. He dropped to his knees and turned the man over, staring in disbelief at Brodie's lifeless face.

The wind soughed through the high branches as Alistair glanced quickly about the field, knowing already he was alone here with a dead man. With deepening shock he noticed the dagger protruding from between Brodie's shoulder blades, the familiar carved stag's head adorning the handle.

"How pretty," Deirdre had said that day in the courtyard, when she was cutting flowers. He had answered, "It was a gift from the laird."

Then he had given it to her.

To Deirdre.

And now here it was again, stuck fast in Brodie Maxwell.

"Hold there! Alistair, what have ye done?" Kinnon Maxwell cried, his voice thin and high with shock.

Alistair looked up as the Maxwells rode into the clearing. At that moment Jemmy arrived from the other side, his men behind him. Kinnon cantered his horse to Jemmy's and spoke urgently, gesturing toward Brodie's body, as the Maxwell men-at-arms surrounded Alistair.

Deirdre sat frozen on her horse, staring at Brodie's lifeless form. Why, Deirdre? Alistair wanted to shout. He had *told* her she would never go back to Brodie, had sworn to her—but she hadn't trusted him to do it.

But no, that was impossible. Deirdre could not have done this. Even if she had, she would not have used his dagger, then sat silent as he was taken. She loved him! Or no, he had been the one to say those words. . . . A shattering wave of doubt seized him and he could not speak, neither to accuse nor deny.

Like a man in a dream, he watched Fitzgerald pull his steed close to Deirdre and encircle her with his arm.

> *"His lady's ta'en another mate-o,*
> *So we may mak our dinner sweet-o."*

How long would it take her? Alistair wondered. How long before she wed the Irishman?

Deirdre swayed in her saddle and Ronan was there, pulling his horse close to her, eyes blazing emerald in a face as pale as parchment.

"He didn't," Deirdre whispered. "He didn't do this."

"Sure and he did. 'Twas—'twas for you he did it, though, just remember that."

Alistair's eyes were fastened on Deirdre, but he did not speak a word. Why does he look at me that way? Deirdre thought. As though it is my fault? Oh, dear St. Brigid, could Ronan be right? Had Alistair really done this thing? *For her?*

A rustle of leaves made Alistair look up. Right on time, he thought with an eerie detachment as the corbies took their places above his head.

"God's blood, Alistair," Kinnon Maxwell cried. "I never took ye for a backstabber!"

The Maxwell men began to move forward. "Let me have him, Kinnon," Jemmy said. "I'll get the truth from him."

"What truth? I can see the truth with my own eyes," Kinnon cried, pointing to his brother's body. "What more do I need? Alistair backstabbed him and he'll hang for it."

Alistair caught Jemmy's eye and shrugged, an infinitesimal movement of one shoulder. Ye canna help me now, he said silently. Don't even try.

"Nay!" Deirdre cried. "I don't believe it! I won't! He wouldn't kill Brodie, not like this!"

The men were still arguing, pointing toward the body. Brodie's body. Even from this distance Deirdre could see the sunlight glinting off the handle of the dagger—Alistair's dagger—that she had left lying on the table, ready to his hand when he stole out this morning without waking her.

She shivered as she remembered his words last night. "I don't need luck . . . tomorrow Brodie Maxwell dies."

"Nay!" she cried again.

Ronan's eyes were wide with shock as he followed her gaze. "'Tis best this way, Dee," he said uncertainly. "Have you not heard what they are saying at Ravenspur? They've known him for years and they believe he's capable of far worse than this."

"What are they doing?" Deirdre cried as Alistair's hands were bound and he was dragged to the center of the field.

"I think—I believe they are about to hang him," Ronan faltered.

Deirdre leaped from her horse and darted into the center of the field. "Is this justice?" she demanded. "In all fairness, he must be tried!"

Alistair was lifted to his horse, hands bound behind him, the noose around his neck. Still he did not speak, nor did he take his eyes from her. Deirdre began to shake, the strength draining from her limbs.

"My lord," she said hoarsely, turning to Jemmy. "You cannot let this happen. He is a Kirallen, entitled to justice. You cannot simply hang him!"

"Oh, aye, we can," Kinnon said, and lifted one hand to give the order.

Jemmy seized his wrist. "Donal," he ordered sharply. "You and Roger get Sir Alistair down from there. Now. He must stand trial."

Kinnon frowned, biting the corner of his mouth. "At Cranston Keep."

"At Ravenspur," Jemmy said evenly. "He's ours, Kinnon, as little as I may like it. We'll see justice done. Tomorrow midday we'll begin."

Deirdre had just begun to breathe again when Alistair's horse reared. Donal and another knight struggled to push through the crowd as Alistair clung to the horse with his knees, trying desperately to control it. He was dragged backward bit by bit, the noose tightening around his neck.

It was Ronan who slipped through and caught Alistair by the knees as he was pulled free from his horse. "Cut him down!" Ronan shouted, staggering beneath Alistair's weight.

Conal galloped over, the men scattering before his mount's steel-shod hooves. Deirdre watched him cut through the rope, seeing Alistair's struggles weaken and finally stop before it was done. When the last strand parted, he and Ronan fell together to the ground.

Deirdre pushed through the crowd about the tree. By the time she reached Alistair's side, he was sitting up, gasping and coughing as he tore the noose from around his neck and flung it aside.

"There's a taste for ye, Kirallen," one of the Maxwells jeered, leaning over to spit into his face. "How did ye like it?"

"I liked it fine," Alistair said hoarsely as his foot shot out, sweeping the man's legs from under him. "How did ye like that?"

"Enough!" Jemmy thundered furiously. "Bring him back to Ravenspur for trial."

Deirdre watched as Alistair was pulled roughly to his feet, every inch of him blazing defiance. "Trial?" he cried. "Still playing laird, are ye, Jemmy? Well, enjoy it while ye can!"

"Oh, I will," Jemmy shouted back. "I'll enjoy every moment. My father cannot help you now, Alistair. 'Tis I you'll have to deal with. And by this time tomorrow, you'll be begging them to finish what they started here today."

Alistair was jerked backward and tied to his horse before he could answer.

"Alistair and I have some old business to settle," Jemmy said, struggling to compose himself as he turned to Kinnon.

"I see that," Kinnon replied thoughtfully. "Mayhap it will work out for the best after all."

"Lady Maxwell," Jemmy ordered. "Mount up."

"She can come back with me," Kinnon offered, holding out his arm to Deirdre.

Deirdre stared at the two men with loathing, not bothering to answer. Back stiff, she walked back to her horse and let Ronan help her mount.

"That was well done," she said, nodding to him as she picked up the reins.

"Was it?" Ronan scratched his chin and watched Alistair ride off through narrowed eyes. "Dee—" he began, turning to her suddenly.

"What?"

"I—oh, never mind." He shook his head and kicked his horse forward. After a moment, Deirdre followed.

chapter 37

"**D**o *you want to make your confession?*" Jemmy asked coldly. "I'll send the priest."

The prison chamber was foul and dank. Jemmy grimaced as he inhaled the noisome stench of the middens running just outside the tower wall. Alistair lay outstretched on the cold stone bench running the length of one wall. When he sat up the chains around his ankles clattered. His face was drawn with exhaustion and his hair hung tangled about his brow.

"Dinna bother," he replied indifferently.

"Talk to him or not, he'll be here before sunset." Jemmy motioned the guard to leave them, adding, "You can go. I'll be but a short time here."

When the door slammed shut, Jemmy shuddered and looked about the small space nervously. Hiding his discomfort, he leaned against the wall, arms folded across his chest.

"Well?"

"Well, what?" Alistair asked warily.

"What the devil happened earlier?"

"Why ask me? Ye were there."

"Oh, so you murdered Brodie Maxwell—backstabbed the man with your own dagger, then stood about waiting to be taken?"

"We all make mistakes."

"You're saying that you did it?" Jemmy asked, amazed.

"I'll not deny it."

Jemmy sank down on the bench beside Alistair. "Master Kerian says he was dead at least two hours before noon."

Alistair shrugged, his mouth set in a stubborn line.

"So you waited there the whole morning just so there would be no mistake? Very thoughtful of you."

"Dinna do this Jemmy," Alistair said tightly. "Just let it go."

Jemmy rounded on him furiously. "In case you have forgotten, tomorrow morning is my father's funeral mass. God knows we weren't close, but he was my father, and I don't expect it to be pleasant. Once that is finished, I will sit in judgment on you, the very last of my kin. Forgive me for *inconveniencing* you, Alistair, but I confess to a certain reluctance to order my own foster brother hanged from the neck until he is dead. I need to know the truth, and I need to know it now."

He leaned back against the wall, willing himself to calmness. Anger would serve no purpose here. It would only cloud his thinking, which was far too muddled as it was. The only thing he knew for certain was that he had no idea what the hell had happened earlier on Kendrick's Field. And Alistair showed no signs of enlightening him.

"You were frightened to meet Brodie in fair combat," Jemmy began, "so you talked him into meeting you alone, two hours early. I can't wait to hear how you managed that! And then, when the two of you were chatting about the weather, Brodie obligingly turned his back so you could slip in your dagger. Is that how it happened?"

"It doesna matter how it happened," Alistair said. "The deed was done."

"Oh, aye, it was done. But who did it?"

Alistair raised his head, and Jemmy thought he had never seen such misery in a man's eyes. For the first time, his belief in Alistair's innocence was shaken.

"Jemmy, I ken ye mean well, I ken ye want to help me, but ye canna. Just walk away now. Please."

His voice broke on the last word and he looked away.

"Very well, Alistair, I'll go. If you can look me in the eye and tell me you did this thing, I'll leave right now."

Alistair turned. His eyes were flat, expressionless. "I did it," he said.

"Why?"

Alistair jumped to his feet with a rattle of heavy chain and turned his back to Jemmy. "Ye said you'd leave if I told ye," he snarled, fists clenched at his sides. "And I have. Now get out."

Jemmy rose as well. "Listen, Alistair," he said rapidly. "I know you don't want to trust me, I understand that, but you must tell me the truth, you have to. How can I help you if you will not?"

"I've told ye all I mean to tell ye."

Had he done it? Jemmy refused to believe it. Why, then, did he not deny it?

"What can I ever say to Malcolm?" Jemmy asked, using the sharpest weapon he could summon.

"I dinna care," Alistair said roughly. "Tell him what ye like. What difference will this make?"

"Aye, you've already broken his faith in you—and don't think I haven't seen what that cost you. Now you'd have him believe you died a traitor, a coward, and a murderer?"

Alistair did not turn, but Jemmy saw the sudden stiffening of his shoulders.

"You are lying," Jemmy said with certainty. "But why?"

Alistair turned, a desperate light in his eyes. "Jemmy, if ye ever—I ken we have never been friends, but we've known each other all our lives. For what was between us, I'm asking ye to do this last thing for me. Dinna ask any more questions. Just let Kinnon Maxwell have his way tomorrow. Believe me, this is—'tis what must be."

"You're asking too damn much," Jemmy snapped. "I am the one who must condemn you—an innocent man—and I will not do it."

Alistair sank back down on the bench and looked up at Jemmy, a hard smile touching his lips. "How can you be sure it wasna me? I wanted the man dead, that was no secret. Why believe anything I've said to you? It could have all been lies, did ye ever think of that? I always wanted Malcolm to follow your father. Maybe I was using ye to force Calder into the open so I could take control."

"I considered that. But I don't think you were."

"Then ye are just as great a fool as I always thought," Alistair grated. "Ye have no reason to trust me! You're well again and if ye have done your work, ye have your supporters now. Here's your chance to be shed of me. If I were ye, I'd take it."

"No, you wouldn't."

Alistair looked up sharply. "Oh, Jemmy, ye canna know that. There have been times I wished—I wanted—"

"And plenty of times I wanted to wring your neck as well," Jemmy admitted, sitting down beside him. "But if you had truly wished to kill me, you could have done it the day I found you. Or the night you came to my chamber. Or you could have let Calder do it for you. You had plenty of chances, but you didn't take them, did you?"

Alistair would not meet his eyes. He stared down at the filthy straw that covered the floor, his face studiously blank.

"Do you really believe I will condemn you to a death you don't deserve?" Jemmy asked. "When all the while there's someone standing back, watching, waiting for me to hang you for his crime?"

Alistair turned to him. "Jemmy, dinna—"

"Or," Jemmy said with sudden understanding, "for *her* crime."

"Nay," Alistair said vehemently. "Ye have it wrong—"

"Do I? Who else would you protect?"

Alistair stood and paced the length of the chamber. "Deirdre had every reason to kill him," he said rapidly. "Ye dinna ken—ye canna begin to ken all he did to her—"

"Why are you so certain it was she?"

"The dagger," Alistair admitted heavily. "I lent it to her and she never returned it."

Jemmy ran a hand across his face, all the events of the past days descending like a leaden weight upon his shoulders. Why did this have to happen now? It was too much, too soon after his father's death. But he had no choice but to see it through.

Frowning, he tried once again to imagine what had taken place at Kendrick's Field that morning.

"She is very slight," he said. "I don't see how . . . and how did she convince him to meet her there?"

Alistair shook his head. "I canna say. But she must have done it."

"But when did she find the time to send a message?" Jemmy insisted. "And whyever would Brodie have agreed?"

"If she said she meant to go back, he would have met her."

"Then she struck him down and left your dagger sticking in him?"

"She panicked," Alistair said. "'Tis natural enough."

Jemmy looked at him curiously. "So you think she will keep silent and let you hang?"

Alistair made no answer.

"Then I wonder why she stopped Kinnon from stringing you up right then and there," Jemmy remarked casually.

"'Twould have been better to let it happen," Alistair said bitterly. "Now we must go through some sort of trial. When it comes to the point, ye must show no mercy, Jemmy. Dinna hesitate. Do what ye must . . . and then think of it no more."

"Thank you. 'Tis all quite clear now. How fortunate I

still have you to tell me what to do! How ever will I manage when you are gone?"

Alistair did not answer. As though the last of his strength was gone, he sank down and buried his face in his hands. Jemmy took a deep breath and released it slowly.

"Alistair?"

"Aye?" he asked dully.

"You are a fool. Ah, there, look, he comes to life! But 'tis the simple truth."

"Think what ye like."

"Do you honestly believe Deirdre murdered Brodie and is sitting silent while you take the blame for it? You wrong her, Alistair. Do you think she has no honor at all?"

Alistair looked away.

"Deirdre would *never* have done such a thing. Oh, I can believe she would kill Brodie—how can I not, when she told us so herself? When she said it, I could scarce believe what I was hearing—and yet that's just the point, isn't it? She *told* us what she meant to do. And I believe if she was desperate enough, if he drove her to it, she would have followed through. But to do it such wise, to stab him in the back . . . and then say nothing when an innocent man is taken? When the man is the one she loves?"

Alistair remained silent, his face averted.

"Do you not know that? How could you not, when 'tis plain to every one of us? How *could* you doubt her?"

He stood and walked to the door, studiously turning his back on his kinsman for a time.

"Christ's wounds," he grumbled, pacing across the floor to peer through the tiny barred window, "I'll have this place torn down, I swear it. I will not condemn any man to this."

His back to Alistair, he asked, "Well? Do you have naught to say?"

"If she didna do it . . . it means . . . it must mean . . ."

"That we have to find the person who did it, and we haven't got much time," Jemmy said, sitting down beside Alistair. "Now, you say you gave her your dagger, but I never saw her carry it. She must have left it in her chamber. Anyone could have picked it up. What if Calder—"

"Nay, Calder couldna get in there," Alistair interrupted. "Not with Finn about."

"Then someone she invited inside," Jemmy suggested. "Fitzgerald?"

"Fitzgerald," Alistair said, his hand tightening into a fist.

"I think Lady Maxwell cares for you far more than you realize," Jemmy said gently. "I will wager Fitzgerald thinks so, too. This would have been the perfect chance for him to be rid of both you and Brodie."

"Aye, it could have happened that way," Alistair said thoughtfully.

"Let's get the harper in here and ask him a few questions."

"Nay." Alistair stood, frowning at the chains around his ankles. "Ye had best stay out of it. Remember, ye are meant to be champing at the bit to hang me. Ye canna start questioning others now."

"Then what?"

"Let me talk to him alone. I can get the truth from him, Jemmy. Two hours, no more than that, and I'll be back. Will ye trust me for that?"

"Aye," Jemmy said. "I will and I do. Come on, then. We'll go to the chapel—we can say you're paying your final respects to the laird. I'll wait for you there."

As he went to the door to call the guard, Alistair put a hand on his wrist.

"Thank ye, Jemmy."

"No need for thanks," Jemmy said gruffly. "It's little enough to ask. You're the only family I have left to me now that Father . . . I need you with me. Alive. So see that you get the truth from that Irishman."

"Oh, I'll have the truth of this," Alistair promised grimly. "One way or another, I'll find young Fitzgerald and make him talk."

chapter 38

❦

"**R**eady to talk, Fitzgerald?*"*
    Ronan kicked backward with all his strength and
twisted in his assailant's grip. But the arms around him
were strong, and the blade against his throat was very
keen.
    "Why else are ye here at this hour?" Calder added, driv-
ing his knee more firmly into the small of Ronan's back.
"Running to Jemmy to spill your guts, were ye? Well, we
canna have that. D'ye think I'll let a wee fool like you
undo all I've done?"
    "You never said—" Ronan gasped. "Never—not mur-
der—"
    Calder laughed. "Nay. I dinna suppose I did. But what's
done is done."
    The courtyard was nearly dark, but Alistair, crouched in
the shadow of a wheelbarrow, had no trouble making out
the two men. Careful not to make a sound, he drew his
sword. He had followed Ronan this far expecting to hear
something very different. But now he understood. It had

not been Deirdre, nor had it been the young harper—now
so dangerously close to death—who had killed Brodie.
Jemmy had been right. It was Calder all along.

He stepped out from the shadows and raised his sword.
To his right, he heard the scrape of a booted foot on cobbles and realized a man stood concealed in the corner of
the wall. Alistair spun to face him, but he was too late. Before he could speak a word, the world exploded into pain
and darkness.

"H ist! *Calder, 'tis Alistair—*"
"What?"

Calder's head whipped toward the figure lying facedown on the cobbles. The moment his attention was di-
verted, Ronan drove an elbow into his belly. When
Calder's grasp loosened, the Irishman twisted, struck out
once more, and disappeared into the darkness.

"After him!" Calder grunted, wheezing. "Find him, slit
his throat—damn ye, man, what d'ye mean by crying out
that way?"

"I'm sorry—'twas the shock—"

"Go on!" Calder ordered curtly. "He must be silenced."

When Calder was alone, he bent and laid a hand against
Alistair's neck. "Still alive," he muttered. "Worse luck."

He drew his dagger, then stiffened at the sound of footsteps and glanced nervously about the darkening courtyard. With sudden decision he righted the wheelbarrow,
heaved Alistair within, and with an armful of hay scraped
hastily from the ground, he covered the prone figure. Just
as the guard rounded the corner, Calder seized the handles
and started for the stable.

R onan *flattened himself against the wall and drew a*
gasping breath, casting a longing glance toward the
lighted window of the tower room. There was no time to
reach Deirdre now. He had to find Jemmy Kirallen and tell

him what should have been told this afternoon. If only he had spoken up at once! But he had not, and now there was no time to berate himself for his own stupid, incredulous folly. If he lived, there would be plenty of time to confess his part in this afternoon's tragedy. And if not . . . well, then there was no point in worrying about it.

Keeping to the shadows, he made his way around the walled courtyard to the doorway. There he stopped, listening hard, hearing nothing but the pounding of his heart.

At last the door opened and a man walked outside and yawned, looking at the stars. Ronan darted inside the doorway and glanced to either side. The hall was just before him and a corridor stretched to his right. As he hesitated, the guard walked back inside, and Ronan dove for the nearest patch of shadow.

Sweat ran into his eyes and he blinked hard, cursing steadily beneath his breath as the guardsman took up his station just inside the door. His eyes trained on the guardsman, Ronan drew a coin from the purse at his belt and threw it past him, into the doorway of the hall. It landed with a muffled clink, and the guard turned in that direction. The moment the man moved, Ronan ran headlong up the stairs toward Jemmy's chamber.

"*Sir Calder!*" the stable lad said, staring at the wheelbarrow. "What are ye doing here? Here, let me take that for ye."

"Nay!" Calder stretched his lips into a smile as he loosened the dagger in his belt. "I have it, lad. No need to trouble yourself."

"But—"

"Good even, sir," a deeper voice said, and Calder eased the dagger back into the scabbard. "Is there something amiss?"

"Nay, nay. All is well. Save for this!" He nodded toward the wheelbarrow and felt the sweat spring on his brow as he saw one booted foot protruding from the straw. "I tripped on it earlier, nearly broke my neck! I'll just leave it here."

"Ah." Sym, the head stable lad, nodded. "'Twas a kind thought. That dappled mare is foaling," he added to the younger man. "Could ye check on her?"

As the lad walked off, Calder leaned the wheelbarrow in a shadowed corner.

"Good night, then, sir," Sym said, holding his lantern high to light Calder's way to the door.

"Aye. Good night."

Calder stopped outside the door and leaned against it. He doubted Alistair would be waking anytime soon, but even if he did, what of it? Calder would deny everything, and nothing could be proved against him. The important thing, the only thing that mattered now, was to silence that damned harper.

But first he had to find him.

R onan crouched behind an arras in a small alcove, lis-tening as two men calmly discussed his murder.

". . . that Irishman," one was saying, a touch of scorn in his voice. "Once across the neck, that's what Calder said, and hide the body well."

Ronan laid a hand across his throat and grimaced as the second man answered in a low voice.

"Who knows?" the first man said with a laugh. "Perhaps Calder doesna care for his harping. Look sharp now," he added in a lower voice. "'Tis Sir Donal."

Peering cautiously around the edge of the arras, Ronan saw the red-haired knight walk down the passageway. He recognized him at once as one of Jemmy Kirallen's personal guard. Someone he could trust. But how to get word to him?

"All's quiet here, sir," one of Ronan's would-be assassins said respectfully.

"Good work."

Ronan thought rapidly. Two on two. It would be an even

fight. If only he could count on the red-haired knight to take his side! He would have one chance to speak, no more than that, and he had better find the right words.

But even as his muscles tensed for the leap, Sir Donal spoke again. "Have ye seen aught of young Fitzgerald, that Irish harper?" he added casually, his gaze moving over the passageway.

"Nay," the men answered just as casually. "No one has been by tonight."

"Keep an eye out for him," Donal said. "If he happens by, keep him here and send word to me."

The two guards turned to watch him go. Ronan did not hesitate. The moment their backs were turned, he slipped from behind the arras. But though he was swift and silent, they heard him. Two on one, it was then, on a mad flight down the stairway.

Ronan was fast, but they caught him just the same.

The chapel smelled of the roses piled high around the bier where three dozen banked candles shed their light over Gawyn Kirallen's lifeless form. He looked younger in death, Alyson thought, the harsh lines of pain and care smoothed from his waxen skin. But his expression was still very stern.

She sighed and touched the shoulder of the man kneeling before the coffin, dark head resting on his arms.

"Jemmy," she whispered. "'Tis late. Come to bed now."

Jemmy raised his head and stared at her with dark and shadowed eyes. "Alyson, love, what are you doing up?"

"Looking for you," she answered simply.

"Go to sleep. I'll bide here a while."

She lowered herself to kneel beside him. "Then I will stay with you. You shouldna be alone here. Oh, Jemmy, I am sorry."

"Don't," he said, twisting away as she stroked his hair. "Don't be sorry for me. I don't deserve your sympathy.

Christ's blood, I am such a fool," he added in a harsh whisper.

"What is it?" Alyson asked. "What is wrong?"

"'Tis Alistair," he answered on a groan. "He is gone."

"Gone? Nay, Jemmy, he's in confinement—until the trial—"

"There will be no trial." He dropped his head back on his arms. "I let him go. Indeed, I almost pushed him out the door! And now he has . . . just . . . disappeared and young Fitzgerald with him. I've had men searching the grounds all night. There is no trace of either of them."

"But how could you have let him go?" Alyson cried, then cast a guilty glance at the laird's still form. "Why?" she said in a whisper.

"Oh, sweeting, 'tis a long, long story. . . ."

Alyson stood and held out her hand. "Then you had best come to bed and tell me all about it." she said, forcing herself to smile reassuringly as he took her hand. "We'll sort it out together."

Alistair stopped at the foot of the tower stairs and leaned weakly against the wall, squeezing his eyes shut. A mistake, he realized as he staggered, nearly falling. But when he opened his eyes, he still saw two dim stairways stretching into darkness. Keeping one hand on the wall, he started up, concentrating on placing one foot before the other.

He knew dimly that he should find Jemmy, tell him something, but he had no idea what it was. The only coherent thought in his mind was that he needed Deirdre. Everything would be all right if he could only find her. What exactly was wrong, he could not remember, and he could not spare the energy to try. Whatever it was, Deirdre would sort it out. He could trust her, he knew that now, though he had no idea why he'd ever doubted her. Memory began and ended in this stairway. He had always been here, putting one foot in front of the other, forcing himself upward with each step.

Through the pounding of his head, he heard a distant clanking sound, but it took some time before he understood it was his sword bumping up each step as it trailed from his hand. He wondered hazily why he had drawn his sword, but there was no answer to that question. He could only imagine he'd had a reason at the time.

Up above a dog was barking. Finn, he thought, so relieved that he had to stop and lean heavily against the wall. He had begun to wonder if he was even in the right part of the manor, but now he knew he was. Finn was here. That meant Deirdre was here, as well. She would open the door any moment now, and he could fall into her arms and rest.

"Quiet, Finn!"

Deirdre's voice was the sweetest sound he'd ever heard. He forced himself to take another step, and from a great distance he heard his sword clatter down the steps behind him. But that was all right. He didn't need it now. Three more steps would bring him to the landing, and from there it was but two paces to the door.

He reached the top of the steps and stood swaying. "Deirdre!" he shouted with all his strength, but the word came out as a hoarse whisper, inaudible over the clamor Finn was making now. Alistair staggered forward and opened his mouth to try again, but before he could utter a word, a hand was clamped hard across his mouth and he was pulled half off his feet.

"Finn, be quiet!" Deirdre called. "What *is* all this about?"

The door opened a little way, but Alistair was pinned against the wall, his shouts muffled by the hand across his mouth. Through a small crack he could see Deirdre standing just inside, a candle in her hand. Her hair was tangled around her tearstained face, and she barely glanced down the stairway before turning back.

"What is wrong with you?" she scolded the dog. "There's nothing out there. Lie *down*, Finn. Quiet!"

Alistair twisted frantically, trying to call out, to kick the man behind him, and then suddenly he stilled. Deirdre could not help him now. If she was to even guess that he was here, it would bring her into danger. Bright spots danced before his eyes and he fought against them, holding on to consciousness with every ounce of his failing strength.

The door closed and she was gone. Finn flung his body against the wood, his paws scrabbling vainly as he howled.

"Ye led us quite a chase, but now we have ye," a voice said in Alistair's ear, and an agonizing pain pierced his skull.

Calder, Alistair thought, and for a single fleeting moment, before the darkness closed around him, he remembered everything.

"F inn, quiet!" *Deirdre ordered, her voice rough with* tears. "Lie down and be still."

The dog whined and pawed frantically at the door, then threw back his head and howled. But there was no one out there, Deirdre had seen that for herself. What was the matter with the dog?

Deirdre thought of Alistair, lying in his prison. Did Finn somehow sense that his master was to die tomorrow? She had heard of such things before.

"I know," she said, kneeling. "There's nothing you can do, Finn. Nothing anyone can do. Just lie down now, that's a good dog, and go to sleep."

But Finn was having none of it. After a time Deirdre stood and pulled the bolt, then opened the door a crack. "Go on, then," she said as Finn slipped through and scrambled down the stairs. "Go find him. Mayhap he'll be glad to see *you*."

She shut the door and leaned against it, hot tears slipping down her cheeks. She had tried and tried to see Alistair earlier, only to be turned away. Jemmy had been no help to her. He was in the chapel, holding a private vigil for his father, and could not be disturbed, nor could Alyson be found.

"If Sir Alistair wants ye, lady, he will send," the guard had said bluntly on Deirdre's third attempt. But Alistair had not sent.

If only she could hear from his own lips exactly how it had happened, perhaps she could believe he'd really done it. Yet he must have done. The evidence had been there before them all, and Alistair had not even denied it.

It must have happened suddenly, she thought. He surely had not planned it. But Master Kerian said Brodie was dead two hours before noon. What had Alistair been doing all that time? Had he just sat there, waiting, too stunned to attempt escape? Oh, if only she could see him once, if only she could hear his explanation. But he did not want to see her.

She remembered the way he'd looked at her when she rode up. There had been more than shock and sorrow in his eyes. There had been blame. And she knew that she had earned it.

It is my fault, she thought, groping her way blindly back to the bed. Whatever I touch, I spoil. If only she had not shown her fear so plainly, Alistair would never have been driven to such desperate measures to protect her. Now he was to pay for her weakness. Because of her, he had lost all claim to honor. Tomorrow he would lose his life.

If he hated her for that, it was no more than she did herself.

chapter 39

T here was a sort of desperate calm that came after all the tears were shed. Deirdre bathed her aching eyes and plaited her hair, dressed and walked down the stairway just in time to see the first light seeping over the trees. The courtyard was empty, the manor dark behind her. The light grew and still she stood, feeling nothing, thinking nothing, simply waiting for this wretched day to begin so she could move through each moment until it ended.

She heard the morning come, the clatter of the bucket going down into the well, the creak and groan of the rope as it was lifted. A cock crowed. The portcullis was raised with a rattle of loose chain. The servants spoke to one another in sleepy voices as they began the morning's work.

Just another day at Ravenspur. When it was done the sun would set, and tomorrow it would rise on the same scene. But the next time the sun rose, Alistair would be dead, hanged by the neck as any murderer must be.

"Mistress?"

Deirdre turned slowly toward a bent old man who

smiled and touched his cap. "I am looking for Sir Alistair Kirallen."

"Then it is well you came today," Deirdre answered, hearing her own voice coming from a great distance. "Tomorrow would have been too late."

The man looked at her strangely, then nodded. "Aye, well, then I'd best be off."

"He cannot see you," she said. "Not today."

"Oh." The man frowned and scratched his nose. "Well. Perhaps then I'd best see the laird."

"He is in the chapel," Deirdre said.

"I wouldna want to interrupt his prayers," the man said, frowning.

"You won't do that. He's dead."

The man stepped back, looking at her warily. Deirdre didn't blame him. She supposed she did sound mad.

"What is your business with Sir Alistair?" she asked. "Perhaps I can direct you."

"He ordered this," the man said cautiously. "I promised I'd see to it at once."

Deirdre stared at the bit of silver in the man's weathered palm, her eyes filling as she saw the sapphire set in the twisted band.

"A ring with a blue stone," she whispered.

"Aye, that's just what he said he wanted, blue to match a lady's eyes."

"'Tis mine."

He stepped back a pace, his fist closing over the ring. "And who might ye be?"

"Deirdre Maxwell."

"Oh! Aye, 'twas the name he said. Here, then, lady . . ."

She slipped the ring on her finger and stared at it. "He remembered. When did he speak for this?"

"Yesterday. Said he was in a hurry for it, so I—"

"Yesterday?" she interrupted. "What time yesterday?"

"'Twas fairly early when he come in," he said. "He took his time about the business and left a bit ere noon. Said he had an appointment he could not miss."

"He was with you?" she whispered. "All the morning?"

"Aye, he was."

"You must see Lord Jemmy!" she cried. "You must tell him! Do you understand me?"

"Aye, lady," he said, backing away. "I'll do that."

"No, wait," she urged, following him. "It is important. You cannot know how important—never mind, there's no time to explain it now, I will come with you."

"Dee!"

Deirdre looked around, startled, at the sound of Ronan's voice, but he was nowhere to be seen.

"I'll see him," the silversmith assured her as he hurried off. "Nay, lady," he added over his shoulder, "there's no need for ye to trouble yourself."

"But—"

"Dee!"

She whirled sharply and there was Ronan, just outside the gate, gesturing frantically. "Hurry!"

"Not now, Ronan," she snapped, keeping one eye on the silversmith. "I must go—"

"Nay, Dee, you won't help him that way. 'Tis too late."

"Too late for what?" she asked impatiently.

"Sir Alistair. He's gone—they took him out an hour ago, Sir Calder and another man. I think he was dead, Dee, but I'm not sure—"

"Dead? What are you talking about?" For the first time she looked at Ronan. His clothes were rumpled, his hair a wild tangle of leaves and stems, and dried blood masked one side of his face.

"What happened to you?"

"I'll explain on the way," Ronan said. "Hurry, Dee, get two horses and meet me out here. I daren't go inside. Later," he said urgently, cutting off her questions. "Do you want to find him or not? They've taken him, do you understand me? Hurry—bring horses—"

She turned and ran without another word.

chapter 40

❦

"Here," Calder said. "'Tis as good a place as any."
He jerked his horse to a halt beside the ruins of an ancient fortress and turned to the man beside him. "Is he dead?" he asked impatiently.

"I dinna think so," Kinnon Maxwell answered, glancing at the horse he led. Calder reached out and seized a handful of white-gold hair, jerking Alistair's head up.

"He looks it."

"Aye, but he moaned a bit before—"

"Then we'd best make sure."

Kinnon turned his face away as Calder raised his dagger. 'Twas a pity, he thought, that it had to come to this. He'd always rather liked Alistair. Then he shrugged philosophically. A bargain was a bargain, after all, and this one was worth the price. He was just thinking he'd have masses said for Alistair when his horse startled, nearly throwing him.

"What the—" Calder cried, holding up one arm to shield his eyes from a dark winged shape fluttering before his face.

Alistair's horse reared as another of the birds flew almost beneath its hooves, throwing its burden down the stony hillside. As Kinnon tried to get his own mount under control, he saw Alistair roll down the hillside and come to rest in a ditch.

"God's blood, what is this? Get off me—" he shouted, flailing wildly as one of the dark-winged shapes dived straight for his eyes. And then there was no more time for words, for his horse, and Calder's and Alistair's as well, all bolted headlong down the road.

It was some time before Calder and Kinnon controlled their panicked mounts and found the spot again. Alistair lay just as they had left him, his gray tunic almost invisible among the bracken.

"We'll just make sure," Calder said, dismounting and starting down the hillside. "Come on, man," he called, and reluctantly Kinnon followed, looking about him nervously.

He didn't like this. There was something strange about those corbies. Carrion birds, filthy, disgusting creatures they were even at the best of times, but these two had some madness in them. Kinnon had never heard of corbies attacking men and horses before—not living ones, at any rate.

As they reached the bottom of the hill, an enormous hound leaped up and came at them, hackles raised and teeth bared in a snarl.

"Get away!" Calder yelled, lashing out a booted foot and catching the dog full in the ribs. It yelped, sprawling awkwardly upon its back.

Kinnon cried out in disgust. The corbies were there before them, one perched on Alistair's chest, the other with its dark claws dug into his hair. Even as Kinnon watched in horrified fascination, one tore a bright strand loose.

"Leave him," he croaked to Calder. "Let's begone."

"Nay. We must be sure."

As Calder strode forward, the hound leaped at him, growling, and the birds flew at his face. He flung up an arm, stepped back and tripped, measuring his length upon the bracken.

"Forget him then!" he cried, scrambling to his feet. "We'll go. Come on, Kinnon—"

The two men fled up the hillside, mounted and galloped off.

"A*listair. Alistair, wake up.*"

"Go away," Alistair mumbled.

The voice went on, urgent, insistent. "Come on, man, get up."

"Oh, God, Ian, let me sleep."

"Later. Now ye must get up. Come on, Alistair, on your feet now."

Alistair stumbled to his feet and stood swaying dizzily. Every muscle in his body ached and his head pounded. He squinted open his eyes and groaned aloud.

"What were we doing last night?" he said thickly. "I canna remember."

"Aye, I know, but now ye must come with me. Come *on*, Alistair."

"All right, all right," Alistair said impatiently. "What's your hurry?"

"Ye have to get back to Ravenspur. Come on, that's right, one step and then another. They're waiting for Jemmy in the chapel."

"Who?" Alistair asked. He tried to focus on Ian, but the effort brought such sharp pain that he had to close his eyes again. "The tinkers?"

"Aye, that's it, the tinkers are waiting for him. Let's go now, Alistair. Ye can do it."

Alistair staggered like a drunken man up the slope. "Where am I? What's happening? Ian, wait. Tell me."

Ian stopped. The breeze ruffled the dark hair back from his brow and his eyes were very bright. "Ye have to get back to Ravenspur," he repeated. Alistair took another step, then dropped to his knees.

"Must rest a bit," he mumbled, wiping his stinging eyes. When he lowered his hand, he saw that it was wet with blood.

"Nay! Alistair, get up, damn ye! Ye lazy, useless bastard, what do ye think you're about here? Get on your feet, man!"

"Aye, all right, I hear ye, Ian. Stop shouting at me."

"That's better," Ian snapped, and though he sounded angry, his face was wrenched with pain. "Now walk."

Each step sent a bolt of white-hot agony through Alistair's entire body. "Ian," he said at last. "I thought—I dreamed—that ye were—"

"Dinna worry about that now," Ian said quickly. "It doesna matter. Just come along."

One step and then another. That was the way. After an eternity Alistair glanced up and saw Ravenspur spinning crazily in the distance. He caught his toe in a tuft of dried grass and went down. A soft rain began to fall, and he welcomed its coolness on his hot face, hardly aware that he was shivering convulsively.

"I ken you're weary," Ian said. "But ye canna lie here. Get up, now, and we'll get ye to your bed."

Alistair managed to open one eye, but he was incapable of speech. Ian stood looking down at him, and it seemed to Alistair that the rain fell all around him, but his hair and clothing were still dry. He raised his head and whistled sharply and two dark birds alighted on his shoulders. He spoke to them and they took off again.

"*You killed them?*" Deirdre asked in disbelief. "*Both of them?*"

Ronan, who was kneeling on the moor as he searched for tracks, cast her a quick look over his shoulder. "I don't know. I might have done. Sure and I didn't stay to inquire after their health! I was in a wee bit of a hurry at the time."

"But why were they chasing you in the first place? What—"

"Damnation," Ronan swore, ignoring her question as he straightened to peer across the empty moor, "we've lost them."

Deirdre lifted herself in the stirrups. "Alistair!" she cried. "Alistair, where are you? Can you hear me?"

The only answer was the wind whispering along the moor.

"Which way, Ronan?"

"How should I know?"

"You used to say that you could see things," she said bitterly. "Was it all a lie?"

"Nay, but—"

"How do you do it?" she shouted. "What do you need?"

"I don't know!" he cried. "It comes when it will, I cannot summon it—I don't know how—"

"Figure it out," she snapped.

"All right, Dee. I'll try. Do you have something that belongs to him? Even something he handled—"

"Aye." She wrenched the ring from her finger and gave it to him. "Ronan, hurry—"

He closed his hand about the bit of silver. "He was thinking of you when he held it," Ronan said. His eyes were wide, and the wind blew dark strands of hair about his face. "He was remembering . . . something you had said about a ring . . . and thinking that you would smile when he gave it to you. . . . He loves you," Ronan said, surprised. "He was thinking that in spite of everything, he would ask you to marry him. . . ."

He sighed and relaxed his hand. "There's nothing else."

"There must be." Deirdre shook her head frantically. "There has to be. Try again. I don't care—oh, nay," she whispered, a thrill of fear racing down her neck. "Nay."

"What is it?"

"Look," she said, her voice high and thin with terror. "Up there. Do you see? Oh, sweet St. Brigid, Ronan, 'tis them, the corbies—do you see them?"

"Of course I do. But what—"

"We're too late—I know it—" she called over her shoulder, already racing after the birds.

She found Alistair lying on his back, one hand outstretched, the rain falling on his upturned face. Finn lay beside him, whimpering. Deirdre fell to her knees and touched his brow.

"Alistair? Alistair, wake up, love, open your eyes—"

Alistair's lids fluttered open. His eyes were dazed, but they fastened on Deirdre's face with desperate hunger. "Dee. Are ye real?"

She bent close to catch his words, and her hair brushed his face. He caught the scent of it and wished he had the strength to raise his arms.

"Aye. I'm here. Nay," she ordered sharply as he stirred. "Lie back. I'll send for help."

"Nay. You help me."

She slipped an arm beneath his neck, catching him as he fell back. "Please, Alistair, lie still."

"Aye. I canna do it. I'm sorry, Ian," he mumbled, and Deirdre and Ronan exchanged frightened glances.

"Ye must." Ian stood behind the two kneeling forms, arms crossed across his chest. "Get up, Alistair. Ye can and ye will. She needs ye now, as does your son."

"I have no son. . . ."

"Nor will ye if ye do not shift yourself right now. She will die," he said, nodding toward Deirdre. "Today. And your child with her."

Alistair raised his head and stared past Deirdre. "Is it true?"

"Aye. Now get up and get back to Ravenspur."

Deirdre put her hands on Alistair's shoulders as he tried to lift himself. "Stop!" she cried. "You mustn't move—"

"Aye, I must. Get me on the horse." He forced his aching eyes toward Ronan. "Ye do it, Fitzgerald—and we'll call it quits between us."

Ronan nodded. "I'll do it."

"Ronan, you can't! He's raving, don't you see that? Get back and bring a litter—"

"Quiet, Dee," Ronan ordered. "Do as he says."

"Deirdre," Alistair said. "Help me. Please."

The desperation in Alistair's last word decided her. "It will be the death of you," she said, but even as she spoke she was putting one shoulder beneath his. He clamped his teeth into his lip as she and Ronan half carried him to the horse.

"He cannot ride," Deirdre protested.

"I can."

She watched through a blur of tears as he slowly climbed into the saddle. "Get up behind me," he said carefully. "Dinna let me fall."

The ride to Ravenspur passed like a dark dream as Alistair swam in and out of consciousness. When he opened his eyes he saw Ian walking beside the horse. The corbies fluttered behind his head.

"Damned birds," Alistair muttered. "Waiting for their meal."

"What birds?" Ronan asked.

"Don't ask," Deirdre said grimly. "You don't want to know."

Ian grinned. "They aren't going to eat ye. That was just for show."

He held up his hands and the birds flew over to him. As they landed, their wings shimmered, changed, and Ian was holding two white doves.

"I meant them for the best," Ian said, sounding faintly apologetic. "But ye would not see it. Ye kept believing they were a portent of your death."

"Twa corbies. Ye ken the song."

Ronan cocked his head. "'The Twa Corbies'? Aye, I know it, but I don't often play it. Too grisly. Though it does have a rather striking melody . . . and that passage at the end—quite haunting, if you can catch the sound of wind blowing over bones. . . ."

"I'd never listened to every word of the damned song, had I?" Ian said defensively. "God's teeth, Alistair, d'ye always have to take everything so literally?"

"Me?" Alistair's laughter was a harsh whisper of a sound. "Oh, 'tis my fault now!"

"Alistair, are you all right?" Deirdre asked, concerned.

"Aye," he said, leaning back against her, feeling the warmth of her through his sodden tunic. "Just hold me."

"The corbies were for your own good," Ian said. "That tower in your vision, Alistair—that was a real place, as ye should know. 'Twas where ye had been living since Darnley struck me down. I sent the corbies after ye to watch over ye, to guide ye. . . ."

"Where?" Alistair mumbled.

"To Deirdre, ye fool! When ye met her in the forest, they were there, weren't they? And ye decided to go with her, did ye no? And why? Because ye saw that life is all too short to waste. Ye needed to see that, Alistair, and I couldna rest until ye did. How do ye think I felt, watching ye pine and suffer for a thing that was my fault, not yours. I had to do *something*!"

Alistair simply looked at him.

"'Twas a good idea," Ian protested. "As far as it went. But I'm afraid those damned corbies caused all sorts of trouble. They set your mind in a certain pattern—oh, I canna explain it in words, but once ye got the idea that ye were about to die, everything shifted a bit—not only you but all around ye. Thoughts are verra real," he added. "I didna ken how powerful they can be."

"Another half-baked plan," Alistair muttered. "Typical!"

Deirdre tightened her arms around him. "Ronan, we must stop. He can't go on like this—he's out of his senses—"

"'Tis not entirely my fault," Ian said, stung. "If not for your fears and your thrice-damned sense of honor, ye would have wed Deirdre long ago. But no, ye would never do anything so simple. Ye always had to twist things up into such a muddle, even ye couldna make sense of it!"

"Alistair," Ronan said. "Look at me. Can you hear me?"

Fitzgerald looked terrible, Alistair thought, dark hair plastered around his ashen face, one eye swollen almost shut and a long gash across his brow.

"Aye, Fitzgerald. I hear ye."

"Who are you talking to?"

"Ian," Alistair replied. "Ye canna see him. But he is there."

"Oh, my God," Deirdre breathed. "Ronan, we cannot go on, we have to stop right now."

"'Tis all right," Ronan said unexpectedly. "There *is* something there—look at the dog!"

Finn was walking stiff-legged beside Deirdre's horse, staring at Ian with hackles raised.

"Off with ye, hound!" Ian cried suddenly, waving his arms. The dog yelped, then ran to the other side of Ronan's horse. Ian laughed.

"Holy St. Brigid, what is it?" Deirdre whispered, clutching Alistair tightly against her as she stared wide-eyed at the space beside her horse.

"'Tis Ian," Alistair said, shooting Ian a withering glance. "Thinks he's amusing."

"Don't worry, Dee," Ronan told her. "If Alistair says to keep going, that's what we must do."

"Not a bad sort, Fitzgerald," Ian remarked. "Young, but he'll get over that. As for your Deirdre—" He sighed dramatically. "If only I were still alive . . . But then again, perhaps 'tis just as well. 'Twould seem her heart is set."

Alistair gathered all his courage into a single question. "Will I see my son?"

Behind him, Deirdre stiffened and leaned forward to look into his face. Alistair tried to smile reassuringly, but from the expression on her face, he didn't think he'd managed very well. "Hold on, lass," he whispered. "Nearly there. Dinna let go of me."

Ian frowned, staring up into the rain. "I would tell ye if I could. But that knowledge wasna given to me. Ye may have fifty years or ye may be dead by sunset. All I know

is that if Jemmy walks into that chapel . . ." He shuddered.

"What?" Alistair asked. "What will happen?"

"This thing between Darnley and Kirallen—'tis old, Alistair, older than either of our families, something that has
always been here, waiting. . . . It takes men—aye, and
women, too—and turns them to its purpose. We've all
been touched by it, me and you and my poor father—all
but Jemmy. He saw it when he was a bairn and ran like
hell. Verra sensible of him, too," he said approvingly.
"Now for some reason it canna get ahold of him. Not like
us. D'ye ken what I am saying?" he asked, peering sharply
into Alistair's face.

"Aye. Vengeance."

"Aye," Ian said. "'Tis an evil thing. Jemmy doesna feel
it as we do. And that lady he wed—she's a bonny thing, is
she no? Seen from here, she burns like fire. The two of
them together are a powerful force. And today, should they
be vanquished—" He shuddered again. "The evil will be
free again, stronger than before. What happened after
Stephen died is nothing compared to what will happen
now. Malcolm will try, but he will no be able to stand long.
'Twill go on for years and years, until the last Kirallen is
dead. And then it will find others."

He looked into Alistair's face. "'Tis a heavy burden, Alistair, I ken that, but there's no help for it. Ye are the only
one to stop it. Jemmy canna rule without ye."

Alistair groaned aloud. "Enough," he said. "I canna
think anymore."

Deirdre halted the horse. "Aye, 'tis enough." She nodded quickly. "Ronan, help me get him down—"

"Nay!" Alistair said firmly. "Go on."

"Just one thing more," Ian said. "I'll no have another
chance. If ye make it through today, ye must let Darnley
go. He'll be taken care of. Dinna fash yourself about him."
He frowned, then added, "Unless . . . ye may still have part
to play in that. If a woman should come to ye and ask

something in my name—then ye must do it. Will ye remember that?"

Alistair sagged forward, saved from falling only by the
strength of Deirdre's arms.

"Hold on," he tried to say, but his lips were too numb to
form the syllables. He tried again and this time the words
were clearer. "Hurry. Get me home."

A listair fell to his knees on the cobblestones when he
dismounted. At his order Deirdre and Ronan hauled
him up, and they walked together toward the chapel.

Ian was gone, if indeed he had ever been there. Alistair
wasn't sure of anything anymore. He only knew he had to
reach the chapel. But halfway across the courtyard, he
staggered and went down.

"Pick him up, Dee," Ronan urged. "Hurry."

"Nay! I will not do this. He's hurt, Ronan, he's been raving all the way back here—why do you insist on acting as
though he's making sense?"

"Because something is wrong. And he's the only one
who knows what it is. Now lift him up and put him on his
feet."

Alistair heard their voices from a great distance, felt
them dragging his weightless body to its feet. And then all
at once, Alistair was standing on the other side of the drawbridge, a chill wind whipping in his face. Mist was rising
from the hollows of the ground. Ian sat on his own horse
looking down at Alistair with a grin.

"I canna waste the morning waiting for ye," he said. "Ye
can catch us—and hurry, man. Try not to miss all the fun."

"Wait!" Alistair cried. "Don't go!"

He began to run, and then he was in the forest again, Ian
racing along the path ahead. "Wait!" he cried, his voice no
more than a whisper. "Don't go. 'Tis a trap."

He rounded the corner of the path and skidded to a stop.
The forest was gone. The corridor of Ravenspur stretched
before him, an endless expanse of gray walls and flag-

stone. At the far end a group of people walked slowly toward the chapel. The door began to open, and a sliver of golden light spilled from within. A cloud of incense rolled into the corridor, and the plainsong of the priests drifted eerily down its shadowed length. At the head of the procession, a dark head rose above the rest.

"Ian—" Alistair began, then stopped and pressed his palms against his temples. Past and present stood side by side, clashed and mingled and became one terrible moment that seemed to stretch into eternity.

D eirdre came breathless to Alistair's side, fearing he had reached the limit of his strength. But even as she reached for him, his hands dropped from his head and he started forward at a run.

"Jemmy, wait!" he shouted. "Don't go in there! 'Tis a trap!"

Jemmy looked back over his shoulder, eyes narrowed as he took in Alistair's muddy, blood-smeared form, eyes burning with a wild light.

"Move," Alistair said in a harsh whisper that only Deirdre, just beside him, heard. "Oh, God, not again—Jemmy, *move*!"

He *is* mad, Deirdre thought, and it is my fault, I brought him here—

Jemmy dropped into a wary crouch, one hand sweeping the dagger from his belt, as with the other arm he pushed Alyson behind him.

The line of mourners was thrown into confusion as Jemmy shouted for his guard. Alistair turned to one of the men. "Your sword," he ordered, and when the man hesitated, he struck him across the face and tore the weapon from his hand with the terrible strength of madness. Deirdre ran after him, calling to Ronan over her shoulder.

"Ronan, help me—stop him—"

Even as they drew even with Alistair, the chapel door flew open and crashed against the wall.

Men rushed screaming from the chapel, weapons drawn. Jemmy had his sword out now, was slashing furiously as he tried to get Alyson to safety. And then Sir Donal was there, his brother just beside him, while the others jostled the panic-stricken men and ladies out of the way.

Deirdre hit the wall hard as Jemmy's guard rushed past her. But they were cut off from him, and he was trapped on the far end of the passageway with only a handful of his closest men.

Alistair walked steadily through the screaming and confusion, looking neither right nor left. A man rushed at him, and Alistair cut him down without pausing. Deirdre watched him, hands pressed against her mouth, as he went on, step after relentless step, making straight for Jemmy.

She looked wildly about for Ronan and saw him in the midst of the fray. He had found a sword and was cutting his way toward the chapel door. Malcolm and Haddon Darnley stood just beside the frame, daggers clutched in shaking hands, Alyson between them. Jemmy stood before his wife, his nephew and his fosterling, shielding them with his body as he fought two men at once.

Jemmy's foot slipped in a patch of blood; he nearly went down, but recovered himself at the last moment, driving upward with his dagger as he straightened. One man fell, but the other redoubled his attack. And Jemmy had been forced from his position, leaving Alyson and the two boys in the open and his own back undefended.

Sir Calder moved with lightning speed to take Jemmy from behind. Deirdre's cry of warning was lost in the confusion. She watched in helpless horror as Sir Calder's sword rose, began its swift descent—and was halted inches from Jemmy's shoulder with a clash of steel on steel.

Calder's face contorted into a mask of fury as he glared down at this new opponent. Alistair retreated a step, his back just touching Jemmy's, and chanced a quick glance over one shoulder, meeting his kinsman's startled gaze. As Jemmy turned back, Deirdre saw the fierce grin flash across his features.

Deirdre let out a sobbing breath of mingled terror and relief. Not a traitor, she thought dizzily. He's not and never has been. How could I have doubted?

Calder towered over Alistair, face flushed and lips drawn back into a snarl. Alistair looked up at him with eyes like chips of ice. His first feint was a sideways slash that Calder caught easily on his sword, twisting his weapon to knock the sword from Alistair's hands. Alistair disengaged before the movement was complete and came at him from the other side, all done in one single, graceful movement that took Calder by surprise. The dark-bearded knight blocked the blow, but only barely, and the edge of Alistair's sword caught him on the upper arm.

Calder leaped back, planted both feet squarely on the floor, and attacked with a rain of heavy blows. Alistair fended him off, though Deirdre could not make out how he did it, for his blade hardly seemed to move. Yet as the encounter wore on, he began to tire. Even Deirdre could see that much.

Alistair was leaning openly against Jemmy now. He blinked and shook his head, as though blinded by the sweat streaming down his face. Calder began to smile; he increased the force of his blows, and Alistair seemed just a bit slower; his blade was sagging, and after one terrible slash that he barely managed to deflect, he staggered and went down upon one knee.

This was obviously the chance Calder had been waiting for. He bent down, sword raised—and Alistair, with a cry that tore through the sounds of combat, leaped up to meet him with a two-handed sweep of his blade.

Deirdre turned away, retching, as the black-bearded head flew from the brawny shoulders in a fountain of bright blood. When she looked again, Calder had fallen to the stone floor. Alistair was nowhere to be seen.

At that moment the door burst open behind her and a crowd of men rushed in; not knights, Deirdre saw, but stable lads, farmers, and drovers by their dress, and the weapons they wielded were the tools of their trade: scythes and cleavers and pitchforks.

"A Kirallen!" they screamed, streaming into the passageway, cutting a path that Deirdre followed. She ran unheeding through the fray, and at last reached the farthest end of the passage. Jemmy had flung open the chapel door and was guarding it as Alyson was helped inside. She looked dazed and sick as she stumbled between Malcolm and Haddon, each of them holding her by one arm.

"Lady Maxwell!" Jemmy shouted. "Get inside."

Deirdre ignored him, her attention fixed on the bodies littering the floor. Her glance passed over one of the red-haired twins—Donal or Conal, she didn't know which—continued past a dozen other men, most of them in Maxwell's plaid, and fixed at last on a spill of bright gold against the flagstones.

A hand jerked her roughly by the arm. "Inside," Jemmy snapped, nodding toward the chapel door.

"Nay!" Deirdre shook him off and dropped to her knees, pushing at the headless body of Sir Calder. At last she succeeded in rolling him over and looked down into Alistair's face.

"Help him!" she cried, turning to look at Jemmy. But Jemmy was already gone, engaged in another fight. She seized Alistair by the arm and began to drag him toward the chapel door. When at last she reached it, she found that it was shut fast, bolted from within.

"Open!" she cried, pounding her fists against the wood. "Alyson—Malcolm, open the door!"

There was no answer. She sank down against the door and drew Alistair's head into her lap, bending over him to shield him with her body as the fighting swept around them.

Someone stumbled over them with a curse, and a booted foot struck Deirdre's cheek hard enough to flood her eyes with tears. The door jerked open, and she felt strong hands beneath her arms, tugging her backward. She tightened her grip on Alistair and they were dragged together back into the chapel. The moment they were inside, the door slammed shut again.

Deirdre could still hear the battle going on, but it was muffled now as though it came from far away. She could hear the harsh sound of Malcolm's breathing as the boy knelt beside her.

"Lady Maxwell," he said. "Are ye hurt?"

She shook her head and smoothed the matted hair away from Alistair's brow, staring down at his still face. Beneath the blood spattering his face, his skin was white as marble, the lashes lying dark and thick against his cheeks. He looked very peaceful, she thought, very young.

"Is he . . . ?" Malcolm gulped and swallowed hard. He reached out a shaking hand and laid it against Alistair's neck, just below the ear. "Thank the Lord."

Deirdre raised her head and looked at him, uncomprehending.

"He lives, lady," Malcolm said. "Here—feel—"

She pressed her fingers to his neck, found the pulse beating quick and light beneath his skin.

Slowly, very slowly, the sounds of battle faded. All that was left were the groans of the wounded and the weeping of the women. Deirdre sat, Alistair's head cradled in her lap, Malcolm moving restlessly between her and Alyson, who was kneeling with two priests on the far side of the chapel. As Deirdre caught their words, she realized they were administering the last rites.

"The chapel guard," Malcolm said in answer to Deirdre's question. "Some of them might live. The others—" His eyes filled and he looked away.

Deirdre bent her head and closed her eyes.

At last the chapel door opened, and Jemmy hurried in, going immediately to his wife and lifting her in his arms.

"Oh, Jemmy!" Alyson cried, throwing her arms around his neck. "I'm fine," she added quickly. "Let me down, I'm fine—but what of you?"

He looked almost too weary to stand, but he smiled. "I am well enough. For now."

Alyson looked as though she might protest, but then Jemmy added quietly, "There are . . . others who need help."

She nodded. "Aye. Of course. Come to me, then, when you can."

Jemmy knelt beside Alistair, his expression grim. "Lady," he said, looking up at Deirdre. "Is he . . . ?"

"Nay."

Jemmy smoothed a strand of blood-soaked hair from Alistair's brow, looking long into his kinsman's battered face. "Where did he come from, earlier?"

"Calder took him last night," Deirdre answered dully. "He left him for dead."

"But you found him."

"Ronan helped me. Where is Ronan?" she asked, looking dazedly about. "He left me—when we first arrived—"

Jemmy touched her hand. "He is being seen to."

"Why? What happened to him?"

"Alyson is going to him now," Jemmy said. "He—oh, lady, he has earned our gratitude today. Whatever can be done for him, she will do."

Deirdre bent her head and shut her eyes, willing back the tears. When she looked up again, she met Jemmy's gaze and understood that Ronan was but one of many he must worry about now.

"Were the losses very heavy?" she asked, knowing already what the answer was.

"Aye. But not so heavy as they would have been without Alistair."

"I thought—you would not heed him," Deirdre sobbed. "I thought—"

"I know. But 'twas never true. All was said and done for my sake."

Alistair's lids fluttered and he looked up at her.

"Dinna cry, lass," he murmured. "Deirdre, dinna—"

His gaze wandered, then fixed on Malcolm. "Jemmy," he said clearly. "Always. D'ye ken?"

"Aye, Alistair. I do now. Why did ye no tell me?" Malcolm cried.

"He could not," Jemmy said. "Nor could I."

Alistair turned his gaze to Deirdre. "Oh, love, dinna cry," he said tenderly. "'Tis all right. We did it. 'Ware, now, I'm bleeding on ye."

"You can buy me a new gown," Deirdre said, her tears splashing on his face.

"Aye." His eyes fell shut. The dark lashes fluttered, as though he struggled to open them, and his voice was only a whisper when he spoke again. "Shall we go to Donegal now?"

"Aye," Deirdre said fiercely. "My father will want to meet the man I wed. For we *will* wed, Alistair. Don't even *think* you can get out of it by dying on me now."

His eyes did open then, only for a moment. "Oh, no, Your Highness." The ghost of a smile passed across his pale lips. "I wouldna dare to try."

chapter 41

Snow was coming, Alistair thought as he walked across the courtyard. Not tonight, but soon. He stopped outside the tower door, the cold wind snapping at the edges of his cloak. He drew a deep breath and studied the frosty stars. The sounds of merriment still drifted from the hall, drunken voices bawling out the words of a particularly bawdy song.

He smiled and went lightly up the winding steps. By the time he reached the top, there was no need to knock, for Finn had already alerted Deirdre to his arrival.

"What are you doing here?" she asked, standing back to let him in. "I thought you'd still be down there."

"The noise was making my head ache."

"Just the noise?" she asked, lifting one dark brow.

"And the wine, as well," he admitted. He wasn't drunk, but he was not exactly sober, either, and now that his head had cleared a bit, he realized he was feeling very fine, indeed.

And why should he not? Today Jemmy had been proclaimed laird of the Kirallen clan, and every man among them had sworn his oath to him.

It had been a fine day altogether, Alistair mused. But tomorrow would be finer still.

"Why are you not abed, lass?" he asked, pinching Deirdre's cheek. "You'll want to be fresh and rested for your wedding day!"

"I was," she answered. "Until you woke me."

"Did I?" He took a step forward and held out his arms. "God's blood, ye are beautiful tonight," he murmured against her hair. "Just like a flower, all soft and rosy with sleep—"

She skipped back. "*Tomorrow* is our wedding night. You must wait."

"I am not sure I can. . . . Oh, fine then," he grumbled as she laughed and slapped his hand. "I suppose one more night willna kill me. Though it feels as though it might," he muttered.

When she smiled, the effect was more dizzying than the wine he'd drunk. "But I didna come here to woo ye—or not only for that. I wanted to bring ye this."

As she took the parcel from his hand, Alistair was riveted by the way her hair spilled over her shoulder, cascading like a rope of black silk across the gentle swell of her breast.

"What is it?" she said curiously, turning the flat package in her hands.

He dragged his gaze to her face. "Open it and see."

She sat down on the bed and undid the string, pulling forth a bundle of yellowed parchments. Frowning, she tipped them toward the candle's light and read the cramped writing. Her dark brows lifted and her lips parted in astonishment.

"Who sent this?"

"Kinnon Maxwell," Alistair answered. "A wedding gift of sorts."

"Blood money is more like it," Deirdre said, folding the

parchment with a grimace and tossing it aside. "Does Kinnon think this will make up for what he did?"

"Ah, but Kinnon says he has done nothing!" Alistair said, his eyes moving over the rumpled bed with longing. "Claims he knew naught of what happened here, that it was a plan Calder and some renegade Maxwells brewed. Says he was shocked to hear of it."

Deirdre gave a delicate snort. "He expects us to believe that? Why, he was there with Calder when they carried you off! Ronan said—"

"Ronan *said* there was a man in Maxwell plaid who might—not *was,* Deirdre, but *might*—have been Kinnon." Alistair shrugged. "And I canna say myself what happened that night."

"You still don't remember any of it?" Deirdre asked.

Alistair frowned as he tried again to recall the events of that strange and terrible day three weeks ago. "Bits and pieces," he said at last. "Naught that makes much sense."

He sat down on the bed beside her and reached for her thick braid, feeling the glossy hair slide between his fingers. He brought it up and set it to his lips.

"Kinnon sent Jemmy a fine destrier, as well," he told her, "A gift to the new laird, his 'trusted friend and ally.'"

"He has more nerve than I gave him credit for!" Deirdre said, whipping her braid from between his fingers. "Jemmy did not take it, did he?"

"Aye, he did."

"But—"

"If he refused, it would have made for bitterness between us and the Maxwells, maybe even come to war. So he accepted. And so should ye, Deirdre. 'Tis what was agreed upon when ye wed Brodie."

"I don't want it," Deirdre said tightly. "I don't want anything of theirs."

Her face had taken on the strained look it always wore when Brodie's name was mentioned. Alistair sighed, almost wishing he had left this for another day. He couldn't have done that, though. Deirdre had the right to know she was a wealthy woman now. But if he had thought the knowledge would please her, he'd been very much mistaken.

"But you think we should keep it," she said. "Why? What do you intend to do with it?"

"'Tis for ye to say."

"Really?" she asked coolly. "Then I shall give it to Maeve."

"A fine idea," Alistair said at once. Relieved to have the matter settled, he slipped his arm around her.

"You don't mind?"

"Why should I?" he said, bending to kiss her neck.

"Have you forgotten that as of tomorrow, by law, what is mine is yours?"

"Oh, so that's it, is it?" He squeezed her close against him. "Take Maxwell's gold and give it to Maeve—or throw it down the well for all I care. 'Tis yours, and I want no part of it. What is ours will belong to both of us together." He hesitated, then looked her in the eye. "Deirdre, I am not Brodie Maxwell."

She looked away, her face reddening. "I know that."

"Nay, ye dinna. Not really."

He drew her against his chest, and she wrapped her arms around him, burying her face in his shoulder. "'Tis all right, love," he said, rubbing her tight shoulders, letting his hands drift down her back. "I dinna expect ye to trust me all at once. I ken it will take time."

"I do trust you," she said, her voice muffled against his shoulder. "I *do*."

"One thing at a time," he murmured. "That's the way. I canna promise we'll never disagree, but I do promise we'll sort it out together." He felt her body soften as she relaxed against him. "It will all be well. You'll see. So long as we're together."

"Oh, I do love you, Alistair," she said, her arms tightening around him.

He smiled. "Whisht, I know that. Why else would ye

agree to stay in Scotland, when ye have told me so often
what a wretched place it is!"

"Not so wretched now," she murmured. "I've grown . . .
quite fond of it lately."

"We'll go to Donegal next spring," he said, unwinding
her braid. "I promise. Ye can show me every inch of it.
We'll stay as long as ye like—"

"We mustn't stay too long." She raised her head and
gave him a brilliant smile. "Jemmy cannot do without you
now."

"Hmph."

"'Tis true! You know it is. Earlier, at the oath-taking,
when he raised you up and set you just beside him—oh,
Alistair, I was so proud! And so was Maeve! The way they
all cheered . . ."

Alistair felt the heat rise to his face. That had been a fine
moment, him and Malcolm on either side of Jemmy, seated
in the laird's great chair. As Alistair stepped into place, the
shouts of approval echoed to the rafters. He remembered
Malcolm's flashing smile, Jemmy looking up at him, a momentary uncertainty passing quickly across his face.

Alistair had seized a goblet of wine and raised it high.
"To the laird!" he cried. "Long may he rule!"

Then the shouts rang out again as he drank and dropped
to one knee, offering the goblet to Jemmy.

"Thank you," Jemmy said, taking it from his hand. And
when their eyes met, any doubts either of them might have
had vanished for all time. As Alistair straightened and
stepped to one side, hand laid on the hilt of his sword, he
had no regrets. They were both exactly where they belonged.

But sweet as it had been, the finest part had come when
he looked up into the gallery to see Deirdre leaning on the
railing with Maeve beside her, knowing that tomorrow
they would truly be a family.

He looked at Deirdre now and felt the breath catch in his
throat. She was so beautiful tonight, her eyes glowing and

her cheeks stained with fresh color. My faerie lady, he thought. My love.

She smiled and lay back against the pillows, holding out her arms. His eyes locked with hers, he unfastened his cloak and let it fall to the floor, then kicked off his boots and pulled the velvet tunic over his head. Still tangled in its folds, he grinned, feeling her hands tugging impatiently at the fastenings of his trews.

When he slipped naked into bed beside her, she turned to him, her warmth enfolding him as he took her in his arms. He kissed her long and deeply, feeling her heart pounding against his chest in rhythm with his own. But that was only right. She was a part of him now—or had she always been? He did not know, nor did it matter, for she was his and he was hers . . . and tomorrow all the world would know it.

He drew back and stroked the hair from her brow, seeing his own wondering joy reflected in the depths of her sapphire eyes.

"Oh, Alistair, I'm so happy. . . . I never thought to feel like this. Tell me it is real," she whispered, her voice shaking. "Say I am not dreaming."

"Oh, no, lady, this is *my* dream, not yours!" She laughed and he bent to her again, his lips just brushing hers. "And a verra pleasant one it's turning out to be."

chapter 42

"Ronan, you would try the patience of a saint!" Alyson said, exasperated. "The start of winter is no time to be setting off. Stay at least until the spring!"

"I thank you, but no," he answered firmly, fumbling with his pack. He muttered an impatient curse, glaring down at his all-but-useless left hand.

Alyson stood in the doorway of his chamber, watching him struggle with the ordinary task of tying a single knot. Though she longed to do it for him, she did not offer any help.

He managed it at last and picked up the piece of wood he carried always now, squeezing his weak fingers around it.

But getting stronger, Alyson reminded herself. Ten days ago he could not move his hand at all.

"Do you have the letter for Sir Robert?" she asked, and he patted his pack.

"I do."

"He will be glad to meet you," she said, smiling a little.

"Remind him to sing you the ballad he made when he last visited us. I think you will be amused."

"I look forward to it."

He spoke politely, but she knew it was a lie. Ronan did not look forward to anything these days. But at least he had made it through Deirdre's wedding, even managing to smile as he kissed her cheek and shook Alistair's hand. That he had been dead drunk when he did it was known only to Alyson and Jemmy, who had devoted himself—quite against Alyson's wishes—to keeping Ronan well fortified with ale throughout the day.

Alyson had expected Ronan to sleep the clock around, given all he had drunk the day before. But he had been up at dawn, a bit pale but still quite determined to be gone.

"Come in, lady," he said now. "You make me jumpy hovering in the doorway! No, don't try to lift that," he added sharply, taking the pack from her hand. "Sit down here—you should have a care for the babe."

"The babe will do quite well," she answered, though she did as he bade her, sinking down on the edge of the bed with a sigh. "If not for you, it would be dead, and its mother with it."

He gave a half-shrug and looked uncomfortable, as he always did when she tried to thank him for what he had done for her that terrible day outside the chapel.

"'Tis a long way to London," she said. "Do you have enough for food and lodging?"

"I can still sing, lady," Ronan answered. "And soon I will play again, as well."

She bit her lip and looked down at his harp. "Aye. But," she added tactfully, "it may be some time before you're healed enough for that."

If ever. But if Ronan heard the words she could not speak, he ignored them. That was a possibility he refused absolutely to consider.

"Oh, Ronan, will you not stay a bit longer?" she pleaded. "Give yourself a chance to mend!"

He shouldered his pack and picked up the harp. "Nay, lady. I cannot." His head bent, he ran his fingers across the strings, producing a plaintive little air.

"I need time. I *am* happy for Dee." He glanced at Alyson and smiled wryly. "At least I'm trying to be. But 'twill be a good bit easier when there is some distance between us." He stared down at the harp, then burst out bitterly, "I feel enough of a fool as it is. All those years—loving her—and it was all a waste, for nothing!"

Alyson clenched her hands together, wondering what to say. At last she decided that no words of hers could make things worse—or better—for him. She might as well tell him what she really thought.

"Love is never wasted," she said firmly. "Think, Ronan, it was your love for Deirdre that helped her survive all those years with Brodie Maxwell. Was that a waste?"

"Well, no, if you put it like that—"

"And even if you did not get what you wanted—or what you thought you wanted—can you really say she gave you nothing?"

"Nay, I cannot say that," he said at last.

She nodded, pleased he could admit that much. It was a beginning.

"You have the right of it, you know," she said. "Much as I hate to say it. You *do* need time. But use it well. And remember, if you need anything—anything at all—you only have to send to us. Or better still, come yourself. Jemmy and I had hoped you would stand godfather for the babe," she added, and he glanced at her, surprised.

"There's no need for that," he said gruffly.

"'Tis custom for a babe to have one," she said lightly. "And who better than you? It willna be here until spring. Perhaps, by then, you'll feel differently."

"Perhaps. Though I would not like to promise . . ."

"No need for that. If you come, we will be glad to see you." She stood and hugged him quickly. "Any time, Ronan. You will always find a welcome here."

• • •

The morning was cool and bright, more like April than November. As Ravenspur faded into the distance, Ronan's heavy heart lifted a bit, and he felt the first faint stir of excitement he usually experienced when setting off on a journey.

By mid-morning he reached the cleft in the hills Alistair had described to him two days before. Ronan had not been able to find a polite way of refusing the favor Alistair asked, and now he must stop and deliver sundry gifts to an old man who dwelt here. With an impatient sigh, he turned his horse's head and cantered up the slope.

At least his errand would not delay him long, he thought with relief as he spotted the bent figure standing on the crest.

"Good day to you, Grandfather," Ronan called. "I bring you gifts from Ravenspur."

"From Alistair?" The old man's voice was surprisingly strong, deep and rich and musical. "So he remembered. Let us see what he sent me."

Yet he made no move to unpack the saddlebag Ronan laid at his feet. He stood leaning on his staff, thick white locks blowing about his high brow, dark eyes fixed on Ronan's face.

"I am Fergus of the clan McInnes."

Ronan bowed politely. "Ronan Fitzgerald, at your service."

"Fitzgerald, is it? Now, that's a fine Norman name on an Irish tongue! Which one might ye be?"

Once, not too many years ago, Ronan could have answered easily. "I am Irish," he would have said, and he would have laughed that anyone thought it necessary to ask. But that was before King Edward had issued his Statute of Kilkenny, declaring that his "wild Irish" lords needed to be brought to heel.

Its purpose had been to remind the Normans of their glorious heritage, lest they begin to mingle too freely with their Irish neighbors. Its result had been to divide neighbor from neighbor, family from family, tearing apart the peaceful society Ronan had taken entirely for granted as a child.

"Who are your mother's people?" Fergus prompted when he did not answer.

What business is that of yours? Ronan wanted to say, but he bit back the rude response. Respect for his elders was too much a part of him to make such an answer possible.

"The O'Donnells."

"An old name," Fergus said, nodding. "A great lineage."

"Not to hear Grandfather Fitzgerald tell it," Ronan said lightly, turning back to his horse.

"Ashamed of your Irish blood, are ye?" Fergus rapped out suddenly.

"No more than my Norman blood," Ronan replied, annoyed.

"I see."

Ronan had the uneasy feeling that the old man saw far too much, perhaps more than he did himself.

He thumped a small cask of wine on the rock between them. "Can you manage this?" he asked, adding pointedly, "I cannot linger this morning. I must be on my way."

Fergus made no effort to lift the cask. "Where are ye bound?"

"To London."

"I never cared for London myself," Fergus said mildly.

I don't like it, either, Ronan thought, wondering what had possessed him to think of going there. He remembered the stench of the crowded streets, the noise . . . and all the musicians, some quite gifted and all with two good hands, competing for a place at court. Once he had no need to fear them, but now . . .

"I am afraid I canna lift this," Fergus said, startling him from his thoughts. "Will ye be so kind as to carry it inside? Or if ye canna manage it, we could take it together."

Ronan flushed, seeing Fergus staring at his hand. "I can do it," he said, bending.

"Just in here," Fergus said, gesturing toward an opening in the hillside.

Ronan looked at the cave's entrance and froze. He had always hated caves. Though his friends had liked nothing better than to explore the caverns winding through the cliffs of Donegal, Ronan had always refused to join them.

Why anyone would willingly venture into such a terrible place, he had never known. Just thinking of it made his stomach clench. All his worst nightmares were of being trapped inside the earth with no way out.

Fergus was watching him closely, eyes hooded and unreadable. If this was some sort of test—and Ronan felt certain that it was—he did not need to prove himself. He could just refuse and walk away. There was no need, none at all, to do as Fergus asked, no matter how simple it might be.

Yet Ronan had the uneasy feeling that Fergus's request was not simple at all. Strongly and without reason he feared that once he walked inside, he would not walk out again unchanged. But would that be such a terrible thing? God knew he could use a change, for he was sick to death of himself, his entire pointless life, and the bleak future stretching endlessly before him.

Was Fergus offering him a new beginning? Or was this some sort of trap? Of course, there is another possibility, Ronan told himself, one far more likely. The man could simply want his wine.

He hesitated, heart thumping wildly in his breast, and despite the breeze, sweat broke out upon his brow.

"Go on, lad," Fergus said gently. "There is no harm to ye in there. None at all."

Ronan swallowed hard, thinking that Fergus must find him ridiculous. God knew he found himself both contemptible and absurd. It was only a cave! But still he could not force himself to move. At last he looked at Fergus.

"Truly?"

"Aye, truly. I'll never lie to ye, Ronan. There will be no room for lies between us."

Ronan studied the sky, so clear and blue, and the road winding down the mountainside toward London. He turned his face up to the sun and felt it warm his skin as the fresh breeze stirred his hair. Then he looked again at the opening in the hillside, black against gray stone. It would be cold in there, he thought, dank and foul, filled with terrifying visions.

"You seemed to be waiting for me," he said, stalling for time. "Did you know that I was coming?"

Fergus smiled. "Oh, aye. Or to be quite truthful, I knew someone was coming. I only hoped that it was you."

"How can that be?" Ronan demanded angrily. "You do not even know me."

"Oh, child," Fergus said, putting one hand on his shoulder. "I know ye well, though before today I did not ken your name. I've been waiting for ye a long, long time."

Ronan glanced at him, surprised, and Fergus nodded, as though answering a question Ronan had not quite dared to ask. His dark eyes were very kind beneath the tangle of white brows.

"Then I—I suppose I could come in. For a bit."

"Unpack your horse and stable it in the shed," Fergus said briskly, turning back to the cave. "'Twill be snow ere nightfall."

Ronan obeyed. At the threshold he hesitated, took the harp from his shoulder, and ran his fingers across its strings, his face taut with concentration as the rippling notes danced in the cool fresh air.

At last he nodded. "If you say so," he murmured, stroking the polished wood. Then he squared his shoulders, bracing himself against whatever dark mysteries lay within, and pushed back the hide stretched across the cave's entrance. He took one wary step and stopped short, staring.

His wondering gaze moved over glittering crystals piled on the shelves, neat rows of parchments, quills and inkpots, bunches of herbs suspended from the ceiling. Half a dozen candles shed a warm light over the homey scene and the scent of fresh-baked bread set his mouth to watering.

"Well, don't just stand there letting in the cold," Fergus said prosaically, looking up from a small table where he was slicing bread and cheese. "Come in and sit."

Ronan laughed and let the hide fall into place behind him as he stepped inside, hands outstretched to catch the fire's warmth.